TEMPERING THE VISCOUNT'S ENVY

The Lords of Vice
Book Three

C.H. Admirand

Dearest Reader;

Thank you for your support of a small press. At Dragonblade Publishing, we strive to bring you the highest quality Historical Romance from the some of the best authors in the business. Without your support, there is no 'us', so we sincerely hope you adore these stories and find some new favorite authors along the way.

Happy Reading!

CEO, Dragonblade Publishing

Additional Dragonblade books by Author C.H. Admirand

The Lords of Vice Series
Mending the Duke's Pride
Avoiding the Earl's Lust
Tempering the Viscount's Envy

Dedication

For Scott Moreland, my wonderful editor whose insightful edits and attention to detail have elevated my writing to a whole new level. You're right, we make a great team!

Acknowledgements

I would not have been able to write this book without the support of my family: sons Phil and Josh, daughter Jess and son-in-law Tom, and grandsons Jack & Hank. You keep me sane while we adjust to the hole in our lives that DJ used to occupy.

I would not have been able to finish writing this book without the support of Tara Nina, wonderful friend and author extraordinaire: thank you for being my lifeline while writing this book. When I realized my "go to guy" for questions wasn't here anymore, who could I ask— "What if their carriage slid off the road…would this happen?" I called Tara crying, and she took the time away from the book she was writing to calm me down and tell me to stop crying because we can figure this out! I love you, Tara Nina…for that, for the second set of eyes, and for just being you, my friend. And to think it all started in a bar in Atlanta with a Hurricane…

CHAPTER ONE

VISCOUNT WILLIAM CHATTSWORTH read the missive in his hand once, and then read it again. Relief filled him. The duke's reply was more than he'd expected and quite timely. An audience with the current Duke of Wyndmere was the first step in regaining what his family had lost in recent years.

The *on dit* circulating the *ton* had been spot on. The duke valued family and duty above all things. Though the connection be quite removed—thrice perhaps on their mothers' side, the duke had still responded in the affirmative and invited William to Wyndmere Hall.

A glance about the sparsely furnished study was a daily reminder of what happened when one's sire threw caution to the four winds and invested all of his blunt in a blasted shipping company! Did his father never consider the possibility the cargo he'd invested every pound in, not entailed, would go down with the ship sailing around the Cape of Good Hope?

William wasn't a sailor but had acquaintances in the Royal Navy who'd shared startling tales of cross currents, rogue waves, and ill-timed journeys around the Cape.

His father's refusal to listen to reason, insisting on backing the fledgling shipping company, had started the family on a downward spiral toward ruin. If that wasn't enough in and of itself, Earl Chattsworth mysteriously disappeared days after the news that he'd lost everything.

William had not received word from his sire in the weeks that followed, or in the year since. Rumors abounded that his father had fallen victim to a midnight holdup at the wrong end of a highwayman's blunderbuss. There was no shred of proof, aside from the disturbing disappearance of his great-grandmother's jewels and silver tea service, along with a number of small antiquities his great-grandfather had acquired while in Egypt.

Along with his father's penchant for backing questionable ventures, he'd developed a fascination for the turn of a card in the underbelly of London. *Had his father pawned the family heirlooms in London to pay gaming debts?* He'd made discrete inquiries but, as yet, had not heard of the jewels or any of the other missing items turning up for sale.

Bloody hell! Where were the *Chattsworth Emeralds?* He could picture the exquisite strand of emeralds and matching earbobs in his mind's eye. They matched his mother's eyes whenever she wore them when attending balls, musicales, and the like. Through his youthful eyes, his mother was as beautiful as a faerie princess. The few times he seen her dancing with his father, he swore he saw her sparkling, iridescent wings!

Declared an *Incomparable* during her first Season, Lady Elizabeth Summerfield had taken the *ton* by storm with her raven hair and flashing green eyes. But it was her laughter and love of life that captivated his father the moment their eyes met across the crowded ballroom. Enthralled, he'd swept her off her feet and into marriage before the end of her first Season.

His mind drifted as he remembered the stories his mother had told him when he was a lad. Stories of a love that knew no bounds. A love destined to be...one that would live forever.

"Rubbish!" He rose from his seat behind this father's desk and walked to the window. The park beyond Chattsworth Manor was in desperate need of attention—and a sharp scythe. He sighed. "The manor needs far more than that," he admitted aloud. "The walls need replastering, and the floors need to be repaired. At least the roof doesn't leak."

Needing to vent his growing frustration, he donned the black greatcoat he'd tossed across the back of a chair. Striding to the glassed doors leading to the terrace, he opened them, and stepped into December's chill.

Ignoring the cold, he breathed deeply. The time of year mattered not as he filled his lungs with the sweetest air known to mankind...the air surrounding his ancestral home, *Chattsworth Manor*. "Colder than I thought," he rumbled.

Taking his time, he walked down the stone steps leading to his mother's rose garden, where her favorite flowers slept until spring. He frowned, knowing he'd be hard pressed to find them among the weeds. All but a handful of servants had left. One more blow he'd been unable to accept, but not the worst of it. His father's overwhelming need for a prodigious amount of coin at the ready—to squander on shipments of goods and the turn of a card, had reduced their home to its present state...on the verge of falling into rack and ruin.

He swore at the realization that he needed his father there in order to vent his spleen and demand to know what in the bloody hell the earl had been thinking! He curled his hands into fists, ready to strike out at anyone, anything, to ease the burning frustration in his gut. Envy curdled inside him, knowing his cousin, the duke, had so much at his fingertips, while William was losing what little he had left.

A breath of frozen air swept past him, clearing his troubled thoughts, scattering them on the wind.

The need to discover what happened to his father kept him company during the day and awake through the night. It was now his responsibility to see to the repairs to the family fortune and his home. Unless his father miraculously returned, the earl's title and their home were all he had left. His elder brother died of a fever when they were young. His mother died giving birth to his sister, who never opened her eyes or breathed that first life-giving breath of Sussex air.

"Why do I feel cursed?" he wondered aloud. The need to quit the house and the grounds that were in such a dismal state had him striding quickly away from them until he stood in front of the barn. The damp air had him pulling his gloves out of his pockets. He rubbed his hands together as warmth was restored. *The leather and fur lining cut the chill quite nicely.*

Mentally tallying a list, he started with the barn roof. It leaked. From there he wandered about the extensive grounds, saddened to note the spring house and the smoke house were literally in danger of falling down if something wasn't done immediately. The fieldstones were still there, some of them askew and needed to be put back in place. Hopefully, the structures would hold and not crumble.

The once grand stables were empty save for one stall which currently housed his only possession of worth—Maximus, a beautiful black Thoroughbred stallion. Striding toward his horse he asked, "Ready to race against the wind, my friend?"

He chuckled when Maximus lifted his head and snorted. Taking that as a yes, he opened the door to the stall and led his horse outside. He saddled Maximus with the ease and efficiency that bespoke of his years spent in the stables. His father used to— no, he thought. *I refuse to go down that road again this morning. It'll only lead to another empty decanter of brandy and an aching head.*

The pair flew across stone fences, galloped through an open meadow, until they eventually slowed to a trot alongside the brook that ran in and around his family's home. William felt better and sensed his horse did, too. "We both needed that all-out run, didn't we?"

Maximus whinnied and William smiled. He dismounted and walked his horse over to the stream, letting him drink from the clear, cold water. The sound of water rushing over rocks and around the twists and turns of the brook was almost musical. He wondered if there were water sprites watching over Max and him. He searched his memory of his mother's stories. *Did they only protect the streams in the warm weather?* Something to ponder as the sun went under a cloud and the chill enveloped him.

"Mother always told us they would know if we were too close to the edge and push us back before we fell in." His thoughts turned dark as he remembered following his brother to this very spot all those years ago.

"Why didn't the sprites warn us, August?" His brother didn't reply...couldn't as he'd been gone these last twenty years. He closed his eyes and remembered the fun they'd had that day, racing through fields, and clambering over rock walls until they'd arrived at their destination—the brook. Mother had warned them not to go without an adult, but they'd been secure in their abilities and had scoffed at the notion.

"It wasn't the dunking in the stream that killed him, you know." Maximus paused to look at him, water dripping from his equine lips. He snorted as if in agreement before he dipped his head to the water to drink once more.

William tamped down on his childhood anguish to confide, "It was the long walk home, drenched to the skin. We both were. But for some reason, the fever took August but not me."

Maximus nudged him in the arm to get his attention. Rubbing his hand along the stallion's neck, he sighed. "Cannot undo what's been done," he said as he mounted. "Let's take the long way home."

The pair settled into an easy cadence. The stark beauty of the land dressed for winter, and the deep blue of the sky, eased the sharpest edge of his sorrow. By the time they'd reached the stable, William noticed a familiar horse occupied the empty stall beside Max's.

"Looks like you'll have company today, Maximus." He took care of his mount, removing the saddle and blanket, and rubbing him down. The routine soothed both man and beast. He gave him a cupful of oats and fresh water before checking to see that his cousin's horse had been duly taken care of.

"I wonder if Marcus received a reply from the duke yet?" Striding into the wan sunshine, he headed to the manor and the cousin who waited for him.

He wasn't left to wonder long. Marcus hailed him as he walked toward him.

"I take it you're here to share news."

Baron Marcus Summerfield stopped and waited for the viscount.

"Well?" William demanded as he closed the distance between them. "Did the duke respond to your query in the affirmative?"

"I was about to ask the same of you," his cousin replied. When William reached his side, Marcus turned around to walk alongside of him, retracing his steps. "When Hargrave said you'd gone for a ride, I was tempted to saddle my horse again. But St. George deserves a bit of a rest after the paces I put him through to get here."

William sensed the urgency vibrating from his younger cousin. His bright blue gaze met that of his cousin's. The Lippincott gene from their mothers' side of the family passed down the piercing blue of their eyes and the rich dark chestnut color of their hair.

"I've received an invitation to Wyndmere Hall," William said.

"Been invited to see the duke," Marcus said at the same time.

The viscount chuckled. "It would appear our cousin is not averse to meeting with extended family. One would wonder, do you think he assumes we're going to stress the familial relationship in order to sponge off him?"

The baron shrugged. "He might be expecting it. Wouldn't you?"

"Absolutely." The viscount's mind wandered as Marcus chatted amiably about what he intended to do with the funds the duke would no doubt be bestowing upon him.

William felt vindicated. The envy curling within him sprung to life as he crossed the terrace. At last, he would be able to reap the rewards he felt entitled to...if not the rather large crumbs he suspected the duke could more than afford to brush his way. After all, it was his cousin's duty to see that the viscount received his due, wasn't it?

William stopped outside the glassed terrace doors leading into the library. "Do you suppose we need to bring the duke's letters with us to ensure our entrance into Wyndmere Hall?"

"I couldn't begin to hazard a guess," the baron mumbled. "Mayhap we should. It's too long a journey to be turned away because of something so trifling."

"I know we discussed the idea and thought through the merits of receiving a stipend from our cousin." The viscount opened the doors, motioning for his cousin to precede him. "Now that the opportunity has presented itself, I'm a bit wary," he admitted. "What do you suppose he is going to ask for in return?"

They stepped inside, and the baron's stomach rumbled loudly. The viscount smiled. "Mayhap I should feed you before we continue our discussion."

He gave a slight tug on the servants' bell pull and wasn't kept waiting long. "Ah, Mrs. Meadowsweet," he greeted the aging housekeeper. "Would you be so good as to ask Mrs. Romney to prepare a light luncheon for me and my cousin?"

"At once my lord," she started to curtsey, but the viscount laid a hand on her arm. "We've spoken of this before, Mrs. Meadowsweet. Please dispense with such formalities. I would not have you injure your knee further."

She smiled as tears glistened in her eyes. "Thank you, my lord. I'll be back in a trice."

Marcus' serious expression had William marveling how closely his cousin resembled the reflection William saw every morning in the looking glass hanging above the washstand in his bedchamber.

"Something wrong, Cousin?"

William paused before answering his question with a question, "Have you ever noticed the strong family resemblance between us?"

Marcus chuckled. "Aye, many a time. The serving wenches down at the Thorn and Rose have mistaken me for my much older cousin—"

"Four years," William interrupted to remind him.

"I daresay, at times it seems like ten."

The viscount silently agreed. His cousin's situation was far better than his own. The baron's parents and three younger sisters were still alive. Though Marcus hadn't had the same number of servants growing up, his circumstances were far more settled than his own.

"Nevertheless, as I was saying, I did not mind being mistaken for you on more than one happy occasion."

William snorted. "By the comely serving wenches Betty and Anne no doubt."

Marcus nodded. "Buxom beauties to be sure and free with their affections...even when they realized I was not you."

William fell silent for a few moments before continuing. "I do believe those days are behind us, Cousin."

"How so?"

"There may be stipulations to the duke's agreeing to lend his support financially."

"You don't suppose he'd insist on certain behavior, would he?"

The viscount stared off into space. "Rumors abound amongst the *ton* that our cousin insisted his own brother end his nightly forays into the stews and gaming hells."

Marcus seemed to be waiting for his cousin to say more. William complied, adding, "I've heard confirmation of such from a trusted source."

"Trusted to whom?" Marcus asked. "Our cousin, the duke, or you?"

A knock sounded on the library door, interrupting them. "Come in."

The door opened slowly. When his housekeeper bobbled the heavy tray she carried, he rushed over to help. "Here," the viscount said, "let me set that down for you."

"Thank you, my lord, it was becoming a bit heavier than I'd

imagined."

Marcus tilted his head as he stared down at the assortment of sandwiches piled high on one plate, nestled next to another filled with confections that tempted him to sample the berry tarts before the more substantial sandwiches. "Please send my thanks to Mrs. Romney."

"Of course, your lordship. Tea is on its way," she informed the men. "Hargrave is bringing it...I couldn't lift it."

William silently chastised himself for ordering his elderly servants about without thought to their ages or abilities. Had his growing need for coin, so like his father's, nearly blinded him to those around him? What had happened to his vow to do better, refusing to follow in his father's footsteps? More than six months ago, he'd promised himself not to treat their servants like shadows, to be summoned only when needed and expecting them to disappear into the wallpaper when he'd finished with them.

Contrite, he reproached himself to the wisp of a woman. "Forgive me for not coming to the kitchen myself."

Why hadn't he noticed she was no longer the same robust figure who ran their household so efficiently after the death of his mother? "I was not thinking," he continued. "Marcus and I are hungry enough to eat anywhere."

"Wouldn't be right for your lordships to eat in the kitchen," she reminded him with her warm, sweet smile.

Hargrave appeared in the doorway with a second tray but managed to balance it better than the housekeeper. The butler was cadaverously thin and must have ten years on the woman. *Good God!* he thought, that would place their aging butler at close to seventy years old! Best to think more of them, now that Father is no longer here to order them about. *Mayhap he could ask the duke's help finding his father as well as the coin needed to pension off those deserving servants.*

A long deep sigh escaped his lips thinking of his father. *Where in the blue blazes was he? Had he fallen ill? Mayhap he had been injured and unable to remember who he was. Bloody hell! Where was the earl?*

Hargrave set the tray on the side table along one wall, and Mrs. Meadowsweet asked, "Shall I pour, my lord?"

"No, thank you. I believe I can manage. Why don't you and Hargrave take some time to rest."

"Unheard of," Hargrave rumbled. "We shall remain on duty and at your beck and call, my lord."

"Marcus and I can manage on our own."

"That may be," his butler continued, his grass-green eyes bright with indignation. "But we would be shirking our duties if we left you to your own devices."

"Even if I insist?" William queried, his tone firm, but not condescending.

Hargrave squared his shoulders but could not keep them from slumping back to his normal slightly stoop-shouldered stance. "Especially then, my lord. It is our duty to serve and serve we shall!"

The butler's impassioned speech had a lump forming in the viscount's throat. He'd been in awe of the man over the years. It was only in recent months that the man seemed to age before his eyes. Right around the time word had reached him of the earl's disappearance.

"Very well," William acquiesced. "However, I insist that you and Mrs. Meadowsweet either join us or repair to the kitchen to enjoy a leisurely luncheon."

His housekeeper lifted the timepiece pinned to her black bombazine gown and sniffed. "We can spare half an hour before we need to return to our duties. Will that suffice, my lord?"

He struggled not to smile at the eminently proper tone his elderly servants always used. They alone were loyal, while others had left when it became evident the funds needed to pay them, were no longer available. Four servants remained: Hargrave, Mrs. Meadowsweet, Mrs. Romney, and his footman/valet, MacReedy.

He was humbled to realize that he wouldn't have survived without them. "Aye, Mrs. Meadowsweet. Thank you."

When the older couple left the room, he sighed. "The duke's reply may resolve my most urgent problem."

Marcus was staring at him.

"Have I crumbs on my coat?"

His cousin chuckled. "No, but I daresay, you should use the blunt to purchase a new frockcoat. One that wouldn't bunch at the shoulder seams or gap a bit in the front."

William pinned his cousin with a hard stare. "There's nothing wrong with the cut of my frockcoat. But not having the blunt to pension off the only people who cared enough to see that I did not starve or let the family estate fall completely to rack and ruin is a crime."

Marcus shrugged. "You could use it to hire younger servants."

His cousin's words echoed what he'd been thinking earlier while riding Maximus. He'd felt he deserved the money the duke should rightly hand over to him. But his mother's voice in his head softly reminded him of his duty to the pensioners who relied on him.

Agitated, William ran a hand through his hair. "With what I plan to wheedle out of the duke, I plan to hire younger staff. But Hargrave and Mrs. Meadowsweet have worked for our family for years—since my grandfather's time. They deserve better than to be still serving what's left of our family...me, as I cannot afford to pay them to retire."

Marcus walked over to the door and closed it, ensuring their privacy. "You need to eat to clear your head, Cousin. Always sets me to rights."

The viscount looked over his shoulder at the closed door and wondered if the duke would balk at his request for money. Mayhap if he apprised his cousin of the desperate situation of his loyal staff, he could pension them off before they keeled over trying to manage tasks beyond their physical capabilities.

The prospect of facing the duke with half-truths had him wondering, could he pull it off? Would he be able to paint a rosy picture, while in his heart he would know it to be a Banbury tale? William slowly walked over to the table where his cousin sat and pulled out the chair across from him. "Shall I pour?"

Marcus waved at the teapot. "Please do."

They ate companionably, while discussing their plans for the money they'd felt certain the duke would bestow upon them. Neither one wanted to return to, or discuss, the subject they avoided—*what the duke would expect in return?* The men knew nothing in life came without strings or was ever free.

After they ate, the viscount rose and went to his desk, retrieving the duke's missive.

Marcus got to his feet and nodded to the note in his cousin's hand. "Mind if see that?"

Thinking he may need it as proof for entrée into Wyndmere Hall, William cautioned, "Careful." Handing it to him, he added, "I may need it to prove who I am."

Marcus read the short note and mumbled, "Bloody hell, I still have trouble believing Jared inherited the title. He was always mucking about the estate, getting his hands dirty—digging a ditch, thatching a roof."

"Our cousin was never one for the life such as he's been living in London," William agreed.

"Never thought Oliver would get caught by Hampton," Marcus admitted. "Though the *on dit* amongst the *ton* had him spending more time in Hampton's wife's *boudoir* than Hampton himself!"

William had to agree. "Deuced bad luck that Hampton returned home unexpectedly. Crack shot, you know."

Marcus agreed. "Bloody hard to miss that broad a target at close range."

William fell silent. The scandal of their cousin's demise, due to a lead ball in the back, had been the talk of the *ton* for months. The Fifth Duke of Wyndmere's reputation for cuckolding peers' wives had cast a pall over the house of Wyndmere—reaching even those distantly related to him. Both the Chattsworths and

Summerfields had felt the sting of social rejection along with their Lippincott cousins, though not on quite the same level.

Despite the fact that the Chattsworth country estate, and most of the furnishings in it, were entailed, a number of the *portable* furnishings had begun to disappear after the fifth duke's death. William had wondered at the time if his father and the duke had been backing the same financial ventures...and frequenting the same stews and gaming hells.

"Our cousin has made great strides filling the family coffers and lifting the Lippincott name out of the mire."

"Still on shaky ground," the baron grumbled. "What with the run-in with Prinny's pet, Hollingford."

The viscount had to agree. "Any suggestion as to what we could do to aid our cousin?"

"Not at the moment. You?"

"No." William wanted to have something to offer the duke...but what? "Whatever we offer, doesn't have to be expensive," he murmured aloud. "Mayhap we could help rebuild something for him."

Marcus chuckled. "Neither one of us is especially talented with our hands in that regard. Though in others—" he grinned, knowing his cousin would be reminded of their times spent at the Thorn and Rose.

William sighed. "The duke values duty to family and steers clear of anything that would lead to another scandal that would harm the family reputation. I doubt he'd approve if we were to cut a swath through the *ton* as his brother, Oliver, had."

Marcus nodded in agreement. "Do you think you can manage to steer clear of the fulsome widows who are constantly looking for a new protector, or the lightskirts hanging on the fringes of the *ton* looking for the same?"

"Once I make the decision to," William said. "Absolutely."

"By the by," Marcus said, "who does His Grace expect to meet with first?"

They looked at William's note first, then Marcus pulled his

out of his waistcoat pocket. "It would seem that you do cousin. Mayhap he decided to start with his older relation."

The viscount frowned. "I'll do my best to make a good impression," he promised. "I'll not do anything to hamper your success with the duke."

Marcus stood and held out his hand.

William did the same. They shook hands. "I shall send word to let you know how I fare after my meeting with His Grace."

"I shall do the same. Why don't we meet at the Thorn and Rose to celebrate your success?"

William slowly smiled, thinking of the inn where he'd spent a good deal of his time on the road south of London before his father abruptly vanished. "I shall send word and meet you there."

Marcus strode to the door and paused with his hand on the knob. "You will be careful, Cousin?"

William noted the unease in his younger cousin's gaze and nodded. "I shall."

Without another word, Baron Summerfield quit the room, his boot heels echoing down the empty hallway.

The viscount walked over to the terrace doors and watched his cousin make his way to the stable. It was up to him to make the right impression upon their illustrious cousin. Their very lives depended upon it.

CHAPTER TWO

L ADY CALLIOPE HARRINGTON held one end of the ivory altar
cloth and ran the tip of her finger over the intricate embroi-
dery that ran along the edge of it. "Your grandmother made this?"

Her good friend, Lady Aurelia Coddington, nodded. "If you
look at the corner on your end, you'll see her initials."

Calliope studied the cloth closely. "Oh! I see it, A.B. What
was her name?"

"Anna Bramwell. She met my grandfather the morning she'd
placed this same cloth on the altar for the New Year's Day
service."

"On Hogmanay?"

Aurelia nodded. "The door opened, and she turned to see
who would be out so early in the morning."

"How early was it?" Calliope wanted to know.

"Just past dawn. My grandmother was supposed to have
finished it the night before but, for some reason, hadn't."

They smoothed the cloth into place and Calliope urged,
"Well? What happened then?"

Aurelia brushed the tips of her fingers along the cloth and
sighed. "Grandmother said her heart stopped and her breath
caught in her chest."

"Was she ill?"

Calliope's friend shook her head and slowly smiled. "The

tallest, broadest, dark-haired man Grandmother had ever seen stood in the doorway staring at her."

Calliope stood stock still and closed her eyes imagining what it must have been like, meeting such a man. Would she have a similar reaction? *Probably not*, she thought. She walked over to the other end of the altar where her friend stood staring at the door to the church, still lost in thought. Calliope started putting the leftover, tiny odd-sized pieces of holly and fresh evergreen boughs into the two baskets they'd carried with them to decorate the church.

"Aren't you going to ask me what happened then?" Aurelia asked.

Calliope was surprised she *hadn't* asked her friend to tell her the rest of the tale. But she, too, had been lost in thought, wondering if she'd ever meet a man who would be able to look past her mean state in life—that of what she'd been reduced to, a poor relation.

"Yes," she replied. "Of course, just woolgathering."

Aurelia frowned at Calliope but, thankfully, didn't prod her about what she had been thinking.

"Their eyes met," Aurelia told her, "the darkest peat brown and softest summer-blue. Grandmother said she knew in a heartbeat that no matter if the dark-haired man walked toward her or turned and strode out of the church, her heart would go where e're he did. It was his from the moment their gazes locked."

Calliope's heart warmed at the long-ago tale of love at first glance. She'd often wondered if she'd be so lucky, but that was before her father died. After her mother died, her life had changed irrevocably. She looked up to see her friend studying her. "Have I thanked you and your uncle recently for making me feel welcome in your family?" Before Aurelia could respond, Calliope added, "No one has ever done that. Not in all the years I'd been shuttled back and forth, from one relative to the next, landing on my second cousin's doorstep."

Aurelia reached for Calliope's hand and squeezed it before letting go. "Yes, you have, my dearest friend." She smiled, "I believe it was just yesterday when Uncle Phineas slipped the kippers from his plate to yours."

Calliope's eyes filled with tears, but she blinked them away. Today was a day for joy, not sorrow. "I've never felt so coddled or loved, Aurelia," she whispered. "I owe you both so much."

"Nonsense," Aurelia said briskly. "You are my friend, and Uncle vowed to take you in and treat you as family that awful night."

Before Calliope could ask her friend not to bring up the night they'd come to her rescue, Aurelia waved a hand in front of her face, a gesture quite familiar to Calliope. Her friend was about to change the subject.

"Let's stand in the middle of the aisle, midway between the altar and the doors, to see if we're satisfied with the greenery, candles, and the cloth."

Calliope nodded and walked over to stand beside her friend as they faced the altar and studied the festive greens and holly branches they'd placed upon the windowsills.

"Do you think the candles detract from the beauty of the greenery?"

"It looks just right," Calliope reassured her. "But if you like, I can remove the candles on one side and—"

The door to the church burst open. Aurelia reached for Calliope's hand—just as they had the night they'd been at the inn on their way to Wyndmere Hall, when her maid had disappeared. Strength and purpose passed from one hand to the other as it had that night, grounding them as they turned to face the intruder together.

The tall, broad, dark-haired man slowly smiled as he walked toward Aurelia and Calliope.

"Edward—" Aurelia stopped mid-step and stared at the man.

Calliope wondered why her friend didn't remind her intended, Earl Lippincott, that it was bad luck to see the bride before the ceremony. And then she noted the way Aurelia's demeanor changed completely from greeting her soon-to-be-husband to speaking to a total stranger. "May we help you?"

"Really, Aurelia," Calliope admonished. "It might be bad luck for Edward to see you before you wed later today, but is it wise to be so decidedly correct in your manner?"

"I do beg your pardon, ladies." The man's deep mellifluous voice filled the church. "I admit to being a bit lost. I'm looking for Wyndmere Hall."

Aurelia and Calliope looked at one another and then at the man who had to be a blood relative of her intended and his brother the Duke of Wyndmere.

Aurelia smiled. "You're only a few miles north of Wyndmere Hall."

"That's a relief," he said. "I was hoping to find someone awake at this godforsaken hour, but no one was about in the village I just passed through."

Calliope was bereft of words...and the power to speak. The handsome man with the toe-curling voice could be Earl Lippincott's twin. They shared the same powerful build, wavy dark chestnut hair, and brilliant blue eyes. Eyes that were now focused on her. She felt as if she'd been caught in a snare, about to be stuffed into a game bag, and carried home to be put into the stew pot!

"Do forgive me," he said quietly, never letting his gaze shift away from Calliope's. "Viscount Chattsworth, at your service." He bowed deeply to her and then to Aurelia. "To whom do I have the pleasure of speaking?"

Aurelia glanced at Calliope before answering, "Lady Aurelia Coddington—soon to be married to Edward, Earl Lippincott. And this is my good friend, Lady Calliope Harrington."

"My congratulations, Lady Coddington." He paused, then queried, "May I be so bold as to ask where your escort is?"

Calliope started to wring her hands and forcibly stopped the telling action. The viscount might think she was afraid of him.

She wasn't. It was the backlash she and Aurelia would face if the man mentioned meeting them to the earl or the duke.

Finding her voice, she answered, "We rode out together to finish decorating the church for Aurelia and Edward's vows."

The incredulous look on his face was accented when he raised one eyebrow—so like the duke it was eerie. "I cannot imagine that the duke or his brother the earl would be pleased to discover you ladies rode out before dawn unescorted." He stared at them until Calliope started to fidget beneath his stern gaze.

"We were supposed to have finished last night, but then Aurelia realized she'd forgotten to bring her grandmother's altar cloth."

"We returned early this morning with more greenery and a few extra candles as well." Aurelia told him. "By the by," she said, "has anyone ever told you that you bear a striking resemblance to my intended?"

"And the duke," Calliope added.

His smile eased most of Calliope's worry. She sensed here was a man one could trust. She'd met a number of people over the years who could not be trusted and sensed the difference.

"Ah, my illustrious cousins."

"Cousins? I didn't realize Edward and Jared had cousins."

"Distant," the viscount corrected. "Thrice, mayhap. I cannot seem to recall. My great-grandmother was a Lippincott before she married."

"That would explain your coloring and impressive stance."

He grinned and Calliope noticed while he shared some of the same Lippincott features, he did not sport a pair of deep dimples. He had a cleft chin and, if she could hazard a guess, was an inch or so shorter than either the earl or the duke.

Feeling emboldened by his bearing and familial connection to Aurelia's intended, Calliope braved the question pressing on her mind. "I wonder if we could prevail upon you to keep this meeting between the three of us?"

His gaze locked with hers once more, and she felt as if he

could see right through to her soul. She fought to still the trembling in her legs but could do nothing to calm the rapid pace of her heart. She hated confrontations and didn't want the earl or the duke to reprimand them for leaving the estate without an escort.

He took a step toward her, hand extended as if to steady her. "Are you ill, Lady Harrington?"

She shook her head in answer, wondering why the room had started to gray at the edges of her vision.

"Calliope!" Aurelia's voice sounded a bit muffled and more than a bit distant. *Dear Lord, where was her reticule with her smelling salts?*

THE DOORS TO the church burst open and a deep voice shouted, "Who are ye and what have ye done to Lady Calliope?"

Viscount William Chattsworth tightened his hold on Lady Harrington and met the angry intruder's stare with one of his own. "Who the devil wants to know?" he demanded.

The man strode to where William stood with the limp lady in his arms. *Was the lady ill? Was this man her husband?* He studied the light-haired man with the piercing green eyes dressed in unrelieved black but refused to back down until he knew who he was addressing.

"Lady Aurelia," the man said, turning toward her. "Are ye hurt?"

She shook her head in answer, looking as if she were afraid. *Bloody hell! Was the man a known rotter? A scoundrel?*

Beyond irritated that the man demanding answers had yet to deign to answer his question, William stepped in front of Lady Aurelia, noting that Lady Calliope stirred in his arms. "I shall see that my cousins, Earl Lippincott and the Duke of Wyndmere, have you put behind bars for harassing these two fair ladies."

The man turned to stare at William, with an odd look on his

face and recognition in his eyes. "So that be the way of it," he said at last.

"The way of what?" William heard the sharp intake of breath and looked down at the woman in his arms. Her skin was the color of fresh cream with a hint of color gracing her cheekbones once more. Her gray eyes and honey-blonde hair added to her air of quiet beauty. Distracted, he didn't realize the man had stepped close enough to place his hand on William's shoulder.

He jolted and damned himself for losing his concentration and, with it, the ability to protect the two women who had yet to explain why they were without escort miles from home at this early hour.

"Lady Calliope?" the man called softly.

Her eyes fluttered open and she rasped, "Patrick! What are you doing here?"

"I have a mind to ask ye the same, yer ladyship," he grumbled before frowning at William. "Why have ye not set her down yet?" he demanded.

"Until I know more than your first name, Patrick," he growled, "I shall not release her, nor will I allow Lady Codding-ton to step from behind me."

Patrick's green eyes shone with a touch of devilment. "And how do ye plan to protect either of them with yer hands full?"

Blast! Good point and hard to answer without risking a heavy blow to his pride. He shifted the lady he held, setting her on her feet while keeping her tucked flush against his side. For a moment, he could swear he felt her heartbeat against him before he shifted her behind him to join her friend. "I've no weapon," William declared. "But I warn you, I excel at bare knuckle fighting."

The other man slowly smiled. "Well now, I'd welcome a chance to have a go at ye, but I've promised His Grace to bring their ladyships home without delay."

Aurelia groaned. "Jared knows we left?"

"Sure and it's me job to see to yer protection, yer ladyship.

Did ye think after everythin' that's happened in the last year, the duke or the earl would let ye off the grounds without someone followin' behind ye?"

"You are acquainted with my cousins?"

"Aye. And as to that, might I inquire as to yer name?"

William knew when he'd come up against a man more stubborn than himself. Patrick was that man. "Name's Chattsworth. Viscount William Chattsworth."

"I've heard His Grace mention ye were expected. Didn't know ye'd be arrivin' before breakfast, though."

With that, Patrick sighed and said, "Yer ladyships can come out from behind yer protector. I've promised to return ye to Wyndmere Hall. And as yer intended told me, I'd best be quick about it."

Aurelia was the first to leave her sanctuary. "Was Edward overset?"

Patrick's face lost all expression as he replied, "Ye could say that."

"Oh, dear," Calliope whispered. "Was Lord Coddington awake when you left?"

Aurelia laughed. "I thought you'd been living with us long enough to realize Uncle Phineas doesn't rise before the sun—ever!"

Calliope blew out a breath. "True. I must confess I was concerned we'd have to listen to another lecture from your uncle, your intended, or the duke."

"Edward may be vexed with me," Aurelia admitted, "but not quite as upset as the duke may be."

"Rest assured, yer ladyships, both the earl and the duke are more than a bit vexed, as ye put it."

They fell silent.

"I daresay, I could use a cup of tea and my horse a warm stable with a cupful of oats."

Patrick's gaze met his. "If ye'll follow me, yer lordship, I'm certain sure His Grace or his lordship the earl will see to both."

He paused before adding, "Name's O'Malley. Head of His Grace's personal guard."

"O'Malley," William said slowly, committing the name to memory. "Thank you for your diligence and duty regarding Lady Coddington and Lady Harrington."

He nodded. "Ye're welcome. Let's be off now. The duke will be hot on me heels if I don't bring ye back immediately."

The viscount wondered why the duke was so protective of the ladies. Well, of course his cousin, Edward, would be of his intended, but why was he so concerned with her friend as well? Was there more to the *on dits* circling the *ton* as to the enemies of the duke? There was a bit of mystery to be solved here and while he loved nothing better, he already had a mystery he hadn't solved—the disappearance of his father.

While he loved solving mysteries, a chance to use his skill bare knuckle fighting with the big man striding toward the door to hold it open for Lady Coddington and Lady Harrington held great appeal. He cracked his knuckles and noted the gleam of anticipation in O'Malley's eyes. Aye, he'd be testing his mettle against the head of his cousin's personal guard before returning home.

A glance at the wand-slim woman smiling at O'Malley as she and her friend walked through the door that the guard held open for them had him wondering again if she had an intended. Bloody hell! Did she have a husband?

He'd come to Wyndmere Hall at the behest of his cousin, the duke, in answer to his request for an audience. Best lend his full concentration on the more urgent matter at hand—refilling his family's coffers so he could woo and win an heiress. A highborn lady to grace his table, greet his guests, and warm his bed with but one thought in mind—begetting an heir to carry on the Chattsworth name.

Lady Harrington was a distraction he could ill afford. Best to steer clear of her. Her lilting laughter had him drawing in a breath at the sound. It reminded him of the faerie chimes his mother used to tell him tales of when he was young.

"*Distraction,*" he mumbled aloud.

O'Malley's gaze met his. "Problem, yer lordship?"

"Not at all, O'Malley," he replied. "Lead the way, and I'll bring up the rear."

The nod of approval from his cousin's guard had him moving with purpose for the first time since his father's death. He had a plan and knew how to accomplish that plan, with the duke's help.

Lord, let the man be willing to lend it to me, Chattsworth silently prayed.

CHAPTER THREE

"Do you think Edward will be overly vexed with you?" Calliope could not help but feel that he and the duke would be and worried for her dear friend. Aurelia had been through so much since that first dance she'd shared with her husband-to-be.

"I hope not, but one never can tell where the Lippincott men are concerned."

Calliope realized she'd been tightening her hold on the reins when her mount started to act fractious. "Er…Aurelia, what am I doing wrong?" She'd only learned to ride a few months ago thanks to her friend and the kindness of Persephone, the Duchess of Wyndmere.

"You're holding the reins too tightly," Aurelia cautioned. "Slowly ease your grip, not all at once. You don't want to spook Millie."

Calliope did as she was bid but couldn't control the fear that she'd already upset her horse. Though she tried to fight against the feeling, it kept building until she unconsciously jerked the reins.

"Lady Harrington!"

Calliope looked over her shoulder to see what the viscount was warning her about, belatedly realizing she'd tugged the reins in that direction. Before she could gather her composure, Millie, well-trained horse that she was, bolted in that direction.

"My cousin's right—I am a bacon-brained female!" She fought to regain control.

A large hand pulled on the reins, forcing Millie to come to a halt. She stared at the gloved hand, gathering her wits while she blinked away tears of fright. Before she had herself fully in hand, Patrick vaulted off his horse and stood beside her. "Are ye hurt, yer ladyship?"

Calliope gulped, knowing Patrick would report this to the duke. *Would he be angry with her for endangering one of his horses? Worse yet, had she put her friend in danger, too?*

"Lady Harrington," the viscount's voice sounded close. *Too close!*

She gathered her courage and lifted her gaze to meet his. Concern was evident in his deep blue eyes. "I...er...thank you, your lordship." His eyes reminded her of happier times when her parents were still alive. She'd lay on her back in the grass and stared at the endless blue of a mid-summer sky while her mother and father took turns reading stories of knights in shining armor rescuing damsels in distress. She sighed.

"Yer ladyship," Patrick called again, reminding her she hadn't answered him.

She apologized. "I am fine, Patrick. Thank you for asking, just a bit rattled. My fault entirely. Please do let His Grace know when you report to him."

The viscount let go of her reins and asked, "Why would he report this to the duke?"

"If His Grace takes ye into his confidence, ye may ask him yerself." Patrick stroked Millie's forehead as if gauging the horse's mood and readiness to let Calliope take the reins once again. Satisfied, he nodded to Calliope and then the viscount. "Ye reacted quickly, yer lordship, thank ye."

"I couldn't very well let her ladyship come to any harm."

Calliope was surprised by his response. He'd only just met her. Why would he feel the need to protect her? If it'd been any one of the distant relations she'd lived with over the years, she highly doubted they would have been overly concerned—or ridden to her rescue.

Surprised to feel comforted by the near-stranger's concern for her safety, she leaned forward to gently stroke her hand along Millie's neck. When Millie turned her head and nodded it up and down, relief flowed through Calliope. "I'm terribly sorry to have confused you, Millie. I'll do my best to concentrate for the remainder of the ride to your stable."

She thought she heard a deep chuckle coming from the viscount, but when she looked at him, he was conversing quietly with the duke's guard.

"I understand there's a cupful of oats waiting for you," she crooned. "Let's see if I can guide you there without further incident."

Aurelia moved her mount closer to Calliope's. "I do believe Millie can get you there in one piece, if you but trust her instincts and use a lighter hand on the reins."

"Oh, of course." Calliope hoped she didn't sound as foolish as she felt. Aurelia's smile reassured her that she hadn't made a fool of herself...yet. There was still time to do so if she did not keep her wits about her.

Her thoughts strayed to the handsome viscount riding behind them. "Aurelia," she called softly.

"Yes?"

"Is it true what they say about Hogmanay? About seeing a dark-haired stranger on New Year's Day bringing you good luck?"

Aurelia nodded. "Absolutely. The new curate from Scotland turned out to be the love of my grandmother's life. Their eyes met...and they both knew."

"Knew?" Calliope queried.

"They were meant to be together...always." Aurelia said with a sigh.

"Like you and Edward," Calliope said. "You two light up the room when you are together."

Aurelia smiled as they guided their horses closer to Wyndmere Hall. "He's everything to me. Happiness and love fill my heart with such joy just standing by his side."

"How wonderful," Calliope confided. Would she ever experience an emotion even close to what her friend described?

"And when he kisses me..." Aurelia's brilliant smile spoke volumes.

"Yes?" Calliope lifted her gloved hand to her lips, waiting to hear what her friend would say. *What would it be like to have a handsome man press his lips to hers?*

"Calliope!"

Aurelia's warning tone reached her in time for her to ease up on the reins again. This time, Millie seemed to expect it and slowed to a stop. "Forgive me, Millie," Calliope rasped. "I cannot think what came over me." Although she knew it had been thoughts of a certain dark-haired, handsome man drawing her into his embrace.

She ducked her head as if to speak to her horse again, so no one would see the embarrassment evident on her heated face.

"You're a treasure, Millie," Aurelia praised. "We're very close to the stables, Calliope. I'm sorry to have roused you so early this morning," she apologized. "I just couldn't bear it if I'd forgotten Grandmother MacTavish's altar cloth."

"I don't mind rising early. I've been up before dawn for years," Calliope reassured her. "I'm not used to being the focus of such attention," she added. "Especially when it's brought on by my ineptitude."

"You are not inept!" Aurelia corrected. "You are still learning how to be comfortable riding a horse. Remember when I told you they can sense our every emotion?"

Calliope sighed. "Yes."

"It's best to remember that until you are more confident in your skill."

"I suppose you are right," Calliope said slowly. "You are the very best of friends."

"So are you. Who else would I have asked to help me with this task before dawn?"

Calliope smiled at her friend. "I suppose you couldn't very well ask Edward."

Aurelia laughed. "He would have jumped at the opportunity, but it truly is bad luck for the bridegroom to see his bride before the ceremony."

Calliope agreed and the pair settled into companionable silence, riding side by side as the sun's rays warmed the air around them.

WILLIAM NOTICED THE way Lady Harrington tensed in the saddle. No doubt, that tension was being communicated to her horse. Ready to leap into action, he paused when he saw Lady Coddington move close and take matters into her own hands.

Relief filled him. Where did this overwhelming need to protect the woman come from? They'd been introduced less than an hour ago. "Curious."

Maximus danced a bit, obviously anxious to pick up the pace, but William reined him in, reassuring him, "We'll be there soon. You'll bed down in a stall with sweet, fresh hay and oats to eat."

His horse lifted his head and snorted his pleasure.

William chuckled. "I could use something to eat myself."

Unease filled him the closer they got to Wyndmere Hall. Would his cousin be on hand to greet him, or keep him cooling his heels? He'd sent the duke his response and advised he was leaving post haste and had unknowingly arrived in time for the earl's wedding.

Had the duke intended for him to take longer to respond? That was a bit of a worry. The viscount breathed in the cold, crisp winter air and set his troubling thoughts aside. He was here now. The duke would either welcome him or send him back to the smallish inn he noted on his way through the village of Windermere.

The ladies picked up the pace as they rounded the bend in the road ahead. The trees thinned out, revealing the awesome splendor of Wyndmere Hall. The viscount had expected the estate to be larger than his own and was not disappointed. The grounds were well kept, the structure standing tall and proud, complete with…

"Good God, are those gargoyles on the roof?"

Soft feminine laughter reached his ears. *Had he said that last out loud?*

Lady Coddington smiled over her shoulder at him. "Yes, your lordship."

"Aren't they marvelous?" Lady Harrington asked.

"Impressive with the sunlight illuminating them."

"Mayhap the duke will bend his strict rules and allow us to give you a tour of the rooftop," Lady Coddington suggested.

"Rules?" William was curious to hear more from his cousin regarding rules and rooftops.

O'Malley turned around and waited for the trio to reach him. "Is there a problem?"

"Gargoyles."

"Lady Aurelia, ye'll not be goin' up to the rooftops today of all days."

She beamed at O'Malley. "I should say not, Patrick. I'd never risk the duke's censure on the day I'm to wed his brother!" Her lilting laughter filled the air and settled around them.

He rather enjoyed the sensation of being included, though how long that would last, he hadn't a bloody clue. There was still the matter of his arrival. Well, he reasoned, he was here now and would have to make the best of whatever his cousin decided to do about it.

"Patrick!"

The viscount glanced in the direction of the shout and noted the man hurrying toward them bore a distinct resemblance to O'Malley—both were broad and tall with fair hair and green eyes.

O'Malley nodded to the man and dismounted, allowing the man to take the reins of his horse. "Is there trouble then, Finn?"

The man turned and stared at the viscount. "And here I was going to ask ye the same."

O'Malley smiled. "'Tis Viscount Chattsworth, come at the duke's request."

"We've been expecting ye," Finn proclaimed. "But weren't expecting ye so soon."

The viscount's heart sank. He had rushed to answer the duke's summons. There was nothing to be done now but soldier on. "I came as soon as I received the reply from my cousin, His Grace."

The two men accepted his response without question. "Ye'll be wantin' to take care of yer mount," O'Malley said. "Me brother, Finn," he said by way of introduction. "Viscount Chattsworth."

"A pleasure, yer lordship," Finn replied. "I'll show ye to the stables."

The viscount was relieved not to be questioned further by his cousin's guard. He wasn't intimated by the men, just curious as to the extent of the need for them. He'd heard of the trouble his cousins had weathered in the last year. The most recent of which still circulated the *ton* though the attack at Wyndmere Hall had been at least six months ago.

"Thank you, Finn."

The man grinned at him. "'Tis a fine bit of horseflesh ye are," Finn said to the viscount's horse.

The viscount smiled. "Maximus."

"Proud name for a proud stallion," Finn led the viscount and his mount to the stables.

William glanced over his shoulder at the two women who were being escorted inside. *Would he see Lady Harrington again, or would he be denied the pleasure and given his marching orders to seek lodging in the village?*

Time would tell.

Chapter Four

"**W**HAT DO THE two of you think you're doing running off like that before anyone is awake?" the Duchess of Wyndmere demanded.

Aurelia and Calliope shared a look before Aurelia answered, "I'm sorry Persephone. It's just that I'd forgotten—"

"Your wits?" the duchess suggested.

Calliope giggled and Aurelia frowned at her, until Calliope apologized. "Do forgive me. I can't think what came over me."

"The dire situation the two of you could have landed in," Persephone continued. "What if Patrick hadn't seen you leave and followed after you?"

This time, Aurelia was the one to giggle.

The duchess glared at them and Calliope worried they had upset her. That would never do, given the duchess' delicate condition. "We had no choice," Calliope explained. "You see, it was Anna Bramwell's altar cloth that she'd forgotten yesterday."

The duchess sighed. "Anna?"

"My grandmother MacTavish."

"I distinctly heard Calliope say Bramwell," the duchess corrected.

"Her name before the dark-haired, dark-eyed Alasdair Mac-Tavish swept into her life on that New Year's Day so long ago." Aurelia proceeded to tell the story of how her grandparents had met on Hogmanay.

The duchess' eyes softened, and her demeanor changed. "Ring for tea won't you, Calliope?"

"Of course."

"I just wish you'd alerted one of Jared's guards as to what you intended."

"Didn't Patrick tell you that he saw them leave and followed after them?" Phoebe asked from her perch on the settee before the fire. "Mayhap it was my darling brother who relayed that bit of information."

The duchess frowned in answer.

Phoebe mirrored the look before adding, "Do you honestly think my brother's guards would not know what Aurelia and Calliope were up to?"

"Not the point, Phoebe."

"It is entirely the point," Phoebe maintained. "Jared has seen fit to secure Wyndmere Hall from the outer perimeter all the way to the village."

"And the inside," Aurelia reminded her soon-to-be sisters-in-law. "No one comes or goes without his knowledge."

"We knew one of his guards would follow us," Calliope added.

"Did you?" Persephone sounded as if she were getting riled again.

"Truly?" Aurelia asked. When Phoebe snorted out a laugh, she sighed. "No. I'd thought Edward might be the one to follow us."

"Bad luck," Calliope reminded her friend.

"I know, but I haven't seen him except for passing him a time or two on my way to the kitchen or the stable."

"As it should be," Persephone reminded her. "We've worked hard to resurrect your reputation from the ashes. Servants talk, even ones as loyal as those on our staff. One little slip of the tongue could put you back in the suds again!"

"Is there really still such a need when more and more of Jared and Edward's father's staunch friends have come forward to lend their support and consequence?" Aurelia inquired.

Persephone was incredulous. "Would you undo all that we have accomplished with the help of our family, friends, and Jared and Edward's peers?"

Immediately contrite, Aurelia fell silent.

Calliope felt sorry for her friend and spoke up in her defense. "Would you have Aurelia ignore her family tradition? It's Hogmanay for Heaven's sake!"

Persephone's gaze slid to Calliope's and opened her mouth to speak when someone knocked on door to the sitting room. "Come in!"

Calliope reached for Aurelia's hand and squeezed it quickly before letting it go.

"Do not suppose for one moment that this conversation is over," the duchess warned. "Thank you, Merry."

"Shall I pour, Your Grace?" their housekeeper asked.

"No, thank you."

When Merry left, Persephone said, "Now then, ladies. Tell me about Viscount Chattsworth. I'm afraid Jared has not filled me in as to the family connection. I confess to being beyond curious as to why he requested an audience with my husband."

Aurelia and Calliope sat on the vacant settee side by side and waited for the duchess to pour the tea. When she passed the teacups, they graciously accepted them, declining the teacakes.

After a few sips and endless silence, the duchess prompted, "Well?"

Aurelia set down her teacup and leaned forward. "He's a dark-haired, handsome man with brilliant blue eyes...and the first one to walk through the doors this Hogmanay!"

The duchess glanced at Calliope and slowly smiled. "Do tell."

Aurelia told of their morning encounter in the church.

Phoebe's eyes lit up as she reached for a currant teacake, took a healthy bite and chewed. When she was finished, she asked, "So, he looks like my brothers?"

Aurelia nodded and Calliope sighed, noting the way the duchess was staring at them. Aurelia squirmed under Persephone's direct gaze. Needing to deflect the attention away from the bride-to-be, Calliope offered herself up as the new target. "He is quite tall, although an inch or so shorter than Patrick when they stood next to one another."

"Ah, so he's tall," Persephone said. "Pray continue."

"He's broad through the shoulders, and his hair was a similar rich, dark chestnut color."

The duchess' eyes brightened. "Did he smile?"

"At one point," Calliope agreed.

"But he didn't have dimples like my Edward and the duke," Aurelia added.

"Pity," Persephone said. "Well then—"

"He has a cleft chin. I didn't notice it at first. Aurelia and I were startled when the door burst open and, at first glance, we thought it was Edward. When we got over our shock—"

"Probably because you'd thought you'd been caught by Patrick O'Malley or one of his kin," Phoebe interrupted, stirring her tea.

"It was an uncanny likeness," Aurelia said. "A bit of a shock and then to find out he is cousin to Edward and Jared."

"Distant, I believe," Persephone told them.

"The viscount said his great-grandmother was a Lippincott."

"That would explain the dark hair and brilliant blue eyes," Phoebe interjected.

"He came to my rescue," Calliope informed them.

"How so?" The duchess set her teacup down and waited.

Calliope felt her face flush with her embarrassment. "You see...I was...to be truthful—"

"No need to dither about it," Aurelia said. "Everyone here knows you're still learning the intricacies of riding. It's far more involved than one would think, especially those of us who have learned to ride a such a young age."

"Were you riding Millie?" the duchess asked.

"Yes."

"She's normally quite well behaved," the duchess said aloud. "What happened?"

Aurelia explained in detail and the duchess' eyes gleamed. "Wonderful, isn't it?"

"That I was unable to keep my head on such a short ride back here?" Calliope couldn't believe Persephone would think so.

"You misunderstand me," Persephone strove to put Calliope at ease. "The viscount volunteered to ride behind you and Aurelia—a position of protection. Obviously pleasing Patrick with the offer. As such, he was able to observe your difficulties and rush to the rescue."

Calliope sighed, reliving the moment…well, except for feeling foolish. She didn't relish feeling that way again anytime soon. She'd have to be on guard and pay closer mind to what she was doing. "No more woolgathering," she mused.

Aurelia was quick to say, "Perfectly understandable. Why not indulge in a bit of a daydream now and then?"

"I wouldn't advise doing such when you're riding," Phoebe suggested. "At least until you've become more proficient."

Calliope agreed.

"I do believe I shall meet with the viscount myself and see what's to be done," Persephone said.

"Done?" Aurelia and Calliope said at the same time.

"About what?" Calliope asked.

Persephone smiled and shook her head. "Never you two mind. It's time to focus on the day ahead and Aurelia marrying the man of her dreams."

Aurelia sighed aloud.

The duchess rose and walked over to the servants' bell pull, motioning Phoebe toward the door. A few moments later, Humphries arrived with one of the footmen to clear away the remnants of their tea. "Do you require assistance with anything else, Your Grace?"

She smiled at their butler. "Not at the moment, Humphries,

but thank you for asking."

When they left, Persephone turned to smile at the others gathered. "Today may have begun inauspiciously, but it shall not end that way. Ladies, we have a wedding to prepare for. I suggest you each refer to the lists my darling husband has supplied to each one of us in the household."

Phoebe chuckled. "Dear Jared does love to plan out his days in detail."

Persephone beamed. "My duke is seldom surprised."

"I daresay, my brother will be a few months from now," Phoebe suggested.

The duchess placed a hand on her stomach and held it there. "It will be a wondrous surprise, will it not?"

Her hand seemed to jump for several moments while the ladies watched in unabashed fascination. "Do not be overly concerned," she reassured them. "One becomes quite accustomed to the movement."

Aurelia was the first to ask, "Does it pain you?"

The duchess shook her head. "Not at all, it started as a flutter, as if I'd swallowed a butterfly. It's gradually developed into a rolling, stretching movement of our babe as he or she grows."

"No one's ever confided such to me," Phoebe whispered, staring at her sister-in-law's hand.

"It has been the way of things for years," Persephone told them. "Probably meant to shield our *delicate* sensibilities."

"Hah!" Phoebe grumbled.

"I felt so unprepared for marriage and the prospect of childbirth and would rather none of you are as ill prepared as I." She positively glowed as she continued, "As Aurelia is to be married today, and you two will surely marry soon, I felt the need to share what I've experienced."

"I'm relieved to know it doesn't pain you," Calliope murmured.

"It has woken me from a dead sleep, and quite unnerves His Grace."

The three friends laughed at the image of the staunchly proper Duke of Wyndmere suffering from a case of nervousness.

"I would ask that you not repeat what I've just told you. My husband has his pride you know."

Phoebe snorted. "Father always said that pride goeth before a fall."

"And he'd be right," Persephone agreed. "Let us allow my darling duke a bit more time. I have a feeling the impending birth of our babe may be his undoing."

Everyone agreed as they followed Persephone from the room to find their task lists. "We have much to accomplish," she told the ladies. "I suggest we meet in the upper sitting room at noon to see where we are and what still needs to be done. This wedding will go off like clockwork!"

"I do believe you've just tempted fate to challenge that prediction, my dear sister-in-law," Phoebe warned.

Calliope and Aurelia hurried to catch up. "Do you think something else will go wrong?" Aurelia whispered.

"Nothing has gone wrong," Calliope reassured her. "Things happened as they ought, just not in the order we'd planned."

"I'm so glad you're here, Calliope."

"I am honored to be here. Would you like to be alone with your list, or shall I fetch mine and meet you in your bedchamber."

"Oh, do bring your list. We can compare them and see just what Edward's brother intends for us to do in the long hours ahead of us until my wedding this evening."

"Just imagine, married by candlelight. The church decorated with fresh greens, your grandmother's altar cloth gracing the altar..." Calliope's voice trailed off as she pictured the image in her head.

Aurelia came to a halt outside of Calliope's bedchamber. "I'll wait here for you."

"I won't be a moment." As promised, Calliope rushed out of her room, holding her list. "Are you as excited as I am?"

Aurelia giggled. "I feel like an absolute bird-wit," she confessed. "My stomach has had butterflies fluttering around in it for the last month!"

"Imagine," Calliope said, linking her arm through Aurelia's. "Butterflies in January."

"They'd never survive," Aurelia said soberly.

"Ah, but since they're safely tucked inside you, they will."

They were laughing as they entered Aurelia's bedchamber.

"CHATTSWORTH," THE DUKE said as he rose, extending his hand to the viscount. "Glad you could make it."

"I understand I have interrupted your brother's wedding day," the viscount started to apologize, only to fall silent when the duke raised a hand to stop him.

"I wasn't sure when you'd be able to get away. Your arrival is not unexpected. No matter the timing, I'm glad to reacquaint myself with family...no matter how distant the connection."

He sat in one of the leather chairs before the fire and motioned for the viscount to be seated.

"Thank you, Your Grace."

"I admit to being intrigued by your request," the duke said. "Our connection is through the Lippincotts?"

"Yes, Your Grace." William wondered if the duke would repudiate the connection or embrace it. "My great-grandmother was a Lippincott before she married."

"Family is all important," the duke said, watching him closely. "Wouldn't you agree?"

"Wholeheartedly," the viscount said with conviction. "I am the last Chattsworth...that is unless I marry and beget an heir."

"An only child?" the duke queried.

William shook his head. "My older brother, August, died when he was ten."

The duke's expression changed to one of understanding. "I know how it feels to lose a brother. I am sorry for your loss."

"My mother died giving birth to my sister."

"How old is your sister?" the duke wanted to know.

William stared down at his hands for long moments to gather himself, he didn't like speaking of the dead. He still held himself responsible for his brother's death, although no one else had.

The duke cleared his throat. "No matter the circumstances or how many family members one has lost, the pain is acute for years. Well, at least I have found it to be so."

The viscount lifted his gaze and found the duke waiting for him to do so. "I had heard your father had gone missing but, at the time, I was mired in my own family's difficulties. Has there been no word of him?"

"None," William said. "I've made discrete inquiries in the last year. There have been a few suggestions, but no one seems to know what happened to him."

"I would be happy to lend assistance."

"Thank you, Your Grace."

"What say we meet tomorrow after luncheon and go over the details of what you do know?"

"I would be most grateful."

The duke steepled his fingers and tapped them together before speaking. "I understand your family has an estate in Sussex. One of my family's estates is located in Sussex as well. Mayhap, we could arrange a visit in the near future."

The viscount wanted nothing of the kind. If the duke found out what dire straits Chattsworth Manor was in, he'd deduce that William only intended to extract a promise of funds. The duke would likely toss him out on his ear! He could not let that happen. Too many things depended upon his gaining the duke's cooperation and financial assistance.

"I was hoping to spend a bit of time in London," he explained. "As the sole remaining Chattsworth, I feel it is my duty to my family to continue the family name."

The duke nodded. "Of course. Looking for a wife, are you?"

The viscount shifted, uneasy with the direct questions he hadn't been prepared to answer. "My father had wanted me to."

"I quite agree. Have you been to London recently? I don't recall seeing you there."

He quickly answered, "I was unable to make the journey last Season, but hope to arrive early—you know, to…" How to put it without giving away his plans? The duke would never lend his consequence, or blunt, if the viscount told him the truth. *Would he?* Before that thought took hold, he dismissed it. His Grace would likely cut all ties with his family, thereby ruining any chance William's cousin, Marcus, had obtaining a leg up from the duke.

"Having floundered myself recently—that is until I met Her Grace, I understand the way may seem unnavigable at first. You may find your way more easily with help from someone accustomed to the ways of the *ton*."

The viscount held his breath, waiting—and hoping—for an offer from the duke to be that someone.

Instead, the duke changed the subject. "Tell me about Chattsworth Manor. How many tenant farmers do you have and what crops do they raise?"

A loud knock on the duke's library door had him looking away from the viscount, who let out the breath he'd been holding.

"Come in," the duke called out. "Yes, Humphries, what is it?"

"Her Grace has need of you, Your Grace."

The duke shot to his feet. "Is she unwell? Has something happened?"

Humphries was quick to reassure him, "Her Grace is quite well. She asked me to deliver the message that she has a small matter that requires your immediate attention, Your Grace."

The duke visibly relaxed. "Very good. I shall attend her at once." He turned toward William. "I have asked Humphries to ready one of our bedchambers for you. If you would be so good as to follow him, you can make yourself comfortable. I shall ask Merry to have tea sent up."

"Please don't go to any trouble on my account," the viscount was quick to reply.

"As our intrepid butler will agree, our housekeeper, Merry, ensures the pot is always on the boil. Our cook, Constance, will have been baking since the fires were first stoked well before dawn. Aside from the specialties she is no doubt whipping up for my brother's wedding this evening, she will have baked the usual tarts and teacakes for this morning and our afternoon teatime."

Humphries bowed to the viscount. "This way, your lordship."

Watching the duke stride down the hallway and up the stairs, he wondered what small matter his cousin would have to attend to. He shrugged and followed Humphries.

He'd been given the gift of time to come up with a proper answer for the duke. What to say? How many tenants or servants should he invent? Chattsworth Manor had a small, elderly skeletal staff and he did not relish admitting that. His father was nowhere to be found, or else he would be able to ask him how to help their tenant farmers whose fields had gone fallow and there was little to be harvested.

Grateful for the time to come up with an appropriate number of staff and answers regarding the rest, the viscount vowed to do his best to recall the names of former servants and their positions. It would be far easier to do than to invent a new fictional staff.

What had he gotten himself in to?

CHAPTER FIVE

"PERSEPHONE!" THE DUKE called out as he strode into their bedchamber. "Is something wrong? Is it the babe?"

The duchess held out her hands to her husband. "I'm fine, my love."

He took them in his and slowly drew her closer until she had to tip her head back to meet his gaze. Silent for a few moments, he finally sighed deeply. "Your eyes are clear, your face slightly flushed, and our babe is performing somersaults between us."

He pressed a kiss to her brow and held her against him without speaking.

"Is aught amiss?"

"Not a thing," he reassured her. "Just the overwhelming feeling that I have no idea how to handle the prospect of impending fatherhood."

She snorted out a laugh and he pulled back from her. "Are you laughing at me?"

Persephone denied it. "I'm laughing at your words because I have been having similar thoughts as to the prospect of me becoming a mother."

He traced the curve of her cheek and then the line of her jaw before pressing a kiss to the end of her nose and finally her lips. "We have one another to rely on, Persephone. How can we fail to meet the challenge as long as we are together?"

Her smile magnified her beauty and filled him with a happiness he hadn't known he was capable of. "Together," he agreed. "Now what had you summoning my presence so urgently."

She sighed, nestling against him. "I wanted to find out more about Viscount Chattsworth. Did you know Aurelia and Calliope thought it was Edward walking into the church?"

"There is a striking family resemblance. I was about to find out more about the viscount's situation. I daresay, the rumors surrounding Earl Chattsworth's disappearance are growing by leaps and bounds."

"Do you think he's still alive?"

Persephone's worry had him immediately striving to soothe her. "Reports are varied. Some say he was held up by a highwayman. Others that he'd been seen boarding one of the sailing vessels he'd heavily invested in. Still others swear he'd been gambling in the bowels of London."

"Busy man."

"Indeed."

"Have you heard from Captain Coventry?"

Jared stroked his hand up and down her spine to ease the knots he felt there. "I have."

She stiffened. "And?"

"As always, my London man-of-affairs has collected the information I required most efficiently."

Persephone eased out of his arms and put her hands on her hips. "Do not toy with me, Jared. I need to know what you know."

"My dear duchess. You most certainly will, just as soon as I finish the conversation you interrupted."

She sputtered and he chuckled. "Your curiosity will be the undoing of us both," he predicted. "Now you shall have to wait as I do not have the time to continue my conversation with the viscount, else Edward and Aurelia's wedding will have to be delayed."

"No, we are not delaying their wedding," Persephone rushed

out. "Let us see where we are in our plans for their perfect day," she said. "Shall we?"

He smiled. "I'll be in my study if you'd care to join me."

"Let me fetch my list."

The duke wondered what the devil happened to Earl Chattsworth and why the viscount hadn't been able to uncover any leads in the last year. A dark thought filled him with dread. *Had the viscount been involved in the earl's disappearance?* As upsetting as the thought may be, the duke had been exposed to more dastardly plots than he'd thought possible in the last year. Nothing would surprise him. His first impression of the viscount had met with his approval. The younger man had met his gaze without shifting it about and had conversed easily. If he'd had something to hide, the man would not have been able to meet his gaze or hold a conversation.

He needed to have a brief meeting with Patrick O'Malley, head of his guard, before he tackled the next item on his list. He had an uneasy feeling they'd be getting to the bottom of the dual requests he'd received recently, both from distant relatives: Viscount Chattsworth and Baron Summerfield.

He wondered how long before Summerfield arrived on his doorstep. Mayhap *the cousins* were behind the disappearance of the earl...he waited a heartbeat for the thought to fully process. His gut and his head were in agreement, the cousins were not involved.

Persephone held up the list he'd penned for her. "Shall we, my darling duke?"

He lifted her hand and feathered a kiss across the back of it. "Indeed."

CALLIOPE TRIED NOT to stare at the tall, dark, handsome man seated beside her. Heat positively radiated from the sleeve of his dark blue frockcoat when he opened his hymnal and held it between them to share. Tingles of awareness shot from her elbow—where she'd inadvertently brushed it against his, to her fingertips. "I do beg your pardon," she whispered. *Would he be overset with her for brushing against him?*

He leaned closer and whispered, "Quite a crush, isn't it?"

Surprised by his comment, she glanced out of the sides of her eyes at him. Bright blue eyes filled with merriment had the tingling sensation moving from her fingers to her belly. *How odd.* First the tingles started where they'd brushed against one another, and then they rushed through her, heating her skin as they traveled from her fingers to her belly.

She felt her face flush but could not do a thing about it now.

"If anyone here knows of any reason why these two persons should not be joined together in holy matrimony, let him speak now..." the vicar paused, "or forever hold his peace."

Thankfully, no one spoke up. Calliope couldn't hold back her sigh of relief.

The deep rumbling of the viscount's voice had her glancing at him once more. "Were you concerned someone would object?"

"'Tis the truth, there are one or two that had both Aurelia and I quite beside ourselves with worry."

Before he could ask who the two in question might be, the groom smiled at the bride and pulled her close for their first kiss as man and wife.

The collective sigh from the women gathered brought tears to Calliope's eyes. Her friend deserved every moment of happiness the years ahead held for her and Edward. Opening her reticule, she shifted the contents to find her lace handkerchief. Before she could, a large linen square appeared in front of her face.

"You are too kind," she rasped as she wiped her eyes and held it out to the viscount.

"Why don't you hang on to it for now?" he suggested.

Bold blue eyes were watching her closely as she met his gaze.

"I...er...thank you, your lordship."

His smile was genuine. She knew the difference, having had more than one of her relatives smile at her while their eyes remained coldly detached. When Aurelia's Uncle Phineas smiled, his face lit up and his eyes sparkled with amusement. He had a wonderful smile.

The viscount's smile deepened his eyes to sapphire, further distracting her, while an emotion she hadn't ever seen before held her attention longer than would be deemed proper.

She caught herself before she sighed aloud again. *That would never do.* She did not want to call any further attention to herself than she already had by speaking to the viscount. Calliope could not seem to help herself. The man captivated her and had since the moment he'd strode into the church just past dawn.

The vicar's wife played the recessional hymn as the couple passed by those gathered to celebrate their nuptials.

Phoebe turned around and asked, "Wasn't it a lovely wedding?"

Calliope sighed. "It was beautiful."

"By the way," her friend began, "what were you and the viscount discussing that could not wait until Aurelia and my brother finished saying their vows?"

Calliope froze. "I am so sorry, Phoebe. It's just that...well you see—"

The viscount smoothly interrupted, "I accidently brushed against Lady Harrington and apologized."

Calliope must have made a sound, as the viscount turned to her and asked, "Shall I apologize again, my lady?"

Shock had her mouth dropping open, but she didn't notice that it had until Phoebe touched her own chin and tapped it. Calliope closed her mouth and shook her head in silent answer. Her tongue was tied and she couldn't have spoken if her life depended upon it.

"Are you ready to return?" Persephone asked. "Constance has outdone herself, preparing their wedding feast."

Calliope and Phoebe assured the duchess that they were.

The viscount waited for the duke and duchess to precede them, and then Phoebe, before stepping into the aisle and motioning for Calliope to proceed. When they reached the doors to the church, the duke was waiting for them.

"Calliope would you mind riding back to Wyndmere Hall with Lord Coddington, Viscount Chattsworth, and Phoebe?"

Calliope smiled. "Not at all." She looked up at the night sky surprised to note the stars had disappeared along with the moon. "There's quite a chill in the air."

"Feels like it will snow," the duke replied. "In you go," he said, extending his hand to his sister.

Phoebe looked over her shoulder at him. "How are you and Persephone getting back home?"

"We'll be taking the chaise," he informed her.

"Aren't you afraid she'll catch a chill?"

The duke chuckled. "Have you noted how often my dear wife comments on the oppressive heat?"

Calliope nudged Phoebe so she would step into the duke's coach. "She's been quite warm these last few weeks."

"But it's January!"

Phoebe's statement wasn't lost on deaf ears. Persephone spoke up. "'Tis the truth, I'm having a devil of a time being in close quarters and dealing with the heat."

The duke raised his eyes heavenward and sighed.

Persephone laughed softly. "Sorry, my dear. I shall have to be more careful with word choice."

"Indeed," Jared replied. "Else the first word our son speaks will put us beyond the pale!"

The duchess laid a hand on his arm, "Don't you mean our daughter?"

Phoebe leaned close and whispered in Calliope's ear, "I daresay, she looks as if she's carrying two babes instead of the one."

Calliope's eyes rounded as Lord Coddington and Viscount

Chattsworth entered the coach and sat across from the ladies.

"Is aught amiss?" Lord Coddington asked.

"Everything's fine," Phoebe answered for Calliope.

Aurelia's uncle smiled at them. "Lovely wedding."

Calliope and Phoebe smiled and started talking.

Lord Coddington held up his hands and laughed as the coach moved forward. "One at a time, my dears."

Calliope nodded to Phoebe. "You first."

Phoebe smiled. "Didn't Aurelia look splendid in that gown?"

Lord Coddington beamed. "Madame Beaudoine outdid herself designing the perfect dress for my niece."

"Did you see how happy they looked standing there gazing into one another's eyes for that heartbeat before they shared their first kiss?"

Lord Coddington cleared his throat. "Yes, well it's as expected," he told her. "Young love and all that."

"It was love at first glance, you know," Phoebe reminded Aurelia's uncle.

"I'll admit I was not certain Earl Lippincott was the man for my niece. After getting to know him better, and observing how he treated her, I had no doubts at all."

Phoebe's eyes danced with glee. "Then it must have been another uncle of Aurelia's that took his time giving his grudging consent to my brother."

Lord Coddington frowned, but the deep lines across his forehead quickly smoothed as he smiled. "I wasn't convinced at first that any man would be good enough for my brother's daughter."

Calliope reached across to place a hand on Lord Coddington's arm. "You are the very best of men, Lord Coddington."

"Now, now," he cautioned, "didn't I insist you call me Uncle Phineas?"

Calliope eased back and tucked her hands in her lap. Gathering her composure at his reminder of his generosity in taking her into his family, she nodded. "You are the very best of men, *Uncle Phineas*."

"It is my cross to bear."

The viscount chuckled, and soon the foursome chatted amiably about the chaotic day, the candlelight ceremony, and the wedding feast to come.

They arrived at Wyndmere Hall a short time later amidst the flurry of servants bustling about and the duke's personal guard keeping watch over them all.

When the duke pulled his horse to a stop, he handed the reins to one of the stable lads. Disembarking, he walked behind the coach and lifted his hand to his wife. "Watch your step, my darling."

Persephone sighed. "It's more than a bit frustrating, trying to maintain my balance as of late."

"Hence my concern," he reminded her.

As they walked inside, she pulled him close and whispered, "Why do I have the feeling you're trying to push the viscount and Calliope together?"

He paused midstride and then shook his head. "Ever observant."

"Well?" Persephone urged.

"Because I am interested in seeing how he will treat our dear Calliope. After all, she won't be a poor relation for long."

"Have you spoken to her yet?"

The duke sighed. "With the viscount's arrival today, I have not had the chance."

"She'll be thrilled," she reassured her husband. "Probably faint dead away when you inform her that you'll be giving her rather a large dowry."

"It's the very least I can do for Phoebe's good friend. She and Aurelia have stood by my sister through thick and thin this last year. I'll not see her reduced to her former status while living with her dastard of a cousin."

"Er...second cousin," Persephone reminded him.

"Yes. Quite."

"Back to Viscount Chattsworth," Persephone urged.

"Ah, yes, my distant cousin is in a difficult position at best. His father has been missing for almost a year. I've heard scuttlebutt—through Coventry, that all but a handful of servants remain at Chattsworth Manor."

"Where are the rest of them?"

"When the earl wasn't there to pay them, and the viscount apparently didn't have the coin to do so, they up and left."

"But not a handful?" Persephone asked.

"Indeed. The butler, housekeeper, cook, and valet—and all of them long overdue to be pensioned off after years of serving the viscount's family."

"Do you plan to involve yourself in your cousin's affairs?"

The duke smiled down at his wife and patted her hand. "I do believe I shall."

"Thank goodness. He's seems a decent fellow and Calliope is quite taken with him."

"That remains to be seen."

His countenance darkened and Persephone asked, "What aren't you telling me?"

"It's not what I'm not telling you, my dear," he reassured her. "It's what the viscount is not telling me."

"Has he not been upfront with you about his situation?"

"I've yet to have an entire conversation with the man," he grumbled. "You do recall that your summons requesting my immediate presence interrupted my meeting with the viscount."

Persephone looked at him for long moments without speaking. "Mayhap."

The duke threw back his head and laughed. It was a joyous sound that had his wife beaming up at him. "I do so love the sound of your unbridled laughter, Jared. It warms my heart."

He drew her closer to his side. "Does it?"

Persephone smiled. "And our daughter dances a jig whenever she hears it."

He shook his head. "Our son," he corrected.

"Daughter," she insisted.

The duke chuckled as he led his wife into the dining room where the bride and groom were happily chatting with the first of their guests to arrive.

Calliope noted Aurelia couldn't take her eyes off her husband, even for a moment. It was as if an invisible bond formed between the two from the moment they were pronounced man and wife. She sighed at the romantic thought, then rationalized it away. *No one could love another that deeply, could they?*

Her thoughts were interrupted by the deep laughter she recognized as belonging to the viscount. She turned toward the sound. The duke and the viscount flanked Aurelia and Edward and were smiling. The family likeness was beyond startling seeing them so close to one another.

Although the duke and the earl were just a bit taller than the viscount, he was just as broad through the chest and shoulders. Their dark chestnut hair and brilliant blue eyes spoke of shared lineage. Lord, they were a sight to see—tall, dark, and handsome men. Her heart fluttered in her breast when the viscount turned his gaze her way.

At the duke's nod, the viscount bowed to the group and headed her way. Breath held, she watched the easy grace with which he navigated his way through the crowd, never once letting his gaze veer away from hers.

She imagined a moth would feel just like this as it danced toward the flame it could not resist. Calliope had no defense against the feelings swamping her where this man was concerned. How or why they started just that morning, she couldn't say, and had no yardstick with which to measure these feelings against. She'd never been instantly captivated before. It was so far out of the realm of possibility in her life that she was left floundering, with no idea what to say or do.

"Are you all right, Lady Harrington?" His concern filled his beautiful blue eyes.

She swallowed against the lump of emotion constricting her throat. "Yes," she rasped. "Quite, thank you."

"You've gone pale." He slipped his arm through hers. "You should sit," he told her, guiding her toward the first empty chair and going down on one knee beside her. "Shall I ring for one of the servants to help you to your room?"

At that last comment, Calliope found her voice and her reason. "I am fine," she insisted. "Just a momentary...er...moment," she said, for lack of a better way to describe that locking gazes with him stole her breath, her mind, and her heart.

Eye level, she was a bit unnerved by his fierce frown, but relaxed when he nodded. "Very well." He rose to his feet in time to meet the duke who must have noted something was amiss.

"Calliope! Are you unwell?"

"No, Your Grace. Must have been the pre-dawn start to my day with Aurelia."

The duke relaxed by degrees as he studied her face. "They will be serving the food momentarily," he told her before turning to the viscount.

"Chattsworth, would you be so good as to attend Lady Calliope? I'm sure the duchess would be reassured all was well in hand if you were her companion during the wedding feast."

The viscount bowed to the duke and agreed. "It would be my pleasure."

Calliope looked from one dark-haired man to the other, and wondered if it was her imagination, or had something a bit more formal just passed between the two men. Neither one said another word, as the duke nodded and turned to leave.

Once he had, the viscount drew out the chair beside her and smiled at her. "How are you related to Lady Coddington?"

Calliope smiled at him and corrected, "Lady Lippincott."

He chuckled. "Of course, the earl's new countess."

"We became friends a year or so ago, having met during her debut," Calliope explained. She left out the pertinent detail that she'd been on the fringes of the ballroom. Delighted to be allowed to attend, while at the same time, a bit unsure of her welcome once all and sundry learned of her status in life as a poor relation.

The footmen carried in enormous trays laden with a sumptuous feast. Calliope's eyes widened as they were being served.

The viscount must have noted her reaction and asked, "This cannot be your first taste of pheasant, is it?"

She didn't want to lie to the man, so she schooled her features and evaded his query. "What an unusual question, your lordship."

Soon, they were chatting companionably as they enjoyed the next few removes. "I do believe that is the best meal I've had in quite some time," the viscount remarked.

Her eyes flew to his and she wondered, wouldn't a viscount have many occasions to enjoy such a wonderful meal? Mayhap he did not enjoy the same level of comfort as the duke and his brother, the earl. As she did not directly answer his question earlier, it would not behoove her to question him now. Instead, she nodded, silently agreeing with his statement.

The duke and duchess rose to their feet and raised their glasses—the duchess being allowed a bit of watered wine for the occasion, as the duke proposed a toast. "To my brother, Edward, and his beautiful bride, Lady Aurelia. May they enjoy every bit of their life together as they enjoy on this day. May they be blessed with children, love, and laughter to the end of their days."

Those gathered to celebrate, shouted at once, "Hear, hear!"

The earl pulled his new wife into his embrace and kissed her breathless, if the way she sagged in his arms were any indication. He laughed as she leaned against him and reached for his glass. "I shall endeavor to provide my brother with nieces and nephews aplenty!"

Calliope felt her cheeks flame, but she raised her glass and joined in the revelry. As she sipped, her eyes met the viscount's. "Do I have something on my face?" She worried that she'd somehow missed a spot.

"You are singularly lovely when you blush, Lady Calliope."

She bobbled the glass she held, but the viscount's quick reflexes prevented her from spilling wine on herself. "Thank you, my lord."

He studied her far too closely for comfort. Finally, he asked, "Would you like me to see if someone can fetch you a spot of tea?"

"That would be lovely, but I do believe the duchess said something about the ladies gathering in the drawing room after Aurelia and Edward bid us farewell."

"Ah, no doubt to do the duke's bidding."

Her hand flew to her heart. Had he just insinuated what she thought? He couldn't not have meant the duke's suggestion, and the earl's comment that he would endeavor to provide plenty of nieces and nephews, did he? Embarrassed by the path her thoughts traveled, Calliope shot to her feet. "Please excuse me."

The viscount rose at the same time. He didn't say a word, but offered his arm, "Shall I accompany you to the drawing room?"

"I can find my way without escort." Her words sounded stiff and unwelcoming to her own ears. She could only imagine how they sounded to the viscount. "Forgive me," she quickly apologized. "I fear, I am more tired than I realized."

His deep blue eyes fixed on hers. "Are you certain that is all?"

"Aurelia had the both of us up and riding to the church before dawn." She latched on to his arm like he was her lifeline, then loosened her hold at his quizzical look.

He nodded and followed a few of the guests already filing out of the dining room. Before she could think of what to say to him, other than the fact that he'd shocked her down to her toes with his insinuation, the viscount bowed at the open doorway to the drawing room. He turned on his heel and left.

Calliope could not collect herself quickly enough to thank him. She merely watched as his purposeful stride led him away from her. Had she missed a vital opportunity to ask if she would have the pleasure of speaking with him again on the morrow?

Ice filled her belly at the thought that she would never see him again. *Surely he wouldn't leave Wyndmere Hall tonight, would he?*

The sound of his booted heels walking away from her added to the realization that she did not want him to leave.

"Calliope!" the duchess called out to her, "won't you come and join us? I've a fresh pot of tea."

"Of course, Your Grace." She forced herself to enter the room and smile, though her heart wasn't in it. Putting on a brave face for the duchess, she joined her on the green and white striped settee and graciously accepted the cup of tea she didn't want, chatting with the others she wished to perdition.

She couldn't help but feel that when the viscount left Wyndmere Hall, he would be taking her heart with him. *Was this what bereft felt like?*

CHAPTER SIX

"I UNDERSTAND IT has been a year since Earl Chattsworth disappeared." Coventry was about to reply, but the duke raised a hand to indicate he was not finished speaking. "You must admit that the timing is suspect."

The duke's London man-of-affairs and longtime friend got up to pace. "The rumors have been confirmed as far as recognizable family heirlooms coming up for sale around the same time."

"Most noteworthy would be the *Chattsworth Emeralds*," the duke added. "Would the earl be that desperate for coin to pawn what is known to be entailed?"

Coventry dropped into the chair opposite his friend. "Bloody despicable, if you ask me."

Jared was amazed at his friend's sense of balance. Despite the loss of his right eye and the use of his right arm, Coventry had regained a good portion of his cat-like grace and more—he'd developed the innate ability to track people in spite of his limitations. "I hadn't, but knew you'd tell me what you thought regardless."

The former Royal Navy captain shed the persona he'd shown the world since being rendered useless after the Battle of Trafalgar and grinned. "Ah, Jared, you know me too well."

"As it should be, Gordon. You've been my friend and mentor for years. I doubt there is much either of us doesn't know about the other."

"That thought may keep me up nights."

Jared chuckled. "What aren't you telling me?"

Coventry nodded to the missive he'd delivered not ten minutes ago. "It's all there, Jared. The list of items brokered by one of the more unscrupulous pawn brokers in London—including the earl's signet ring."

"When would that have been?"

Coventry's bright green eye darkened with what the duke recognized as disgust. "Nearly a year ago."

"Do you have any information as to who pawned the items?"

"It's a delicate process, gleaning information from one who exists beneath the veritable underbelly of London."

The duke nodded. "In other words, you're working to convince someone to talk who doesn't wish to. How much do you think it would require to loosen the man's tongue?"

Coventry's bark of laughter had the duke joining him. "It's a difficult business, as I am known about town as your man-of-affairs—hard to miss the black eye patch and matching sling."

"I rather thought it was your well-cut dark blue coat."

They shared a smile—the duke at having gifted his friend with the coat, and Coventry for finally accepting the gift as it was meant, from one old friend to another.

"As to being recognized, it does hamper my ability to glean information," Coventry admitted.

The duke got up and reached for the servants' bell pull. A few moments later, a loud knock sounded on the library door. "Enter."

The head of the duke's personal guard, Patrick O'Malley strode in. "Ye have need of me, Yer Grace?"

"Yes, for a rather delicate matter."

O'Malley nodded. "Aye. Does this have to do with yer cousin the viscount?"

The men shared a look and the duke answered, "It does. There isn't much Coventry can do to disguise himself. We need someone who can blend in, someone who knows his way around the bowels of London."

O'Malley grinned. "I'm yer man, Yer Grace!"

The duke did not want to quell Patrick's enthusiasm, but he was loath to let the man leave his post at Wyndmere Hall. Any one of his guard was more than capable of guarding his wife and unborn child but, bloody hell, he depended upon Patrick.

"Who will be taking your place here at Wyndmere?" Before O'Malley could respond, the duke added, "Correct me if I've missed any other additions to my personal guard but, at last count, we have eight O'Malleys, four Garahans, and four Flahertys."

"Aye," O'Malley replied, "divided between yer estates."

"Who have you decided will travel to Lippincott Manor in Sussex with my brother and his new bride?"

"As a matter of fact, me cousin, Sean, has expressed an interest."

"Edward requested that Sean head up his personal guard," the duke advised. "The situation is not as dire as it had been. But still, I'd prefer if Sean not leave his current post until his replacement has arrived."

Patrick's gaze met the duke's and understanding flowed between the men. "I understand, Yer Grace," O'Malley said. "I'd be honored to remain with ye here."

The duke let go of the breath he'd been holding. "Thank you, Patrick. My brother and his new bride will require an escort from Wyndmere Hall to Lippincott Manor. I'll leave it to you and the men to decide who will take this first temporary assignment."

Coventry queried, "Do you mean to have four guards per residence, or will you be hiring on more men?"

The duke walked over to the window. Staring at the newly rebuilt stables, he remembered the night lightning struck the nearby tree that fell on the stables setting it ablaze. It was the same night Hollingford and his men attacked. There had not been any threats since Hollingford had been turned over to the constable nearly a year ago. "At present, I believe that is the best course of action."

"Even your crumbling tower in Cornwall?" Coventry asked.

"Especially at Penwith Tower," the duke replied. "It would be far too easy to dispatch one of my family members visiting the site. Accidents happen when in the midst of such a vast project as the reconstruction of our tower."

"Ye have the right of it, Yer Grace."

Coventry rose and joined the men by the window. "Have I missed any recent acquisitions on your part, Your Grace? Or is it just the four residences: your London town house, Wyndmere Hall, Lippincott Manor, and your crumbling tower in Cornwall."

"Penwith," the duke said again.

O'Malley cleared his throat to cover his snort of laughter.

The duke raised an eyebrow at the interruption but couldn't contain his grin. "Devil take it, O'Malley...you've yet to behold its historical significance."

"Beggin' yer pardon, Yer Grace," he readily agreed. "Me family has a similar residence in Ireland."

Interest piqued, the duke urged, "A Norman round tower?"

O'Malley's lips twitched as he fought not to smile. "A faerie hill fort, Yer Grace."

Coventry's brash laughter echoed through the library. "Sorry, Your Grace. I've been to Ireland and seen more than one faerie hill fort. I've been to Cornwall and seen your crumbling— Penwith Tower."

"Indeed."

"They bear a striking resemblance to one another," Coventry told him.

O'Malley seemed relieved that he hadn't upset his employer. "I meant no disrespect, Yer Grace."

"I know. Your sense of humor is quite similar to my brother's." With a glance at Coventry and then O'Malley, the duke continued, "Four guards at each of my residences, you and Sean to pick who goes where."

"Would it be all right if me brothers and cousins were allowed to choose for themselves?"

"Of course," the duke responded. "If there aren't any takers for Penwith Tower—"

O'Malley sighed, admitting, "I'm more than afraid there will be too many takers for the protection of yer tower in Cornwall."

"Are you?" the duke questioned.

"Aye, me brothers and cousins like to work with their hands—while guardin' Yer Grace is a privilege and a pleasure, they've been itchin' to get back to workin' the land and buildin' somethin' that will last."

"You could rotate the guards, so everyone will become acquainted with the particulars of each of your residences," Coventry suggested.

The duke nodded and slowly smiled. "I daresay, you've got the right of it. See to it, won't you?" he asked O'Malley.

"Consider it done, Yer Grace." O'Malley bowed before leaving the room.

"You do realize how fortunate you are to have hired on O'Malley and his kin, don't you?"

"As fortunate as I am to count you as my friend and man-of-affairs," the duke replied.

"You will keep digging for clues as to what happened to Earl Lippincott, won't you?"

The determined gleam in Coventry's green eye reassured the duke that he would.

"Without question. I'd best be on my way," his friend replied. "I need to get back to London."

"Thank you for coming."

"It was a pleasure to be included among the wedding guests."

The duke grumbled, "You are my friend first—"

Coventry nodded. "It was still a pleasure."

"Indeed."

"By the by, Jared."

"Yes?"

"Wasn't there anything else you wished to ask me?"

"Not that I can—" the duke paused, then locked gazes with his man-of-affairs. "Did you get it?"

Coventry reached inside his frockcoat pocket and pulled out the sheet of foolscap. "One Special License as requested."

The duke took the paper and thanked his friend. "I'm not certain when I'll be using this, but I have a feeling I will have need of it."

"For your sister?"

"Mayhap," the duke admitted. "Then again, mayhap for Calliope."

"Has Coddington received an offer for Lady Calliope's hand?"

"Not that I know of, but I have a feeling my cousin is quite taken with her."

"The cousin whose father went missing under mysterious circumstances?"

"Yes."

"Who stands to inherit the earldom if his father is declared dead?"

"Quite."

"The same cousin who quite possibly did not deign to confide his true circumstances when you asked him?"

"Our conversation was cut short before he could confide anything in me."

"And you have yet to continue that conversation because?" Coventry urged.

"You know bloody well why."

"I confess to being quite baffled."

The duke raked a hand through his hair and started pacing. When he stopped, he glared at his friend. "I completely understand how it feels to have lost both his father and his way in the world. He'd been living one life and now has been thrust into limbo."

Coventry nodded. "I do not doubt that you understand and sympathize, but don't sympathize too much until we get to the bottom of the earl's whereabouts."

"Do you think he got on board a ship to the Americas?"

"Escaping his creditors?" Coventry asked.

"Just a thought. One could be on board a ship for months on end, without a way of communicating to his family."

Coventry's intense frown had the duke nodding. "I see you understand my line of thinking."

"I do believe I have another avenue to investigate!"

The duke stood in the doorway and demanded, "Where are you going?"

"I need to speak with O'Malley before I return to London."

"About what?"

Coventry looked around him before answering, "The earl."

The duke nodded and spun on his heel to return to his library. There was much to be done before O'Malley returned to London. He'd best get his lists in order.

WILLIAM STARED OUT the window of the guest bedchamber he'd been staying in. It had a pastoral view of the wooded expanse beyond the stunning park-like acreage surrounding Wyndmere Hall.

He clenched his hands into fists at his sides. By comparison, his family's estate was in dire need of someone to take care of the vast grounds surrounding it. "Am I not deserving of such a view?"

He'd worked with their steward and family solicitor to disburse what little funds were left in the family coffers to pay them. The mass exodus of servants a month after his father vanished still cut him to the bone. "Why do I have to deal with a shortage of servants who've left their posts after years of loyalty to my family?"

The viscount ignored that still small voice inside of him that insisted he *do* something other than try to wheedle coin from his illustrious cousin. That voice grew louder as it reminded him the *duke* had restored his family's fortune, although he hadn't a clue how Jared managed that feat. "Mayhap I should ask him that instead of seeking a handout."

The knock on his door interrupted his brooding. "Come in."

Humphries cleared his throat before saying, "His Grace would like to speak with you, your lordship."

Chattsworth nodded. *The time had come to tell his cousin the truth of his circumstances...mayhap he should continue to evade the duke and ask for an allowance.*

"Of course." He let the butler lead the way and announce him before entering the duke's library.

"Thank you, Humphries." When the butler bowed and retreated, the duke motioned for the viscount to have a seat. "Sorry for the delay in continuing our conversation."

The duke leaned back and tapped his fingers together. "I believe we were discussing the staff at Chattsworth Manor."

A bead of sweat broke out on the viscount's brow. His stomach roiled as his innate need to tell the truth warred with the need to get his hands on the coin to begin repairs on his home, a visit to one of the smart tailors on Bond Street, and lastly to pay his aging retainers. Mayhap he should pay them first, they deserved far better than he'd been able to provide them since his father's disappearance.

What in the bloody hell had happened to his father? People don't just disappear. Well, unfortunates of the lower classes do...but certainly not an earl!

He'd have to send word immediately to his cousin, Marcus, to meet him at the Thorn and Rose—either that or send him a missive. *Forewarned is forearmed.*

The viscount nodded and started to list the servants who had been employed just prior to his father's disappearance. It was the truth. *They had been servants at Chattsworth Manor at one time—just not at present.*

The duke listened intently, never letting his gaze waver from the viscount's. When he'd finished listing the former staff, the duke asked, "Thank you for the list of former servants, but I am interested in the current staff at Chattsworth Manor."

CHAPTER SEVEN

C ALLIOPE THANKED THE duke's housekeeper and rushed up the stairs. "I wonder what the duchess wants to speak to me about. I daresay—"

Deep male voices arguing had her thoughts shutting off and her heart picking up speed. *Whatever could be wrong? Who was yelling at the duke? Who would dare to?*

The door to the duke's upstairs study burst open as her foot touched the top step. Before she could move out of the way, the viscount turned and barreled into her.

She swung her arms out to keep her balance, but she lost her foothold. She couldn't even summon the breath to scream. It had been knocked out of her on impact. Her vision grayed as she felt herself falling backward into thin air.

"Lady Calliope!" the viscount reached out and pulled her to safety. "Good God!" he rasped cradling her in his arms.

"What in the bloody hell is going on out here!" the duke demanded, glowering at his cousin.

William was too busy brushing a hand to Calliope's pale as parchment cheek. He pulled her closer and laid his ear on her breast. The beat of her heart and gasping breath told him he'd knocked the wind out of her but reassured him she would recover. *What if he had cracked one of her ribs on impact?* "Lord, forgive me!"

"Unhand Lady Calliope at once!"

"Shall I summon the doctor?" Humphries called from where he stood at the bottom of the staircase.

"I'll have one of the footmen bring hot water at once!" Merry dashed to the kitchen.

The viscount met the duke's glare but did not let go of his burden. "I have to fix this," he rasped.

The duke heartily agreed. "And so you shall, Chattsworth. As soon as Lady Calliope regains consciousness, you shall be married at once!"

"I...she...we—marry?"

"I was not the only one to see you with your head on her...person. You have compromised her in front of my servants."

"I saved her from falling down the stairs and breaking her neck!"

"She would not have fallen had you not lost your temper and stormed out of my study."

"I cannot marry—"

"Yes," the duke interrupted. "You can and you will. Her reputation is all that she has, Chattsworth."

Confusion filled him as the duke bade him to follow him to Lady Calliope's bedchamber.

Ice slid through the viscount's gut at the realization the duke could and would force this marriage upon them. "What do you mean by all that she has?"

The duke opened the door and waited while William gently laid Calliope on her bed. "Mayhap you were unaware, but Lady Calliope is a poor relation—without a pound or pence to her name."

William could not have heard the duke aright—could he?

"How is that possible when she's dressed as equally fashionably as your sister or your wife?"

Merry rushed in, interrupting further conversation as she directed the footman, who carried the pitcher of hot water. He poured it into the large pale pink and white ceramic bowl on the washstand beside the armoire and bowed before leaving.

"Shall I sit with Lady Calliope, Your Grace?"

"If you would, please, Merry. We need to keep her from moving suddenly," he advised, meeting the viscount's gaze once again. "There is the possibility that she injured a rib when her future husband nearly knocked her down the stairs."

Could he feel any worse? He'd lied by omission to the duke and before the duke called him on it, sensed that the duke knew that he had. *Why then would the duke insist that Lady Calliope—good friend to his sister, his wife, and his new sister-in-law—marry the viscount?*

"A word, Chattsworth."

He started to follow his cousin out of the room but stopped dead in his tracks at the sound of the duke's housekeeper's voice.

"There now, my lady. You're safe, thanks to the viscount."

Calliope's gaze sought his. Why had he let his anger loose at his cousin? If he'd kept it under control, he wouldn't have knocked the breath out of Lady Calliope. Had he caused her further injury trying to keep her from careening down the staircase?

"I am beyond sorry to have caused you to suffer an injury, Lady Calliope."

She closed her eyes and seemed to be collecting herself. When she opened them, he could not help but notice the tears shimmering there. "Not your fault," she managed to say.

"If I hadn't bolted out of the duke's study—"

"What's done is done," the duke interrupted. "I have a Special License and you can be married as soon as O'Malley returns with the vicar."

"Married?" Calliope squeaked.

"Now?" the viscount challenged.

"I do not think I need to remind you that even the most loyal servants talk," the duke informed them. "I am certain that even now, the stable lad knows what occurred and will be telling the farrier who arrived this morning."

"And he'll no doubt carry the news with him to his next stop," Merry added. "Not to worry, my lady," she was quick to add. "They will be sure to mention that you and the viscount are to wed at once."

"But he didn't ask me," Calliope sounded confused.

The hell of it was that he was as confused as she. "All I did was—"

"One more word, Chattsworth," the duke warned, "and I'll have O'Malley remand you into the constable's care for the foreseeable future."

The viscount shut his mouth and followed the duke back to his study. As the duke reiterated the need to stem the gossip and preserve Lady Calliope's reputation, the viscount knew his life was destined to continue on its downward spiral.

No trace had been found of his father. The staff at Chattsworth Manor had been reduced to an elderly skeletal one. He'd inadvertently injured the lovely Lady Calliope, and he would be forced to marry her to save her reputation.

The bloody hell of it was that she was a poor relation without the means to help him repay the few servants who'd stayed on, or the tenant farmers who needed repairs to their homes and seeds to plant in the spring.

Good God, what was to become of them?

If only he hadn't been so envious of his cousin, he'd never have hatched the plan to seek an audience with him with an eye toward asking for the duke's help in the form of coin or the loan of a few servants.

The viscount realized the duke had finished speaking and appeared to be waiting for him to reply. He opened his mouth to speak, but what could he say? *Sorry, I wasn't listening?*

"I see you are beyond speech," the duke nodded. "As I would be if I were reduced to your current circumstances."

"But—"

The duke held up a hand and stated, "The vicar should be

arriving shortly. You'll want to change, I'm sure, while you wait for my summons."

"I would—"

"Thank me for not having you hauled off to the village where you'd be waiting to be transported to London to stand trial? Yes, I would imagine so."

"Trial? For what?" the viscount demanded.

"Grievous injury to Lady Calliope. Tearing her reputation to shreds before my household staff. Seeking an allowance under false pretenses...need I continue?" the duke inquired.

The viscount squared his shoulders, accepting his fate, even if he didn't agree with the duke. There was no one to back the viscount's claims at the moment. No one at all. "I shall be ready and waiting for your summons."

When the duke waved him away, he bowed and quit the room. This time, opening the door with great care before slowly making his way to his bedchamber where he would await his fate.

"ARE YOU CERTAIN you should be getting out of bed?"

Calliope brushed a strand of hair out of her eyes. "Quite sure. Now that I am able to draw in a deep breath."

"You must have been terrified!" Phoebe murmured.

"Actually, I remember reaching the top of the stairs...and that's where things get muddled," she said slowly. "I heard shouting and then the door to the duke's study thrust open. But I do recall the moment of impact because I could not catch my breath. Then my vision began to gray."

Calliope felt the heat rush to her cheeks as she remembered a bit more. The way it felt to be swept into Viscount Chattsworth's arms—for the second time. The strength in them. The swiftness with which he acted, no doubt saving her from catapulting down the staircase and breaking her neck.

"How are you feeling, Calliope?" the duchess asked as she stepped into the room.

"Much recovered, as I was just explaining to Phoebe."

"Hmmm." Persephone studied Calliope's eyes for long moments. "What is the name of the horse you rode to the church at dawn on Hogmanay?"

Calliope snorted out a laugh before answering, "Millie."

"Your eyes are clear, and apparently so is your brainbox," the duchess declared, slipping her arm through Calliope's. "Let's go to my room, so we can find something suitable for you to wear when the vicar arrives."

Calliope planted herself more firmly, so that the duchess had to slide her arm free or be jerked off her feet. "Is there any way you can change your husband's mind?"

Persephone smiled. "About anything in particular?"

Phoebe put her hands on her hips and frowned. "You know very well what she's asking."

The duchess sighed loudly. "Why would I want him to change his mind? It's evident that you and the viscount have spent the last two days in one another's company and seemed to enjoy doing so."

"That does not mean I want to be forced to marry him," Calliope groused.

"Do you mean to say you do not hold with the notion that it's good luck to see a tall and handsome, dark-haired man on Hogmanay?"

"I did not say that," Calliope countered.

"Or that you do not find his blue eyes rather distracting?" Persephone continued as if Calliope had not answered.

"Well...I really—"

"I further understood that you found the cleft in his chin added to his considerable charm."

Calliope gave up trying to reason with the duchess. "You *want* me to marry the viscount?"

"Jared and I agreed that he would make a suitable husband

for you."

Calliope couldn't begin to understand why the duke and duchess were trying to make decisions for her without her consent. "You did not ask how I felt."

"My dear Calliope," the duchess soothed. "You cannot hide what you're feeling when you glance at the viscount. Your eyes give you away."

She placed her hands on her face as if she could hide her embarrassment or how she felt about the viscount from the duchess or Phoebe. It was at that moment in time that she realized she could not hide from the truth. She'd developed a tendre for the viscount from the moment he'd strode into the church.

"What am I to do?" she implored her friends.

"About what?" Phoebe wondered.

"I cannot marry the viscount," Calliope insisted.

"Whyever not?" Persephone wanted to know.

"He does not wish to marry me."

"How do you know?" the duchess asked.

Calliope's eyes filled with tears that slowly fell. "I heard the duke tell the viscount he had to marry me."

"And?" Phoebe prompted.

"He gave a number of reasons why he could not. But—"

"But?" Persephone echoed.

"He was appalled to learn I was a poor relation."

"Did Jared and the viscount know you were awake at the time they were discussing your marriage?"

"I was feigning unconsciousness," Calliope admitted.

"What?" the duchess sounded quite astonished.

"Why?" Phoebe demanded.

"It's how I learned anything of import over the years, feigning sleep or unconsciousness."

Persephone's eyes filled, but she blinked the tears away. "I do not believe I shall ask how many occasions you had to pretend to be unconscious—else I would have to insist my husband do something about those horrid relations of yours."

"It's not too late to do so," Phoebe reminded her sister-in-law. "After all, her second cousin and his wife still have not returned the monies they stole from Calliope." She turned to Calliope, asking, "Have they?"

Calliope shook her head. Her life had been a series of misfortunes since that one tragic moment in her life when her father was killed in a freak carriage accident and her mother died shortly after. From that moment on, she'd been shuffled from one relation to another, never staying for any great length of time with any of them, until landing on her second cousin's doorstep. It was there that she'd been on the receiving end of physical and mental abuse unlike anything she'd experienced before.

"I am quite certain my darling duke will get to the bottom of things, now that Aurelia and Edward have married and are on their way to take up residence at Lippincott Manor."

"But what of the viscount?" Calliope insisted. "He truly does not want to marry me."

"My husband is correct in his assumption that our servants will talk—and not unkindly, mind you," the duchess reaffirmed. "There are those who will hear of the tale of his rescuing you from a fall that could have been fatal and find it romantic, while at the same time others will turn it around when they retell the tale to another."

Calliope did not understand why anyone would turn it around. "Why would they?"

Persephone sighed. "People do what they will do."

"And say what they will say," Phoebe added. "Whether it be truth or Banbury tale!"

"I have no say in the matter," Calliope said. "Do I?"

"Jared is at this moment in deep discussion with Lord Coddington. Cooler heads shall prevail. Let us wait until they have finished their meeting before we throw caution to the four winds and decry the situation as desperately hopeless."

"I suppose you are right," Calliope admitted. "But I cannot

seem to move past the fact that the viscount has no desire to marry someone of my station in life."

"You are the daughter of an earl!" Phoebe reminded her.

"He died without male issue," she reminded her friend. "Leaving my mother and I at the mercy of Uncle Silas."

"The bloody fool who tossed you out without a backward glance?" Persephone wanted to know.

"Uh...yes," Calliope answered. "He did."

"Unconscionable." Persephone muttered. "There should be a law against it."

"What about the viscount?" Phoebe asked. "Could we not appeal to him to aid you in recovering your stipend that your cousin and his wife robbed from you?"

"Second cousin," Calliope reminded her.

Phoebe waved her hand in the air, "Second, third. It does not matter. What matters is that they be made to repay you. That way, you shall not continue to be a poor relation."

"And the viscount will no longer have a reason *not* to marry you," the duchess crowed. "It is obvious to all and sundry that he is captivated by you."

Hope filled Calliope's breast. "Truly?"

"Sparks flew between the two of you whenever you were together these last few days," Phoebe told her friend.

Calliope stared off into space. It was not just all in her mind? Could it be true? "I would be willing to marry the viscount, if he were not so averse to marrying me."

"I can guarantee in a few hours' time, when you are standing in front of the vicar, that the viscount will have come around and will embrace his good fortune in marrying my very good friend," Phoebe concluded.

"But—"

"We have much to do before then," the duchess reminded her. "Come and we'll see which of our gowns will best suit you for your wedding."

Calliope let herself be led from her bedchamber, where she

would have to confess, she'd been secluding herself since the doctor had left, pronouncing her fit as a fiddle. Finding her Scots' backbone, ready to face her future with honor and pride, Calliope slowly smiled at the duchess. "As long as it is not one of your infamous yellow-green gowns, Persephone," she teased.

The duchess' delighted trill of laughter echoed behind them and down into the entryway.

Patrick O'Malley nodded to his brother, Finn. "All will be well. Ye'll see."

"I still think we should have a word with Chattsworth."

"Aye. We shall," he reassured Finn. "The duke gave *his* word."

Finn smiled at his brother. "Do ye think we'll need to convince him with our fists?"

O'Malley's smile mirrored his brother's. "Lord willin'."

CHAPTER EIGHT

WILLIAM SAT WITH his head in his hands. How had his plans to set things right veer off course? Plots and machinations had turned completely around on him.

He shot to his feet. Bloody hell! He had to get word to his cousin as soon as possible. Marcus had to know that the duke already knew about the earl, the viscount, and the state of Chattsworth Manor! But how? When? Stripping off his shirt, he walked over to the washstand. A glance at his reflection in the looking glass had him grimacing. *Married?* He shook his head as every fiber of his being fought against the marriage his cousin would force upon him.

If the duke had his way, William would wed the wand-slim Lady Calliope of the soft gray eyes and honey-blonde hair by nightfall. Pouring the now-cold water in the bowl, he splashed his face. Shuddering at the cold, he reached for the round of soap and slowly worked up a lather. The scent of sandalwood had him lifting his hands to draw in the fragrance. There used to be scented soaps aplenty at home before his father had lost his mind and his way.

Don't think of Father now. Nothing could be done until he returned to Chattsworth Manor and contacted his network of acquaintances. *Would any word have surfaced as to his father's whereabouts?*

The knock on his door had him drying his face and hands, reaching for the freshly laundered shirt someone had thoughtfully laid out for him. Swiftly donning the shirt and tucking it in, he called out, "Come in."

"Are ye ready, yer lordship?"

The viscount studied the men standing shoulder to broad shoulder just inside his bedchamber. *Imposing. Unnerving.* Did the duke feel the need to send the head of his personal guard and his brother to ensure his cooperation? From the way they flexed their fists and grimly smiled at him, he wondered what course of action would be taken if he disagreed with the Irishmen.

"Nearly," he answered, ignoring the deep-seated need to use his fists on someone—anyone, to rid himself of this overwhelming feeling that he'd failed on all counts. He'd been unable to locate his father. The family name was in danger of being stricken to a new low. If the *on dit* presently circulating the *ton* was to be believed, it would be ground beneath the heel of polite society. The family coffers were nearly empty.

But the acute failure that kept him awake most nights was his inability to pay the longtime, aging, servants who remained at Chattsworth Manor. They'd been loyal to his grandfather during his time as earl, then transferred that loyalty to his father. No one knew better than the viscount that he did not deserve the loyalty the four remaining servants lavished upon him. He could not marry a poor relation! He needed to pay Hargrave, Mrs. Meadowsweet, MacReedy, and Mrs. Romney their back wages.

"'Tis time," Patrick O'Malley reminded him.

The viscount blinked and realized he'd been standing stock-still while his thoughts raged inside of his aching head. There was no way out—but there had to be, he reasoned with himself. There had to be!

Donning his white waistcoat and dark blue frockcoat, he ran a hand over his hair and checked his reflection one last time. It would not do to appear before his cousin, the duke—or his unwanted bride-to-be, inappropriately attired.

With a nod to the two men, he indicated his readiness to follow them to a future being forced upon him, leaving him unable to reconcile his past.

CALLIOPE STARED AT her reflection as Persephone and Phoebe fussed and flitted about her. Could they not see that she was dying inside? She was about to be forced to wed a man she'd hoped was developing an affection for her, but was not certain would accept her.

When last she'd gazed into his eyes, the anger and frustration darkening his crystal blue eyes was definitely not what she'd hoped to see. What if his frustration grew? What if it fueled the anger she'd glimpsed? Was she destined to continue to live a life filled with drudgery and scorn?

What about love? Did she not deserve the smidgeon she'd discovered living with Aurelia and her uncle? With Aurelia newly married, she could not imagine herself continuing to live with Lord Coddington. He'd declared that she was now a part of their family, insisting she call him Uncle Phineas. He could easily change his mind now that Aurelia no longer lived with him.

Dear Lord, what was she to do? How was she to survive life with a man who so obviously begrudged her very existence in his life?

"Calliope!"

"Hmmm? What?"

The duchess frowned at her. "I understand that you may feel as if only disaster lay ahead of you, but Phoebe and I do not believe it to be so."

"We've noted the way the viscount sought out your company above all others," her friend reminded her.

"And my husband approves of this union."

Calliope wrung her hands until the duchess stopped the action with a mere touch. "Don't do this to yourself. Happiness is a choice, Calliope. I chose happiness when I agreed to marry Jared."

"I thought it was a love match," she whispered.

"I turned him down at first as I never intended to marry."

Calliope could not believe it. "You turned down the Duke of Wyndmere?"

Phoebe giggled. "She did—not that I was there at the time, but I heard all about it."

She had to ask. "What made you change your mind?"

The duchess stared off into the distance, silent for a few moments before continuing. "When he rephrased his question—"

Phoebe cut her off, "Don't forget to tell her how he asked the first time."

"I do believe he told me he asked mother's permission," the duchess remarked. "When I asked him why he wanted to marry me, the answer was not one I'd expected to hear."

Calliope was totally engrossed in the tale. "Well what did he say?"

Persephone frowned. "He was in need of a wife!"

"Is that all?"

Phoebe snorted. "No, it's gets better. Tell her, Persephone!"

The duchess smiled. "I'd have the distinction of his title, his wealth, etc., etc.—oh, and his protection."

"Was that important?" Calliope asked.

"At the time," the duchess agreed. "But my father promised, before he died so suddenly, that if I did not find someone I wished to marry, that I could retire to our country estate and enjoy living my life the way I chose."

"But you married him," Calliope prompted.

The duchess sighed. "Yes. It was after I thanked him for the offer but refused him that I finally heard what rang as the truth from Jared."

Encouraged that the duchess had given the duke a second chance, seeing as how they were happily married and expecting their first child, Calliope waited to hear what the duchess would add.

Before Persephone could continue, Phoebe spoke up. "He told her he needed her guidance in a rather personal nature."

Calliope could not even begin to imagine what that would entail. She cleared her throat. "Do go on."

Persephone smiled. "He fumbled through admitting his sister was in need of a chaperone, someone to guide her through her first Season."

The story had her full attention, "And?" she urged.

"I had to fill in the blanks, as the duke was quite unsure how to put things that didn't sound as if he were asking for something far different and not at all proper."

"I see."

"When I asked him if the marriage would be in name only, or if he intended to beget his heir and a spare, I rendered him speechless."

Phoebe and Persephone's laughter filled the room, adding warmth where Calliope had only felt the chill. "I cannot believe—" she began only to shake her head. "That would not be quite true. I absolutely do believe you asked that. From what I've observed from the moment I met you and His Grace, you two were destined to be together. It's plain for all to see you share a deep and abiding love."

"It's what I want," Phoebe confessed.

"I never thought I would be in a position to marry as I have no dowry…and little family who would claim me. Especially not my uncle, the earl."

"But you are now," Persephone reminded her.

"And am being forced to wed."

"Can you not see the duke is protecting your reputation, literally all you have left, until he can sort out the legalities and criminal charges that have been levied against your second cousin and his wife? These things take time, as my darling duke would want to provide proof that would not be questioned at a later date."

Phoebe nodded. "My brother wants to see your inheritance returned to you in full," her friend told her, "but he also would like nothing more than to see you happily wed."

"Happily? How is that possible when he's forcing the viscount to marry me?"

"It may appear that way," the duchess conceded. "However, many's the man who has acted inappropriately...stolen a kiss, too ardent and unseemly an embrace. Some have been stranded with a lady without a chaperone. They have all done the gentlemanly thing as their honor would have it. They've married the lady they unwittingly compromised."

"You'll see," Phoebe said. "The viscount will come around to understanding that it is his only course of action."

Calliope knew it was the only course of action, but that did not mean she would willingly accept her fate when the man in question had such a strong opinion against marrying a poor relation. She tried one last time. "What about my lack of dowry?"

"Jared and his solicitors are working toward the return of your inheritance," the duchess reassured her. "Surely that will make a difference in the viscount's unreasonable attitude toward your monetary situation."

Calliope sighed. "I am not certain how long he will be amenable to waiting, should the wheels of justice continue to turn so slowly."

"Let us think of happier things," Persephone urged, circling Calliope and smiling. "You look lovely. The sheer dove gray overdress and deeper blue beneath enhance your gray eyes— they're sparkling."

Phoebe nodded. "Although dear Calliope's eyes do have a similar look when she's agitated beyond reason."

"Are you still agitated?" the duchess asked. "Can you not trust the duke?" When Calliope did not answer, Persephone rasped, "Can you not trust me?"

A single tear slipped across Calliope's cheek, sliding behind her ear. "I am sorry. After all you and your family have done for me, of course I can. Do forgive me for being obtuse and ignoring all that I should be grateful for."

"You'll give the viscount a chance to prove he cares for more than coin?"

Calliope grasped the duchess' hand and Phoebe's, promising, "With an open mind and willing heart."

Persephone nodded. "We cannot ask for more."

TWO HOURS LATER, Lady Calliope Harrington and Viscount William Chattsworth stood beneath a fragrant swag of evergreen. Giving witness to their union were the Duke and Duchess of Wyndmere, Edward, Earl Lippincott, and his new wife, Lady Aurelia, and the duke's sister, Lady Phoebe Lippincott.

Calliope's hands trembled as the viscount repeated the vicar's words. Her heart fluttered as she took in his black eye, bruised jaw, and split knuckles. The serious look on the viscount's face did not bode well. *What had happened? Who had he fought with?* Certainly not Lord Coddington, who was not present...mayhap they had exchanged blows. It did not fit with what she knew of Aurelia's uncle—yet still...

"Lady Calliope," the vicar's sharp tone called her back to the present as she repeated the vow to love, honor, cherish, and obey.

Dear Lord, she was exhausted. She did not think she could bear it if he placed the blame for his obvious beating on her head as well. Would he always be angry with her? Would they never have a chance for happiness? It was not her fault she happened to be at the top of the stairs when he stormed out of the duke's upstairs study.

When would he cease to blame her? Was there more that he was not telling her? Her belly roiled at the thought that the viscount hid a checkered past behind his handsome face and winning smile. The road ahead seemed uneven and filled with ruts. The questions filling her mind and her heart plagued her, leaving her head light and her knees weak.

At her wits' end, she did what her parents had taught her from a very young age—she prayed. *Dear Lord, please don't let him hate me!*

William noted the fear creeping into Calliope's eyes but could say nothing to stave it off. He had attempted to seek her out, but that had brought about a conversation with Lord Coddington that left him wondering if the man would follow through on his threat to ruin him if he so much as harmed a hair on Calliope's head—physically or emotionally.

He'd been escorted from his meeting with Coddington to an outbuilding beyond the duke's stables where a satisfying bout of bare knuckle fighting, with opponents who relished the encounter as much as he had, occurred. The result—he had not been permitted to speak to Calliope before taking their vows. That would come later—after the hastily prepared wedding supper, when they were alone as man and wife.

By all that's holy, what was he going to do tonight? He did not want her as his wife, but he knew his duty. He was raised a gentleman and would do as he'd been taught. He'd marry the chit. But that didn't mean he had to consummate their marriage. *He could wait and have it annulled.*

Though the satisfaction he felt pummeling the O'Malleys eased his frustration, the pounding he'd received in return did little to assuage the helplessness he felt mired in this situation. He was bound till death to the woman trembling before him who could do naught to help him in his quest to find his father or replenish the family estate and refill the coffers. But the worst of it—she had no dowry, and he could not repay his father's loyal servants what he owed them.

How in God's name would he feed them—or his new wife? He'd added yet one more failure to the long list trailing behind him. It hit him between the eyes like one of the O'Malleys' blows—he did not even have the means to transport his new wife to Sussex. He had no carriage and they could not very well ride double on Maximus.

What was the duke thinking?

"Ahem." The vicar cleared his throat. "You may kiss the bride, your lordship."

William stared down into eyes the color of morning fog over the lake behind his home. Tears glistened in her eyes, but his wife of but a few moments gamely blinked them away and stilled her trembling. If she could bravely face the unknown, then by God, so would he.

He bent his head and brushed a wisp of a kiss across her mouth. His eyes widened at the jolt that seared his lips and his heart. *What was that?* He had expected a bolt out of the blue to incinerate him where he stood for nearly mowing down the woman earlier and would deserve it. Just as he would deserve the same for adding one more link to the chain of failures that would surely drag him under—forced to wed an innocent because of his explosive temper.

Her mouth rounded in a perfect "o". Calliope's eyes grew misty with an emotion he was not quite sure it was wise to encourage. He was sorely tempted, but temptation led down the road to ruin. Hadn't something of the sort happened to his father?

Intoxicated by her, unable to resist, he lowered his lips for another taste. Forbidden nectar. Sweet with a hint of Heaven. He could not bring himself to end the kiss until he'd drunk his fill. When he finally drew back, Calliope sagged against him. Much to the delight of the duke and the earl.

The duchess, Aurelia, and Phoebe showered them with felicitations. The vicar nodded as if all was right in his world now that he'd performed the marriage necessary to protect their reputations amongst the *ton*.

"Constance has prepared a wonderful supper," the duke told them. "Please join us in the dining room."

If he lived to be one hundred, the viscount would never forget the hopeful look in his bride's eyes as she waited for him to escort her to their wedding feast. Fear that she'd come to know him, only to revile him, filled the viscount to bursting. He bowed over her hand. "If you will excuse me…" he could not think of what else to say as he spun on his heel and quit the room.

The muffled voices mixed with alarm had him glancing over his shoulder in time to see the duke sweep a limp Calliope into his arms. Brilliant blue, met brilliant blue—anger simmering on both sides of the expanse. If he didn't escape now, he had no doubt he would do something utterly unforgiveable. His soul was black enough.

The sound of weeping followed him down the long hallway and into the night. As he reached for the door to the barn, an animalistic growl him had him looking over his shoulder. It was all the impetus Finn O'Malley needed to level him with a solid right cross.

The viscount's head swam and his jaw ached. His eyes finally focused enough to see that he was staring up at the clear night sky. Stars twinkled in the inky blackness. "Cold," he rasped, wondering if the bloody guard had broken his jaw.

Before he could gather himself to ask, he was summarily jerked to his feet. He swayed between the same two men he'd fought earlier before having to stand in front of the vicar and his bride.

"Ye coward!" Patrick O'Malley roared. "Did ye have to leave her like that?"

As his head cleared, disgust filled him. "Yes."

A sound to his left had him bracing for another blow. Finn O'Malley's jab was followed by an uppercut that leveled him a second time.

When he came around, he was no longer outside, but lying on his back on a cot. His brain tried to piece together what he was seeing and what had brought him to wherever he was. The only thing he could remember was a kiss that tasted of Heaven and eyes that begged him to stay.

The bucket of cold water cleared his head in a heartbeat.

"I'm thinkin' ye may have finally mastered leanin' into the jab, Finn."

He shrugged, before admitting, "Ye've reminded me more oft than not that I needed to follow through, not pull back, me punches."

"'Tis a proud moment for the O'Malleys," Patrick agreed. "Da would have been proud."

The viscount groaned as he tried to sit up, then noticed his feet and his hands were bound. "What in the bloody hell?"

"His Grace wanted to have a word with yer lordship," Patrick explained.

"And he did not want to have to send one of us to track ye down," Finn added.

"You didn't have to punch me."

"Would ye have stopped if we'd asked ye nicely?" Patrick wanted to know.

The viscount tugged and pulled against the ropes that bound him. It was no use. The brothers had trussed him up tight. "Mayhap."

"I'd venture to say, nay," Finn said cheerfully.

"If I untie ye," Patrick asked, "will ye try to go for yer horse again?"

This time, the viscount relaxed to ease the bite of the ropes holding him prisoner. "You don't understand," he told them. "I have to leave."

"Ye'd leave Lady Calliope behind?" Patrick sounded incensed.

"How in the blazes would I transport her? Riding double all the way to Sussex on Maximus?"

"He's a fine Thoroughbred," Finn admitted. "Strong, but not strong enough to travel the distance required carrying the both of ye."

"I did not travel here with a carriage and cannot conceive of my wife being made to travel the distance to our home on horseback in the dead of winter."

"Another fine point ye've made," Patrick agreed. "Have ye not thought that His Grace would be offerin' one of his carriages for yer journey home, then?"

He had to admit he hadn't. "It matters not. I have unfinished business to attend to," he told the brothers.

His words fell on deaf ears, as Maximus chose that moment to whicker loudly, distracting the O'Malleys.

"He needs a good run," the viscount told them.

"I'd be more than happy to oblige," Finn said.

"But what about my wife?"

The O'Malleys glared at him. "The one ye were bent on leavin' behind?" Patrick asked.

Shame washed over him. He had thought to do just that. After the brief encounter...for lack of better word for what passed between him and the O'Malleys...earlier, he hadn't had time to speak to the duke about borrowing a carriage. He hadn't thought past much of anything, except getting through the blasted ceremony and leaving.

"Bloody hell...I am a coward!"

"Well now that ye've admitted it, we may be untyin' yer ankles so ye can walk with us. The duke would have another word with ye."

As the ropes fell from his ankles, he slowly stood. "Would this conversation involve fists?"

The O'Malleys chuckled, then sighed. "Alas, no. His Grace was a bit put out with us for our earlier...discussion...with ye," Patrick admitted.

"Without question, he'll have more to say," Finn grumbled.

The viscount could only imagine. "Lead the way."

The O'Malleys walked one on either side of the viscount, leading him to believe he was still most definitely a prisoner. Walking toward the dark outbuilding near the edge of the wide expanse of the open ground, he wondered if he was headed toward his doom.

Would he disappear without a trace just like his father?

CHAPTER NINE

"**I** SIMPLY CANNOT believe he kissed you and turned on his heel and walked away from you!"

Calliope watched the duchess pace back and forth in front of the fireplace in her sitting room. How could she answer that burning question? She had no idea...and after a kiss that had opened her heart and liquified her bones!

"Before my oldest brother died, Edward was like that," Phoebe confided. "If he did not have the answer to a question or did not like the way a situation was unfolding, he'd just turn and walk away."

Calliope stared at her friend for long moments before commenting, "You're not joking, are you?"

"No. But I am delighted to advise that he has since outgrown that horrid habit and has become the man we all know—and Aurelia loves."

An odd sense of loneliness filled Calliope as she thought of her friend, Aurelia, on her way to her new home with Edward. They were so very happy to be off to share their new life together. They'd prepared for it...when it came right down to it, they'd fought for their happiness. They'd had to battle against wagging tongues and small minds of those with nothing better to do than to belittle others and spread false rumors.

With the help of Edward's family, Aurelia's Uncle Phineas,

the duke's personal guard and servants, they'd spread the truth in and around the village of Windermere and all about London. Whenever a new rumor would crop up to defy the truth, the duke staunchly defended his brother and Aurelia until the *ton* lost interest in rumors that simply refused to circulate amongst the quality. That had been a day to celebrate.

And now, she doubted she would see her friend for quite some time. Aurelia and Edward deserved to start their new life unencumbered by rumors from the past, or friends that were at loose ends, waiting for their so-called family to return monies they'd stolen.

"Are you all right, Calliope?" Persephone asked.

"I am not quite sure how to answer. I'd thought my life had suddenly begun when William kissed me at the vicar's urging...and then—" she fought back the tears that sprang to her eyes. "I felt as if it ended abruptly when he left me."

"If I were a man, I'd have rattled his brainbox!" Phoebe declared.

"A lovely sentiment, sister dear," the duke murmured entering the sitting room, leaving the door open. "Hardly appropriate."

"Do you condone what the viscount did?" his sister asked.

Calliope wished she could melt into the carpet, so acute was her embarrassment.

"Mayhap we can save this conversation for a more appropriate time."

Phoebe acquiesced, all the while glaring at her brother.

Persephone cleared her throat and asked, "Shall I ring for tea?"

"I asked Merry to see to it on my way up, my darling."

The duchess smiled. "Thank you, Jared. I'm certain we could all do with a cup."

Their housekeeper arrived with one of the footmen a few moments later. "Do come in, Merry," the duke invited.

"Shall I pour for Your Graces?"

"Thank you for offering," Persephone replied, "but that will not be necessary."

"Very good, Your Grace."

The footman set the heavier of the two trays on the table in the middle of the room and bowed before following Merry.

"Now then," Persephone said, "shall we discuss the awkward situation we all appear to be in, or will we continue to ignore it while poor Calliope becomes even more distressed?"

The duke gave his approval. "Cutting through to the heart of the matter. Well done, my love."

Persephone smiled.

"Why don't you pour," the duke suggested, "while Phoebe passes out the tarts and teacakes?"

The duchess poured while Phoebe filled dessert plates.

"Calliope? Berry tart or teacake?"

"Neither, thank you, Phoebe. Just tea please."

"Now then," the duke said after taking a sip from his teacup. "I spoke to your husband."

At that last word, Calliope jolted, spilling tea into her saucer. "Oh, dear!"

Without a word, the duke rose from his seat and took the cup from her and set it on the table and took another from the tray. "Darling, please pour a half-cup for Calliope, would you?"

Persephone did as he bade her.

Calliope sipped from her teacup, and the duke began again, "I know you must be anxious about what happened earlier. I can assure you that your husband did not abandon you as it would appear."

She carefully placed her teacup on the table between them, drew in a calming breath and replied, "I see."

"I have asked Chattsworth to travel to London to attend to some rather urgent business for me."

"The viscount?" Phoebe asked. "Why?"

"Patience, Sister," he cautioned.

"How long do you think he'll be gone?" Calliope wrung her hands, then stopped the telling motion. "What shall I do while he is away?"

"I have taken care of those arrangements as well. You are to travel to Chattsworth Manor with two of my personal guard and Mary Kate as your lady's maid."

"I am?"

"Of course, it is your home now, is it not?"

Calliope nodded, all the while wondering why the duke had not answered her first question. How long would her husband be gone? Instead of asking again, she decided to wait and ask him later.

"Mary Kate is packing your trunk. You will be able to leave mid-morning, providing the weather cooperates."

"I see. Does William know I will be going to his home?"

"I did not have the opportunity to tell him before he left."

Calliope felt hollowed out...like an empty shell. "He's gone?" She blinked back the tears gathering in her eyes. "I didn't get to say goodbye."

The duke nodded and changed the subject. "Now as to your protection, I would advise that you and Mary Kate pay close attention to whatever my personal guard would have you do. Their main objective is to see the both of you safely delivered to Sussex."

"Yes, Your Grace."

"As we are now related, Calliope, please call me by my given name."

"Yes, of course, if you wish...Jared," she stammered.

The duke smiled. "There. That was not so difficult, was it?"

"I confess it will take some getting used to."

"I have no doubt you shall soon be quite comfortable addressing me as such."

Calliope would not dare to gainsay His Grace. As she'd be leaving in the morning, it would undoubtedly not be an issue much longer.

The duke rose to his feet, bowed graciously over his wife's hand and pressed a kiss to the back of it.

Calliope wondered how it would feel to have such a deep affection between oneself and one's husband. Her time to discover that was apparently not to be for some time. If only she knew how long she would have to wait before seeing the viscount again.

A sinking feeling filled her. If they did not consummate their vows, were they still married in the eyes of the church? Would the viscount now have the ability to set her aside if he chose to do so?

The tea in her empty stomach sloshed about. The sour taste of it reached the back of her throat. *Not good.* She should have listened to Persephone and at least eaten a bit of bread earlier that afternoon. She'd been beside herself once she awoke to find it wasn't a dream that she'd had the wind knocked out of her and nearly hurtled backwards down the stairs.

Hand to her mouth, she fled the room, bumping into the immovable form of one of the duke's guard. She was saved from the embarrassment of landing on her bottom or emptying the meager contents of her stomach on the man's boots by the man's quick action and a nearby urn.

"Are ye all right, yer ladyship?"

Calliope wished she could curl up and die as mortification swept up from her toes. She couldn't answer and desperately wished she'd had the foresight to have a handkerchief on her person.

As if by magic, a large linen square appeared in front of her. She blinked, but it did not vanish. Delicately blotting her mouth, she managed to thank him.

"Ye'd be most welcome, yer ladyship."

She dared a glance at her rescuer and tried to smile but didn't quite manage it. "I know we've met before...in London I think, but I'm afraid I don't remember your name."

"'Tisn't necessary that ye do," the tall dark-haired, dark-eyed man replied.

Feeling a bit better, she eased a step back and met his curious gaze. "You're one of the Garahan brothers, are you not?"

His grin was swift and a bit lethal. "Aye. Aiden Garahan at yer service, yer ladyship." He bowed, then asked, "Are ye feeling better?"

She folded the handkerchief in half and then in half again. Searching for something else to say to the man who'd witnessed such unladylike behavior, she finally managed, "I am, thank you. I shall launder this myself and return it to you."

His dark eyes twinkled, surprising in a man whose countenance a moment ago appeared quite threatening. "I have another. Ye can keep it if ye like."

"Thank you, Mr. Garahan."

He chuckled. "Just Garahan'll do."

"What if you and your brother are together?"

He smiled fully this time. "That'll be good luck indeed for all concerned."

She found her first smile since her husband turned his back on her. Thinking of William had her staring down at her toes. Her head felt light and her vision grayed at the edges.

"Easy, yer ladyship." Garahan scooped her off her feet and into his arms. "Ye'd best have a lie down. Their Graces would have me head if I let ye fall on yers."

Before she could summon the strength to respond, his ear-splitting whistle echoed through the hallway. Answering footsteps pounded toward them.

"What's happened, Aiden?" Patrick O'Malley demanded. Before his cousin could reply, he asked, "Are ye injured, yer ladyship?"

"Her ladyship had an upset stomach," he said, cradling her a bit closer as he shifted his hand to pass off the urn he'd yet to set down.

Patrick nodded, passing the urn to the footman who stood off to the side. "I'm thinkin' it wouldn't require ye to be carryin' her ladyship if it was her stomach."

The deep rumbling had Calliope opening her eyes. "I'm so

sorry to be a bother. He only caught me when my head went light and I felt myself falling."

O'Malley nodded. "Well then, that's fine. Do ye think ye can walk?"

"I, uh...I'm not certain," she whispered. Wishing herself anywhere but standing between the two giants.

"Carry her ladyship back into the sittin' room, while I let His Grace know we may be needin' his physician again."

"I'm sure I shall be fine, Patrick. Just a bit of an empty stomach," she reassured him. *And an aching heart.*

The head of the duke's personal guard met her gaze and held it for long moments before nodding in agreement. "I need to speak with the duke if ye'll see to her ladyship."

"Aye." Her rescuer had suddenly become a man of few words.

"Calliope!" the duchess called out as Garahan carried her into the sitting room. "I knew I should have followed you. I am so sorry."

"It would only have added to my embarrassment." The duke's guard eased her onto the settee, and she smiled. "Thank you, Aiden."

He nodded to her, bowed to the duchess, and left the room without a word.

"We may have been too hasty, thinking you'd fully recovered from having the wind knocked out of you," the duchess murmured. "I'll let Jared know that you need to rest for a few days before leaving for Chattsworth Manor.

The mere mention of leaving the safety of Wyndmere Hall had tears gathering, threatening to turn her into a watering pot. That would never do, she reasoned. She'd been through far worse than this. After all, her husband-in-name-only had not raised a hand to her. He'd only left her. *Left her...*

Unaware that her tears had begun to fall, she was surprised when the duchess sat beside her and pulled her into an embrace. "It's quite all right to cry, you know."

"Never solves anything," Calliope replied before blowing her nose in Aiden's handkerchief.

"I do not relish being reduced to tears and beg to differ. It does solve something."

"Really?" Calliope didn't think so. "What would that be?"

"It releases the tension and frustrations coiled inside of one. An outlet if you will."

Calliope relaxed against the duchess until she felt a distinct jolt to her side. She sat up and stared. "Did you feel that?"

The duchess laughed as she rubbed her belly. "I must apologize for my daughter's manners."

Calliope smiled. "I must say she has a way of making her presence known."

They were laughing when Merry entered carrying a small tray. "Constance said you were to eat every bit, your ladyship."

"Oh, but I'm—" she fell silent under the stern look from the duchess. "I will, thank you, Merry. Please thank Constance for me."

"I will," the housekeeper replied. "All of it, mind?"

She nodded as Merry retreated. Staring at the bread and mug of what smelled like beef broth, she rasped, "I don't know that I can eat."

"Give it a try," Persephone urged. "Once you have a bite of bread and sip of broth, you may be surprised that you are able to."

Doing as the duchess bid, she felt the tightness in her throat ease swallowing the warm broth. Miraculously, her belly slowly settled down. A few sips, later she was ready to confide what happened.

Persephone listened, patting Calliope's hand partway through the telling. "I have been where you are," the duchess confided, "and have felt a bit of what you're feeling. Life can overwhelm one at times, but don't let it control you. Dig deep for the courage I know you possess and take life by the horns! You are stronger than you realize, Calliope. I have faith in you."

Such a simple thing, Calliope thought. To have the duchess speak from her heart and say something so unexpected. "You do?"

"Have faith in you? Yes. Believe you possess courage? Without question."

Under the direct gaze of the duchess, Calliope felt a bit of that courage, and her resolve, returning. Mayhap someone to believe in her was all she needed to find it again. "Thank you, Persephone."

"Are you ready to see how the packing is going? There may be a few things you'll require for your trip."

"I'm afraid I don't have any pin money."

"What sort of friend would I be if I let you go off on such a journey without reassuring myself and Jared that you had all you required? I am not certain when I will be able to make the journey as it's becoming most uncomfortable getting about these days."

Calliope blinked away tears of happiness. "I do not know what I ever did to deserve your friendship, Persephone, but I shall treasure it always."

The duchess inclined her head. "See that you do, as I value yours. Now then, do you feel well enough to walk or shall I summon Aiden to carry you?"

The laughter in Persephone's eyes, and teasing note in her voice was not lost on Calliope. She stood and immediately put the back of her hand to her forehead. "I feel faint!"

Persephone laughed. "Too theatrical. You'll have to do better than that."

Arms linked, they walked out of the sitting room and up to Calliope's bedchamber. "How is the packing going, Mary Kate?"

"I was wondering if I should have been making a list, as there are a few essential items that seem to be missing from Lady Calliope's toilette."

"Really?" Calliope couldn't think of what she was missing.

"A sound notion," Persephone agreed. She walked over to the

lady's desk beneath the window, smoothed out a bit of foolscap and dipped the quill in the inkwell. "Now then, what's missing?"

An hour later, the list had been completed and decisions made as to what should be added to Calliope's wardrobe to make the journey in such cold weather.

"Now then, Mary Kate," the duchess said. "We need to go over what you'll need in your new role as lady's maid to Viscountess Chattsworth."

Calliope silently wondered how long her marriage-in-name-only would last.

PERSEPHONE STORMED INTO her husband's study. "What are you about, Jared?"

He returned the quill to its holder and pushed to his feet. "My dear?"

"Do not play that card with me! I know there is more afoot here than you have deigned to confide in me."

The duke walked to where his wife stood halfway between the doors and his desk. Lifting her hand to his lips, he pressed a gentle kiss to the back of it. "My dear, there are matters we have yet had the time to discuss that threaten the very fiber of Calliope's and Chattsworth's lives."

"And you believe that separating them right after they've wed is the answer?"

He gently tugged on the hand he still held, drawing her close. When she was tucked in his arms, he sighed. "Do you trust me?"

She sighed before answering, "You know that I do."

"Excellent. Will you try to be patient while we sort through this morass we've waded into?"

"Jared, I—"

He eased back to look into her eyes. "Please?"

"Aye. But—"

His lips cut off her reply. When she leaned against him, she confided, "I do so want Calliope to find happiness. She's had so little for so long."

"I am endeavoring to get to the bottom of Earl Chattsworth's disappearance," he informed her. "But there are circumstances that need to be carefully and quietly investigated before answers can be found or assumptions made in this matter."

Their gazes met and held. "I see."

"I've entrusted the lead in this to Coventry."

"Do you believe the earl is still alive?"

"It is too early in Coventry's investigation to determine, but I will say that we need to follow this through to the end. I've taken the measure of the man and do not believe the viscount is in any way involved in his father's abrupt disappearance."

"Are we taking unnecessary chances with Calliope's safety, encouraging her to marry Viscount Chattsworth?"

"I do not think so, but that is in part why I have instructed Calliope to listen to the guard I am sending as her escort and protection."

He paused and then continued, "There is another possible curve in this coil we have been in since I inherited the title."

"Oh, and what might that be?"

"There is an outside chance another henchman of Hollingford or Lady Hampton could slink out from wherever they are hiding—most probably under a rock, to cause trouble for our family—or extended family,"

Placing a hand over his heart, Persephone soothed, "Say no more, Jared. You've done the right thing, keeping them apart while Coventry works to uncover the truth...for both their sakes."

The duke gathered his wife close again. "My dear, have I told you—" His sharply indrawn breath and surprised look on his face had the duchess dissolving into giggles.

Having felt the strength of the babe's kick, she cleared her throat to speak. "Our daughter begs your pardon, my darling duke."

He tried to frown but ended up smiling at her. "Our son."

"Do you know Phoebe mentioned I appear large enough to be carrying twins."

Jared fought to stiffen legs that had gone weak on him at his wife's pronouncement. "Good God!"

Persephone's eyes filled as she agreed. "He is assuredly good and has blessed us."

The duke caught the first tear on the tip of his finger and swept it away. "Indeed He has, my dear. Indeed He has."

CHAPTER TEN

"**D**O YOU THINK the viscount has let his staff know that he's married?"

Calliope turned to look at Mary Kate. "I have no idea. One would hope, but then again..." her voice trailed off as she bit back the rest of what she'd been about to say. One would have hoped he would have stayed and spoken to her after that mind-numbing kiss. Instead, he'd left Wyndmere Hall without saying a word to her, while the duke made plans to whisk her away to the viscount's estate.

She could not fault the duke for making arrangements to see that the viscount's volatile temper had time to cool off, while at the same time seeing that she was dutifully settled in his home. What she could not get past was the feeling she'd received the ultimate *cut direct*. As if the viscount had said, *"I may have been forced to marry you, but I'll be dashed if I'll reside in the same abode as you!"*

"Her Grace was wonderful to insist we have a few things added for our journey."

Calliope sighed, setting those tortuous thoughts of her husband aside. Appreciating the change of subject, she responded, "There are so many things she thought of."

Mary Kate nodded. "Dried herbs, tinctures, salves, and tonics."

"Don't forget the calves' foot jelly and the huge pile of linen she had us cut into strips just last evening," Calliope added. "I sincerely hope we shall not have to use them, or the slats of wood she insisted we would need."

"I confess to being quite worried I'd have to help set a few broken bones—minor injuries and stitching wounds back together I learned from my mother—but not resetting bones." Mary Kate confided, "Francis and Mollie described what happened last year when that madman attacked before I joined the staff there."

Calliope visibly shuddered. "When we were under attack by Hollingford and his men. Francis and Mollie were a Godsend, helping us take care of the injured that day."

"Did you note what else Her Grace added to those supplies?"

"A few extra jars of calves' foot jelly?"

Mary Kate shook her head. "Some of the soaps we made, along with two bottles of Constance's blackberry cordial, and two bottles of sherry."

"Between Persephone, Constance, and Merry, we shall be well prepared to care for my husband's staff and tenant farmers."

"Shall I be attending them with you, your ladyship?"

"I would welcome that and be most appreciative of your help." She met Mary Kate's gaze and asked, "We've been traveling together for a few days now. How long do you think it will take for you to do as I asked and address me by my name?"

Mary Kate's cheeks flushed.

Calliope understood how her maid felt, having suffered from similar feelings when the duke asked the same of her. "Mayhap you can call me Calliope when it is just the two of us."

"Er...yes...Calliope," Mary Kate murmured.

"Excellent. I confess I am not quite certain what to expect when we arrive at Chattsworth Manor."

"It would have been helpful to know what to expect," Mary Kate said.

"It is unfortunate neither the duke nor the duchess were

familiar with the viscount's estate. Though we cannot say the duchess has not sent us more than prepared for any emergency."

Mary Kate agreed. "How many more changes of horse before we arrive?"

Calliope had been keeping track of the stops along their journey and pulled her journal out of her reticule. "Our last change of horse was when we stopped for our midday meal. We should be nearing the end of our journey."

"Are you excited?"

Calliope slipped the thin volume back into her reticule. "I confess to being torn between excitement and apprehension."

"As the new Viscountess Chattsworth, why would you feel that way?"

Calliope had confided bits and pieces of her years as a poor relation to her maid on their journey. "Although my earliest memories were of a loving home and family, the years after I lost my parents were filled with learning to work as one of the servants for my extended family."

"We have much more in common than I'd realized," Mary Kate marveled. "While at the same time, you are indeed a lady and as such should not have to toil like the rest of us."

Calliope begged to differ. "I may have been a lady from birth, but my relatives spent years instilling one thought—I was a poor relation who existed in life to serve them."

"Her Grace and Lady Phoebe have always treated you with affection and as their equal," Mary Kate reminded her. "You are a viscountess now."

Calliope sighed. "And that is what frightens me. I have no idea how to be a viscountess."

"Surely you've observed your relatives and noted how they ordered their servants about," Mary Kate urged.

"Yes, and I was appalled by more than half of them. They treated their staff abominably and as if they lived and breathed only to serve—at all hours of the day!"

"My previous employer treated me that way," Mary Kate told

her.

"How fortunate that you'd found your way to Wyndmere Hall," Calliope ventured.

"I was building up the courage to run away," Mary Kate whispered.

"From the duke and duchess?" Calliope could not countenance it! "They would never treat a servant poorly."

"No," her maid agreed, "they would not. I was a scullery maid for a lady in London and had been treated as you've described you had been."

"I had nowhere to run to," Calliope said.

"Neither did I," Mary Kate said, "but I thought about it every day when I received a beating because I wasn't fast enough or had not performed a task to my mistress' liking."

Calliope was riveted to a tale so like her own that she took hold of Mary Kate's hand to reassure her. "How did you escape?"

"It was one of the duke's guard that saved me."

"One of the O'Malleys?"

Mary Kate shook her head, "One of their Garahan cousins...James. He's among the guards stationed at the duke's London town house."

"Ah, one of the tall, dark, and handsome cousins—Aiden's brother."

Mary Kate nodded. "He was there when Lady Kittrick's cook kicked me out of the kitchen at my mistress' orders."

"Good Lord! Were you hurt?"

"Bruised and battered, but nothing out of the ordinary, and what I'd received from the first working for Lady Kittrick."

"What did James do?"

"He picked me up and brushed me off. I was a bit afraid of him—he's quite tall, very broad, and intimidating to behold."

Calliope had to agree.

"He bid me accompany him while he walked the earl's horses around the block."

"Edward?"

"Aye, Earl Lippincott had called on my mistress."

"I see. Then what happened?"

"Mrs. O'Toole, the duke's cook in London saw to my bruises, fed me, and took me under her wing."

"The duke has a way of rescuing people, too," Calliope said. "How did you end up in the country?"

"When the duke asked Mrs. Wigglesworth and Mrs. O'Toole which servants should accompany Her Grace and Lady Phoebe on their journey north last year, she suggested I go to help their maids. The duke has a reduced staff there as you may have noticed."

"Have you spoken to James since then?"

Mary Kate shrugged and looked out the window. "He saved me and, for that, I will always be grateful."

Calliope could tell from what her maid didn't say that she cared for the man. She had no idea if the duke's guard had feelings for her maid—or the time to examine if he had feelings for Mary Kate. She planned to speak to Aurelia and ask what she knew about the duke's plans to rotate his guard. Mayhap between the two of them, they could arrange for James and Mary Kate to meet again.

Even though her life had not been filled with romance, she'd been flattered and attracted to the darkly handsome viscount from the moment their eyes had met on Hogmanay. If only they hadn't been forced to wed, they might have developed an affection for one another that may have led to something more.

As they lapsed into silence, she wondered if the viscount *had* sent word ahead of their arrival, would he have mentioned her former status in life? She knew so little of the man she'd wed. Facts were facts: she had no dowry, no property, nothing of value except mayhap her years of toil and servitude to her extended family. How in the world would she convince her new staff that she was more than a poor relation? She knew how to clean and cook for a large household. Beyond that, she knew how *not* to treat one's servants.

She sighed. It was as good a place as any to begin.

The carriage slowed, and Calliope pushed the heavy curtain to the side to peer out of the window as the coachman guided the horses onto a narrow lane. "We must be getting close—"

Calliope's words were cut off as the carriage wheels slid on a patch of ice and careened to the right. The women braced themselves as the carriage tilted at a precarious angle then jolted to a stop. Mary Kate screamed as she flew off the seat, landing on top of Calliope.

The door burst open. "Are ye all right, yer ladyships?"

Mary Kate shifted, trying to move off of Calliope, but the angle of the carriage was too steep. She slid back on top of her mistress, eliciting a soft moan from Calliope. Before she tried again, Seamus Flaherty reached into the carriage and deftly pulled Mary Kate out, handing her off to the footman.

The carriage tilted further toward the ditch as the weight distribution changed.

Flaherty reached for Calliope's hand and warned, "Do not let go."

Her eyes filled with tears, but she blinked them away, promising, "I won't."

White hot pain sliced through her hip, and she fought against the need to move to ease the abominable ache. Her eyes locked with Flaherty's.

"What's wrong?"

"Nothing," she rasped, hanging on to his hands with all of her might.

He looked over his shoulder and shouted, "O'Malley! Get yer arse over here!"

Calliope's eyes widened at Flaherty's words, but wisely kept silent.

The auburn-haired giant, turned back and apologized, "Begging yer pardon, yer ladyship."

The fair-haired Michael O'Malley peered over his cousin's shoulder. "We don't want ye to move, yer ladyship."

"Will the carriage turn over on its roof?" She imagined the scene Aurelia had described to her when her friend had confided Lord and Lady Coddington's carriage had overturned on an icy road all those years ago, leaving Aurelia an orphan. And then there was the harrowing fact that her own father had perished in a carriage accident.

The men glanced at one another and then back at Calliope. "Don't borrow trouble," Flaherty told her.

"I want to thank the both of you for trying to extract me," she told them. "You and your family have bravely protected Aurelia, Phoebe, Her Grace, and me for the better part of a year."

Flaherty grinned at her. "Ye didn't make it easy on the lot of us with yer disobeying His Grace's instructions, now did ye, yer ladyship?"

Her mouth opened, but she bit back on the retort poised upon her tongue. *He was right.* They had made the job of protecting them much harder. "Do forgive me."

Flaherty said something to his cousin, but was speaking so softly that she couldn't quite make out what was said. But she heard the coachman talking to the team of horses, calming them.

Capturing her attention once more, his face was devoid of amusement as he said, "I need ye to listen closely and do exactly as I say. Will ye do that, yer ladyship?"

"Yes," she rasped, silently praying that no harm would come to anyone outside of the carriage—or their horses.

"I'm going to pull ye out, but mind, the carriage may move beneath us. Will ye trust me to free ye?"

She swallowed against the lump of fear lodged in her throat to answer, "I trust you." Calliope closed her eyes and silently prayed, *"Dear Lord, please don't let the carriage turn over and crush us."*

She felt the carriage move, and her eyes shot open. Flaherty had slid forward and wrapped his arms beneath hers, lifting her off the floorboards. As she hung suspended for a heartbeat inside the shifting carriage, she wondered if her parents would be the first angels she met in Heaven.

"Don't worry, yer ladyship, O'Malley's got me by the ankles."

Calliope tried to see past him, but he warned her with a look. "Me cousin and I are strong enough to pull ye to safety, but ye have to work with us to save ye."

Fear replaced worry, but the steely determination in his blue eyes reassured her. "I will."

"Put yer arms around me neck and hold tight!"

She wrapped her arms around his neck as one of his arms banded around her back and the other behind her knees.

Before she could push away from the intimate contact, he cautioned, "Don't move, yer ladyship!"

Her injured hip hit the edge of the seat. She grit her teeth to keep from crying out until O'Malley hauled his cousin and Calliope out of the carriage.

"Are ye hurt?" O'Malley demanded, as he lifted her from where she and his cousin landed on the ground at his feet.

Calliope offered up a prayer of thanks to her Maker and the strength of the duke's guard. "I am sure I shall be."

"Me ma would say that yer prevaricating, yer ladyship," Flaherty said, getting to his feet.

She moved to take a step back and groaned aloud.

"Where are you hurt, your ladyship," Mary Kate asked, slipping her arm around Calliope's waist. "That jolt lifted me right off the seat. I'm ever so sorry to have landed on top of you."

Calliope shook her head. "It's nothing that I haven't suffered before," she reassured them. "I'm strong, and I'll mend."

The men towered over her, but she felt calm instead of the fear that slid through her belly when she realized their predicament. Flaherty's fierce frown and O'Malley's clenched jaw actually soothed her.

"I'll carry ye," Flaherty offered at the same time O'Malley did.

She found her first smile since the duke's carriage slid off the road. "I am quite capable of walking, thank you," she told them. "How are we going to right the carriage?"

Flaherty's blue eyes danced with merriment. "We?"

"I will do whatever needs to be done to help," she replied. "After all, it is my fault."

O'Malley's frown deepened. "What a load of—"

"Language," Flaherty warned.

She opened her mouth to respond but decided against it as the guards stood side by side, feet braced apart—a broad-shouldered, impenetrable wall.

"I...er—"

"Trust me, and just nod," Mary Kate whispered.

Calliope nodded and the men immediately relaxed their stance.

Flaherty called out to the coachman to keep the team steady. The coachman made short work of the task and the powerful geldings were under control once more.

"How can two men possibly right a carriage of this size?" Calliope asked.

The men shared a look before helping the women move to safety well off the road. "We've done this a time or two, yer ladyship," Flaherty announced before turning back to the task at hand.

While she and Mary Kate watched, O'Malley climbed onto the wheel and tied off a rope to one of the side rails atop the coach.

Mary Kate's sharply indrawn breath had the man grinning at her as he pushed off the carriage, landing on his feet, rope taut in his hands.

Just when Calliope thought they were through, a sharp whistle sounded, and O'Malley's horse trotted over to where he stood.

"There's a lad," he crooned, tying the rope to his saddle. "Toss another rope, Seamus!"

His cousin complied, and O'Malley repeated the move, this time standing on the rear wheel. Flaherty led his horse over to where O'Malley stood waiting to tie off the rope to his cousin's saddle.

Impressed with their strength and ingenuity, Calliope and Mary Kate watched the men walk their horses to the opposite side of the road. The ropes pulled taut and the carriage shifted, but it soon became evident it wasn't going to move.

"We need to brace the front wheel and lift the back wheel out of the ditch," Flaherty instructed.

"Do ye think—" he started to say, while his cousin blurted out, "...that pile of deadfall."

They backed their horses up for a moment to ease their burden and headed to the pile of heavy limbs and branches a few yards off the road. Working swiftly, the pair found what they were looking for.

Calliope asked, "How can that possibly aid them?"

Mary Kate was quick to reply. "You'll see. I watched my father use limbs and branches when our wagon loaded down with supplies got stuck after a heavy rain."

Calliope watched Flaherty pull a knife out of his boot and cut the smaller branches off one of the tree limbs and then the second before tossing them to his cousin who placed them on the large patch of ice by the rear of the coach. "Truly?"

"Father usually worked alone, so he had to use what tools he had to get himself out of scrapes like getting stuck in the mud."

While they watched, O'Malley tossed one of the limbs he'd trimmed to the other side of the ditch like a caber. With a running leap, he landed beside it. Shifting the weight in his hands, he slid the end of the limb between the spokes in front of the wheel hub. Moving off to the side, he waited for his cousin to toss the second one across the ditch before watching him take the same running leap, landing beside his cousin.

The coachman stood at the ready by the front of the carriage with the geldings, while the footman waited by the rear wheel with Flaherty's and O'Malley's horses.

Working together, they threaded the second limb through the spokes behind the wheel hub. Flaherty nodded to O'Malley then called out to the coachman and the footman, "Are ye ready, lads?"

"Ready!"

Calliope realized the safest place to be was where they were—across the road from the carriage while the cousins combined their strength to bear down on the limbs lifting the wheel out of the ditch.

Braced, straining against the weight, Flaherty shouted, "Now!"

The coachman urged the horses forward, straining against the weight. This time, with the cousins using the limbs to raise the wheel higher, the carriage shifted as the wheel touched down on the evergreen-covered ice.

All at once, the carriage tilted toward the horses, but Flaherty's quick thinking and the spare rope he'd tied to their side of the carriage, kept the heavy conveyance from leaning too far the other way.

When the creaking stopped and the dust settled, the small group began to talk all at once.

"Did you see that?" Mary Kate asked Calliope.

"Haven't attempted that with a town coach," Flaherty admitted to O'Malley.

"Never saw the like," the coachman said to the guards.

Silence descended as the group performed their tasks. The coachmen and the footman worked together to shift the trunks back into place and climbed onto the coach. O'Malley untied and coiled the ropes, returning them to where they'd been stored atop the coach. Flaherty moved the tree branches back off the road and filled the deep ruts with the smaller branches he'd cut off.

The women waited until the men completed their tasks and walked over to where they stood.

"Let's get ye out of this cold," Flaherty said.

Before he could lift Calliope into his arms, she moved behind Mary Kate and smiled. "Thank you, but I can walk."

Flaherty opened the door and held out his hand to assist Calliope and Mary Kate into the carriage once more.

Moving the curtains aside, the women watched as the duke's guards mounted their horses. With Flaherty once more taking the lead and O'Malley bringing up the rear, they followed the road to the end.

"It looks abandoned," Mary Kate murmured.

"There's a flicker of light in that window," Calliope pointed out.

"The grounds are overgrown."

Calliope had observed more than one gardener at work over the years. "A sharp scythe will take care of that."

"Not a wisp of smoke is coming out of the chimney," her maid remarked.

"We know where there is sufficient wood to start a fire," Calliope said with a smile. "It would appear we have our work cut out for us, Mary Kate."

"I wonder where all of the servants are?"

"Performing their daily tasks, I would imagine." Calliope decided it would be up to her to maintain a calm she did not feel. The notion that the viscount was resistant to marry for more than one reason filled her. Of a certain, he had no wish to be forced into it. Another reason lay before them in all its run-down glory.

CHAPTER ELEVEN

W ILLIAM STARED AT the duke. Anger and envy combined to serve up a noxious brew he had to swallow before he responded. "You thought it best to send my wife to Chattsworth Manor without consulting me? All the while letting her believe I'd already left here without saying goodbye?" It was not to be borne! He had to do something to assert his will over that of his autocratic cousin.

Before he could think of what to say or do, the duke responded, "Your decision to leave this estate without a by your leave— especially to your viscountess, was inexcusable. You left me no choice."

Their gazes met and held...again William noted it was disturbingly akin to staring into his looking glass. Tamping down on his anger, he bit out, "And yet you order me to London? I do not answer to you, Your Grace, and I do not intend—"

"I beg to differ, Chattsworth," the duke interrupted. "Your actions earlier today have disgraced Lady Calliope, who has been under the joint protection of Lord Coddington and me, which indeed places you in the same position."

"I do not see it as so." His anger simmered, dangerously close to exploding. Drawing in a deep breath, he was able to quell the worst of it, but he was unsure what to say to extricate himself from the situation.

"As I see it," the duke continued, "you need time to become accustomed to your new state."

"By that, I take it you mean my marriage."

The duke placed his hands on his desk and shoved to his feet, the first indication he was angry. "Bloody hell, Chattsworth, it is not the fault of Lady Calliope that she happened to be in such a vulnerable position at the top of the stairs! Have you thought what might have happened had you not reacted so swiftly?"

William's gut roiled as bile threatened to shoot up his throat. With a will of iron, he fought and controlled the urge to retch.

Before he could reply, the duke continued. "Had she been beyond your reach and catapulted down the staircase, any one of the steps—or the handrail, could have broken her neck!"

William saw something then in the duke's gaze that should have been in his own...remorse. Why would the duke harbor that emotion? His cousin wasn't responsible for Calliope's situation. That fault lay directly at William's feet.

The duke blinked, and the glimpse inside the man he'd thought so remote, was closed off once more. William would question him another time.

"Who did you send with my wife?"

The duke seemed pleased at the question. "One of our maids has been elevated to Lady Calliope's lady's maid, as she will need one."

"And for protection?"

"Astute of you to ask," the duke intoned. "Seamus Flaherty and Michael O'Malley."

"And I assume a footman?"

"Indeed."

William relaxed. He may not have wanted to marry...*that was not true.* Before he'd been told Calliope was a poor relation, he had briefly considered her a suitable candidate. That the duke saw fit to send her with a lady's maid from his own staff, a footman and two of his personal guard was commendable. In his anger, he had not thought of his wife—*his viscountess,* at all.

"Do forgive my outburst, Your Grace," he apologized. "I have been struggling with more than one calamitous situation this past year."

The duke nodded. "I still intend to lend my considerable connections. Then mayhap we can get to the bottom of your father's disappearance."

William could not for the life of him imagine why the duke would lend such support after he had clearly been beyond angry with the events that had transpired since that morning. "If I may be so bold to ask, why would you lend such to me?"

The duke sighed. "Though you may not realize it, I value our familial connection and would do all in my power to help our family—no matter how distant that tie may be."

As his cousin's words sank in, William felt ashamed. He'd planned to use that which he knew the duke held sacred to his own ends. Envy struggled to resurface, but the viscount beat it back in order to thank his cousin. "I would be beyond grateful for your assistance. I have exhausted the avenues open to me...as well as the ready coin to do so."

"I am well aware the cost is high, having struggled with much the same at the time of my brother's death."

The duke walked over to the fireplace and stood with his hands behind his back.

Not wishing to encroach upon the duke's musings, William wondered what he could say or do to repay the duke for his offer. He should have been honest with the duke from the beginning. It became crystal clear he would honor the duke's request that he head to London to take up residence in the duke's town house. He would willingly handle the affairs the duke indicated he would need assistance with.

"I mean no disrespect but am compelled to ask for your reassurance that my wife will be well protected."

The duke turned around and stared at William for long moments before answering, "I would ask the same in your place. You have my word that Calliope and her lady's maid will be well protected."

William opened his mouth to speak but quickly closed it. He could not give the duke the real reason he feared for his wife's safety. His new wife had no idea of the ramshackle condition of his family estate...or his finances. He highly doubted the duke did either, or else he would never have sent Calliope to Chattsworth Manor. *Then again, the duke did know about the number of servants. Was that the man's reason for sending two of his personal guard with them, or did the duke fear for their safety for reasons connected with the duke's troubles?*

He bowed to his cousin. "You have my gratitude. Shall I leave you to compile the list of duties you'd have me oversee?"

The duke smiled and walked back to his desk and sat down. Waving to the chair in front of the desk, he nodded when William sat. "Not necessary." He lifted a bit of foolscap. "I have enumerated them and indicated who would be best to seek counsel from should you need it."

Impressed with his cousin's foresight, William thanked him. "That would ensure the duties will be handled to your satisfaction, Your Grace."

"I have no doubt you can handle them, Chattsworth. Mayhap your time in London will help you to see past your anger at the situation you feel has been unjustly foisted upon you."

"I will do my best to accustom myself to it."

"In time, you will realize the delicate jewel I have placed in your care. Time spent in London attending to the small portion of duties I am placing in your hands should open your mind...if not then, your heart."

William was about to disagree that his mind was not closed but thought best to leave that discussion for another time. Mayhap a few weeks from now, after he'd met with his wife again...had the duke just said open his heart? Surely he'd misheard that last.

The duke waited for him to reply, but the thought that his future did not seem quite so out of his control tantalized him with what might be. He held the reins to a number of the duke's duties, he never expected to have it so. The viscount frowned. He had no doubt whatever the duke required of him could easily be handled by the duke's man-of-affairs but was wise enough not to say so. But he would benefit from learning to handle the affairs, mayhap using that knowledge in taking the reins of the twisted mess his father had left behind.

"I shall do my utmost to follow your direction to the letter and seek wise counsel from those you've indicated."

"I believe you shall exceed my expectations, Chattsworth." The duke stood and offered his hand.

William rose and accepted it as it was meant—a bond between them. The duke's trust in him, and William's word that he would honor that trust.

He left a short while later, anticipating the journey to London. It would be shorter as he would travel on Maximus. Time alone on the road, with none but his stallion as company, would do much to clear his head. He was not certain he would ever come to value Lady Calliope as the duke indicated, but he would not discard the possibility that he may…in time.

As THE DUKE and the head of his guard watched the viscount round the bend out of sight, Patrick O'Malley asked, "Do ye think his lordship's time in London attendin' to the list ye've given him will change his mind about Lady Calliope?"

The duke took his time responding. He needed to search his heart to answer O'Malley honestly. "Given time, I hope he will see beyond Calliope's circumstances to the loyal, strong, loving woman we know her to be."

"'Twas lucky the viscount is quick on his feet."

The duke's gaze met that of O'Malley's. "My hope is that a month from now, the viscount will realize his good fortune and return from London a changed man. One with purpose, who is not blinded by what he feels he does not have in life, recognizing and able to embrace what he has."

"Before me brothers and I left home, Ma liked to remind us that men needed to use the gifts God gave them for the good of others."

"A wise woman, your mother."

Patrick grinned. "Aye, she is that. If we dared try to gainsay Ma, she'd add that if we were lucky enough, someday we'd meet women who'd put up with the bone-headed lot of us."

The duke's rolling laugh had the horses in the stable lifting their heads, but only the duke's Thoroughbred stallion sent up an answering wicker.

Persephone and Phoebe watched the men from the rear sitting room and smiled at one another. "It appears your brother has found something that makes him smile and laugh," Persephone confided.

"He's been worried about far more than enemies coming out of the woodwork," Phoebe remarked.

The duchess' sigh was audible. "I cannot seem to assuage the unnatural fear he harbors where our babe is concerned. Although it probably did not help matters when I mentioned you thought I looked as if I carried two."

Phoebe's eyes widened. "I am certain the thought will plague him until you are safely delivered of your daughter." She linked her arm through her sister-in-law's as they watched the man they loved. "It is not just the heir to the dukedom that he worries over and you know it, Persephone."

"I know," she admitted. "But women have been bearing children for ages. Can you but imagine if the duke had to bear his heir?"

Phoebe's jaw dropped and it was moments before she could collect herself enough to close it. Her delighted laughter filled the room. When she collected herself, she confided, "The illustrious Dukes of Wyndmere would end with my brothers if that were the case."

Persephone smiled as she uttered her husband's favorite expression, "Indeed. I'm feeling a bit peckish. What say we see what sweets Constance has been baking this morning?"

They walked into the kitchen as the duke entered from the outside door. "Why are you not resting?" he demanded.

"Is that any way to greet your wife?" his sister fired back. "Should you not be asking how she feels?"

The duke raised his eyes to the ceiling and sighed before addressing his wife. "I beg your pardon, my dear. How are you feeling?"

Persephone smiled and replied, "Quite peckish."

"I'm certain Constance has something to take the edge off your hunger. Haven't you?" he asked their cook.

The older woman smiled at the trio as she poured hot water into the silver teapot sitting on the serving tray on the large oak table in the center of the room. "How would you feel about sampling the warm batch of cream tarts I just removed from the oven?"

Persephone's stomach growled and the duke's eyes danced with glee. "That sounds fine for my lovely wife, but what about the rest of us? She's sure to gobble the entire tray."

"Mind your words, Husband," Persephone grumbled, "else you'll be bedding down with your stallion tonight," she warned.

The duke glared at her. Obviously still not used to her volatile changes of mood Dr. McIntyre had warned of.

Persephone disliked having to deal with the emotions herself, but she was sorry to have lashed out at her husband. Her exaggerated sigh was quite loud. "Fine, I won't insist you sleep in the stables if you promise not to make any further unkind remarks about my appetite."

He closed the distance between, wrapped an arm around her back and pulled her against his side. Leaning down, he whispered, "I am truly sorry. It was a jest in poor taste. I promise not to do so again. You are responsible for the feeding of our son—"

"Daughter," she interrupted. "Do go on," she urged.

"As I was saying, you are eating for two, therefore I should not comment on what you eat or the quantity."

"We are in agreement. Now as to your untoward comments—"

"I shall refrain from this moment forward. I should have taken into account your fragile feelings during this time."

Persephone narrowed her gaze at him. "See that you do not forget."

Cook shooed everyone out of her domain, professing she needed the time to set up the two trays. "Shall I have one of the footmen deliver it to your upstairs sitting room, Your Grace?"

"That would be lovely. Thank you, Constance."

"My pleasure, Your Grace."

"Do you truly have the time to take tea with us, Jared?"

He smiled at Persephone. "I do believe I can shift a few items in my appointment schedule to accommodate my lovely wife and delightful sister."

Phoebe and Persephone eyed the duke with skepticism. Persephone doubted it would be an easy thing to clear his overly long list of duties. Grateful for the time to sit down with her husband and his sister, she smiled when the tea was delivered. Merry entered the room followed by one of their maids and a footman.

"Thank you, Merry. Please set it on the table by the window."

The housekeeper did so, offering, "Shall I pour?"

"I believe it's Phoebe's turn to act as hostess," Persephone said. "She could use the practice, you know."

Phoebe's face flamed as Merry curtseyed and left with the servants. "I most certainly do not."

The duke covered his snort of laughter with a cough. "Pardon me."

The women were not fooled, especially the duchess. "Do you recall our conversation of not twenty minutes ago?"

His gaze met hers and he sighed. "I take it you are referring to my promise not to jest?"

"That is correct," she agreed. "I would have you do the same for your sister. She needs your encouragement, not your jests."

The duke gave a brief nod before lifting his teacup to his lips. He sipped and set his teacup on its saucer on the table between them. "Phoebe, would you be so kind as to serve the cream tarts?"

Persephone watched her sister-in-law's impeccable manners before noticing her husband's wide smile. "You are most jovial this morning, Husband."

He agreed. "I'm having tea with my beautiful wife and lovely sister. Indulging in one of Constance's delectable confections— cream tarts. That would put anyone in an elevated mood."

Persephone narrowed her gaze at her husband, studying him before nodding her agreement. "Are you ready to stop ignoring the obvious and impart what conversation took place between you and the viscount before he left this morning?"

The duke set down his dessert plate and half-eaten cream tart. "It went far better than expected. The viscount will be working closely with Coventry for the next few weeks, at which time, I hope he will have had the time to cool his volatile reaction to Lady Calliope."

"And?" Persephone urged.

"He will be traveling south to Sussex to take up residence with his new wife."

"Do you think Phoebe and I should be there when he arrives?"

The duke considered it for a moment before shaking his head. "I do not believe that will be necessary. I have faith in the viscount."

"What if he has not changed?" Phoebe wanted to know.

"Do not forget that Seamus Flaherty and Michael O'Malley accompanied Calliope and her maid to Chattsworth Manor."

"Did you give them instructions to stay on until the viscount is settled."

"Indeed I have."

Persephone reached over to lay a hand on her husband's arm.

"Thank you, Jared. I am quite concerned about Calliope and Mary Kate."

"Have faith, my darling duchess."

Phoebe snorted out a laugh. "Shall I leave you two alone to billet and coo?"

The duke's jaw dropped open, but Persephone ignored him and seemed to consider Phoebe's offer. "Now that you mention it…"

"Oh, do be serious, Persephone!" Phoebe barked. "I was jesting."

Persephone glanced at her sister-in-law before locking gazes with her husband. "Could we please cease and desist with the jests?"

Brother and sister smiled at one another before he answered, "Of course, my love."

"Yes, Persephone."

"Excellent. More tea?" Persephone asked.

The duke and Phoebe declined.

"Would you care for another cream tart, Persephone?"

The duchess smiled at Phoebe. "Two please."

CHAPTER TWELVE

C ALLIOPE SMILED AT the butler and housekeeper as they were introduced and made welcome at Chattsworth Manor.

"I had no notion that his lordship planned to marry," Hargrave intoned with a glance at the housekeeper.

"Nor I," Mrs. Meadowsweet added. "We would have made certain to have a celebratory dinner planned for your arrival. I take it his lordship is riding Maximus?"

For a heartbeat, she froze before answering, "I am certain his lordship is riding Maximus."

The butler and the housekeeper were obviously waiting for her to advise when he would be arriving.

Calliope ignored them and could not help but notice the shabby outward appearance of the manor was mirrored on the inside. There were faded outlines on the walls where she imagined paintings had once hung. There were a number of occasional tables—standing empty. Would they have once displayed a vase, small bit of artwork, or mayhap a miniature of one of the viscount's ancestors?

She tried not to show her surprise at the layer of dust, or the fact the entryway could use a thorough scrubbing. A brief glance at the elderly housekeeper revealed her worry. Did the woman doubt that she had indeed married the viscount or was it something else entirely?

C.H. ADMIRAND

It was then she remembered the missive the duke had entrusted her with. "The duke penned a missive addressing the viscount's staff." She opened her reticule and pulled out the sealed note and handed it to Mrs. Meadowsweet.

The woman looked to the butler before speaking, "I am certain His Grace would want to reassure me and Hargrave that everything is in order and that we should welcome your ladyship to your new home."

"We will do our utmost to see you settled, your ladyship," Hargrave added.

"Thank you." Calliope noted a distinct change once she'd handed over the duke's missive and silently thanked him for having the foresight to do so. She resolved not to comment on the state of her new home until she had met the rest of the staff and toured the viscount's home.

The duke's guard appeared in the still open doorway, each balancing the two largest trunks on their shoulders. "Where would ye like us to deliver the trunks, yer ladyship?"

"I shall leave that to Mr. Hargrave or Mrs. Meadowsweet to direct you," she said before introducing the men.

Hargrave cleared his throat. "Just Hargrave, your ladyship." To Flaherty and O'Malley, he intoned, "Follow me."

Mrs. Meadowsweet fluttered her hands and appeared most agitated. Instead of asking outright if there were a problem, Calliope sensed she and her party were the problem. In that moment, her resolve to put the elderly woman at ease had her offering, "Mary Kate and I would be happy to accompany our trunks."

"Shall I help you unpack?"

She was right in her assumption. A housekeeper would normally oversee the task of unpacking, directing one or two of the upstairs maids, while Calliope would direct her lady's maid. Calliope had not seen any other servants and noted their conversation seemed to echo in the house. *There were probably no upstairs maids.*

"Thank you, but Mary Kate and I shall manage."

"If that be your ladyship's wish." The older woman hesitated before asking, "Shall I ask Mrs. Romney, our cook, to see about putting a tea tray together? You must be chilled to the bone."

Calliope smiled and reassured the housekeeper she was not overly chilled, but that tea sounded wonderful. She didn't dare admit to having been warmed by the blood rushing through her as the coach slid, then tipped over and then having to be rescued by Mr. Flaherty. Best to leave that discussion for another time...in a year or two from now...or never.

They passed a number of closed doors along the upper hallway before the butler opened the second to last door the right. "In here, if you please."

Flaherty and O'Malley ducked their heads to enter the room and set down their burdens beneath the large window. Calliope and Mary Kate followed them into the large room. The curtains had been pulled back on the window in the wall opposite the door.

She asked Hargrave what direction it faced. If he thought the question odd, he gave no indication. "East, your ladyship."

Taking in the mahogany four poster bed, chest at the foot of it and lack of a rug, she sighed. It was lovely in comparison to the tiny attic rooms she'd been living in before Uncle Phineas had come to her rescue. Not quite as sumptuous as the bedchambers at Wyndmere Hall or the duke's town house in London.

Calliope smiled at the butler. "How wonderful to wake to a room filled with sunshine."

"Do ye want us to bring yer other trunks up here as well, yer ladyship?" Flaherty asked.

Thinking of the supplies the other trunks contained, she nodded. "That shall do nicely for the moment, thank you."

Watching the men leave, she felt a bit uneasy beneath the direct stare of the viscount's butler. Unsure if it was the man's personality or due to his advanced years and length of service to the Chattsworth family, she spoke up. "I do hope that will not be a problem, storing them in here as well."

Hargrave inclined his head. "I am sure his lordship will inform us if that is not to his wishes."

Not willing to impart the news that her husband would not be returning for a number of weeks, leaving her in charge of his home, she nodded. "Of course, thank you, Hargrave."

The butler walked over to the closed door along one wall and opened it. "The connecting door to his lordship's room is on the other side of the dressing room."

Calliope peered inside, noting the space just beyond the door was empty, save for a wardrobe and a lovely mahogany dressing table with a mirror attached. The connecting door stood open to the viscount's side. There was a lovely copper hip bath and a larger wardrobe. No doubt filled with the viscount's clothing.

"Thank you, Hargrave. I shall be more than comfortable."

"Here now, what's this?" a gruff voice demanded from behind them. "Who are you?"

"Mind your tone, MacReedy," Hargrave huffed.

"You are well aware that his lordship agreed his dressing room is my domain."

Hargrave cleared his throat and announced, "Viscountess, may I introduce his lordship's valet, MacReedy."

MacReedy's face showed shocked surprise. "I had no idea his lordship married. Begging your pardon, your ladyship."

"No need, I assure you, Mr. MacReedy."

"Where is his lordship?"

MacReedy asked the question Calliope was certain the others had wanted to ask but had thought better of it. She answered as truthfully as she could, "The viscount is acting on the duke's behalf in London for the next few weeks."

"Is he now?"

Though the question sounded impertinent, she answered, "Yes. He'll be staying at the duke's London town house and will no doubt let us know when he is expected."

"Very good, your ladyship," Hargrave responded.

MacReedy stared at her for long moments, leaving her to wonder what the man was thinking. Instead of letting his manner upset her as she would have in the past, she turned to Mary Kate. "Mrs. Meadowsweet has promised us tea. Shall we see if it has been prepared?"

"Of course, Lady Calliope."

They swept from the room, only to encounter the duke's guard as they hauled the rest of the trunks up the stairs.

"Is everything all right, yer ladyship?" O'Malley asked.

"Yes, thank you, Mr. O'Malley. When you've finished, please do join us in the kitchen. I am certain Mrs. Meadowsweet can advise where we can put you and the others up until you are ready to make the return journey to Wyndmere Hall in the morning."

At the incredulous look that passed between O'Malley and Flaherty, she wondered just what she had said to cause such a reaction. She would have to ask them as another more pressing thought occurred to her. They were leaving in the morning, weren't they? Surely the duke did not send them to act as her personal guard until the viscount returned? That would be wholly unnecessary.

"Aye, yer ladyship," Flaherty answered for the both of them.

The butler swept past them. "Allow me to show your ladyship to the kitchen."

"Thank you, Hargrave. Please do lead the way."

Following behind the man, she noticed the sad neglect that permeated throughout the viscount's home. Did the viscount send to the village for additional staff to run Chattsworth Manor when he was in residence? She wouldn't ask outright, not yet. Time to observe first and see what she could do to amend the situation.

"Viscountess, may I introduce Mrs. Romney, our cook." He turned toward the cook and finished the introductions.

"A pleasure to meet you, your ladyship."

The cook was much younger than the butler or the housekeeper. It was a bit harder to pin down the wiry valet's age, possibly somewhere in between.

"Lovely to meet you, Mrs. Romney. Mrs. Meadowsweet mentioned something about tea?"

"Of course, it's all prepared. Mrs. Meadowsweet suggested that you would be most comfortable in the sitting room."

She noticed that the guard was still shadowing her. Obviously on the orders of the duke. Knowing the men had to be ravenous after the ordeal involving their coach, she asked, "We've traveled a good distance since dawn this morning. I wonder if I could impose upon you to prepare a meal for the duke's men."

"Of course, your ladyship. Just let me serve your first."

Calliope glanced at the size of the tea tray and the plateful of teacakes and then her maid. "I do believe the kitchen is the coziest room in the house, don't you agree, Mary Kate?"

"Aye, your ladyship."

"With your permission, Mrs. Romney—and a few more cups, I think tea in the kitchen would warm us all up."

"All of you?" Uncertainty laced the cook's words, though her expression was neutral.

"Ye don't need to worry after the lot of us, yer ladyship," Flaherty told her. "We've—"

"Worked harder than I have today," she finished for him. Turning back to the cook, she smiled and said, "We had a bit of an accident with our coach at the end of the road leading to the manor."

Mrs. Romney's face lost all its color. She set down the stack of cups she'd brought to the large oak table and gasped. "Was anyone hurt? Shall I send Mr. MacReedy to fetch the physician?"

Calliope looked at each one of the faces gathered around her and shook her head. "Just a bit bruised, nothing a bit of the healing salve the duchess supplied me with won't take care of."

"What about yer injury?" O'Malley asked, his gaze locked with hers.

She couldn't believe that he would bring up something so

personal. "Not that this is the time or the place to discuss such, I will attribute it to concern on my behalf and reassure you that I shall be fine."

"The duke would have our heads if ye don't let us help, yer ladyship," Flaherty reminded her. "Would soaking in a hot tub take care of it?"

His dark frown didn't deter her from seeing those that made the journey with her were promptly taken care of. She'd never put herself first. It would take a bit of time—and a lot of convincing that she should start doing so now. Being forced into a marriage with the viscount was not reason enough to do so.

"Well now," Mrs. Romney said to Hargrave, "I'll start heating water for her ladyship's bath, if you and Mr. MacReedy would be so good as to carry it upstairs when it's ready."

Calliope could not have heard the cook correctly. From the look on Hargrave's face, and slightly pained expression, she knew she had. Well acquainted with the narrow design of most servants' staircases, she would never condone having someone the man's age haul bath water for her up that flight of stairs.

"Me cousin and I will be happy to fetch and carry bath water for her ladyship," Flaherty announced to the room at large, causing everyone to shift their gazes away from Calliope and Hargrave.

"Do you have a small room off the kitchen where a tub could be set up?" Calliope asked. Well aware her suggestion was more than a bit unconventional, she waited for the cook's reply.

"As a matter of fact," Mrs. Romney remarked, "the pantry is quite large and we do keep a large wooden tub in there for those of us to use—nothing fitting for your ladyship, along with a smaller wooden wash tub."

Calliope drew in a deep breath and squared her shoulders. If she was now the viscountess, it was time she took charge. "Let me be the judge of that, Mrs. Romney," she advised before asking, "Does the tub hold water?"

"Of course."

"Is there a door to the pantry that could be closed for privacy?"

"Yes, your ladyship."

"Perfect." She'd already acted unconventionally including the duke's guard in the tea prepared for her. Asserting her will over the cook by demanding she not receive the preferential treatment due her position as the viscount's wife would no doubt be repeated. *Had she just consigned herself to perdition?*

A glance around the room had her drawing on her newfound courage, holding out her hand and nodding to the teacups and saucers. Finally, the cook passed a few to Calliope who, with Mary Kate's help, set the table. The coachman and the footman entered through the outer door to the kitchen, wiping their feet before noticing Calliope. "How are you feeling, your ladyship?" the coachman asked.

"A bit hungry. Are you?"

The coachman looked to the guards first, and the footman second, before nodding. "I could eat a little something, if it's not too much trouble."

"Not at all," Mrs. Romney announced. "Her ladyship decided to have tea with the lot of you in my kitchen."

Calliope caught the underlying note of annoyance and immediately wondered if her first duty as viscountess would be an issue with the cook. *That would never do.*

"Mrs. Romney," the butler rumbled, "you will not speak to Lady Calliope in such a manner again, or I shall report you to his lordship."

The cook's face flushed a bright red as she bowed her head. "Do forgive me, your ladyship, I cannot imagine what came over me."

"Probably having our party descend upon you without notice so late in the day," she said by way of excusing the woman's sharp reply.

Hargrave harrumphed. "See that you do not speak to her ladyship in such a manner again." Bowing to Calliope, he said, "I shall leave your ladyship in Mrs. Romney's care. I need to see if Mrs. Meadowsweet has need of me."

"Shall I send Mary Kate to you after she has a bit of tea?"

"Thank you, but no, your ladyship." He turned on his heel and walked out of the kitchen.

Flaherty walked over to large cooking stove when he noticed the cook struggling to move a large pot onto it. "Let me help you."

Before she could refuse, he had the pot on the burner. "What can we use to fill the pot for you?"

"We?" the cook asked, staring up at Flaherty.

"Aye, me and me cousin. The job will go faster with the two of us filling the pot."

Mrs. Romney smiled. "Right you are. Please everyone, have a seat. I'll be back in a moment to pour."

"I can handle the serving. You've put together such a lovely tea for us, Mrs. Romney. Thank you."

The woman goggled at the praise and Calliope's offer to serve but remembered her manners. "You're quite welcome."

By the time she returned, Calliope had emptied the first pot of tea and was preparing more. "I'll take care of that for you."

"It's no trouble," Calliope assured her. "Shall I pour you a cup as well?"

Her eyes were as round as saucers. "No thank you, your ladyship."

Mary Kate served Calliope and then passed teacakes to everyone, saving some for Mrs. Romney. Calliope poured one last cup of tea for the cook. "Do please join us," she urged. "We're quite a merry group and we've quite taken over your kitchen."

Mrs. Romney shook her head. "Never would I imagine a day when a viscountess would be in my kitchen making tea and pouring it for her servants!"

Calliope smiled at those gathered around the table. "Servants are people, too. We've had a long trip, and I wouldn't want anyone to have to wait to have a nice cup of tea. Now," she said, pulling out the chair for the cook to sit. "What can I help you prepare for supper to feed the duke's men?"

Mrs. Romney held up her hands. "Not a thing. That's my job, your ladyship."

"But you could not have been expecting so many mouths to feed tonight," Calliope said with a glance about her.

"True, but I can manage. Enjoy your tea everyone, then let me start supper."

Flaherty flashed a grin at the cook. "Sounds just like me ma. What she's meaning is drink up and clear out."

The cook's laughter filled the room. "Well, that's putting it in plain speaking. If you and Mr. O'Malley will stick around to haul the water upstairs—"

"Just O'Malley," Michael interrupted.

The cook nodded that she'd heard.

"Downstairs if you please, Mrs. Romney," Calliope insisted.

Mrs. Romney frowned over the rim of her teacup at Calliope but agreed. "Downstairs, your ladyship."

Calliope nodded. *She'd done it!* She was relieved that she'd won her first challenge asserting herself in her new position as lady of the house. Now if she could convince the small staff that she did not want to change how things were run. Today was an exception, with her unconventional way to see that the duke's men would be taken care of quickly. After all, they'd saved her life when the carriage slid across the icy road.

She would need the help of the viscount's staff to run his home the way he was accustomed to. Then all would be well when he came home.

If he came home.

CHAPTER THIRTEEN

C ALLIOPE STOOD WAITING in the doorway to her bedchamber. Mary Kate dashed up the servants' staircase and slipped into the room.

"What did you find out?"

"You were right," Mary Kate rushed to tell her mistress. "There are only four servants in the whole of the estate!"

"I suspected something to that effect when we arrived and saw the state of the viscount's home. After hearing that the coachman and footman took care of the horses, I worried that there is more that needs to be done here than I may have been prepared for." Calliope sighed. "You didn't press the staff about the state of affairs here, did you?"

Her maid reassured her, "I was careful not to ask too many questions. The cook is the youngest—and the strongest from what I observed when I returned your breakfast tray."

"Did you have a chance to peek into the pantry? I didn't have a chance to do more than hurry through my bath last night."

"I tried, but Mrs. Romney is quite protective of her territory and a bit on the defensive."

"Best not to push too hard too quickly," Calliope advised. "My mother's cousin and his wife were so generous to me but hid the fact they had pockets to let. They took me in for the first month after my parents died but couldn't afford to feed one more in addition to their growing family."

"I'm ever so sorry, Calliope."

"Thank you." Calliope was pleased that her maid had taken her words to heart, using her given name when it was just the two of them. She had no idea how soon she'd be able to visit Aurelia, who lived a few miles away, and she would need someone to confide in if she were to settle into her new role as mistress without issue.

"I asked about lending a hand as my duties for the morning had been taken care of," Mary Kate explained. "But she shooed me out of her domain."

"I do believe I shall venture downstairs and see if anyone is about to give us a tour."

Her maid smiled. "They would expect you to ask questions."

Calliope nodded. "If the viscount was here, I would not dare to pry. As the viscount has been sent to London, and we have been sent to his home, I feel it is my duty to do all I can to help my husband."

"There," she thought, *"I said it aloud...my husband!"*

"I'm not afraid to work hard," Mary Kate confided.

Calliope felt at ease for the first time since they'd arrived yesterday. "We shall be able to accomplish twice as much together!"

Mary Kate looked around the room and sighed. "I see that I do not have to make the bed or see to your wardrobe this morning."

Calliope smiled. "You carried the breakfast dishes down to the kitchen, and I straightened the room. See what I mean? We are, indeed, a wonderful team."

"And tended to your traveling clothes."

"A chore I am well used to doing—taking care of myself."

"Do you have other duties for me?"

"Not at present. I wanted to ensure that you accompanied me on our tour. A second set of eyes is always best."

"You could have had a leisurely morning, writing your letters or reading, while I went about my duties."

"Mayhap on the morrow. Oh, that reminds me. I'd better sharpen my pencil. It'll just take me a moment."

While her maid waited, Calliope opened the reticule she'd left on the ornate lady's writing desk. She removed her small journal, pencil and folding pen knife—a gift from Aurelia's Uncle Phineas. Having nicked her knuckles on more than one occasion opening the knife, she did so with care. Holding the pencil just so, she carved away bits of wood until satisfied that the one end would have enough graphite exposed to last for the whole of the tour.

Journal and pencil in hand she smiled. "Let's be off."

"And here we have the earl's study." Hargrave opened the door with a flourish and stepped back. As she thanked him and entered the room, she noted his face was devoid of expression, though Calliope thought she detected a hint of emotion in the man's brilliant green eyes.

The room could benefit from a good cleaning. Calliope opened her journal and made a note that the room needed an airing—it was a bit musty, leading her to add: launder the heavy drapes, beat the rugs, floor's quite dull. Her hand cramped before she finished.

Hargrave appeared interested in her notations but did not question her until she opened her journal and began to make notes while in the sitting room, the dining room, and the library.

"I do not wish to be presumptuous, your ladyship," he said as he gave a slight nod, indicating her journal. "Is something amiss?"

"Not at all, Hargrave," she answered readily. "I'm taking note of duties to be performed to discuss with Mrs. Meadowsweet."

He paused and drew in a deep breath before squaring his shoulders. "As you are our new mistress, I feel it is my duty to inform you of Mrs. Meadowsweet's difficulty with her knees."

Calliope was immediately drawn to the man for confiding something that any of her relations would have sacked a servant for, feeling they would not be up to performing their duties.

"I have a wonderful salve the Duchess of Wyndmere maintains is wonderful for joint pain. I shall deliver it to Mrs. Meadow-sweet as soon as we are finished with the tour."

The terribly correct butler relaxed for a brief moment as he said, "I am certain she will be pleased. Thank you."

"You are more than welcome. It is my duty to see that our staff is well looked after in his lordship's absence. In that regard," she advised, "I will be working alongside everyone to lend a hand."

His look of abject horror was amusing, but she dare not laugh for fear of insulting the man.

"I hope to meet with you and Mrs. Meadowsweet to go over the lists I'm preparing. With your invaluable input, we can prioritize which duties are the most pressing and attend to them first."

"I have no doubt of your sincerity, your ladyship," Hargrave said. "However, I cannot help but think his lordship would not approve of his viscountess performing such menial duties."

Calliope could not hold back the bubble of laughter that erupted. "I am no stranger to getting my hands dirty, or pitching in wherever needed, Hargrave."

He inclined his head, accepting her words.

"Furthermore, I realize I will be thought most unconvention-al. There are very good reasons for my actions, Hargrave. I trust you will not try to gainsay what I would very much like to do."

As the viscount's wife, she could demand what she wanted out of the servants. But Calliope's past would not let her demand anything of her husband's staff. She would offer, hoping to be accepted as it was meant—for the benefit of their master, Viscount Chattsworth.

After long moments of silence, Hargrave spoke. "I daresay, the viscount is most fortunate to have married your ladyship."

Calliope blinked away tears at his approval of what she hoped to accomplish at the viscount's home. "Thank you, Hargrave. You have no idea how much your words mean to me."

He nodded. "Shall we see if Mrs. Romney has tea ready?"

"That would be most welcome. Thank you." Calliope and Mary Kate followed the butler to the kitchen.

Mrs. Romney was just placing the silver teapot on the tray. "Just in time, your ladyship. Tea's ready."

"That looks wonderful. I am a bit parched."

"Shall I serve you in the sitting room?"

"As you seem to be in the middle of preparing our midday meal, I think that would be best." Her decision obviously pleased the cook. She intended to reach for the tray, but the sound of Hargrave clearing his throat gave her pause.

A direct look from the man had her nodding her understanding he would carry the tray and smiling at Mrs. Romney. "Everything looks delicious, thank you."

The cook beamed. "My pleasure. I hope you enjoy the biscuits. It's my grandmother's recipe."

"I am sure we shall." Calliope and her maid followed their intrepid butler to the sitting room. When he'd placed the heavy tray on a table situated between two velvet lady's chairs and a striped settee, she asked if he would ask Mrs. Meadowsweet to join her.

"At once, your ladyship." He bowed, turned, and retreated, closing the door behind him.

"Now then," Calliope said, setting her journal beside her teacup. "I'd be happy to hear what duties you feel are the most pressing and difficult for our aging staff to accomplish."

Mary Kate met her gaze. "Shall I pour your tea first?"

"That would be wonderful."

The pair were in the middle of going over the last of their observations when they heard someone knock. "Come in."

When the housekeeper entered, Calliope rose to her feet. "Ah, Mrs. Meadowsweet, just the person we need to speak to. Won't you have a seat?"

The older woman nodded and walked over to join them. "Thank you, your ladyship."

Calliope wanted to set her at ease, so she poured a cup of tea and passed it to her. "I hope we're not taking you away from your more pressing duties, Mrs. Meadowsweet. I am sure Hargrave has already informed you that I have been preparing a list of duties I feel need attention. Given the number of staff currently working for my husband—" *there was that thrill again,* "Mary Kate and I will be working alongside you and the others until the viscount returns and we are able to discuss the possibility of hiring on additional staff."

Mrs. Meadowsweet sipped from her teacup and nodded.

"I know it is rather unconventional of me, but there are times in life when one must perform whatever tasks need to be done, without worrying whether or not it is proper for one to do them."

The older woman carefully placed her teacup and saucer on the table and folded her hands in her lap. Calliope noted the faint trembling in them. Was it worry, or something more? She hoped to ease the woman's burden immediately—and that of the rest of the elderly staff, and speak to the viscount as soon as that time presented itself.

Until then, she would have to use her wits and keep her head down as she ticked off one chore after another. She desperately wanted the viscount to be pleased with what she hoped to accomplish...not berate her for interfering.

That was a bit of a worry but, with time on her hands, she could not remain idle when there was work that needed to be done. Mindful of the possibility of one of the servants talking, she vowed to be as circumspect as possible, garbed in her finest whenever she and her maid traveled into the village. She would not shame the viscount by appearing unkempt or ill-clothed. While she was in the viscount's home, she would wear one of her older work dresses and roll up her sleeves. *Hang convention!*

"Does that meet with your approval?"

Mrs. Meadowsweet smiled at last. "I cannot think the viscount would approve of his viscountess working alongside his staff. However, when I weigh the outcome against the duties that are too many and too taxing for us, I cannot help but be appreciative of your kindness and willingness to bring about the much-needed change in the master's home. Thank you, your ladyship."

"It will most definitely be my pleasure, Mrs. Meadowsweet." Leaning forward, journal in hand, Calliope shared, "Here is what Mary Kate and I have listed. We definitely need your advice as to what is most important."

"I would be happy to help."

"Wonderful. I believe Hargrave will have time to look over the list before our midday meal."

"I was hoping you would be asking him. Has he spoken to Mrs. Romney and Mr. MacReedy as yet?"

"I confess I do not know. But I am certain to find out this afternoon."

With that, the women got to work, adding to and subtracting from the duties listed, then ordering them by importance.

An hour later, they had the list completed to everyone's satisfaction. "I am so pleased that you could spare the time to help, Mrs. Meadowsweet. Pray tell me," Calliope said, "what tasks have I taken you away from and how can we help?"

The housekeeper frowned, leaving Calliope to wonder if there were tasks not easily noted when she toured the manor. Deciding to suggest what she knew would be the most pressing, she asked, "Are there linens to be laundered? We can enlist Mr. Flaherty and Mr. O'Malley to help haul the water to the kitchen and empty the wash tub when we are through."

The woman's thin face lifted at the suggestion. "That would be most appreciated, your ladyship."

"I understand they have been sleeping in the room at the back of the stable, while the coachman and footman are in the servants' quarters."

"Yes. Mr. MacReedy apparently offered the room as a possibility when the duke's guard mentioned they would be sharing guard duty and did not want to rouse the household."

"I see." The guards must have been instructed by the duke to remain, but for how long? Why did they not speak to her about it? Setting that thought aside for later, she asked, "Any other pressing duties for the day?"

"I believe we should speak with Hargrave before we begin any other tasks."

"Do you think Mrs. Romney will need assistance preparing the midday meal or tonight's meal? After all," Calliope mused, "there are six more mouths to feed."

"After we speak to Hargrave, I believe he will be able to convince our cook to accept help."

Relief flowed through her at Mrs. Meadowsweet's acceptance of Calliope's offer of assistance. "Excellent. We all want the same thing, you know."

The housekeeper nodded. "To bring back the polish to the viscount's home until it shines."

"My sentiments exactly."

Mary Kate stood and reached for the tea tray. "I'll just return this to the kitchen."

"Thank you." Turning to the housekeeper, Calliope offered, "If you wouldn't mind accompanying Mary Kate to the kitchen, I need something from upstairs and will meet you shortly."

"Of course, your ladyship."

Calliope watched the housekeeper's stiff-gaited retreat and dashed up the stairs to retrieve the duchess' healing salve. While she was there, she decided to strip her bed and Mary Kate's. For expediency's sake, her maid was in one of the smaller rooms just down the hall. She carted the linens to the servants' staircase and heaved them down the stairs.

"Are ye trying to knock me down the stairs, yer ladyship?"

Hands covering her mouth, Calliope stared at the shrouded form of Michael O'Malley. With a grunt, he shrugged out from under the linens. "I am so sorry, Mr. O'Malley! I didn't know anyone was on the stairs."

"From what I could see, yer ladyship, the door opened, and the pile of linens hurled through it."

"Please forgive me. I promise it was unintentional."

He chuckled and waited for Calliope to reach his side. "Of course."

She let go of the breath she was holding. "Thank you."

"I was on my way to see if ye needed help collecting the linens. Glad I could be there to catch them for ye."

They were laughing as they made their way downstairs. "Allow me," he opened the door, stepped through, and held it for her. He turned back to gather the laundry.

"Thank you, Mr. O'Malley."

"Do ye think after ye tossed the linens on me head, ye might call me by me given name?"

"Of course, if you wish, Michael."

"I do, and ye're embarrassing me cousin as well, calling us mister."

"I see, so I should call him by his given name, too?"

"Aye, Seamus asked me to broach the subject with ye if I happened to see ye before he did."

"I really am sorry."

"Not at all. Me ma used to get our attention with cold, wet linens when we ignored her."

"When you were much younger?"

His eyes twinkled with devilment as he replied, "Oh, aye, last year when I went home to visit."

She was smiling as they entered the kitchen. Mary Kate and the tub of hot water were waiting for her. They easily developed a rhythm, working together, scrubbing the bedsheets and then wringing them out. Mr. MacReedy hung a makeshift clothesline across from the large fireplace, as she tossed one of the linens across the line, she felt something she hadn't in a number of months...useful. Having spent so much of her life working, it was difficult to accustom herself to being a lady of leisure.

She hummed softly as she reached for another bedsheet to hang on the line. Before long, the linens were washed and hanging up to dry. Mrs. Meadowsweet returned from her meeting with Hargrave with a few additions to the task list. Grateful for the chance to sit down, she urged Mary Kate to do the same.

Mrs. Romney placed two glasses of water on the table. "We wouldn't have been able to get to the laundry today without your help. Thank you."

"Our pleasure," Calliope assured her. "Well, what's next?"

"We feed you," the cook said with a smile. "But you two are a bit on the dampish side. Mayhap you should eat here where you can dry out by the fire."

"Wonderful idea!" Calliope drained her glass and started to rise, but the cook shook her head. "Let me get your stew."

There seemed to be an abundance of flavorful vegetable stew and fresh bread. For that, Calliope was grateful. Tomorrow, she'd ask Hargrave about the tenant farmers. If he was willing to continue the tour, after she and her maid spent the morning working, mayhap she could convince the butler or the house-keeper to show her the accounts.

"Oh, that smells delicious!"

Calliope agreed with Mary Kate. They made short work of their meal and were preparing to wash their dishes, when Flaherty and O'Malley walked into the kitchen. "Are ye ready for us to haul out the wash water?"

"We are."

O'Malley sniffed the air. "Something smells heavenly."

Calliope had not seen them for a few hours. "Have you eaten?"

"Not as yet."

"I'll set a place for you," Mrs. Romney told them, "while you empty out the tub."

"Thank ye," O'Malley replied.

"Should we leave the tub outside?" Flaherty wanted to know.

"Yes. I'll bring it in later."

"Just give a call, and me cousin or I will be happy to haul it back inside after it's drained."

Appreciation lighting her features, Mrs. Romney nodded. "I will."

"If you have time this afternoon, we'd like to go over the list of duties so we can divide them up between us. Many hands—"

"Make for lighter work," her maid finished for her.

"Too many cooks spoil the broth," Mrs. Romney muttered.

"We do not intend to be underfoot, Mrs. Romney," Calliope reassured her. "We want to bring a shine to the manor—to please the viscount."

The cook's gaze met hers. "We all want the same thing, your ladyship."

Calliope smiled. "Then let's work together, shall we?"

Mrs. Romney agreed.

"Excuse me for a moment, I need to speak to Mr. O'Malley." Calliope hurried outside to catch up with the duke's guard. "Mr. O'Malley!"

He and his cousin straightened, the wooden wash tub between them. "Ye agreed 'tis Michael, yer ladyship."

"Yes, of course, forgive me, Michael."

"What can I do for ye?"

"How long are you intending to remain at Chattsworth Manor?"

"Are ye anxious to see the back of us?" Seamus asked.

She felt her face flame. "Of course not. I don't know what I would have done without your help on the journey, and here while we are settling in."

"His Grace asked that we stay and see to yer protection."

"Until..." she added, hoping one of the men would answer her question.

O'Malley and Flaherty shared a look before answering, "The viscount returns."

"I see."

"Do ye now?" Seamus asked. "'Twould make our job easier."

"Am I making it more difficult for you?"

"To tell ye the truth, yer worry has us wondering if there is something more on yer mind that we need to know in order to fulfill our duties to the duke."

She sighed. "I do apologize."

"And?" O'Malley prompted, making her smile.

"My only concern at the moment is cleaning the viscount's home until it shines. Then I intend to move on to the gardens. Although I do plan to visit with the tenant farmers."

"Leave the outside work to us. As to visiting the tenant farmers, ye'll need one of us to escort ye, yer ladyship."

"I don't think—"

"His Grace's instructions, yer ladyship," Flaherty told her.

"Very well then. I shall keep you informed."

"Ye promise not to go off on yer own at dawn, yer ladyship?" O'Malley asked.

Calliope's first reaction was disbelief, then she slowly smiled remembering how difficult she and Lady Aurelia had been while at Wyndmere Hall months earlier. "You have my word."

"Be sure ye keep it, yer ladyship." Flaherty's tone was ominous.

"I'm not certain it is at all proper for you to speak to me that way."

"'Tisn't," Flaherty agreed. "But yer life is at stake, yer ladyship. And I'll not tolerate yer interference while me and me cousin are trying to protect ye."

Calliope let her gaze meet that of the duke's loyal guard as she placed her hand over her heart. "I promise not to go off on my own."

"I'm thinking she means it this time," O'Malley said with a grin.

Flaherty flashed one of his own. "Aye. I'm thinking we can trust her."

CHAPTER FOURTEEN

W ILLIAM WONDERED NOT for the first time what he was
doing in London sleeping beneath the sumptuous
bedlinens of his illustrious cousin, the duke.

He tossed aside the covers and got out of bed. Reaching for
the pitcher, intending to pour it into the ceramic bowl, he
marveled that the water was warm. He hadn't heard anyone
enter the bedchamber—or leave it.

Had he been dozing and thought himself awake? The proof
was in the temperature of the water. "Can't do anything about it
now." He reached for the round of soap and worked up a soft
lather. The scent of sandalwood soothed his frayed nerves,
though he'd never admit it if anyone asked.

A glance at his reflection startled him yet again. The strength
of the Lippincott genes was astounding. He could pass for the
duke—or his brother, from a distance. As he shaved, he wondered if he could use that to his advantage. Doors he had not
anticipated opening to him, would, as word circulated among the
ton that he was in London handling the duke's affairs.

He dried his face on the soft linen towel, inhaling the hint of
lavender. His mother always placed dried lavender among the
linens. The scent brought back the memory of helping her with
the chore, pleased that she'd asked for his help.

Would his wife do the same with their son? "Bloody hell!

There cannot be a son until we've—"

"I beg your pardon, your lordship."

William lifted his gaze to the looking glass and met that of the valet he'd been assigned while he was in the duke's residence. His movements measured, he turned slowly and acknowledged the man's presence. "Turner."

The man's posture bespoke military training as he held the viscount's deep blue frockcoat in one hand and a small brush in the other. "You were asleep when I had the maid leave the pitcher of warm water. Jenkins advised that no one was to disturb you."

William relaxed the hands he'd unconsciously clenched. "Thank you for the water. I see the duke's London household runs as efficiently as Wyndmere Hall."

The valet returned the frockcoat to the wardrobe and was reaching for another when the viscount stopped him with a question. "Do your duties extend beyond the care and keeping of the duke's clothing and personal needs?"

Turner locked gazes with him. "That would depend on what His Grace requires of me on any given day."

"I see." William could only guess at what else the duke would require. Thinking of his father's valet—who now served him, the viscount frowned. MacReedy was a man of many talents that the viscount had no choice but to enlist, given the fact he'd begun to run out of funds as his father's return seemed less likely as time passed by.

"Is there anything I may do for your lordship?"

The viscount took the man's measure, placing him five to ten years older than himself. Broad frame, weathered features, and scarred hands...serious countenance. "As I go about the duke's business, I may require your assistance."

"I'm at your service, your lordship."

"Excellent." Turner's offer sounded sincere. William had no idea if he'd need the man. Knowing Turner was willing, eased the mounting worry that he'd been sent to London where the duke

could keep an eye on him.

Had that particular task been assigned to each of the duke's servants? Was there no one he could trust in this mausoleum? He hadn't thought he'd given away the fact that he'd been less than truthful when last they'd met, yet his cousin had known the truth and called him to the carpet about it. That's when he stormed out of the study and run into Calliope and his heart had stopped until he'd pulled her to safety. Were the tasks he'd been assigned a way to gain back the duke's trust?

Mayhap the duke's reasons for separating him from his bride had more to do with the duke's mistrust of him...mayhap it was for her benefit. The duke's wife and sister were good friends with Lady Calliope. It was quite possible one of the ladies had suggested the separation to give Calliope time to adjust to her married status.

Time and a bit of digging would uncover the truth. *No amount of time had uncovered the whereabouts of his father.*

"Thank you, Turner. I shall be in the duke's study for the better part of the morning." Truthfully, he had no idea what tasks would be on his cousin's list. Best to get to it and start ticking them off. He intended to make the most of his current situation and be seen amongst the *ton* as a man of consequence.

As he descended the staircase, he wondered who he could trust regarding the disappearance of his father. He'd best keep his thoughts close to his vest and not trust anyone until they'd proven they were worthy of it.

Resolved to spend the morning attending to the duke's affairs, he asked one of the footmen to direct him to the duke's study. He'd make it a point to ask for a tour of the grand town house after the midday meal.

COVENTRY ANSWERED THE door and demanded, "What have you learned?"

Sean O'Malley grinned. "Anxious to hear me report, are ye?"

The duke's man-of-affairs shook his head at the Irishman and motioned for him to enter his lodgings.

This wasn't the first time one of the O'Malleys guarding the duke and his family met Coventry where he lived. There were too many servants with eyes and ears at the duke's town house. To ensure their meeting would go unnoticed, he'd asked Sean to meet him here.

"To answer your question, O'Malley," Coventry drawled, "yes, I am anxious. The duke is depending upon me to ferret out as much information as I can surrounding the disappearance of the viscount's father, as well as information about the viscount."

O'Malley nodded. "Yer information was confirmed by the pawn broker. Scraggly man, stank of the drink and in want of a bath."

Coventry expected the man's report to confirm at least that much. "Were you able to convince the man to forego his 'ethics'?"

"'Twas an even trade—a name for a bottle of *Blue Ruin*."

"I would have thought the name would be worth far more than a bottle of gin," Coventry murmured. "Do you think the proprietor was capable of telling you the truth? Did he have any tells? A twitch under his eye? Unable to meet your gaze when speaking to you?"

"None that I noticed."

Coventry hesitated, then asked, "You're certain the man told you all he knew?"

O'Malley met Coventry's single-eyed gaze. "The gin was akin to gold to the man." He scrubbed a hand over his face before adding, "Had an uncle who worshiped a jug of *Poitín* as if it were life and breath to him."

"*Pocheen?*"

O'Malley chuckled. "Aye, ye could pronounce it that way. 'Tis illegal homemade brew."

"Ah. I sailed under a rear admiral who preferred a spoonful of tea in his morning cup of rum." Coventry paused before stating, "I see we are both skirting around the most important news. Who sold the *Chattsworth Emeralds* and the rest of the entailed items?"

O'Malley's merriment vanished. "Percival Fauncewater."

"Of the merchant class?"

O'Malley shook his head. "More like the working class, those that can be found plying their trade by the docks."

Coventry knew it was time to share what he'd discovered with the head of the duke's London guard. "I have a possible lead as well."

"Do ye now?"

A sharp pain sliced through his useless arm. Coventry rubbed at it, calling attention to his injury.

"Does it still pain ye, Coventry?"

"At odd times. Though why I should feel anything when I have little strength to move it baffles me."

"Can ye do anything for the pain?"

"Ignore it mostly, these days."

"Ye sound like me da."

"He was injured in battle, too?"

"Aye, in a local skirmish."

Coventry knew better than to ask for more information that would likely lead to hard feelings on both sides. "Did ignoring the pain work for your father?"

"At times...at others, he'd visit me uncle and share a bit of his jug."

"I confess to having relied on whiskey and brandy for a time. When one doesn't have the use of both arms...and has only one eye, it's harder to defend oneself."

Their gazes met and held. O'Malley asked, "Ye don't do yer investigating after dark do ye?"

Coventry chuckled. "Some of my best work is done then."

"Do ye go alone?"

Coventry glared at him.

The emotion in that one green eye had O'Malley realizing that although the man was at a disadvantage, he would be a formidable foe. "When do ye want to go after Fauncewater?"

"Tonight. We'll need two more men, whoever you suggest from your ranks."

"Me cousins."

Coventry chuckled. "You have six of them here in London at the moment."

Sean laughed, "Well then, a Flaherty and a Garahan."

"That's more specific," Coventry remarked, pulling the time-piece out of his waistcoat pocket. "Meet back here after eight o'clock. We should endeavor to be in place on the docks before the dregs start plying their evening trade."

"Ye forgot to tell me about yer lead," O'Malley reminded him.

He smiled. "I am not sure yet if it is as viable as I hope it will be. I will know more tomorrow and will share what I've learned."

"Fine then. I'll return with me cousins before eight."

Closing the door behind O'Malley, Coventry wondered what the duke would make of this latest development in their search for the missing earl. "What would Chattsworth make of it?"

Time would tell. In the meantime, they had more information to extract and other quarry to question.

CHAPTER FIFTEEN

FLANKED BY HIS cousins, Sean O'Malley led the trio to the duke's man-of-affairs' abode. They were ahead of schedule, as O'Malley preferred to be. The men moved with ease through the throng that still filled the streets. They were men to be reckoned with and they knew it. It was a source of pride that not many who challenged O'Malley, or his kin, walked away unscathed.

"Ye're in a hurry tonight," Rory Flaherty remarked.

James Garahan grinned. "He has a female on his mind."

O'Malley grumbled. "No female, mind's as clear as a bell."

"Ah, so the lovely Bridget Callahan has stood ye up then?" Flaherty asked.

"'Tis a fact, she's meeting me later for a quiet dinner," Garahan announced.

The two men stopped in their tracks, while Garahan kept walking. "Keep up lads, ye know how Sean hates to be late."

Sean shoved Garahan from behind. "Are ye after me woman?"

"Didn't know she was yers. Besides, are ye not leaving soon to take up the position at Lippincott Manor guarding his lordship and Lady Aurelia?" His cousin had been expecting the shove and stepped double-time to keep from tripping. "Ye'll have to do better than that to get the best of me, Boy-o."

Flaherty grinned. "Can I hold yer coats, lads? I've been waiting to have a go at Sean meself."

Shaking his head, O'Malley wondered why their cousin, Patrick, had thought the men could work together. There was always a disagreement over a female, and prideful boasts as to who held the best record as a bare knuckle fighter. "Lads, I'm still in charge here until I leave for me new post in Sussex. Best mind yer tongues and yer surroundings."

Immediately contrite, his cousins agreed. They left the area surrounding Grosvenor Square turning onto Duke Street. It always amazed O'Malley that those with far less would live so close to those who had it all. "On yer guard, lads," he warned as they made their way onto Hart Street. Coventry lived on the corner of Hart and Lumley. Although his lodging was in a well-kept building, it was surrounded by others that were not in the best of shape.

His cousins' miens immediately changed from casually conversing to alert and expecting trouble. As they walked, Flaherty asked, "Do ye know if Coventry has known the duke long?"

"I know it is more than a few years," O'Malley answered.

"If ye'd paid attention and listened to their conversation," Garahan advised, "ye'd agree with me, 'tis longer."

"Ye could be right." O'Malley stopped on the sidewalk. "We're here."

They entered the brick building and ascended the narrow stairway to the second floor. On edge, expecting trouble from all directions, they were in tune to their surroundings and the sounds of life behind closed doors.

Garahan knocked. No one spoke while they waited for Coventry to answer the door.

"Glad you could make it. So, it's Flaherty and Garahan tonight?"

"Me cousins, Rory Flaherty and James Garahan," O'Malley informed Coventry.

The men nodded as they entered Coventry's lodgings.

"I hope you men are ready for anything."

"Ye could say we've lived that way for years now," O'Malley told him.

"Have you?" Coventry's interest was piqued. "How so?"

"Once ye're the reigning bare knuckle champion, there's no end of lads trying to convince ye to fight at the drop of a hat."

"Are you all champions?"

The trio grinned at one another as O'Malley replied, "Aye, in our counties back home."

"Is it important?" Garahan asked.

Coventry slowly smiled. "No, but very useful."

A FEW HOURS later, those words were tested.

"Excellent way to slip him a convincer, Garahan," Coventry said. "I do believe our gentleman friend here is ready to talk."

The thug slumped at their feet groaned.

Flaherty cracked his knuckles. "Shall I give it go?"

"Enough," the ruffian growled. "I didn't plan to pick yer bloody pockets!"

O'Malley reached down and hauled the man to his feet. "Weren't ye now?"

The man's eyes widened, but he didn't reply.

"I'm thinking the man needs a bit more convincing, Flaherty."

The man ducked his head down and shielded his face. "I said enough!"

Coventry sighed. "If you'd tell us what you know, we'll stop."

The man had the temerity to glare at him. Coventry knew then it would take more than a beating to get the man to talk. "I do believe he should accompany us down to Bow Street. Gavin King would no doubt enjoy the pleasure of his company for the next little while."

"Bow Street? I'm not going there!"

Coventry got in the man's face, ignored the stench of soured sweat and rum—a scent he was all too familiar with. He'd faithfully served His Majesty in the Royal Navy—until that last battle...*Trafalgar.*

"Give us a name. Where did you get the *Chattsworth Emeralds?*"

"I told you. I found them."

"O'Malley, I do believe it's Flaherty's turn."

The auburn-haired giant moved like lightning, delivering an uppercut that knocked the man senseless.

"Impressive. Let's haul his carcass to Bow Street. I'm sure he'll talk...eventually."

"What reason will ye give King to detain the man?" O'Malley wanted to know.

"He had the *Chattsworth Emeralds* in his possession nearly a year ago," Coventry told him. "Earl Lippincott disappeared at the same time. That should be sufficient cause to question him."

"When ye put the two together," Garahan added, "it makes sense. I'll take the left side, if ye'll take the right, Flaherty."

O'Malley stared at Coventry for a moment before speaking. "'Tis glad I am that ye're not questioning me and me cousins."

The duke's man-of-affairs slowly smiled. "To borrow his favorite expression—indeed!"

O'Malley hailed a hackney.

"'Ere now," the driver protested. "I ain't taking—"

"You will drive us to Bow Street without complaint," Coventry quietly commanded.

The driver looked from the two men who had a death grip on the man between them to the one who'd hailed the carriage before answering, "Yes, my lord."

O'Malley climbed in and motioned for his cousins to hand the thug off to him.

When the men were seated, Coventry knocked on the roof of the carriage and it lurched to a start. "He takes up more room than I expected," Coventry commented.

"Are ye meaning that the lot of us do as well?"

"Not at all, Flaherty. I am well acquainted with the size and stature of each and every man employed in the duke's guard."

When the men remained silent, he added, "His Grace and I are beyond grateful to have men of your stature and experience guarding His Grace's family."

O'Malley chuckled. "Stature is it? Me ma would love that one."

His cousins agreed. "Aye, Aunt Eileen bragged her sons were destined to do more than shovel *shite.*"

Coventry shook his head at the image they painted. He thoroughly enjoyed working with the O'Malley clan, which included the Garahans and the Flahertys. "Are there any more of you?"

The trio looked at one another and grinned. "Are ye meaning men ye'd hire on?"

"Yes. It may be to our advantage to hire on a few more men, given the fact that the duke will be in residence at Wyndmere until the birth of his son—or daughter. He's sent two guards with his brother to Lippincott Manor and two more have accompanied Lady Calliope, Viscountess Chattsworth, to Chattsworth Manor."

O'Malley made eye contact with his cousins before speaking. "Well, now that ye've asked," O'Malley paused, waiting for Garahan and Flaherty to nod. "There are six Mulcahy cousins on me ma's side, but half of them aren't old enough to leave the farm and the others are needed to work the farm."

Garahan was listening intently. *What was the man thinking?* Coventry wondered.

His question was soon answered when the man spoke up. "Do ye know of any former naval men such as ye who are in need of work?"

Silence fell in the carriage. The steady clopping of the horses' hooves on the cobbled streets echoed in the night.

Coventry's gut twisted into a painful knot, but he had learned not to jump to conclusions years ago. He waited a beat then cleared his throat. "I take it you are asking if I know of any injured military men in need of work?"

Garahan nodded. "Aye. Military men have training that

would be useful to His Grace."

Coventry wasn't mollified by the compliment. "Why would you think the duke would hire on any other injured men—aside from me? I am hampered by the loss of one eye and less than half the use of one arm."

Flaherty was quick to add, "We've watched ye handle yerself with amazing balance and dexterity. We don't agree with yer thinking that ye've no use in a fight."

"Aye," O'Malley said, "and ye've a head for ferreting out information. King respects yer opinions. The duke trusts ye."

"What me cousin is not making clear enough," Garahan clarified, "is that ye're the man the duke wants at his back. We agree with His Grace. Ye're the man I'd want leading us, coordinating our efforts in the protection of the duke's family. Why can ye not see that ye're not a hindrance to him—or us? Like as not, there are others ye know who would be of equal value to His Grace."

Coventry gave a brief nod. He didn't know what to say, how to respond. He'd listened to the surgeon drone on about the devastating loss of his sight and the use of his arm until he thought he'd go mad. That Jared's father, and Jared, had said as much as these good men wasn't lost on him. It wasn't easy to believe their claims. He'd lost faith in his physical abilities after the battle. He fought to regain his strength and had reached a point where he knew he was as physically healed as he would ever be. He'd accepted it, but he did not have to like it.

The moan from their prisoner ended what might have been an awkward discussion. Coventry hated to air his troubles. If he were honest with himself, he had wondered if to truly heal on the outside, he'd have to heal on the inside where his injuries still cut through to the bone.

The hackney slowed to a stop, and Flaherty jumped out. "If ye'll pass his head and shoulders out, I'll steady him."

His cousins did as he bid and, soon, they were following Coventry's lead to the building where the Bow Street Runners were housed.

"Coventry!" King boomed. "Who have you brought this time?"

He smiled. "As you can see, I've brought a small contingent from the duke's personal guard." With a glance at the man who was slowly coming around, he added, "And a special guest who would like to spend some time getting acquainted with you."

"Would he?" King locked gazes with the man. "To whom do I owe the pleasure of this visit?"

O'Malley chuckled. "Captain Coventry here followed the lead that led us to his man, but me and me cousins helped convince him he should meet ye."

"And tell ye the story of how he'd come to be in the possession of the *Chattsworth Emeralds* last year."

King's gaze sharpened. "I do believe we should take this discussion to my office. This way, gentlemen."

CHAPTER SIXTEEN

"**V**ISCOUNT CHATTSWORTH TO see you, sir."

Clayton Roxbury rose from his seat to welcome William to his office. "A pleasure, your lordship. His Grace indicated you would be in London for at least a month handling his affairs. Welcome."

"Thank you, Roxbury. It's a pleasure to be able to help my cousin while he and his duchess remain at Wyndmere Hall. I confess I am not quite sure why he would agree to do so."

Roxbury settled into his chair and leaned back, hands folded across his expansive middle. "I've known His Grace since he was a lad, but not as well as I knew his older brother during his tenure as the fifth duke."

The solicitor paused to go through the neat stacks on his desk. Finding the one he wanted, he pulled a document off the top of the center pile and gave it a cursory glance. "His Grace has a good head on his shoulders. I am certain in his bid to lend his aid to more of his family, he means for you to learn a bit of what may lie in store for you, if your current situation does not change."

The hair on the back of William's neck stood on end. "What situation might you be referring to?"

The solicitor met William's irritated gaze with one of compassion. "It is no secret that your father is still missing. The duke is doing all in his power to lend his aid in trying to find him."

The viscount's hackles settled down. "It is very gracious of him, but I find myself wondering why he would at such a critical time."

"Critical for you or His Grace."

William felt the prick to his pride but decided against acknowledging it. He would need the duke's solicitor to report back that he'd been eager to discuss his new duties with Roxbury. What he did not need was to rouse suspicion that he was here on a quest of his own.

"For His Grace of course."

The older man nodded. "Captain Coventry and I discussed the situation at length, and it was our considered opinion that Her Grace would be more at ease settling in at Wyndmere Hall."

Safer, the viscount silently added given what he knew of the events this past year. "It is beautiful, and Her Grace seemed in quite good spirits when last I saw her."

"Excellent," Roxbury beamed. "As to your own situation, I have been instructed by His Grace to keep you abreast of any information my brother or I happen to uncover as well."

The viscount wondered if His Grace was real or a product of his imagination. The duke's level of society was decidedly above his own. Why would he be so generous with his time, attention, and connections to a distant relative such as him? He could not credit it. He would have to send word to Summerfield. Mayhap, between the two of them, they could get to the bottom of what seemed so unlikely.

Did the duke have a hidden agenda?

Don't you?

"It is most generous of my cousin. I will be sure to thank him when next I see him."

"Just so." The solicitor leaned forward in his chair. "Now, let us go over the duke's instructions for this first week. Shall we?"

By the time Roxbury had gone through the list of names and places the duke required him to be during this next sennight, he could only stare at the duke's solicitor and shake his head. "I am afraid I do not quite understand."

The older man placed the list on the desktop and leaned back in his chair. "His Grace is providing you with an entrée into society, despite the distant connection between you. At the same time, the duke is trusting you to act as his emissary. There are functions he cannot attend while residing with his duchess at Wyndmere Hall awaiting the birth of their first child."

"I cannot fathom why he would."

"His Grace is unconventional but knows exactly what he is about. Best not to worry over the whys and wherefores, your lordship. I am certain you will do the duke proud."

The viscount could not think of what to say. He gave a brief nod which seemed to appease Roxbury.

"Now then, your lordship, as the duke instructed, you have an eleven o'clock appointment at Weston's after which time you have a three o'clock appointment with—"

"I am not in need of any new clothing," the viscount interrupted. He had to clear up this misconception of the duke's at once.

Roxbury stared at the viscount's waistcoat, leaving the viscount to wonder what was wrong with it. Then he remembered Marcus' comment about the ill-fitting shoulder seams.

The solicitor finally continued, "The duke prefers to have his business conducted the way he sees fit."

Still annoyed to realize he might not be up to snuff in the duke's estimation, he queried the solicitor, "And that includes the cut of my waistcoat?"

"Do not look upon it as a requirement, your lordship. The duke sees it as a gift, especially outfitting you in something befitting your rank for evening wear as well."

"I'm expected to attend the frivolous round of evening entertainments?"

"Balls, musicales, and the like. Yes, the duke has secured invitations on your behalf."

"Good God," the viscount mumbled.

His solicitor ignored that last and continued, "You are to meet with Lord Coddington at three o'clock at Tattersalls."

He clenched his jaw. "We've met—at Wyndmere Hall." He'd been on the receiving end of the older lord's blistering lecture concerning Calliope. *How the devil was he to speak to the man now that he'd been sent to London as the duke's errand boy?*

Roxbury waited for a moment before continuing. "Above all things, the duke wanted you to meet with a familiar face your first week in London. Coddington has an excellent eye for horseflesh. His Grace is in need of two pair of matched grays for his London residence."

Suspecting the duke's solicitor had been apprised of the discussion he'd had with Coddington at Wyndmere, he did not bother to ask the question plaguing him: *Would Coddington berate him publicly?* Instead, he remarked, "The duke has an excellent team of horses at Wyndmere."

"Exactly. Which is why he requires another team here in London while you are in residence. The duke has more than one carriage at his disposal."

Irritated beyond belief at the duke's high-handedness, the viscount shot to his feet. "I do not require anything of the sort! I'm perfectly capable of hiring a hackney."

The solicitor locked gazes with the viscount, waiting until he mumbled an apology for the outburst before retaking his seat. "The duke was most explicit. While you are staying at the duke's town house, and attending to the duke's business, you are to appear wearing proper attire as befits your station and be seen riding in the duke's carriage. Members of the *ton* would expect no less."

"Why?"

Roxbury raised a hand and the viscount fell silent. "While it is perfectly acceptable for you to question me," the man grumbled, "you do not question His Grace."

William squirmed in his seat, feeling as if he were two and

ten. He did not like the feeling or being reminded he should not gainsay his cousin. Envy sharp and swift sliced through him before reason once again ruled his thoughts. If he were to do any investigating on his own into the disappearance of his father, he would first have to be seen attending to the duke's errands.

The next three names were known to the viscount. All three lords were acquaintances of his father and he suspected they played a part in his father's ruin. Andrews encouraged Earl Chattsworth to invest in shipping ventures. Darnley encouraged his father to invest in the *ill-timed* shipping venture that bankrupted him. Chellenham's reputation amongst the *ton* was well known. He used to carouse with the duke's older brother, Oliver, when he'd held the lofty title.

His blood boiled as anger and frustration surged through him. He'd long suspected Chellenham had been responsible for his father's mad scheme to recoup his losses by gambling in the stews of London. *What he needed was proof.*

The solicitor went over the duke's instructions for meeting with the lords. Oddly, they were all the same. The duke felt it would be of great benefit for the viscount to meet with the gentlemen as they were good friends to Earl Chattsworth.

Was this the duke's way of helping him uncover the truth as the duke was still ensconced in the country? He would have to be on guard. Until he found the answers he sought—no one could be trusted.

The last name on the list, Lady Farnsworth, was a surprise and brought him sharply back to the discussion.

"The duchess' mother?"

"Yes. Have you met?"

"I have not had the pleasure."

"Good *ton*. Have known her for years through her husband prior to his untimely passing. His Grace has sent missives to each of the lords—and lady—on this week's list. Your entrée is assured."

William wanted to ask why the duke did not send his man-of-affairs around to handle these errands but kept silent. Mayhap the duke felt the need to orchestrate meetings with the men who may have indirectly—or in Chellenham's case, directly been involved at the time his father vanished. *Was this the duke's way of helping him get to the bottom of his father's disappearance?* If he asked outright, he had no doubt the solicitor's answer would be the same as before, *His Grace required it of him.*

"Did His Grace give any reason for only scheduling one appointment a day? I am quite certain I could take care of at least three in one day and move forward with the rest of the tasks."

Roxbury smiled. "He thought, perhaps, you'd enjoy further discussions at White's, accompanying those you've handled the duke's business with."

White's. It was the club his father frequented...well it had been before he'd taken to trying his luck at games of chance on the seamier side of London. "I see."

"That would give you plenty of time to return to the duke's residence and enjoy an excellent meal prepared by Mrs. O'Toole before dressing for the evening. I have had the pleasure, on more than one occasion, of being a guest at the duke's table and can vouch for Mrs. O'Toole's skill in that regard."

This was not at all what the viscount envisioned when the duke first discussed it with him. He'd mistakenly thought the duke needed someone of the viscount's expertise to handle...his thoughts trailed off. What expertise did he possess that the duke did not? *Not a bloody thing.*

But it did speak of the duke's willingness to help family, no matter which branch of the extensive Lippincott family it may be. Instead of being envious of all the duke possessed, the viscount realized he would owe the duke his eternal gratitude if it led to the whereabouts of his father. Was that too great a hope? After a year's time, would they locate him alive—and if not, his remains?

Chattsworth inwardly shuddered at the ghastly thought.

Taking the viscount's silence as agreement, Roxbury reminded him, "You have but to send word should you need anything from me. If not, then we can reconvene next week at the same time."

"I am not expected to report back to you?"

Roxbury smiled. "Not at all."

William surmised from what the solicitor did not say. The man would be receiving reports from the duke's contacts, disclosing how the *"tasks"* went. The viscount rose and bowed. "Thank you for your time and excellent advice, Roxbury."

The solicitor stood and opened the door for the viscount. "My pleasure."

On the carriage ride home—*and just when had his beleaguered brain begun calling the duke's town house home?* That question snapped him out of the daze he'd slipped into at the names of the lords the duke expected him to meet with in the next few days.

The month before him loomed with pitfalls aplenty. He sighed, wishing he was back home at Chattsworth Manor. A vision of his wife, Lady Calliope of the quiet beauty and delectably delicious lips, filled his mind. Letting his thoughts drift south to Chattsworth Manor, he wondered how she was filling her time.

His thoughts kept time with the steady beat of the horses' hooves. Would she be appalled by the lack of amenities? Would she castigate his longtime staff for not performing their duties to the fullest? Did she regret the circumstances that forced them to wed? Did she think of him kindly?

Did she think of him at all?

Mayhap, he could complete his duties to the duke ahead of schedule. He would ask Roxbury again, when next they met. If he could either find the time, or make the time, he would ride to Sussex and check on his wife.

His conscience plagued him. *The one you turned your back on. The one you didn't want.* He could not afford a wife but, by law, he had one...albeit in name only for the moment.

As the carriage slowed to a halt, he remembered the taste of her lips and how she melted in his arms. *She's still my wife!* He

would have to attend to the duke's affairs first, then he intended to claim his wife-in-name-only.

The door to the carriage opened, interrupting his train of thought. "Your lordship," one of the duke's footmen acknowledged. "You have a visitor."

He stepped down from the coach. "Who might that be?"

"Jenkins did not say. He only asked that I inform you when you arrived."

"Thank you—" He couldn't for the life of him remember the man's name. "Forgive me for not remembering your name."

"Hoskins, your lordship."

"Thank you, Hoskins."

Before he could reach for the handle to the front door, it swung open.

"Your lordship," Jenkins greeted him. "Captain Coventry awaits you in the duke's study."

William sighed. He did not need the daily reminders—he was *not* the duke. "Thank you, Jenkins."

"Allow me." The butler reached for the viscount's hat and gloves and handed them off to Hoskins.

Surprised he was still uncomfortable with the constant hoovering, he nodded to the older servant and was relieved at the satisfied look in the man's eyes. Obviously, he was learning the way he should act around the duke's staff.

He followed the butler, wondering why it should matter to him what the staff thought of him. *Dissention.* His father had raised him to avoid it among the staff and tenant farmers by listening to their grievances and resolving them in a manner that would benefit all.

With that in mind, he would make it a point to pay close attention to all that went on in the duke's household, from the head of the staff to the lowest level servant. There was much he could glean from observing Jenkins, Mrs. Wigglesworth, and those who reported to them. He would put the knowledge to good use at Chattsworth Manor.

The thought that he would have to take a firmer hand in running the household—and in refilling the family coffers in his father's absence, helped him resolve to learn all he could while in London. Those who depended upon him could wait no longer. He had to do something to reverse their fortunes and help those who in turn helped him.

Where in God's name was his father?

Jenkins opened the door to the duke's study. "Viscount Chattsworth."

It was odd to hear himself announced. He would have to become accustomed to it for the next few weeks. "Thank you, Jenkins."

Captain Coventry rose to greet him. "I trust I have not come at a bad time, your lordship."

"Not at all. I just returned from meeting with Roxbury."

The former captain nodded. "Excellent solicitor and very good friend to the duke's father."

The viscount wondered why the man would feel the need to explain the connection to him but did not respond. He waited for Coventry to continue.

"I have news."

That caught his attention. He motioned for Coventry to be seated, choosing the chair across from him. "About my father?"

Coventry's one-eyed gaze met his. "Yes."

William braced himself to hear they'd found his father's remains. *Good God, would they need him to identify the body?*

"...Chattsworth Emeralds."

That snapped him back to attention. "What about them?"

Coventry frowned. "I take it your mind was elsewhere."

"Forgive me. Would you mind repeating what you just said?"

"We received information and followed the lead to the docks."

Did this have anything to do with the shipments his father heavily invested in? Did Lord Andrews or Darnley know of this? Had either had a hand in his father's disappearance?

"I see."

"Unfortunately, we were not able to urge the man to tell us all he knew, but I'm confident that King will have been able to do so by now."

The viscount was unfamiliar with the name. "King?"

"Gavin King, the duke's contact at the Bow Street Runners."

"I see." He didn't know the duke's reach extended quite that far. It might be useful to the viscount to make use of it. "Does this contact in King's custody have a name?"

"Fauncewater."

"I don't recognize that name."

"Wouldn't think so. He plies his trade on the docks."

"Thug for hire?"

Coventry agreed. "Our information points to Fauncewater as having pawned the *Chattsworth Emeralds* to one of the more disreputable pawn brokers in London."

"Are there more than one in that class?" It wouldn't surprise him, but he'd only questioned the two he'd discovered.

"At least half a dozen, why?"

William decided in that moment he would not only trust the duke, but he would put his trust in Coventry, too. "I was only able to locate two and questioned them last year."

"There are a handful who do not have a specific location."

The viscount wondered how that would be possible. "How do they stay in business?"

"If they do not hold on to their merchandise for more than twenty-four hours," Coventry relayed, "it is very easy to be on the move constantly."

"Avoiding the constable or the Runners," the viscount said.

"Precisely."

"Profitable no doubt."

"Without question," Coventry remarked.

"Where are the emeralds now?"

"King has men investigating that lead right now."

The viscount got to his feet and paced from the window to

the door and back again before coming to a halt in front of the fireplace. "Do you believe it will lead to my father?"

Coventry remained silent for so long, William wondered if the man was preparing a fabrication or how to bluntly tell him the truth. "I have high hopes that it will. There are other inquiries being made through my connections in the Royal Navy."

"My father was never a member of the king's navy."

Coventry's gaze met his. "I am sure you've heard of press gangs?"

William's hands clenched into fists. "Do you mean to tell me you think someone found my father near the docks, overpowered him, plied him with rum and then shanghaied him?"

"In a word, yes."

"Good God! It boggles the mind."

"Don't ignore what could be a possibility. It could very well be the reason no one has been able to trace your father since the night he vanished."

"It's been over a year's time. His ship could have gone down."

"Or run afoul of bad weather and had to limp the ship into the nearest port to make repairs. Neither circumstance is unheard of."

"But why not report the ship has been waylaid for such?"

"I am certain that has been done." Coventry held the viscount's gaze and as if he sensed that the viscount needed confirmed, he said, "There would be no reason for the captain of the vessel to report the names of sailors who'd recently been pressed into service."

The viscount returned to his chair and sat down heavily. "He's by no means a young man and wasn't in the best health when last I saw him. He could be ill. He could have died and been buried at sea!"

"Let us wait until the information I've requested comes through from the Admiralty."

"They keep records of all men the press gangs have taken in?"

"Aye. Once we have the information, we can either continue to follow the lead in that direction or be satisfied we've exhausted that lead and need to look in another direction."

William raked a hand through his hair—twice, before nodding. "A sound conclusion. Thank you for keeping me abreast of your search for my father."

"Have you met with Lord Andrews yet?"

The viscount met Coventry's questioning gaze with one of his own. "What do you know about Andrews?"

"More than I am able to share with you at this time. Meet with the man before you form an opinion."

"But—"

"You would do well to remember there are those amongst the *quality* who believe that you had a hand in your father's disappearance. It would not be the first time something like this happened."

William's mouth opened and shut, but no sound emerged.

"I see you begin to understand why we must be vigilant in our endeavors, but with a clear head and defined purpose."

"I am grateful to the duke and you for your aid in locating my father."

"It is our duty and pleasure."

"Duty?"

"Aye, as kin to the duke, your father is family…as are you."

"Family," the viscount murmured. Somewhere in the world, his father still lived, mayhap on board one of the king's naval vessels. Aside from his cousin, Marcus, he had no other family.

A soft voice reminded him, *"You have a wife in Sussex."* It suddenly became so very clear to him that until he had the opportunity to travel to his family home and meet with his wife, she would occupy his thoughts.

Calliope haunts me.

CHAPTER SEVENTEEN

"LADY LIPPINCOTT TO see you, your ladyship," Hargrave announced.

Calliope jolted upright and smacked her head on the table leg she was polishing. She stood and rubbed the sore spot on her head while trying to think of the best place to meet with her friend. "Please show her to the library."

Hargrave shook his head. "Your maid is waxing the floor."

She frowned, going over the list of chores being tackled today in her mind. "His lordship's study?"

Again, the butler shook his head.

Exasperated, she asked, "Where do you suggest?"

His lips twitched as he fought to keep his expression neutral. "Here."

"But I'm not finished polishing the furniture!"

"The rugs and draperies have been beaten and the floor waxed—it truly is the best option."

"Very well. Please show her in."

"Shall I take your ladyship's apron?"

She looked down at the dirt-smeared apron she wore over her oldest day dress. "I'm not fit for company, but we cannot very well keep her waiting." Calliope removed her apron and handed it to the butler.

"Very good, your ladyship."

She only had time to check her reflection in the looking glass that hung over the small burgundy velvet settee. "No dirt on my face," she mused, then sighed noticing she would have to receive her friend with her hair falling out of its pins.

"What will she think of me?"

"Lady Lippincott," Hargrave announced.

"Calliope how wonderful to see—" Aurelia stopped mid-sentence. "What have you been doing?"

She laughed. "What does it look like I have been doing?"

Aurelia frowned at her friend, grabbed her by the hand and dragged her over to other side of the sitting room, so as not to be heard. "Tell me what is going on! Where are the viscount's servants?"

"It's wonderful to see you, too." Calliope had missed the daily chats with her friend, their outings, but most of all watching her friend fall in love with Edward, Earl Lippincott.

The stolen glances when they thought no one was looking. The utter joy on their faces as they danced. The whispered conversations while she'd been chaperoning their visits from the other side of the room.

"Are you listening to me?"

"Oh, sorry. I confess my mind was wandering."

"I demand to know what is going on here."

Calliope sighed. "As you can see, you interrupted me cleaning the sitting room."

"Why are you cleaning?"

"It's my home."

"Not the point," Aurelia grumbled. "Where are the maids?"

"Mary Kate is in the library."

"Reading?"

Calliope giggled. "If I am polishing furniture, you can be assured my lady's maid is most definitely not reading."

"I should hope not."

"Can you keep a secret?"

Aurelia frowned. "From whom?"

"The duke, the duchess, any one of the duke's guard."

Aurelia threw her hands up in the air. "It's a little late for that."

"Why?"

"Edward received a missive from Jared, asking him to see, and I quote, 'what in blue blazes is going on!'"

The two women dissolved into gales of laughter. When they were able to catch their breath, they were still smiling. "His Grace would be most upset if he heard either of us repeating such language."

"Indeed," Aurelia quipped.

Calliope fell silent.

"What are you not telling me?" Aurelia asked.

"The tenant farmers' homes are in need of repair."

Aurelia nodded. "Edward took me around to meet with our tenant farmers our first week at Lippincott Manor."

"Did they appear happy? Did they have enough food to eat?"

Aurelia studied her friend for long moments before asking, "What can we do to help?"

Calliope reached for her friend's hand and squeezed it briefly. "I've made lists."

Aurelia smiled. "Of course you have. Where should we start?"

"How long can you stay?"

"Darling?" The deep voice had Aurelia answering, "In the sitting room, my dear."

At Calliope's shocked expression, she shook her head. "You didn't think Edward would let me visit alone, did you?"

"Didn't you bring along your guards?"

"Can you imagine the uproar if I did not?"

Calliope smiled. "In truth, I cannot. Surely you don't need guards when Edward accompanies you."

Aurelia shook her head. "You know Jared."

Calliope sighed. "No doubt, he insisted before letting his guard accompany the newly wedded couple.

Before Aurelia could reply, Edward strode into the room. "Calliope, you look—" His eyes widened as his gaze collided with his wife's.

"Like she's been cleaning," Aurelia said. "Yes, she does, and she has."

"I can speak for myself, Aurelia."

"Please do," her friend urged. "Tell my husband where your staff is."

Edward locked gazes with his wife before turning to Calliope. "How can we help?"

Calliope brushed at the tear that slipped past her guard at his suggestion. "Mary Kate and I have everything well in hand but thank you for the offer."

The earl nodded and turned to his wife. "My dear, would you mind if we stayed the night? Michael O'Malley and Seamus Flaherty insist I accompany them on a tour of the grounds."

"They do, do they?" Calliope was not normally given to anger, but frustration was quite another thing altogether. Hers was a living, bubbling thing inside of her. "I shall speak to Michael and Seamus at once."

Calliope jumped up from the settee and raced out of the room before Aurelia or the earl could stop her.

"Shall we follow her?" the earl asked.

"This is her home," Aurelia reminded her husband. "Why don't we give her a head start and follow along behind."

"Excellent." The earl held out his hand to his wife, who let him help her to her feet and into his arms. He placed the tip of his finger beneath her chin, tilting it up. "Shall we give them a bit longer?"

Aurelia was smiling when she slipped her hand around the back of his neck. "We wouldn't want to wrest the management of her home from her."

Their lips met and time stood still.

"And I say ye're not using yer head," a deep voice rumbled just outside the sitting room. A muffled grunt and loud thump followed.

"I'd best see what the trouble is."

Aurelia sighed. "We can finish our discussion later."

The earl's gaze lingered on her face. "Later." He walked across the room and through the doorway. "What seems to be the problem?"

The duke's guard assigned to the earl froze. Thomas O'Malley ran a hand over his tousled hair and grinned. "Not a thing, yer lordship."

"Settling a matter of opinion," Aiden Garahan replied.

"If it requires more than words," the earl stated, "take it outside."

"Aye, yer lordship," Garahan was quick to reply.

The earl suspected he'd been the one to headbutt his cousin against the wall.

"Aye, yer lordship," O'Malley was quick to agree.

"We have much to discover in a short amount of time," he told his men. "I may ask one of you to take the carriage and return to Lippincott Manor."

"Ye don't need our help?" O'Malley sounded confused.

"I need one of you to bring back a few supplies."

"And a trunk with some clothing in it," Aurelia added, walking over to join the men. "We may be staying a bit longer than anticipated."

O'Malley nodded. "I can see why the viscount wanted an audience with His Grace."

"Aye," Garahan readily agreed. "Their servants aren't young enough to handle the heavier duties any longer."

"The lack of food is more of a worry at the moment," the earl told the men. "If you leave now, you can bring back enough food for the next few days."

"If they go together," Aurelia suggested, "one can gather the food with the help of Mrs. Wyatt, while the other can ask Finch and Mrs. Jones to pack our clothing and see to their own needs for the next few days."

"See to it, men."

The men agreed and left to do as instructed.

"I've always admired your ability to organize things quickly, my dear."

Aurelia beamed. "We must see where Calliope has gone off to. She may need us."

"Do I have no say at all in my life?" Calliope trembled with the frustration and embarrassment swirling inside of her. "Does the duke believe I am not capable of handling my own affairs?"

"Yer ladyship, that's not—"

She interrupted Michael. "He insisted that the viscount and I marry."

"But yer ladyship, 'tisn't what ye—"

Calliope cut Seamus off. "He sent the viscount to London and me here! The very least His Grace can do is grant me the opportunity to succeed or fail on my own!"

O'Malley and Flaherty shared a look, and O'Malley answered, "We cannot go against our orders, yer ladyship. We will protect ye with our lives."

"And if that be meaning yer feelings be hurt because of our duty to protect ye," Flaherty told her, "we're sorry for it."

"Sorry for it," she repeated. "But not willing to go against your orders to see that I have the freedom to live my life the way I choose."

Flaherty curled his hands into fists and then relaxed them. O'Malley clenched his jaw.

Calliope held the sides of her head in her hands as if to contain the thoughts she wished she could say but knew she could not. "I'll take your silence to mean you shall do your best to quell my freedom and only do as His Grace instructed no matter how high-handed I believe his actions to be."

"So happy to hear you've come into your own, my dear Calliope." Edward entered the kitchen with Aurelia hot on his heels.

Aurelia rushed to Calliope's side—facing down the united

male front of the duke's guard and her husband. "Can you not bend your brother's rules while you are here? I am certain Calliope is well able to direct her own staff."

Edward glared at his wife. "I happen to agree with Jared on this. Our women will be protected at all costs!"

"If I belong to any man," Calliope said, "it is to William. Not you. Not the duke."

"Begging yer pardon, yer ladyship," Michael O'Malley said. "But the viscount isn't here. We are."

Aurelia grabbed hold of Calliope's hands to keep her from tearing her hair out. "Well," Aurelia said brightly, patting the hands she held. "That's settled then. Tea anyone?"

Calliope stared at her friend but could think of nothing to say. At that moment, Mrs. Romney walked into the kitchen. Calliope cleared her throat to speak. "Mrs. Romney, would you be good enough to prepare tea for our guests? They've only just arrived."

"Of course, your ladyship. Would you all excuse me?"

O'Malley laughed. "What she's meaning to say is clear out of me kitchen."

The earl led the women from the kitchen, while the two guards headed back outside to speak with their cousins before the earl's guard left on their errand to Lippincott Manor.

Calliope didn't know what had come over her in the kitchen just now. She'd never raised her voice to anyone. *Ever.* The anger and frustration now roiled in her belly. With a will of iron, she fought to contain the emotions. It would not do to allow them to erupt in a more embarrassing way than raising her voice. She did not need a repeat of what happened at Wyndmere Hall.

"Calliope, you must understand my brother and I only wish to protect you."

Unsure of how to respond to the trite statement from the earl, she nodded.

"You do know how much we care for you?" the earl asked. "Don't you?"

She sighed. "I suppose, but it is beyond vexing to not have

control of one's life." Had her mother felt this way after the death of Calliope's father, when the new Earl Harrington swept into their lives...sweeping them out of their former home?

Aurelia slipped her arm through Calliope's. They walked the rest of the way to the sitting room in silence.

Her friend's touch comforted her. Calliope hadn't realized how much she missed the hugs, the friendly pats on the arm, or walking arm in arm with Aurelia, Phoebe, and Persephone. Women friends understood far more than a man ever could. Even if the man in question was her husband-in-name-only.

Would the viscount want that to change? Would she want it to?

Heaven help her, she did not know.

CHAPTER EIGHTEEN

"Thank you, Aurelia, for the additional supplies to our larder." Calliope smiled. "Mrs. Romney was over the moon having a full pantry at her disposal."

"It is definitely my pleasure when she's prepared such a wonderful breakfast buffet for us this morning."

"Has Edward already eaten?"

Aurelia finished chewing and smiled. "He wanted to check on the horses and see if there was anything to report from last night."

"Does he truly believe I am in a precarious position as my husband is not in residence?" Calliope hardly thought so. Then again, their servants were not as spry as the duke's, or from what Aurelia told her yesterday, the earl's.

"Edward and Jared will not take any chances with the women in their lives."

"I am not married to either of them and still do not see why they would bother with me."

Aurelia set down her teacup and reached for Calliope's hand. "You are my dearest friend, and for nearly a year, we lived together after Uncle Phineas opened his home to you. Do not forget he, too, is concerned for your welfare and protection. Given the fact that your dastardly cousin and his wife have agreed to repay the money they stole from you, but have yet to do so, the general consensus is that they plan to abscond with even more."

"How could they do that, now that I am aware of their theft? Why has no one spoken to me about this?"

"The men in our lives seek to protect first, apprise us of their worries after the fact. As to your cousins, if they were to somehow threaten to silence you—"

"Heavens! What could they possibly do that they haven't already done?" Calliope demanded.

"Kidnap you and demand a ransom."

"From Uncle Phineas?"

"He is one possibility," Aurelia agreed. "Now that you're related to the duke—"

Calliope interrupted, "Distantly."

Aurelia frowned. "Related all the same. What's to keep your cousin from demanding payment from Uncle Phineas and Jared?"

Calliope fell silent as she mulled over those disturbing possibilities. "And you feel that Jared, Edward, and Uncle Phineas are all of a mind on this?"

"Yes."

"I cannot help but wonder if the past year has not colored their vision of life and they are seeing villains around every corner. I really do not think the duke or Edward should be so concerned about my welfare."

"It is our pleasure," the deep voice of Aurelia's husband interrupted. "You are the dearest friend to my wife, my sister, and my sister-in-law—and married to our cousin. Therefore, you are part of our family. We will do our utmost to protect you, Calliope. No matter how irritating that protection may feel at times. Our honor and conscience will not allow us to do otherwise."

Aurelia rose from her seat and walked over to wrap her arms around her husband.

Their loved radiated warmth into the room. In that moment, loneliness filled her even while the memory of the viscount's kiss gave her hope that happiness may one day be hers.

"We're ready, yer lordship."

Calliope jolted. How had she not heard these four men walking down the hallway? They were so huge. Their footsteps could normally be heard from the entryway all the way to the sitting room.

Standing beside one another were the light-haired O'Malley brothers, Michael and Thomas, and two of their cousins, dark-haired Aiden Garahan and auburn-haired Seamus Flaherty. Though their hair and eye color were different, their rough-hewn facial features and the proud way they stood identified them as kin.

"Was there something ye wanted to ask, yer ladyship?" Michael O'Malley inquired.

Had she been staring? A quick glance at her friend suggested she must have been. Aurelia was on the verge of laugher. Calliope sighed. "Actually, now that you ask—yes. I was wondering if you could ready the small wagon for me. I'd like to visit with some of our tenant farmers and their families today."

"We were on our way to collect his lordship for the same purpose."

Confused, she asked, "The earl wanted to take me to visit the families today?"

"Er...not exactly," Flaherty answered.

"In a way," Garahan added.

"Ye should tell her the truth," Thomas O'Malley grumbled. "The earl was planning to make the rounds."

"Without me?" Calliope felt the surge of anger twist her belly into painful knots. "It is not to be borne, Edward!"

"You are reacting without thinking, Calliope," he observed. "I was about to ask you to accompany me. You mentioned your plans to do so yesterday."

She only heard the first part. "Reacting? Not thinking?"

Aurelia sighed. "Dearest, please give us a moment, would you?"

The earl practically vibrated with what Calliope guessed was indignation. She had pricked his pride. *Botheration!* Her life was decidedly easier to navigate when she had been forced to slave for her cousin. Listening to what she could not, and should not do, would drive her to bedlam!

The earl bowed to Aurelia, while the duke's guard left without comment.

"Won't you please tell me what's wrong?" Aurelia asked. "You're not yourself."

Calliope's shoulders slumped as tears gathered in her eyes. "You wouldn't understand even if I told you."

Aurelia frowned. "I daresay I never will if you do not tell me what's troubling you."

True, Calliope thought. *Would her worries lessen if she shared them?*

"Are you worried about William?"

The first tear fell. "Yes."

Her friend waited for a few moments before asking another question. "Have you heard from him?"

Calliope shook her head.

"I see. Have you written to him?"

Calliope's gaze locked with Aurelia's. "No."

"Why not?"

"I did not wish to disturb him."

Aurelia tugged on Calliope's sleeve to get her to follow her to the table. They sat beside one another. The warmth of the sun streamed in through the tall windows. Calliope lifted her face to the beams. "I miss the warmer weather, and I'd be outside in the cold if I could spare the time."

"If you apologize to Edward, I am certain you can go outside and visit the tenants as you planned yesterday."

Calliope wondered why she should apologize when she'd done nothing more than speak her mind.

As if her friend knew what she was thinking, Aurelia sighed. "The Lippincott men have frightful tempers and too much pride, but it keeps them moving forward and doing what must be done."

"Do you think I was wrong to question him?"

"No, but I do think the manner in which you spoke to him, and the way you worded your question, were not well done of you."

"I see." And she did. Although she did not think she was in the wrong, Aurelia did have a salient point. She should apologize to Edward. "Let's see if we can catch him before he leaves."

Aurelia smiled. "I am quite sure he will wait. Why don't I help you gather the baskets we prepared last night?"

Calliope nodded.

"Would you still like me to accompany you?"

"If you would, please. It might seem odd if I were to arrive with your husband."

Aurelia laughed. "That would be interesting, wouldn't it? Hello, I'm the new viscountess and this is my very good friend's husband, Edward, Earl Lippincott."

Their shared laughter lightened Calliope's heart. "It is wonderful to have you here. I was feeling quite alone. Without Mary Kate, I don't know how I would have managed thus far."

"I'm glad we came. I was worried about you. When we return, you should pen a note to your husband."

My husband. The words still gave Calliope hope that the viscount would wish to remain so.

A LITTLE WHILE later, Calliope walked outside and stared. "This is not the wagon. How are we to carry the baskets Aurelia and I prepared?"

The earl was waiting by his carriage. "It's quite cold today, I didn't want to risk you and Aurelia catching a chill. I spoke with Hargrave and MacReedy, who gave me the names of those they felt in greatest need of assistance. I thought we would visit with those half-dozen families today."

"I confess I didn't consider the weather when Aurelia offered to join me today."

"Having recently spent time visiting our tenants in all sorts of weather—clear and cold, wet and miserable, the weather is now the subject of our everyday plans."

"Thank you for your thoughtfulness, Edward. We would probably be quite chilled on our return."

He inclined his head, accepting her thanks.

"I brought the list of tenants the viscount entrusted to Hargrave in his absence. I thought I would jot down any specific needs when we visited them."

"Excellent notion, Calliope."

"I do hope you will forgive my miserable conduct, Edward. I am feeling overwhelmed and have not been myself as of late."

He helped her into the carriage. When she was seated across from Aurelia, he entered and sat beside his wife. With a knock on the roof of the carriage, he signaled the coachman to proceed.

"You are forgiven. I have been in a similar situation as you, Calliope. When change was happening all around me, and the direction I planned to continue to move forward in was suddenly no longer available, I had to change my thoughts and direction." Lifting Aurelia's hand to his lips, he pressed a brief kiss to the back of it. "My life is far richer for accepting change."

Calliope felt a sense of peace wash over her. Was it the earl's words or simply being in the presence of the loving couple? "Thank you." She wondered yet again if it was too much to hope for that she, too, could find happiness.

The coach slowed to a stop and the door opened. The earl stepped down and thanked Garahan for accompanying them today.

"Me pleasure. 'Tis beautiful out here. The land stretches for miles. Do ye think the farmers have their seeds sorted, anticipating the spring planting?"

"I hope they do. Our farmers were enthusiastic and welcoming when Aurelia and I visited with them to discuss their plans for planting."

Garahan listened as he helped Calliope from the carriage.

"Mind yer step, yer ladyship."

"I will. Thank you, Aiden."

He nodded and turned to assist Aurelia.

"Their roof looks as if it needs repair. What do you think, Garahan?" the earl asked.

"I'd have to take a closer look but, from down here, I'd say it should go on the list."

Calliope opened her reticule and pulled out her journal. "The Jones family. Two sons aged five and seven. Was their roof the reason Hargrave and Mr. MacReedy told you about them?"

"MacReedy advised Mr. Jones injured his leg a fortnight ago."

"Has the physician been around to see him?"

"MacReedy did not say," the earl advised.

Calliope made a notation next to their name about the thatch needing repair and the possibility of the viscount's physician being summoned. "Shall we introduce ourselves?"

The earl and Aurelia motioned for her to precede them. Calliope knocked on the door and was greeted by the hugely pregnant Mrs. Jones. "Welcome to our home, yer ladyship. Oh! I didn't know you were bringing guests with you."

"I'd like to introduce my very good friends, Edward, Earl Lippincott, and his wife, Lady Aurelia."

The woman had a death grip on the sides of her apron as she started to curtsey. Calliope rushed forward to keep her from doing so. "A woman in your condition needn't curtsey."

"Thank you, your ladyship. I've a pot of tea brewing and brown bread, if you're hungry."

Calliope thanked her and offered her basket. "Aurelia and I have a gift for your family."

Mrs. Jones' eyes widened at the full basket Calliope handed to her. "Oh, this is so very thoughtful of you! Thank you."

Calliope sensed Mrs. Jones wanted to dig into the basket and encouraged her. "Why don't you sit down with Aurelia while I pour the tea."

"I wouldn't hear of it, your ladyship. You are a guest in my home. Let me pour the tea and fetch the bread and butter."

"Thank you, Mrs. Jones."

"It's Lizzy."

"Thank you, Lizzy."

Edward announced, "I'll go and have a look at your roof."

Lizzy looked up from slicing the bread. "As we told the viscount when last he called, it'll do until spring."

The earl smiled. "If it would be all right, Garahan and I will have a closer look."

"Thank you, your lordship. I'm certain you will agree with my husband. It can wait."

"I'll leave you ladies to your tea." He bowed and quietly left the cottage.

The temptation to see what was in the basket was too much for Lizzy. She had a sip of her tea and beamed when Calliope suggested she look inside. "The Duchess of Wyndmere gave me a supply of calves' foot jelly along with a wide assortment of tinctures and dried herbs to share with the viscount's tenant farmers and their families."

"The duchess?" Lizzy whispered as she lifted out a jar of the prized jelly. "Oh, this is wonderful. Please thank Her Grace for me."

Calliope smiled and explained, "Aurelia's married to the duke's brother."

Lizzy nodded and Calliope suspected she was only half-listening as she oohed and aahed over each item she removed from the gift basket.

Calliope had been on hand earlier in the year to collect and dry the lilac, rose petals, and lavender buds. They used the lilac to make the duchess' favorite soap and the rose petals to make Calliope's. Lavender for one's linens was an important addition to any household. "I hope you like the last few items."

Lizzy reached for the ball-shaped object wrapped in paper. "Soap?"

Calliope nodded. "Her Grace favors lilac. I prefer the rose. I hope you enjoy them both."

Lizzy unwrapped the first soap and held the ball close to inhale the delicate scent. "Your ladyship, this is so thoughtful." She rewrapped the soap to sniff the rose-scented one. Sighing deeply, she admitted, "I've never had such a luxury before."

"Open the embroidered bag," Aurelia urged.

Lizzy didn't need to be asked twice. She opened the bag and gasped. "Oh, lavender! This reminds me of home. Thank you."

"You are most welcome," Calliope assured her.

The women drank their tea while becoming acquainted. Calliope learned Lizzy's babe was due in February, but confessed she thought he or she would come before then.

"Who will attend the birth?" Aurelia wanted to know.

"Old Miriam, the local midwife."

"I should like to meet her," Calliope said.

Lizzy's eyes widened and Calliope was quick to reassure her that she was not expecting but would like to meet everyone involved in the lives of the viscount's tenants.

"Of course, your ladyship. I can send word to her for you."

"That would be wonderful, Lizzy. Thank you."

They bid Lizzy goodbye and visited the other families Hargrave and MacReedy suggested. It did not surprise Calliope that the families knew one another quite well. In spite of the fact their homes needed repair, and they lacked certain amenities, they were generally happy. It was such a change from the last household Calliope resided in.

On their return journey, the earl listed the major repairs he and Garahan discussed for each of the families. Calliope made note of each one. It would take time and the coin to make the repairs. Added to the ones she noticed at the viscount's home, she could only imagine how much coin it would require. She had a sinking feeling the reason the viscount did not want to marry a poor relation had to do with the state of his home, and the welfare of his staff and tenant farmers.

Lost in thought on the carriage ride home, Calliope was relieved no one questioned her hasty marriage to the viscount. She was delighted to have been able to share her time and gifts with the first of his tenant families.

As the carriage pulled to a stop in front of Chattsworth Manor, she wondered how the viscount was faring in London.

CHAPTER NINETEEN

THE VISCOUNT DREW in a deep breath and sighed as he entered Tattersalls. Nothing lifted his spirits like spending time around horses. A good portion of his boyhood had been spent in his father's stables. He'd pestered the stable master with questions and offers of assistance until the man had gone to the earl, asking for permission to teach his son.

Between running wild through the meadows and woodland surrounding Chattsworth Manor with his brother, hanging around the stables occupied the rest of this time—well, except for his studies. He'd been diligent there but hadn't enjoyed being cooped up inside as much as he'd enjoyed being out of doors.

He pulled his timepiece out of his waistcoat pocket, noting he was a bit early. "Time to see what's on the auction block today."

"Chattsworth!"

Blast! Coddington. Just when he'd begun to hope the man would not show for their appointment, he'd arrived. "Lord Coddington."

The man inclined his head in greeting and immediately turned his attention to the horseflesh the viscount was inspecting. "Going to bid on this beauty?"

Chattsworth shrugged. "Maximus would be quite put out if I brought another Thoroughbred stallion to share his quarters."

The older man grinned. "Tricky business, introducing a new

stallion into the mix. What of your other stock?"

William wasn't sure if he should take the man into his confidence, then remembered he was interested because of his connection to Lady Calliope. He owed the man a direct answer. "Due to circumstances beyond my control, I had to sell off all but one horse."

Coddington nodded, and from the look on the man's face, already knew of the viscount's situation. He shouldn't be surprised. Anyone who had ties with the Duke of Wyndmere was well in the know. The duke had connections everywhere.

"A sorry business, Chattsworth. His Grace and I are using all of our connections to uncover any leads that may have been missed in discovering the whereabouts of your father."

Why had the lord joined forces with the duke?

Before he could voice the question, the lord answered it. "Lady Calliope is like a daughter to me. As my niece's very good friend, I opened my home to her when it came to light that she'd been sorely mistreated by her own kin. Despicable people."

"What's this?" The viscount really had no idea what his wife's homelife had been like.

"Second cousin, I believe. The rotter and his wife siphoned off Calliope's allowance, without her knowledge. Forced her to become a servant to them when they should have opened their home and their hearts to her."

And what had he done to Calliope? Turned his back on her and walked away, without a word. "I did not realize what her situation had been."

"You hardly had the time to ask before you nearly tossed her down the stairs and broke her neck!"

Coddington's eyes promised retribution, and William was more than ready to accept the challenge.

"I say, Coddington!"

A man of middle years approached, hand extended. "Haven't seen you in an age. Where have you been keeping yourself?"

William noted the man's frockcoat was of the best cut—he'd

been to Weston's and knew from experience what the renowned tailor was capable of. The ring on the man's little finger brought him up short. *Where was the earl's ring with the family crest on it?* The earl used it to seal his correspondence and was never seen without it. One more thing to find the answer to.

"Don't believe we've met," the man said at last. "Name's Wadsworth."

"Chattsworth," Coddington supplied. "Married my niece's friend, Lady Calliope Harrington."

"Harrington? The earl's daughter?"

Coddington frowned. "The current earl's niece. Her father, the previous earl, died without male issue. Calliope's mother followed shortly after her husband."

"Sad business that," Wadsworth replied. "Hadn't heard the news, married her recently?"

"A sennight ago," Coddington answered quickly. "The duke asked Chattsworth here to attend to some of his affairs."

"The first of which is why Lord Coddington and I are here," the viscount remarked.

"The business of purchasing reliable horseflesh is always of great import," Wadsworth agreed. "What have you looked at?"

William admitted he'd been ignoring the duke's needs in favor of a look at the Thoroughbreds. "I'm to secure two matched pair of grays."

"Ah, carriage horses. Mind if I tag along?"

Coddington readily agreed, much to the viscount's relief. Their interrupted conversation could continue later, hopefully in more private surroundings.

A FEW SURPRISINGLY enjoyable hours later—none that included the need to seek seconds for a dawn appointment, the grays had been purchased and Wadsworth remained behind at Tattersalls.

"Care to join me at White's?"

William was unsure if he should accept. Would Coddington continue their conversation where they'd left it before

Wadsworth had interrupted them?

"Excuse the earlier outburst," Coddington admitted. "I cannot abide anyone who mistreats Calliope—or any other female for that matter. Goes against everything I hold dear."

"I did not know she was there when I burst out of the duke's study."

"How could you, when you apparently didn't take the time to look?"

"Perhaps we should conclude our conversation another time," the viscount suggested.

They waited for their carriages to be brought around and were about to part company when William knew it would be up to him to set the older man's mind at ease. "I would never intentionally harm Lady Calliope."

"But you would turn your back on her," Coddington said.

The viscount took his time responding. Finally, he did. "If I felt it would be in her best interest, yes."

"Do you dare to mock Lady Calliope? How in God's name would turning your back on her be in her best interest?"

Coddington's distress was more than evident. William had to tell him the truth. "I do not have the coin to feed another person, let alone support her in the style she deserves. What little my father left behind is divvied up between our elderly staff, tenant farmers and their families." He looked away, wishing he hadn't confessed the state of his affairs. "So much is in need of repair, seeds still to be purchased for the spring planting…"

Coddington laid a hand on the viscount's shoulder. "I may have been hasty in my conclusion," he stated. "You did not intend to give her the cut direct, leaving her after you'd said your vows."

His throat tight with emotion, the viscount could only shake his head. He had not meant to do anything of the sort.

Coddington urged, "What say we discuss your plans for your estate over a glass of whiskey or port? I may not enjoy spending time at my country estate, but I have an excellent steward and estate manager. Mayhap I can be of assistance in that regard."

"I would value your input, Lord Coddington."

"Let's be off then. Here's my carriage now. I shall meet you at White's."

>>><<<

COVENTRY LISTENED AS Sean O'Malley gave his report. When he finished, Coventry asked, "Did the horses arrive?"

O'Malley smiled. "Aye, they did. I was there when they arrived. Beautifully matched in height, coloring, and temperament. His Grace should be well pleased with them."

Coventry gave a slight nod, as he'd learned to do after recovering from his injuries. Too deep or fast a movement would throw off his balance. Something he could not afford to do if he were to succeed in any future endeavors. He had no desire to be the subject of anyone's pity. He would live life on his own terms.

"And the viscount? What have you heard from my contact at Tattersalls?"

"Wadsworth had no trouble inviting himself to tag along—the ruse that he was a friend to Coddington was never questioned by his lordship. Yer man stayed behind after the viscount purchased horses for the duke."

"Did he have anything insightful to report? His character judgment has always been spot on."

"I spoke with Wadsworth meself. Said the viscount was amiable. Got on well with Coddington, after a bit of a dust up."

"What happened?" Coventry demanded.

O'Malley shrugged. "'Twas before Wadsworth joined them. If ye ask me, he interrupted at a crucial moment."

Coventry's interest was piqued. "In what way?"

"It was Wadsworth's opinion that one of them was about to demand satisfaction."

"The duke would not be pleased."

"Aye, 'tis why he chose that moment to interrupt."

"I see." He'd have to assign another man to shadow the viscount. He could not take a chance that their plans would go awry. "Who's stationed at White's?"

"A friend of one of the Garahans works there. He knows how to blend into the background while serving drinks to the high steppers who frequent the establishment."

"Excellent. Has the duke advised when you'll be taking up residence in Sussex?"

"A fortnight."

"I'll be sorry to see you go, Sean. I'll be glad when the duty rotation brings you back to London."

O'Malley grinned. "Ye haven't seen the last of me, and I'm sure ye'll enjoy having me brother, Michael, back in town."

Coventry smiled. "It's been a pleasure and an honor to work with you and your family, Sean."

"Sure and ye'll not be rid of us anytime soon."

"That's a relief," Coventry confirmed. "Who is your connection on the Andrews' staff?"

"Actually, 'tis the former butler of Lady Kittrick."

"Didn't Edward have something to do with that?"

O'Malley smiled. "The earl was properly angered by the woman's treatment of her staff."

"Wasn't there a scullery maid that one of the Garahans brought back with him from the earl's visit?"

"Aye, 'twas James. He could have hardly left the poor lass languishing on the sidewalk...the cook had shoved the poor *colleen* out the door! Her hands and knees were a mess."

"I take it Mrs. O'Toole took the young woman in hand. I don't recall seeing any new maids."

"The earl thought it best to send her to the country with the duke and duchess."

"Ah, that would explain why I don't recall meeting her. Anything else to report?"

"Aside from the news that me cousin, Finn, is apparently sweet on another of the duke's maids, nay."

Coventry grinned at the thought. "Let us hope he doesn't break her heart."

Chuckling, O'Malley added, "'Tis time for me to check in with the men guarding the perimeter. I'll see ye tomorrow, then."

"Thank you, Sean."

"As I said, 'tis me pleasure, Mr. Coventry."

He chuckled. "Just Coventry."

"Aye, Coventry."

CHAPTER TWENTY

"LORD ANDREWS," THE butler intoned as the older gentleman entered the study.

The viscount quickly rose to his feet to greet the man.

He had been waiting for close to three-quarters of an hour. Every moment spent wondering if the man would send his servant to advise Andrews would not receive him today after all.

The viscount quickly buried those thoughts and grasped the hand Lord Andrews extended to him.

"Wondered what the duke had in mind suggesting we meet. But now that I've had time to mull things over a bit, I've decided the duke's idea has merit." Andrews sat in the chair behind his desk, motioning for the viscount to have a seat.

William sank into one of the chairs across from the lord. What was the man talking about? "I'm not quite sure I follow."

Andrews harumphed. "Tell me, Chattsworth, what's been done to locate your father?"

His stomach lurched as knots of tension threatened to double him over. "I've used every connection I have to discover his whereabouts."

"Details, Chattsworth," Andrews demanded.

"When I did not hear from him for a few days, I traveled to London."

"And?" the man prompted.

"I knew he'd invested heavily in a shipping firm and heard rumors that he'd been…" How to tell the man in front of him that he'd confirmed the *on dit* that his father had developed a gambling addiction?

"Your father sought my advice on more than one shipping company," Andrews expounded. "However, he did not heed me when I warned him to pay close attention to when those shipments would be made. Weather is key when investing in such."

"I see. Thank you for your elucidation. I have a few acquaintances in the Royal Navy who'd shared their tales of ill-fated voyages around the Cape of Good Hope."

"Sailors who've survived such treacherous weather would have advised your father the same."

William hesitated in responding. He did not want it to seem that his father pushed forward without heeding sound advice from one who knew the dangers involved in financing shipping companies.

"I take it from your silence you've discovered another possibility behind the earl's investments."

Blast his father's reputation! If the truth would save the earl's life, then to bloody hell with his family's reputation! "I have it on good authority that my father spent an indecent amount of time in the seamier side of London."

"The stews and gaming hells," Andrews confirmed. "Bound to empty your pockets and drain every last pound from your estates if you don't keep your wits about you."

"I know," William rasped. "There were so many conflicting stories from his cronies he'd befriended there. I ended up chasing my tail more than any truly solid leads." There was one lead he suspected but hadn't followed. The duke had somehow discovered information that would either confirm or deny Chellenham had encouraged his father to recoup his extensive losses in the gaming hells.

Andrews turned to stare at the fireplace, as if entranced by the flames steadily devouring the wood. Abruptly, he asked, "What about the reports of him being robbed by a highwayman?"

The viscount locked gazes with Andrews. *Did the man know something?* No noticeable twitch…and the man met his gaze straight on. He wondered, not for the first time, how could the man help him, if he didn't know anything?

"Well?" Andrews asked, when the viscount remained silent.

"I spoke with the constable near Chattsworth Manor, who was able to confirm no crimes were reported in the area at the time."

Andrews leaned forward in his chair. "Followed every lead?"

He had, and still he'd failed to locate his father. "Yes."

"Any other news that may shed some light on your father's whereabouts?"

Should he tell Andrews? Is that what the duke intended when he'd arranged this meeting? *Bloody hell!* He was tired of evading questions in regard to his father. If it came to light his father had gambled everything on an ill-fated shipment of goods, so be it. If he'd tossed every last coin into the pot, betting it all on the turn of a card, at least he'd be one step closer to an answer.

"There was one other *on dit* I felt worth looking into. Led me to a pawn shop."

"Ah," Andrews seemed satisfied with that last bit of information. "Found some items that had gone missing from the manor?"

The bottom dropped out of his stomach. Had the man sitting across from him aided his father or helped him escape? "As a matter of fact, the broker perfectly described a few of the antiquities my great-grandfather collected while in Egypt."

"Any jewelry?"

William shot to his feet. "If you know something, tell me!"

His demand was met with a measured look. Andrews motioned for the viscount to be seated. When he complied, Andrews related, "I'd heard more than one rumor the famed *Chattsworth Emeralds* had been pawned—and purchased."

"Bloody hell! Who bought them?" the viscount demanded.

"I'm afraid that was not part of the *on dit* I'd heard about them." He waited a beat before asking, "If the purchaser's name comes to light, what would you do with the information?"

His ire bubbled inside him; a roiling mess of emotions best kept to himself. It would not do to admit he wanted to beat the truth out of whoever had purchased the emeralds. "I would seek the man out and demand to know the details."

"You wouldn't buy back your family's heirloom?"

Shame had him looking away. He curled his hands into fists. God, what he wouldn't give to beat the hell out of whoever had his mother's emeralds! The childhood memory haunted him and would always be tied to the happier moments in his life, before his brother, August, died...before his mother died in childbirth, taking his unborn sister with her.

"I have not the funds to do so, your lordship."

"Do you plan to declare yourself earl as your father all but vanished in thin air?"

"His solicitor sought me out and advised me to take over the running of the estate and do what I could to recoup a bit of what my father lost."

"Sound advice. What did he say about the earldom?"

"Nothing can be done for six more years."

"Nothing?"

William slowly rose and held out his hand to Andrews. "Thank you for your time and suggestions."

Andrews rose to his feet and accepted the viscount's hand. "Asking questions and digging deeper is doing something."

The viscount shrugged. "My father is still missing."

"Missing isn't always synonymous with death, Chattsworth," Andrews advised. "Remember that."

"I shall. Thank you."

"A moment, Chattsworth." Andrews walked over to the fireplace and tugged on the bell pull. He wasn't kept waiting long.

His butler appeared. "Yes, your lordship?"

"Summon my carriage, I shall follow Chattsworth to White's."

"Very good, your lordship."

A FEW HOURS later, Chattsworth was greeted by Jenkins. "There is a letter that arrived in today's post for you, your lordship."

He paused for a moment then proceeded to remove his gloves. Had his cousin, Marcus, replied to the letter he'd sent telling him of his marriage and duties to the duke? *No, he reasoned. His cousin was more apt to take action than to write a letter.* Something was wrong. Handing his hat and gloves to Jenkins, he asked, "Do you recall who it was from?"

"Viscountess Chattsworth."

That last had the brandy he'd had at White's curdling what little he'd eaten earlier in his stomach. Had something untoward happened to his wife? Keeping tight control on his emotions, he replied, "Thank you, Jenkins."

"I left it on the duke's desk in his study."

William sighed. *The duke's desk.* "Very good." Was Calliope ill? Did she write to ask when she could expect to see him? Mayhap she was simply asking after him. He walked quickly, not wanting to alert the butler that he was anxious to read her letter.

Devil take it, he was!

Closing the study door behind him, he strode to the desk and slipped out of his frockcoat. Tossing it across the arm of his desk chair, he rifled through the first stack before realizing it had been sorted and contained calling cards. The next stack was an orderly pile of invitations to balls, musicales, and the like. Off to the side was a single letter atop the morning *Post* he had yet to read.

He picked up the folded note and turned it over, recognizing the imprint on the wax seal as one his mother had used—a rose in bloom. Rather than feel annoyed his wife had used his mother's seal, he was pleased she had found what she needed to write to him. He broke the seal and began to read.

Dear William,

I hope you do not mind my writing to you. I find my thoughts drifting to London, wondering if you've settled in on Grosvenor Square. Having spent time there with Aurelia and Phoebe, I know it to be quite lovely and an exceedingly comfortable place to reside.

My maid, Mary Kate, and I arrived in one piece and are keeping ourselves quite occupied in your absence. Aurelia and the earl came for a visit. We prepared baskets and delivered a few of them to your tenant farmers and their families. I expect to be delivering the last of the baskets with Mary Kate as Aurelia and the earl have returned to Lippincott Manor.

I hope you continue to be in good health.

Yours,
Calliope

William read the letter three times before setting it back on the desk. Her written words reminded him of the conversations they'd had at Wyndmere Hall. Though not many, he'd still enjoyed them.

Should he answer her letter?

"Of course," he grumbled. "You'd have to have half a brain to even consider ignoring a letter from your wife."

Wife.

What had she meant by telling him she and her maid had arrived in one piece? Had something happened while en route to his home? Would she have told him? Did she have all she required? Their food stores had been running low when he'd left for Wyndmere Hall. He hadn't given it much thought at the time as he'd intended to return to Chattsworth Manor directly—not after a four-week stay in London.

Another question plagued him. *Was there more to the earl's visit?* Granted their estates were relatively close in proximity and their wives were very good friends. His gut churned. The duke had connections. By now, he must have ascertained the truth of the viscount's empty coffers and with his brother's visit, the true condition of Chattsworth Manor.

He had much to atone for the next time he met with the duke. Hopefully, he would have the answer to what had happened to his father and found a way to bring honor back to his family name and refill the family coffers.

Calliope was first and foremost on his mind. He penned a reply and sanded and sealed the missive to his wife. He'd ask Jenkins to take care of it for him.

Should he enlist aid from one of the duke's guard or Coventry to find out how his wife was faring? He'd have to give it serious consideration before broaching the subject. Another task awaited him on the morrow. It was the meeting he dreaded with Lord Chellenham, the man he suspected had lured his father to the gaming hells in the stews.

Mayhap he should send word to his cousin, Marcus, and ask him to check on the state of things at Chattsworth Manor. A loud knock interrupted his train of thought. "Come in."

The door opened to reveal Jenkins standing in the doorway. "Yes, Jenkins?"

"Sean O'Malley to see you."

"Thank you, Jenkins." The look in O'Malley's eyes had William pushing to his feet. He met O'Malley halfway across the room. "Trouble?"

"Could be brewing. Ye're to meet with Lord Chellenham tomorrow."

The viscount nodded, waiting to hear what the man had to

impart.

"The duke hired me away from Chellenham before he married the duchess."

What did that have to do with his meeting with the lord tomorrow? "I see."

"There are times when I'm not sure meself why he did, but I'm grateful to be away from that house. I would warn ye not to believe all Chellenham has to say. From me time serving as his footman..."

The viscount had the feeling O'Malley was about to tell him something he needed to know but was hesitating. "You may speak freely. I'll not castigate you for speaking the truth or your mind."

O'Malley seemed to be considering whether or not he could trust him. William did not take offense; he would do the same if their positions were reversed.

"Chellenham and the duke's older brother were bent on following the road to perdition as me sainted mother would say."

The viscount acknowledged the information, deciding to question O'Malley to better judge what possible motive or plan lay behind his doing so. "I take it you know of the rumors about my father?"

The duke's man was quick to respond. "I've heard a few. I don't trust the man and wouldn't lift a pint with him."

In William's book, that last said it all. "Thank you for the warning. I'll be on my guard."

O'Malley nodded. "I need to check in with me men standing guard on the perimeter."

William was impressed by the way he moved—with an economy of movement and little or no sound. *He'd be a good man to have at my back.*

He was still standing in the doorway when Jenkins returned. "Dinner is served, your lordship."

"Thank you. Oh, Jenkins?"

"Your lordship?"

"Will you post a letter for me?"

"Of course, your lordship."

He walked back over the desk, retrieved the letter. Handing it to the butler, he thanked the man.

"Will you be going out this evening, your lordship?"

"I had planned to, but I've had a change in plans."

"Very good, your lordship."

After an excellent meal, the viscount retreated to the duke's study. A few hours later, he'd compiled his own list of recent conversations, and information about his father's disappearance. He'd added notations to the list of repairs he planned to make at Chattsworth Manor. The first of which would be a deep cleaning, although where he'd find the money to hire on additional staff for the task, he had no idea.

CHAPTER TWENTY-ONE

C ALLIOPE WAS ON her hands and knees scrubbing the hearth in the library when Hargrave called her name. She sat back on her heels and wiped the back of her hand across her brow. "Do you need my help with something?"

He smiled—a rarity in the time she'd been at Chattsworth. They'd worked together to decide which tasks needed to be done immediately and which ones would need to wait. No matter the task, she approached whatever needed to be done with conviction and fortitude. With or without William's blessing, she'd do her utmost to bring his home back to life.

"A letter for your ladyship."

Pushing to her feet, she used the rag in her apron pocket to wipe her hands before reaching for the letter he held out to her. Not recognizing the handwriting, she turned it over and noted a similar imprint to the one she'd used to seal her letter…a rose in bloom.

Could it be from William?

Carefully breaking the wax seal, she unfolded the note.

Dear Calliope,

I was happy to receive your letter. The duke's town house is everything you described. I'm curious about something you said in your letter. Was there a reason you and Mary Kate would not arrive at Chattsworth Manor in one piece?

I'm happy you enjoyed visiting with your friends. I am in quite good health and would inquire after yours and caution you not to tire yourself looking after our tenants. Please be patient with our aging servants, they have served my family for years.

Yours,
William

She'd read the note a second time before realizing Hargrave had remained.

"Is his lordship well?"

The butler obviously recognized the handwriting. "He is." She decided against sharing the viscount's request to have patience with his elderly staff. They were older, but they were proud of their service to the family and deserved her respect. "Although he does not send news of London, only that the duke's town house is quite comfortable. I do hope the duke has not tasked him with too many duties."

Hargrave was quick to assure her. "His lordship is up to any task, no matter who asks it of him."

"I have not known him as long as you," she observed, "but from my conversations with the viscount, I agree. It is the number of them that I question," she added. "It would be wonderful if he were able to return earlier than expected."

The butler nodded. "We have much to do in the next fortnight."

Calliope was about to tuck the note in her apron pocket when she thought better of it. She had more than a bit of ash streaking across the front of her. Holding out the note to Hargrave, she asked, "Would you please have Mary Kate put this upstairs for me. I don't want to spread cinder and ashes on it."

"At once, your ladyship."

Calliope watched the retainer walk away. The staff was loyal to the viscount, and she'd overheard more than one comment about the viscount shirking his duty here at home by spending it in London at the duke's behest. She, too, wished William were here. Would he stay if she was in residence? Should she leave before the humiliating prospect of her husband asking her to?

Did he want her to remain his wife?

Her thoughts in turmoil, Calliope did not hear the front door open. The sunshine poured in around the tall, dark-haired man standing in the entryway staring at her.

"You're here!" she rushed to him, smiling, ready to welcome him home. Would he be pleased with the efforts she, Mary Kate and the staff made on his behalf? Mayhap he'd be vexed with her for taking initiative without consulting him. Reaching for his hands, she remembered hers had been scrubbing the hearth just moments before.

She hid them behind her back as the man closed the door behind him, blocking out the sunlight. "It's so good—oh, forgive me. I do beg your pardon."

"Not necessary," his brilliant blue eyes sparkled with mirth as he stared at her.

"I thought you were..." Who was this man who bore an uncanny resemblance to her husband? He'd let himself in, obviously accustomed to doing so. If he didn't resemble her husband so closely, she'd have run to the library and come back with one of the fireplace pokers to defend their home. His smile was familiar—although without the duke's dimples or her husband's cleft chin.

"Has anyone ever told you that you bear a striking resemblance to Viscount Chattsworth?"

"Yes, actually, numerous times," his deep voice drawled. He

continued to stare at her for long moments before saying, "I do not believe we've met."

Did most women mistake him for the viscount? She noticed he did not bow as a gentleman would in the presence of a lady. She sighed, of course not you bird-wit! Calliope was wearing one of her oldest gowns and a borrowed apron from Mrs. Romney...covered with the former contents of the hearth.

Before she could explain, he took a step closer. Quite close actually, making her more than a bit uncomfortable.

"I did not realize my cousin had hired a new servant." He reached out as if to touch her face.

She jerked backward, nearly stumbling in her haste. "Cousin?"

"Skittish," he murmured, his gaze caressing her face. "Easily remedied once we've become better acquainted."

Shocked to the core, she opened her mouth to set the man straight when she heard Hargrave's voice echo down the hallway. "Your ladyship, Mrs. Meadowsweet needs you to approve the menu for the evening meal."

It was all Calliope could do to keep the snort of laughter from escaping. They'd been eating the same hearty vegetable stew for the last few days. Before she could respond, the butler greeted the man looming in front of her. "Baron Summerfield! Apologies, I did not know you had arrived."

The baron locked gazes with Calliope and then the butler. "Hargrave, did you say ladyship?"

The older man beamed. "As his lordship is not in residence, allow me to introduce you to his viscountess, Lady Calliope."

"I do beg your pardon," the baron stuttered. "But your appearance—your manner of dress...forgive me for not realizing you were William's wife, Lady Calliope."

His look of shocked surprise did not in the least excuse his untoward behavior, nor the fact that he'd been about to...to...to what? Touch her face, or had he planned to do something more? She recoiled at the thought of anyone but William letting his finger trail along the line of her jaw. Worry that the man would not be above seducing one of her husband's servants filled her.

"Baron Summerfield," she said with as much aplomb as she could muster, still garbed in her work dress and soot-stained, borrowed apron.

He had the temerity to grin at her. "I daresay my cousin did not deign to share where he met you, your ladyship. He kept that particular *on dit* close to his vest, but deuced if I am not delighted to make your acquaintance."

He bowed to her and then turned to Hargrave. "I've settled St. George in Maximus' stall. Fine looking beasts he has for company. By the by, who do those four roan geldings belong to?"

"Yer ladyship!" Seamus Flaherty called as he strode toward her from the kitchen. "O'Malley and I need a word with ye."

"Who the devil are you?" Summerfield demanded, straightening to his full height, glaring at the auburn-haired giant.

"I might be asking the same of ye, if word didn't reach us when we returned from making the rounds telling us who ye are."

Summerfield got in Flaherty's face and reiterated, "I asked, who are you?"

Flaherty chuckled. "Faith, don't ye remember? Ye asked, who the devil are ye?"

Calliope watched in fascination as the baron's face turned a deep red. She would later swear he all but had steam pouring out of his ears. Mayhap he shared a bit of what her friends had warned was the Lippincott pride and temper. "Baron Summerfield, may I introduce one of His Grace's personal guards, Seamus Flaherty."

"His Grace?"

"Yes," Calliope replied. "The Duke of Wyndmere. His brother, Earl Lippincott, recently married my very good friend, Lady Aurelia."

The baron's face visibly paled, and Calliope was about to ask if William had left that part out of his letter to his cousin, but thought better of it as her worry about her lady's maid filled her. The man had been about to make overtures to her when he thought her a servant. Would he truly dare to treat a servant in his cousin's home in such a familiar manner? It didn't bear thinking.

Did one accept such treatment of her staff? She thought not. The situation never arose, that she knew of, while her parents were alive. Her earliest years were spent in a loving and well-run household. But she was quite young and may have missed the undercurrents that had become more evident the older she got—the more households she'd lived in.

What did his actions say of the baron? What did that say of her husband? Heaven help her, she hadn't a clue. Time to take back control of the situation. "If you will excuse me, my lord. I must speak with our housekeeper. Shall I ask Mrs. Romney to prepare tea?"

Flaherty crossed his arms and glared at the baron. "O'Malley will be along shortly. I'll keep his lordship company until ye return, yer ladyship."

She smiled, relieved that she had two men she knew without question would guard her with their lives. "Thank you, Seamus. Mayhap our guest would like to wait in the drawing room."

He inclined his head. "Yes, yer ladyship."

As she turned and walked away, she heard the low rumble of Flaherty's voice warning the man to watch his step and mind his ways where she was concerned. Warmth filled her. This was the second time Seamus had come to her rescue.

As she hurried to the kitchen, she hoped it would be the last time she needed rescuing—at least for the next little while.

"Mrs. Meadowsweet! You wanted to speak to me?"

The older woman shook her head. "Not that I recall."

Calliope paused and then smiled. She suspected Hargrave had manufactured the summons to ease his way into the awkward situation she'd found herself in moments ago. "Baron Summerfield has just arrived, and I offered him tea."

Mrs. Romney looked up from the pot she stirred. "I have some teacakes that would be just the thing." As if she had just noticed the state Calliope was in, she gasped. "Er...would your ladyship care for a bath before serving tea?"

Calliope wondered if she had a smear of soot across her face. She remembered using the back of her hand to brush the hair out of her eyes. "Have I dirt on my face?"

Mrs. Romney sighed. "More than a bit." She grabbed a fresh linen towel off the stack on the hutch along one wall. While Calliope watched, she dipped the large copper ladle into one of the pots on the stove, poured it into a bowl and then dipped the corner of the towel in. "May I?"

Calliope nodded. "If you would, thank you."

As gently as if she were bathing a small child's face, the cook smoothed the warm, damp towel across Calliope's brow and then her cheeks. "There. Much better. If you like, you can use the pitcher and bowl in the pantry to wash your hands."

Mrs. Meadowsweet was shaking her head at the cook. "Her ladyship should change in order to properly serve tea to the baron."

"I wasn't thinking," Calliope told her. "Please let the baron know I shall be down shortly."

O'Malley walked in through the door as she was speaking. "Baron, ye say?"

"Yes. William's cousin."

O'Malley frowned. "Is Flaherty with him still?"

"Yes, and he—"

Before Calliope finished speaking, Michael O'Malley hustled through the kitchen, giving a brief nod in her direction before exiting the room. "I guess he wanted to speak with the baron as well."

Mrs. Meadowsweet and Mrs. Romney shared a satisfied look. "His Grace's guard are honorable men who would never shirk in their duties."

Calliope wondered what the women were hinting at. "Their

duties?"

"Protecting you, your ladyship."

"From the viscount's cousin?"

The housekeeper sighed. "He has a reputation for taking advantage of young women."

"Does he?" Calliope was not surprised, but she hesitated to say as much.

"Before the other servants left, Mrs. Romney and I had our hands full whenever the baron came to visit."

"Did my husband speak to the baron about his behavior?"

Mrs. Romney nodded. "More than once. Though the baron often stops by when the viscount is not at home."

She wondered why that would be. The best way to find out was to ask. "Does the viscount travel much?"

"Spent nearly a year making trips back and forth to London after the earl..." Mrs. Meadowsweet cleared her throat. "Well, that was then."

Knowing it was a subject she needed to broach with her husband, and not their servants, she nodded. "I'd best wash up and go upstairs to change. Mary Kate should be finished scrubbing the hearth in the upstairs sitting room. I'll send her down to see if there is anything else on the list that needs doing for today."

"Thank you, your ladyship."

The water in the pitcher was cool, but Calliope was well used to making do. A few minutes later, she'd washed and dried her hands. She used the servants' staircase to the second floor. She opened the door, and nearly jumped out of her skin.

"Baron Summerfield!" she gasped. "What are you doing up here?" She glared at the man until he took his hand off the doorknob to her sitting room—the room Mary Kate was in.

"I left something in here the last time I visited William," he explained. "I need to collect it."

She did not believe him for a moment. "I'd be happy to go and get it for you. Was it a book?"

From the frown on his face, he did not like being questioned.

Another thought occurred to her as they stood facing one another in the empty hallway. Had William asked him to come and see how she was faring, or had he sent the baron to ensure she was treating the servants kindly? Although she had not known the viscount long, she highly doubted her husband would approve of the baron's behavior toward their servants.

He still had not answered her question. She asked another. "Did my husband send you? Was he concerned with my being here without him?"

The baron was not quick enough to respond. Bright blue eyes challenged her. Did the man think she would be cowed by his connection to William and allow him to behave in such a manner in her husband's absence?

"I am quite sure William would not approve of your conduct, your lordship."

Duly reminded of his behavior toward her, he replied, "William mentioned that he recently married and that you were here while he was in London."

"And?" she prompted, not about to give the man one inch until she was satisfied with his answer.

"His concern for you was genuine, your ladyship."

Although he'd answered her questions, she noted he'd once again reached for the doorknob. He turned the knob.

Calliope had had enough! Drawing in a fortifying breath and called, "Seamus!"

The baron blanched. "Here now, your ladyship. There is nothing wrong here. I told you I left something—"

The pounding of footsteps on the stairs had the man taking three steps back.

"Lady Calliope!" Flaherty nearly ran into the baron in his haste to answer her summons. "Are ye hurt? What's wrong?" He turned to the baron and inquired, "Were ye not going to check on yer horse, your lordship? The stables are that way." Flaherty pointed out the window. "Are ye lost?"

The baron gaped at Flaherty but did not reply.

Calliope wanted the man as far away from her maid as possible. "Please escort the baron back to the drawing room…and keep him there."

Turning to glare at the baron, she informed him, "I shall gather what I need to pen a note to my husband. I am certain he will be interested to hear of your *visit*."

Confusion and anger suffused the baron's handsome features, contorting them into what she recognized as a mix of anger and pride. She had the distinct impression the man was vexed in the extreme but didn't care one wit. That could all be rectified once William returned. Apologies could be made; fences could be mended. But until then, he would believe whatever he wanted about her high-handed way of treating him.

"I shall be down shortly," she told him. "Mrs. Romney is preparing your tea."

The baron had the intelligence to know when to retreat and did so. Flaherty was hot on his heels.

O'Malley called her name as she heard him thundering up the servants' staircase a moment later. "Lady Calliope!"

The baron froze and looked from one guard to the other. "Does His Grace know how you feel about my cousin's wife?"

The import of his words struck Calliope like a blow. Barely married two weeks and the possible threat of a scandal was brewing and all because the duke's men were diligent in their assignment to guard her with their lives.

Tears filled her eyes, but she blinked them away. She would not give the man the satisfaction of knowing he'd scored a direct hit. "Have I mentioned that His Grace, Jared, and his wife, Persephone, are good friends of mine as well?"

The self-important expression on the baron's face disappeared as did every ounce of his color.

"Seamus and Michael are here at Jared's request. He did not want anything untoward to happen to me while my husband was in London attending to Jared's affairs."

Summerfield inclined his head. "William mentioned he was

attending to the duke's affairs, but not your connection with the duke. If I gave the impression that I intended anything that would offend, pray forgive me, your ladyship. Nothing could be further from the truth."

Flaherty clenched his jaw.

O'Malley curled his hands into fists before relaxing them.

"You are forgiven, your lordship. I am quite sure William would not have us at odds. We're family now."

The three men walked downstairs, with O'Malley and Flaherty speaking in low tones. She could not hear what they were saying but had a feeling they were warning the baron to watch his step.

The door behind her slowly opened. Mary Kate peered through the opening. "Is it safe to come out?"

Calliope sighed. "For the moment. If you will help me change, I will fill you in before I have to serve tea to the viscount's cousin."

"Would you like me to accompany you?"

She smiled. "That would be wonderful. I am certain either Flaherty or O'Malley will be remaining as well."

Mary Kate's eyes rounded in surprise. "While I unbutton the back of your dress, you can tell me what that man was up to."

Calliope sighed. "I fear we're going to have to be vigilant until he leaves."

"Is he staying for luncheon?"

"I sincerely hope not."

A short while later, Calliope's hopes were dashed when the man announced his intention to leave immediately *after* luncheon.

Chapter Twenty-Two

"A MISSIVE FROM O'Malley," Humphries announced.

The duke paused. "Which O'Malley? We do have eight in our employ."

Humphries coughed to cover his laughter.

"I have seen you laugh on rare occasion, Humphries. Feel free to do so at any time."

"Yes, Your Grace."

"Humphries?" The duke held out his hand. "The missive?"

The butler handed the sealed note to the duke, explaining, "No first initial, just the last name."

The duke nodded as he opened the note. "It's from Thomas."

"Stationed at Lippincott Manor?"

"Indeed," the duke replied. "Is the messenger still here?"

"Taking care of his horse. Constance is preparing a meal for the man. He appeared chilled to the bone."

"At times, a thankless job, delivering urgent messages." The duke rose. "I need to speak with him."

"Of course, Your Grace."

An hour later, both horse and messenger were sufficiently rested and warmer on the inside. The horse, happy to have eaten a portion of oats, and the messenger a hot meal. The pair would need them on their return journey.

Persephone was waiting for the duke when he returned from

the stable. "Are you ready to share the contents of the missive?"

The duke held out his hand to his wife. "You should be resting, my dear."

"I would rest easier if you'd tell me which O'Malley sent word to you."

"Thomas."

"Has something happened? Is Aurelia unwell?"

"Yes and no."

Persephone drew in a deep calming breath. "Yes, something has happened, and Aurelia's fine."

"Precisely."

"Would you cease with the abrupt answers and tell me what Thomas said."

"Very well." The duke filled his wife in on the contents of the message.

"I had no idea the viscount's finances were in such dire straits," Persephone murmured.

"I cannot say the same."

"Why not?"

"Given the length of time the earl has been missing, and the rumors that he'd invested heavily in that ill-fated shipping venture—"

"And the gambling," Persephone added.

"That, too, my love," the duke agreed. "The viscount would not have had the time to refill the family coffers when so much surrounding his father's disappearance is suspicious."

"Do the suspicions point toward the viscount."

"Most definitely."

"You cannot truly believe he is in any way responsible."

Jared drew Persephone closer to his side and guided her toward his study. "Come sit with me in front of the fire."

"Are you planning to distract me instead of answering?"

Jared chuckled. "You know me too well. However, now that you mention it—" he tilted her chin up and pressed his lips to hers for a lingering kiss. "Distracting you is one of my many daily pleasures."

She sighed and rested her head in the crook of his shoulder. "Do you believe the viscount had anything to do with his father's disappearance?"

"I do not."

Persephone sighed. "I would not believe it of him either. Any word from Gavin King about the return of Calliope's inheritance?"

"I've written to Coddington suggesting we give Calliope and William their wedding gifts from us now, rather than when the viscount returns from London."

"The dowry?"

"Aye."

"What will Phineas be sending them?"

"Calliope's inheritance—in full. Not the monthly stipend, though he intends for her to be able to drawn upon it monthly."

"I thought Calliope's cousin hadn't repaid her."

"He hasn't."

"That is extremely generous of Phineas. Will it help Calliope and William?"

"Most assuredly. Now do be quiet and kiss me."

Persephone was smiling when their lips met.

"YE CANNOT HAVE heard it aright," Seamus Flaherty argued with Michael O'Malley. "No one would say such things about Lady Calliope—especially the man she married."

O'Malley shrugged. "I wouldn't have thought the viscount would spread such wicked lies about his wife."

"Bride," Flaherty reminded him. "Ye know the duke saw to it they were separated the moment the viscount turned his back on his her."

"He seemed a better man than that," O'Malley said. "Could

we have misjudged the man?"

"I doubt it."

"Ye're sure?"

Flaherty fairly growled his reply. "I am."

"How are we to get to the bottom of who started the rumor then?" O'Malley asked.

"Coventry will know. Best send word to him at once."

"He'll have heard the rumors by now."

"What can we do then?" Flaherty asked.

"Shield Lady Calliope as best we can until we either hear from Coventry or see the whites of the viscount's eyes."

"Mayhap we should pay him a visit..." Flaherty suggested.

O'Malley grinned. "Aye, but me cousins already used their fists to convince him once, he'll not likely fall for that a second time."

"Seeing as how Chattsworth's not here," Flaherty begain, "why don't we go a couple of rounds?"

O'Malley grinned. "But no aiming for me face, ye know Lady Calliope frets something fearful when she sees the bruises."

"Ye have me word."

"Mary Kate, have you seen Seamus or Michael?"

"Last I saw they were heading out behind the barn."

Calliope frowned, remembering the last time the cousins disappeared for an hour. "If they are fighting again—"

"You know they don't see it as such, Calliope," Mary Kate reminded her. "It's how they stay in fighting form. Practicing their moves and—"

"Beating one another senseless? We'll just see about that," Calliope promised as she grabbed her shawl off the peg by the back door and swept out of the house.

"Couldn't they toss bags of feed up to the hayloft instead of pounding on one another?" With each step, her frustration continued to build. By the time she'd reached the barn, it was a living breathing thing. "Seamus! Michael!" she shouted as she walked around the back of the building.

Michael paused with his left hand guarding his face, and his right ready to deliver a blow to Flaherty's midsection. "Yer ladyship," O'Malley gasped.

"We didn't see ye there," Flaherty admitted, giving his cousin a shove.

Calliope put her hands on her hips and glared at the two. "You promised no more fighting!"

"We're not fighting," O'Malley reassured her.

"Practicing," Flaherty said with a grin.

She threw her hands up in the air and spun around, only to slip on a patch of ice. Arms flailing, she managed to regain her balance before ignominiously landing on her face.

"Ye've a wonderful sense of balance, yer ladyship," O'Malley told her.

"Ye didn't strain anything, did ye?" Flaherty wanted to know.

Drawing in a calming breath, she thanked Michael for the compliment and reassured Seamus she was fine. A thought occurred to her. "Was there a specific reason you two needed to...er, practice just now?"

They shared a look that bordered on guilty.

She sighed aloud. "The last time you two were beating—"

"Honing our skills, yer ladyship," Flaherty corrected.

"So you said at the time," she grumbled. "I distinctly recall you'd heard some disturbing news."

They stared at her but didn't answer. "Well?"

The cousins shrugged.

"A shrug is not a proper response," Calliope reminded them.

They grinned at her.

"Neither is a—oh, never mind," she huffed. Mindful of any other icy patches, she carefully made her way back to the house.

"Do ye think she suspects? Flaherty queried.

"Aye, but she hasn't heard anything yet," O'Malley stated. "Else, we'd know it."

"Ye're right. We'd best be ready for the backlash."

"Ye'll speak to MacReedy and Hargrave?" Flaherty asked.

"Aye, and ye'll speak to Mrs. Meadowsweet and Mrs. Romney," O'Malley said.

Their bodies well battered, their heads clear, the men went off in separate directions to lay the groundwork necessary to prevent Lady Calliope from hearing the vicious *on dits* bandied about London and now Sussex.

Lady Calliope Harrington was never mistreated or rescued by Lord Coddington...she earned his favor and a place in his home—on her back!

Viscount Chattsworth believed it of her and left his bride at the altar rather than tarnish his family name.

Even the best laid plans often went awry.

CHAPTER TWENTY-THREE

"I BEG YOUR pardon?" William could not believe what he'd just heard.

"'Tis your wife who should beg yours," Chellenham told him. "Not the first time a man's been rushed to the altar. Beguiled by a pretty face and presented with his *heir*, seven short months later."

William locked gazes with the lord and leaned close. "Where did you hear that claptrap?"

Chellenham chuckled. "It's in the betting book, Chattsworth." Chellenham swept his arm in its general direction. "Odds are she delivers a red-headed brat!"

The viscount shot to his feet and grabbed the man by his heavily starched cravat. "I could kill you for that."

The man's face was turning red, but he managed to rasp, "Didn't start the rumor...or the betting."

William released Chellenham and stepped back. *Who hated him enough to bandy about such gossip? Moreover, who hated his wife?*

Not satisfied until he'd seen the wager in White's book, he stalked over to it and flipped through the pages. Nearly two days after he and Calliope had wed, someone placed the wager without leaving their initials. *Was that done? Hadn't he heard one could not leave a bet without their initials?*

Gut churning, head pounding, he left Chellenham and White's behind with but one thought—Calliope must not hear this vicious lie!

Bursting through the door to the duke's town house, he raced up the stairs and pulled out a small traveling case, tossing in a change of clothes and the lists he'd been preparing for the duke and for himself.

Jenkins met him at the bottom of the steps. "Are you leaving us, your lordship?"

"Urgent business. I must get to Chattsworth Manor at once."

"But the duke—"

"Tell His Grace I have to protect Calliope!"

Before the butler could respond, the viscount was halfway to the stable. Reaching for his saddle, he rasped in his horse's ear, "Ride like the wind, Maximus!"

Sean O'Malley stood at the other end of the darkened stable, observing the frantic motions of the viscount. He knew of the rumors involving the viscount and Lady Calliope. His replacement had only just arrived, and he was free to leave. *Luck or destiny?*

It didn't matter which, the duke's town house would not be shy one guard. That's all that mattered. He'd already spoken to Coventry, his brother, and his cousins. They had been made aware of the situation and were prepared to handle anything that came their way, while working to stem the tide of the gossip, and uncover who placed the blasted wager at White's.

He saddled his horse and took off after the viscount.

WILLIAM'S MIND WHIRLED with unanswered questions all revolving around the bet placed after he'd been forced to marry Calliope. What had the person placing the wager hoped to accomplish? Was it connected solely to him and the missing earl? Was it connected to Calliope and her connection to the duke?

He stopped at a posting inn along the route to Sussex to take care of his horse. He wasn't going to bother to eat—his stomach still roiled trying to discern who could be behind such slanderous gossip. From the tone of Chellenham's voice and the smirk on the man's face, he was at the top of the list.

"What would he have to gain by striking out at my wife?"

"If ye'll pause for a moment, I'll be happy to tell ye."

The viscount spun around, grooming brush raised as if to strike a blow, but lowered it when he recognized the head of the duke's London guard, Sean O'Malley. "O'Malley?"

"Aye, did ye think just because ye left as if yer saddle were on fire, that one of us wouldn't be following ye? The duke would have me head."

Relief had him lowering has hand. "I never even gave it a thought."

"Ye'd be right not to trust Chellenham. Didn't I warn ye about the man?"

"You did." William finished brushing Maximus and proceeded to check his hooves and fetlocks. He'd pushed Maximus, but not beyond what he knew his mount was capable of. Mindful of the cold weather and letting his horse cool down, only to push him in the cold air to reach Chattsworth Manor, he debated stabling Maximus and hiring a horse.

"Did ye know the duke keeps a number of horses at the inn as it's halfway to Lippincott Manor?"

The viscount's gaze shifted from his horse to O'Malley. "I did not."

"He'd want ye to leave yer Thoroughbred here for a bit of a rest. Why don't ye settle him in that empty stall, tuck him in and come with me? I'll introduce ye to the gelded lads."

William chuckled at the expression.

O'Malley shook his head at the viscount. "Don't be laughing at them when I introduce ye. They don't like being reminded of the fact, if ye get me meaning."

"Do you always look for the humor in life, Sean?"

"Aye. 'Tis one of me failings, but I am serious about the lads—they know they don't have all of the equipment yer fine stallion has."

The viscount met his gaze and saw the sincerity there. "You

have my word."

The men walked down the length of the huge barn until O'Malley stopped in front of the last four stalls. "Gents, I'd like ye to meet Viscount Chattsworth."

William nodded to the roan beauties. "His Grace has an eye for excellent horseflesh. Why did he need me to oversee the purchase of four horses, when there are four perfectly good horses right here?"

O'Malley pulled an apple out of his pocket and quartered it, handing half to the viscount. As they fed the horses their treat he explained, "The duke wanted to ensure his family would be able to make the trip to any of his estates without the worry of hiring a team when they stopped to change horses."

"His Grace is a fortunate man."

O'Malley's gaze met the viscount's. "His Grace takes care of family."

William wasn't sure if he deserved to be considered part of the duke's family after he'd withheld pertinent information from his cousin. The need to warn his wife overrode that worry.

"I'll be speaking to the innkeeper for ye on the duke's behalf. He'll see that yer horse is well cared for until ye return."

The viscount held out his hand to O'Malley. The man shook it as he said, "I'll be changing me horse as well."

William was glad to have Sean O'Malley at his back. "Thank you. I'll let your brother and cousin know to expect you."

They parted company shortly thereafter. Although he hated to leave Maximus behind, he knew it was best. Settling into the gelding's easy cadence, they made good time, arriving at Chattsworth Manor a few hours later.

Knowing there wasn't a stable lad waiting to attend to his mount, the viscount followed the drive around to the back of the manor. Shock had him staring at the once dilapidated stable. He dismounted and led the gelding over to his temporary home. Someone had recently made repairs...but who? And where did they find the materials or coin to do so?

He opened the door and froze. The inside had been put to rights. The stalls had been repaired, tools hung in their proper places, and the tack he rarely used had been cleaned. Shame filled him remembering he hadn't thought to take care of that chore before he left. He only used the one stall. Four horses took up the newly repaired stalls, leaving two empty and waiting.

The viscount took care of his mount, settling him into one of the stalls with the promised feed and handful of oats. "Thank you for bringing me the rest of the way." The horse lifted his head and nodded as if to acknowledge the viscount's thanks.

Walking through to one of the side doors, he let himself out. Chilled, but not ready to change into the dry clothes he carried in the small traveling bag just yet, he headed to the outside entrance to the library. "Bloody hell!" he tried the doors again. "Locked!"

Stomping around to the kitchen door, he found it, too, was locked. Instead of walking around to the front, he banged on the door, knowing Mrs. Romney would be in the kitchen at this hour.

The door swung open. He was greeted by warmth, and the scent of freshly baked bread, and if he was not mistaken, Mrs. Romney's meat pies.

Seamus Flaherty stepped back from the doorway. "Yer lordship. We didn't expect ye."

Without preamble, William asked, "Have you heard? Does she know?"

Flaherty's expression hardened. "Is that why ye're here? To apologize?"

Taken aback by the rebuke from one of the duke's guard, anger boiled inside him. It took all of his control not to take a swing at the man. "I only just learned of the slander against my wife late last night. I rode straight through to get here."

"Who's banging on her ladyship's back door?" Michael O'Malley asked. He stopped to stare at the viscount. "So 'tis his lordship come to apologize."

The viscount curled his hands into fists at his sides and pushed his way into the kitchen. "I was just explaining—why the devil should I explain anything to either of you?" he demanded. "I don't answer to you. You are here to protect my wife, nothing more."

"That's where ye'd be wrong, yer lordship," Flaherty corrected him. "We answer to the duke, and Lady Calliope."

"Where is my wife?"

Mrs. Romney stopped and stared. "Your lordship! Have you come to ap—"

"If anyone needs to apologize, it will be the duke's guard and you," he grumbled. "I do not owe the lot of you an explanation. This is my home."

His cook nodded vigorously.

"I repeat, where is my wife?"

Mrs. Romney grabbed hold of her apron and twisted it in her hands. "She's resting abovestairs."

Worry hit him hard. "Is she unwell? Has the physician been summoned?"

The duke's guard exchanged a look but didn't respond.

Mrs. Romney looked away.

The viscount drew in a deep breath to calm his racing heart and burst of anger that demanded to be set free. "I shall deal with the three of you later."

Stalking from the kitchen, he took the quickest route—the servants' back staircase to the second floor. He surprised the young woman coming out of the bedchamber adjacent to his.

"Your lordship! We didn't expect you."

He clenched his jaw to keep from shouting. She looked familiar. Had he seen her at Wyndmere Hall? When he was certain he was in control of his temper, he asked, "Has the physician been summoned?"

"Physician? Is someone ill?"

Finished with unanswered questions and being questioned in his own blasted home, the viscount stepped around the woman and opened the door.

The worn draperies were pulled closed. For some reason, the

darkness bothered him until he noticed Calliope laying on her bed. Drawn to her, he walked slowly toward the bed and stopped when he noticed she was curled into a ball. *Were those tears on her cheeks?* God in Heaven, he would find out who placed that bloody wager and call him out!

Hands fisted at his sides, the viscount turned around and left as quietly as he'd entered his wife's bedchamber.

It was time for some answers to his bloody questions!

He found not one, but two O'Malleys—Michael and Sean, and one Flaherty in his kitchen...and no sign of Mrs. Romney or Mrs. Meadowsweet, Hargrave or MacReedy. *Where were his servants?*

Before he could put the question to the men, Sean O'Malley spoke. "I've filled me brother and cousin in. They've something to say to yer lordship."

"We heard that 'twas yer lordship that started the ugly rumors about her ladyship."

William glared at Flaherty. "And you believed it of me?"

"'Tis the truth I didn't even stop to consider ye hadn't said it. When me temper is up, me brain takes a bit of time to catch up to it."

William swallowed the chuckle at the man's words. He'd often suffered from the same when angered. Not wanting to let the man off that easily, he turned to O'Malley and asked, "What about you?"

Michael O'Malley shrugged. "What Flaherty said holds for me as well."

He sighed. Best to let that go for now. "Where did you hear the rumor?"

"In the village, picking up supplies for Mrs. Romney," Seamus Flaherty told him.

"Meeting with one of yer tenant farmers," Michael O'Malley added.

William had to be careful or he was going to reach for the closest man's neck and start squeezing. Drawing in a calming breath, he asked, "Did you tell them it was an out and out lie?"

Flaherty snorted to cover the laugh that escaped. He cleared his throat. "Apparently me cousin had words of a sort with yer tenant."

"Did he?"

O'Malley shuffled his feet. "I didn't mean to clip the man in the jaw."

"Didn't ye now," Michael's brother asked.

"I didn't, Sean. Ye know me. Me temper is fierce. Flaherty's is nothing compared to mine."

Sean looked at the viscount. "I'm afraid 'tis true. Ye won't want to be taking Michael with ye, if ye'll be needing a clear-headed man beside ye."

"Now that's not true," Michael said.

"Isn't it?" When no one answered the viscount's question, Flaherty's snort of laughter had the O'Malleys joining in.

"What have ye done to curtail the gossip?" Sean wanted to know.

"With only the two of us working alongside MacReedy, there hasn't been time," Flaherty answered.

"Did ye notice the repairs to yer barn?" O'Malley asked.

William nodded. "I'm grateful."

"Something has to be done, but we need more mouths to spread the truth," Sean O'Malley told his kin.

"I'm thinking we could follow the duke's example," Flaherty suggested. "Remember how his servants and everyone staying at Wyndmere Hall took turns going to the village?"

Michael nodded. "They quickly turned the tide, when every-one realized Lady Aurelia and the earl had the duke confirming their innocence."

"We don't have the same number of servants here," William reminded the men.

"But ye have tenant farmers," O'Malley reminded him.

"Didn't you punch one of them?" the viscount asked.

"Half-heartedly," Flaherty reminded him, standing up for his cousin. "Michael didn't put his full weight behind it. I'm thinking it doesn't count."

William shook his head. The men looked as if they believed it did not count. "Who was it, by the by?"

Flaherty sighed. "'Twas Peters."

The viscount recalled the man was prone to spreading tales without ascertaining the truth. "I'll speak to my wife. I think if the two of us speak to our people and they see that we are of a mind, they will stand behind us."

The duke's guard murmured between themselves for a few moments before agreeing to the viscount's plan.

"Thank you, men. I know you have little reason to believe me after the way I acted at Wyndmere Hall. I was overwhelmed by what happened and knew I could not afford to feed those already depending on me. If Calliope is willing to give me a second chance, I hope you will, too."

His heartfelt words reached the men. One by one, they pledged to do their utmost to help the viscount in his quest to right the wrong that had been done to his wife, while they continued to lend their backs wherever needed.

Now, if only the conversation with his wife would go as smoothly.

CHAPTER TWENTY-FOUR

C OVENTRY THANKED KING as they parted company. The information his contact at the Bow Street Runners confirmed what he'd suspected. Although there were no initials next to the wager in White's betting book—a policy most everyone followed, he and King had come up with the same name as to who the culprit was.

A man whose past was tied to the duke's older wastrel of a brother. A man who spent his time in the very bowels of London. One who made a tidy sum off unsuspecting young bucks looking to try their luck in London's underbelly. The same man suspected as the last man to see Earl Chattsworth alive.

Chellenham.

King sent one of his men to deliver his findings to the duke in person. Coventry would make the trip to Chattsworth Manor to do the same.

The hackney driver pulled to a stop outside of Coventry's building. He stepped down and heard a shrill whistle. He turned in time to avoid being knocked unconscious by the club his attacker wielded. Though he tried to see who'd alerted him to the attack, the man was a blur of movement as he swept past Coventry, tackling the thug before he escaped.

Turning his head to see out of his eye, Coventry watched James Garahan deliver one last blow, subduing the attacker.

"I owe you, Garahan."

The duke's man disagreed. "Nay. We work for His Grace. Me family has adopted ye. Best get used to having one of us—or all of us, guarding yer back."

The driver had disappeared as soon as the attacker made his move but reappeared with the constable in tow. "Looked like you had help, my lord. So I fetched the constable to take that one off your hands." He pointed to the man Garahan still held by his collar.

"Thank you for your foresight," Coventry replied.

The constable frowned, "Aren't you the duke's man-of-affairs?"

Coventry nodded.

"Seems trouble still follows the duke, and anyone acquainted with him."

Neither Garahan nor Coventry disagreed.

After the constable left with his prisoner, Garahan remarked, "I was waiting for ye to arrive."

"Is there a problem?"

"Nay, me replacement arrived, and I'm off to Chattsworth Manor."

Coventry smiled. "As it happens, I am on my way there myself and would appreciate the company on the ride."

Garahan shook his head. "I'll meet ye there, but I prefer making me way on horseback."

Coventry laughed. "My favorite way to travel."

They were on their way to Sussex an hour later.

CALLIOPE'S LOVELY MOUTH parted as she gasped in surprise. "William?"

He strode toward her, noting she was as pale as milk and looked as if the rest hadn't done her a bit of good. That was about to change. He'd nearly caused the woman grievous injury. Had been forced to marry her, and then left her. Now he would begin to earn her forgiveness and make it up to her.

The duke knew what he was about. The time spent apart had put Calliope front and center in his mind. His first thought on rising and last thought before retiring was of his wife. After the letter she'd penned, he could no longer fight the fact he'd been entranced by her from the start. The only thing that held him back was her lack of fortune and his goal to marry an heiress.

"Calliope. You're tired. Come join me in the library," he held out his arm. When she slipped her arm though his, he felt her tremble. The need to soothe her filled him. He pitched his voice low as he advised, "Mrs. Romney has prepared a tea tray for us."

"Tea would be lovely, thank you."

He opened the door for her and escorted her to the deep green settee across from the fireplace. The fire burned brightly, lending warmth to the room. Taking his time, he eased his arm free and took her hand, seating her before joining her.

"I understand you are partial to Mrs. Romney's teacakes." He placed two on a small plate and handed it to her. "Would you mind pouring?"

"Not at all." She filled his teacup and added a bit of sugar.

That she remembered after only sharing tea with him less than a handful of times spoke volumes. Warmth filled him. *She remembered how he liked his tea.* He vowed to go slowly and lay the groundwork for what he hoped would be a lasting friendship that could blossom into so much more.

He watched her add a splash of cream to her cup and take a dainty sip. Looking around the room, he noted the high polish on the floors and wood furniture. The drapes and rugs appeared to have recently been cleaned. "Where did you find the money to hire on extra help?"

She set her teacup on the table and folded her hands at her waist. *Was she afraid of him?* Needing the answer, he urged, "It would have cost more than I left in the household fund to hire on servants."

"I didn't use any household money."

"How do you explain this?" He swept his hand indicating the room. "From the entryway to the upstairs bedchambers. It had to have taken an army of servants to accomplish the task."

She shrugged.

He would not accept a non-verbal response. He needed to know how she managed the feat of bringing Chattsworth Manor slowly back to life. "I am not angry," he reassured her. "But I need to know so I can properly thank whoever is responsible."

She slowly smiled. "If one puts one's back into it, any task can be accomplished."

"You cannot expect me to believe you had a hand in cleaning our home."

She shrugged again.

"Calliope..."

"William."

Their gazes met and held, and a fleeting glimpse of pride filled hers. She blinked and it was gone. "Do you trust me?"

She countered, "Do you trust me?"

He sighed. This was not the homecoming he'd envisioned. Why were they having tea and a difficult conversation? Why wasn't she crying in his arms over the vicious rumors circulating among the *ton* and in their village?

He cleared his throat. "I do trust you, Calliope. I just cannot fathom how such was possible. Won't you trust me enough to tell me?"

She sighed. "I am no stranger to hard work. I spent most of my life as the poor relation no one wanted, shuttled from relation to relation, forced to work as a servant in their homes."

"But you're the daughter of an earl!"

"Who died without male issue, so the earldom and all that was entailed along with it went to my uncle."

"How long did you live with your uncle?"

She sighed and took so long to answer, he was afraid she

wouldn't. Finally, she said, "As long as it took to pack a few of our dresses and leave."

"You and your mother?"

Tears filled her eyes. She blinked them away. "Yes."

He reached out a hand to her, and she grabbed hold of it. "Calliope. I am deeply sorry for the trials you faced after your father died."

She sniffed and he moved closer. "Mother didn't last long after that. I think her heart simply broke with missing my father."

He gathered her close to his side and urged her to lean against him. Her small sigh was the first hint she'd given him of acceptance. Mayhap he would be able to salvage their marriage.

Enjoying the moment, holding his wife against him, he watched the flames lick the logs as his eyes grew heavier.

CALLIOPE FELT HIS body relax as sleep claimed him. Daring a peek, she marveled at the strength the viscount held in check. She knew him capable of holding his own against the duke's guard...she had seen his bruises and knew he'd landed a few solid jabs of his own. Unable to keep from memorizing the line of his jaw by touch, she brushed her fingertips on his chin. The dark whiskers on his face were surprisingly stiff.

After another glance to ensure he slept on, she touched her index finger to the cleft in his chin. "So beautiful," she whispered as she brushed a strand of dark chestnut hair off his long eyelashes.

"Handsome," came the deep reply.

She jolted, but before she could leap to her feet, he had a hold of her. "I didn't mean to startle you, my dear."

My dear?

"Don't let me interrupt." His smile was wicked as he leaned close and whispered, "I believe you were about to kiss me."

Her gasp was audible.

His chuckle reverberated through his broad chest, sending shockwaves of emotion she'd never experienced before sweeping through her.

Their eyes met and he leaned closer. "Kiss me, lovely Calliope."

Her lips parted of their own volition and his lips claimed hers. The kiss consumed her. She slid her hands around his neck to hang on as he took the kiss deeper, plundering, demanding her response.

Something moved deep inside. She remembered her first kiss—shared with the viscount the day they wed.

"Calliope, you fill my senses until I'm mad for you."

She wasn't certain what he meant by that but was afraid to ask him. So new were the feelings he'd aroused in her.

The look in his eyes changed to something darker, desperate, dangerous.

She eased back and placed her hand to his chest, stopping him.

He collected himself and pulled her against him once more. "I'd best not kiss you again until you answer the rest of my questions."

"Questions?"

He nodded. "I came as soon as I heard."

"Heard what?"

He tightened his hold on her. "The false, ugly rumors. I hope you haven't heard them, because—"

She looked away from him. "I have."

He touched the tip of his finger to her chin and gently urged her to look at him. "I will find out who is behind these falsehoods and make them pay."

"Don't do anything that would further bring censure to your good name, William."

His surprise was evident. Did he not believe her? He'd said he trusted her. "You would be concerned about me?"

She had to trust him with the truth. He was bound to leave no matter what she said. A few kisses do not a marriage make...especially when they were not truly wed in the eyes of the church. "The duke forced you to marry me. I knew you were angry, but you gave me the protection of your name, in spite of how you felt about me."

"Calliope, I—"

"Please," she rasped, "let me finish."

He nodded.

"The duke sent you on an errand to London, and you've been working for him since the day you left Wyndmere Hall. I cannot give you back your name unless you set me aside."

His jaw clenched, but he did not speak.

"I will not try to stop you or stand in your way if an annulment is what you seek."

"Is that what you want, Calliope? An annulment?"

His anger added a sharp edge to his words and, for the first time, she felt uneasy in his presence. Would he strike out at her as she was accustomed to when living with her cousin?

The viscount closed his eyes and slowly opened them. "I would never do anything to hurt you."

"I never said—"

"Ah, but your eyes speak volumes."

She stared down at her hands. Again, he tipped her chin up so he could look into her eyes. "Do not be afraid of me, Calliope. It wounds me."

"I shall do my best not to. Then you do not wish an annulment either?"

He pulled her against him until she could feel the rapid beat of his heart. Was he afraid? Her heart raced when she feared something.

"I do not."

"Then why are you here earlier than expected? Does your cousin have anything to do with your being here?"

"Marcus?"

"Yes. He arrived unexpectedly and mistook me for a newly hired servant." Remembering the encounter and the way it made her feel had her indignation growing.

Her husband's eyes narrowed. "I did ask if he was going to be heading this way if he would stop in and—"

"Check up on me? See that I was treating your staff well?"

"Nothing of the sort."

"You sent him here knowing of his penchant for trifling with servants?"

He raked a hand through his hair until it stood on end. "I rather thought he would be a help, not a hindrance. I apologize for not alerting you to the fact that he would drop by. In my defense, I had no idea when—or if he would."

"But you asked him to."

"Of course, I was worried about you knowing the state of my home...which has changed drastically thanks to you."

"And Mary Kate, Seamus, Michael, and your staff."

"I am beyond pleased that you have taken an interest in our home, and working with our staff, but I do not want you to overexert yourself on my behalf."

"It is our home, is it not?"

"Yes."

"And you are pleased with what you've seen?"

"Beyond pleased."

"That is a relief. I was worried you would be vexed with me. I did not ask your permission but hoped you would understand my need to help."

"Thank you, Calliope. For caring enough to give so unselfish-ly."

She looked into his eyes and saw the truth of his words. "You are more than welcome."

"I am truly sorry my cousin acted in such a manner. He will have much to apologize for. I shall see to it that he does."

She nodded. Her husband was obviously close to his cousin. An apology would go a long way toward smoothing over the disturbing situation. Now that she had his attention, she asked, "Are you ready to tell me why you are here earlier than expected?"

He mumbled something she could not quite make out. "What did you say?"

"I came to protect you."

Her eyes sought his. When their gazes met, they held steady. "Protect me? From whom?"

"Whomever it was that placed that blasted wager in White's betting book that started this vicious rumor."

Aghast, she asked, "Someone wagered on your honor?" She'd never imagined anyone would do so.

"And yours," he told her.

"But what can be done?"

"What I told you before. I intend to uncover whoever it was and make him pay!"

"Please, can you not just forget it? I am sure it will pass, given enough time."

The incredulous look on his face had her guessing he could not. "I do not want you to jeopardize your family name on my account."

"You. Are. My. Wife!"

"In name only, and that can easily be changed, if you wish it."

"I just told you I did not *wish it*, as you so aptly put it."

Confused more than ever, she asked, "What do you want?"

"You, Calliope. I want you." When she remained silent, he asked, "What do you want?"

She reached for his hand and dug deep for the courage to tell him what was in her heart. "You, William."

"Me?" he asked, as if he hadn't heard her.

"You."

"Despite the fact I have little or no coin to keep you in the manner in which you are accustomed?"

She laughed, a light and lilting sound. "You have been doing just that from the moment I arrived at your home."

"But you just finished telling me you've been cleaning and working like one of the servants."

"Did you not hear me tell you that was how I lived most of

my life?"

"I thought it an exaggeration."

"You thought wrong."

"You shall not have to work until you're worn out, Calliope. I shall do my best to find a way to refill my family's coffers and help see that our tenant farmers have a bountiful harvest, and—"

"Pension off your staff?"

"What makes you say that?"

"I am a good listener and Mrs. Meadowsweet and Hargrave have sung your praises until I hear them in my sleep."

He tried to hold back the smile but could not. "They've been with my family as long as I can remember. They deserve whatever I can do to see that their years of service are repaid."

Calliope agreed with him, then shared what she hoped would help take care of the first obstacle he felt obliged to remove. "Persephone told Aurelia when she and Edward were the subject of such slanderous lies that people will say what they will. It is how we react to those lies that shows our true character."

"The duchess is a gracious woman of keen intelligence."

"And quite crafty. Once everyone put their heads together, we were able to stem the tide of the gossip in the village near Wyndmere Hall."

"What about the *ton?*"

"Aurelia and I spent a few months attending the rounds of entertainment. And while the earl was also in attendance, he would only dance one dance with Aurelia. Gradually, the *ton* became convinced they were telling the truth, while more and more of Jared's father's supporters rallied around them."

"Who would rally around you?"

"If I asked, Aurelia and Edward for a start."

"Would the duke and duchess?"

"If I asked it of them, but I don't intend to. Persephone is nearing the end of her confinement and does not need such a worry plaguing her."

The knock on the library door had them pause in their conversation. "Enter," he called out.

The door opened and Hargrave announced, "Captain Coventry and James Garahan here to see your lordship."

William and Calliope rose together to greet them.

"Your lordship, your ladyship," Coventry said walking toward them, while Garahan hung back.

"It is lovely to see you again, Captain Coventry, Mr. Garahan," Calliope remarked.

"And you as well," Coventry replied.

"No mister," he reminded her. "Just Garahan."

She smiled.

The viscount frowned. "What brings you to Chattsworth Manor?"

Coventry glanced at Garahan before speaking. "Trouble, your lordship."

The men swept William from the room before Calliope could protest. Whatever the trouble was, she intended to stand by her husband's side whether he wanted her to or not.

Intent on her mission to find out what trouble William was in, she rushed out of the room and nearly collided with Seamus and Michael.

"His lordship has asked that ye stay here," Flaherty advised.

"'Twill be but a moment or two and he'll return to ye," O'Malley added.

"But I want to know—"

"Ye're making this harder than it needs to be, yer ladyship," Flaherty remarked.

"His lordship will come back and tell ye what ye need to know," O'Malley told her.

The duke's guard were steadfast in their orders and would not budge, nor would they let her.

Calliope turned around and walked back into the library and closed the door with those five words echoing in her aching head...*what ye need to know*. "Botheration!" she grumbled. "I need to know everything!"

CHAPTER TWENTY-FIVE

"**I** HAVE TO return to London."

"You've only just arrived," Calliope whispered.

The turmoil in his gaze tore at her conviction not to tell him more of what was in her heart until she had the courage to do so.

His handsome face, so dear, so familiar to her tore that conviction to shreds. She'd dreamed of him every night since that dark day he'd turned his back on her. Calliope understood why he left and vowed to give him his freedom. A half-hour ago, he'd told her he didn't want an annulment. Now he was poised to leave her again! How could she bear it?

"Please tell me why," she begged.

In the quiet of the library, they were alone again. He reached for her hands. The strength in his grasp suffused her. She must be strong for him—stronger than she'd already striven to be.

"To protect you. I ask that you trust me, my love."

Love? The endearment was a balm to her frayed nerves and aching heart. How could she refuse the man she'd come to love? She met his gaze and gave her promise. "I trust you, but that doesn't mean I am not worried for whatever danger lay ahead."

He drew her close, wrapping her in his embrace. "I will do everything in my power to protect you—even if it means my life."

She jolted. "You will not risk your life for me. I would have you here with me! Send someone else in your place. Don't go, William," she pleaded.

His heart pounded a furious beat as he bent his head and claimed her lips in a kiss that stole her senses. A kiss of promise, of passion, of love.

"Wait for me."

Tears threatened, but she blinked them away. She could weep later. "Come back to me."

He hesitated a heartbeat too long.

Fear for him threatened to overwhelm her. She dug deep for the will to tamp it back down. *Did the trouble threaten his life as well?* "Can you not tell me why you have to go? What is so important that you'd leave me—again?"

"There are things you do not know about me. You would not ask me to stay if you knew the whole of my situation."

She shook her head at him, but he held a finger to her lips. "Listen to me. Please?"

Calliope slowly nodded.

"My father has been missing for a year. When he disappeared, a number of the family's heirlooms—entailed to his estate, went missing." He looked away for a moment.

Was he trying to decide how much to tell her? She squeezed his hands to encourage him to continue.

The intensity of his gaze dimmed. Sorrow filled the depths of his bright blue eyes, darkening their hue. "There are those who suspect that I had something to do with—"

"No," she cried. "I will not listen to such lies. You would never have done anything to harm your father."

"You don't know me, Calliope."

She corrected him. "I know enough about you from those who have known you since you were a young boy. They've watched you grow up, told me of the way you did your best to step into your father's shoes, though news of his disappearance was rife with rumors tied to you."

His Adam's apple bobbed as he struggled with whatever he

refused to tell her. "Hargrave and Mrs. Meadowsweet are servants. As such, they have not accompanied me and my cousin, Marcus, on our forays to inns, raising a mug of ale, sweet talking any one of the pretty maids who'd served us."

His words stung as they painted a picture of a young man who was no doubt living his life to the fullest. She'd grown up watching members of her family doing the same. Not all, but one or two had then turned their attention to doing something more important with their lives than seeking their own pleasure. She had no doubt the viscount had been doing just that when he'd traveled to Wyndmere Hall to speak with the duke. He'd been working to that end while living in the duke's town house. And now…

"You will not convince me that you have been spending your time in London chasing after women when I've heard the duke's men praising the way you've stepped into the role the duke had for you."

"Not everyone seeks their bed before midnight."

"Not everyone has the duke's men guarding him—day and night."

He traced the line of her jaw with the tip of his finger. "Pretty Calliope."

She trembled at his touch. "No one's ever said that to me before."

He raised his brow at that. "No one?"

She smiled at him. "Well, there was someone."

"I knew it. What was his name?"

"Aurelia."

"Who else?"

"Phoebe."

He frowned down at her. "There must have been someone."

"Do you mean someone special in my life who wasn't a female friend?"

"Precisely."

"Lord Coddington."

Coddington! The name tore through his soul as Chellenham's words reverberated through him. He shook himself free of the vile gossip. He could not, would not believe it of her.

"Pray what did he say to you?"

She hesitated and his gut roiled. "It was the night Aurelia and her footman came to my rescue."

"Rescue? Were you in a carriage accident?"

She shook her head. "I was living with my second cousin and his wife at the time."

Was there the tiniest shred of proof Chellenham was right? "What happened?" he had to know.

"I'd sent a note to Aurelia asking for her help. I couldn't live one more day with the beatings."

Unconscionable! "Good God, they beat you?"

She shrugged. "I thought they'd broken my jaw when they hit me with the fireplace poker. Aurelia and her footman arrived at the same time—she'd sent him to bring the constable."

"What about Lord Coddington."

"He arrived by the time the constable and his men were about to take my cousin and his wife into his custody."

"I see." Nothing out of the ordinary with her story so far, he reasoned. "Then what happened."

"He apologized for not heeding his niece's fear for my safety. He promised I would never be beaten again and vowed to open his home to me."

"Did you go with him?"

"Yes, and Aurelia. He sent for his physician. They were concerned that my jaw had been broken and worried about a possible concussion."

"My God, Calliope. How did you bear it?"

"I thought it was my lot in life after my father and then my mother died. It wasn't until I'd met Aurelia that I'd had a true friend."

"What about her uncle?" *He had to know.* He wasn't proud of the fact that he had to hear her speak of it.

"He made me laugh. He fed me kippers every morning."

"Laughter and kippers?"

"If you'd grown up without them, you'd understand how precious they were to me. No one ever took the time to see me— as a person, until Aurelia. Her uncle hadn't seen past what I strove so hard to hide, that I was a poor relation relegated to the position of servant who deserved the daily beatings I'd received."

"Until?"

She met his gaze. "Until the night he saw the truth of what I'd confided in Aurelia. Even the constable was horrified." She sighed. "I guess I looked as bad as I felt."

"I thought he told you that you were pretty," he urged.

She laughed. "The side of my face was a multitude of colors. He would smile at me at breakfast and delight in comparing the shades of purple and blue—which slowly changed to green and yellow—to that of sunrises and sunsets." Tears filled her eyes, but she didn't blink them away. "He told me I was as pretty as a sunrise and lovely as a sunset, though I knew he didn't mean it. My face was swollen and the colors were dreadful. Aurelia reluctantly let me see myself in her looking glass."

He swallowed against the lump of self-disgust lodged in his throat. A part of him had begun to believe what Chellenham had hinted at. He should have believed his first reaction, that Calliope was innocent of any wrongdoing. She had lived with adversity most of her life. Served her distant relations to earn her keep. She would never ease her way out of that difficult situation in such a way as the vicious lies suggested.

"Forgive me," he rasped, brushing a strand of honey-blonde hair from her damp eyelashes. Her eyes were the gray of a moon-dappled stream or a mist-covered pond. Gazing into them, he saw the stark truth of her words and was even more determined to protect her with his life. He'd die if it would avenge her honor. He would see that it was restored. Chellenham and all who placed wagers on the vile bet would lose.

She stood on her tiptoes, wrapped her arms about his neck

and whispered against his lips, "There's nothing to forgive, but you shall have forgiveness if it will ease your mind."

He plundered the softness of her mouth, sipped from the sweetness of her lips. "I don't deserve you, Calliope."

He pressed a kiss to her forehead, cheeks, and the tip of her nose.

She sighed and hugged him close. "I love you, William."

"Calliope."

"You don't have to love me. It's enough that you want me."

"But I—"

Her fingertip against his lips cut off his words. "It's enough for me. I never expected to be kissed by a man as handsome as you, let alone wanted—for whatever it is that men desire women for."

He groaned aloud. She had no idea her innocent words added kindling to the flame of his desire. "You are killing me, my love."

"You don't have to say endearments to ensure I will still be here when you get back. I do love you, William. I've come to know you working alongside your staff and your tenants. The protection of your name is far more than I ever thought to have. I will never do anything to bring censure to your name. You have my word."

With the strength he hadn't known he possessed, he stepped back from her and bowed. "I shall do my best to honor the gift of your love and your trust. When I return..." *Lord willing*, he prayed. "We shall continue this conversation...among other things," he promised.

"You are not riding out alone, are you?"

"Coventry and Michael O'Malley will accompany me."

"Will Mr. Garahan and the others remain here?"

He smiled at her continued use of "mister". "Garahan will remain with Flaherty. Sean O'Malley is to report to Lippincott Manor."

"The duke's changing of the guard," she murmured.

"His men are loyal, and each have special talents that can be used at any of the duke's estates."

"Even the crumbling tower in Cornwall Phoebe has told me of?"

He nodded. "Most especially Cornwall."

"Why most especially?"

He knew the men were waiting for him but couldn't bring himself to part from her just yet. "It's in a state of disrepair—"

She giggled. "Crumbling," she reminded him.

He smiled. "Indeed."

"You sound like Jared."

"My illustrious cousin," he quipped.

"He's a good man who loves his wife and family and would do his utmost to protect them," Calliope reminded him.

The faintest hint of envy swirled through him, but he was able to ignore it. Put it in its place at the back of his mind. He had duties to see to: protecting his wife's honor and upholding his family name. There was no time left to dally.

"Do not work too hard, my love."

"God go with you, William."

"Do not venture out alone," he warned.

"Remember that I love you," she reminded him.

"I shall not forget." He wanted to tell her what was in his heart, but knew she was not ready to believe him.

After he'd defeated Chellenham in a duel of honor, she would.

CHAPTER TWENTY-SIX

C ALLIOPE STOOD ON the front steps of Chattsworth Manor
watching the departure of the man she loved and his two
companions until they were specks in the distance.

"Calliope, won't you come back inside?" Mary Kate urged.
"It's frightfully chilly out here."

Calliope looked over her shoulder. "Have you packed my
bag?"

Mary Kate nodded. "Won't you reconsider and stay?"

"How can I, knowing that William races back to London to
issue a challenge to Lord Chellenham? I have to be there with
him. Can you not understand that?"

Mary Kate sighed. "I know you think you do. But is it safe?
Who will make the journey with you? You cannot go alone! I
won't allow it."

"Neither will I," a deep voice boomed from behind the wom-
en, so intent on their discussion they did not know they had an
audience.

"Mr. Garahan!" Calliope cried. "I did not see you there.

"Ye weren't meant to and for the love of God, 'tis James or
Garahan. Please pick one!"

"Er…yes, of course, James."

"Ye won't be going to London."

She took a step closer to the huge man glowering at her, put her hands on her hips and glared at him. "Oh, yes, I will."

"Not if we lock ye in yer bedchamber, yer ladyship," Seamus Flaherty shouted as he rounded the side of the house and walked toward where the group stood.

"You do not have the authority to do any such thing."

"Well now, ye see, his lordship thought it necessary if ye took it in yer head to follow after him."

"You wouldn't dare," she challenged Flaherty.

He grinned. "Ah, James, isn't it grand to be working for the duke's family?"

"Aye," Garahan replied. "Strong, stubborn women...reminds me of home."

Their shared laughter irritated the life out of Calliope. She was about to speak when she decided it might be best to hold her tongue while she worked out an escape plan. She had to leave soon or she wouldn't arrive in London in time.

An idea formed. She visibly shivered. "You're right, Mary Kate. It is bitter cold. Let's go back inside."

Garahan watched Mary Kate's every movement like a hawk, delighting Calliope. Whatever she decided to do, if Mary Kate came with her, she hoped Garahan would be the one to follow them.

"Shall I ask Mrs. Romney about tea?"

"Yes, thank you. Would you mind waiting for it and bringing it to my bedchamber?" That ought to keep the meddling Irishmen from following her every move.

"Not at all," her maid replied. "I'll see if there are any of your favorite teacakes left."

"Thank you." Calliope waited while Flaherty opened the door. When he would have followed Mary Kate to the kitchen, she called his name. "Seamus, may I ask you a favor?"

"Of course, yer ladyship." He nodded to Garahan who followed Mary Kate. "What can I do for ye?"

"Please don't try to stop me from leaving," she pleaded. "I cannot let him go alone, knowing what he plans to do. It's my honor he'll be fighting for. I'm not worth it, Seamus. Please don't try to stop me."

Seamus clenched his jaw and drew in a deep breath. "I cannot let ye go. I gave me word to yer husband. He trusts me. I will not break that trust. Yer life is in me hands."

His eyes gave voice to what was in his heart. "Ye are most definitely worth fighting for, yer ladyship. Never doubt it. Let his lordship prove it ye."

Tears gathered and fell. She ignored them and thanked Flaherty for listening before turning to go up the staircase to her bedchamber.

Garahan strode down the hallway to his cousin's side. "What now?" he demanded.

"She wants me to let her go to London."

"His lordship suspected she would. What did ye tell her."

"No. What else?" Flaherty asked.

"Well, ye could have said ye'd think about it."

"She's worked so hard here bringing the shine back to his lordship's home and hope to his people."

Garahan's gaze met his. "Ye have feelings for Lady Calliope." It wasn't a question.

"Aye. But I'll never act on them."

"See that ye don't."

"Ye know how fast the mail coach travels," Flaherty remarked, changing the subject.

"Aye. What of it?"

"If we were to convince her ladyship and her maid to take the duke's carriage, we could hitch two more horses for a total of six pulling the carriage."

"And travel faster," Garahan said slowly. "Might be something to consider."

"Ye know she'll try to sneak out past our guard, don't ye?"

"I know it," Garahan agreed. "But we gave our word."

"We also told his lordship that if she was insistent on going, we'd appear to let her go and follow along behind her," Flaherty reminded his cousin.

"But it's the dead of winter and not weather a lady should be traveling in unless it's inside of a carriage."

"Agreed. Let's ask Mrs. Romney to prepare some bread and maybe one or two of her meat pies for our journey to London."

"Are ye mad, Seamus?"

His cousin laughed, tugging on Garahan's arm to get him moving. "That I must be."

"How do you think to get past the duke's guard without their notice?" Mary Kate asked.

"I'm still working that out in my mind," Calliope answered. "Do you think we should pack some of Persephone's healing salve and some bandages?"

"It's always good to be prepared," her maid replied.

"I wonder if Mrs. Romney would pack a light meal for us. She's awfully fond of my husband."

"All of his staff is," Mary Kate stated. "Maybe we should enlist MacReedy and Hargrave to help elude the duke's men."

"Wouldn't it be better if we had one of them traveling with us for protection? Then my husband might not be as angry with me."

Mary Kate shook her head. "Calliope, that man will be furious when he sees you, knowing that you'd traveled the distance against his wishes in the middle of winter."

"Mmmm...you might be right. Did you ask Sean to deliver my message to Aurelia?"

"Yes. He should arrive at Lippincott Manor shortly."

"All we need to do is wait for Seamus and James to go on their rounds. Then we can make our escape."

"Um...Calliope?"

"Something wrong?"

"Just one tiny thing," her maid answered. "I've never ridden a horse."

Calliope stared at her maid for several moments before she started to laugh. Mary Kate joined in and, before long, they had tears in their eyes and sounded like a pair of loons.

"Did ye hear that?" Seamus asked, from the other side of the viscount's closed bedroom door.

"Aye. They'll have to take the carriage. That fool maid would never try to ride a horse just to accompany Lady Calliope."

"Ye haven't been here, James. She's loyal to the bone to her ladyship. She'd ride a lion if Lady Calliope asked it of her."

"The lass has come a long way since I helped her to her feet after she'd been kicked to the curb by Lady Kittrick's cook."

Flaherty motioned for Garahan to follow him out of the room. As they took the back staircase to the kitchen, he remarked, "Sounds like a story that bears repeating."

The third time Mary Kate fell out of the saddle, Calliope sighed. "I'm still new to riding a horse, but have to admit, this is not going to work."

"You cannot leave me behind!" Mary Kate wailed as she brushed straw and dirt off the back of her skirts. "I'm going with you. One way or another."

"Can you help me hitch the team?"

Mary Kate paled. "I can try."

"The lass is going to need to sit on a pillow for a week," Flaherty observed from his position behind one of the empty horse stalls.

"She's afraid of horses," Garahan rasped. "The next time she falls, she's sure to break her neck. Have ye told MacReedy and Hargrave we'll be driving them to London?"

"Aye, Seamus. I have. Hargrave wished us Godspeed, while MacReedy reminded me to keep our powder dry."

"Let's go before they manage to leave without us," Flaherty grumbled. "Lady Calliope!"

She spun around, hand to her heart. "Seamus! James? What are you doing here?"

They looked at one another and then stared at the two women. "We're taking yer ladyship and Miss Mary Kate to London."

Calliope's mouth opened and closed, but not one word came

out.

Flaherty nodded. "Well, don't just stand there, climb aboard, while Garahan takes the saddles off yer beasts and puts them to bed."

Calliope found her voice, proclaiming, "I can hitch the team for you."

"Sure and that would be grand, but I'll see to the chore, if it's all the same to ye."

"I want to help, too," Mary Kate told him.

"Will ye help me change her ladyship's mind and stay here?" Flaherty asked.

The maid shook her head.

"Then ye'd best be climbing aboard the carriage with her and be quick about it. With luck, we may reach London before morning."

CHAPTER TWENTY-SEVEN

J ENKINS GREETED THE viscount when he arrived at the duke's
London town house.

"Welcome back, your lordship."

"Thank you, Jenkins." He did not want to be rude, but time
was of the essence. He needed to pay Chellenham a visit and
demand the man meet him on the field of honor.

"Have you heard?" Jenkins asked.

The viscount met the butler's intense gaze and asked, "About
the blasted wager at White's? Yes."

A sound had Jenkins looking past the viscount as Coventry
and Michael O'Malley entered behind him.

Coventry asked, "Has the challenge been accepted?"

"I haven't had the chance to challenge Chellenham yet," the
viscount grumbled. "How the devil could he possibly accept it?"

Jenkins looked at the duke's man-of-affairs and shook his
head.

William knew then there was more to the bad news than
Coventry had divulged. "What didn't you tell me, Coventry?"

The man's green eye met his gaze and held it. "It appears we
did not arrive in time for you to challenge Chellenham."

"What reason could the man have for not accepting my challenge?"

"He's already meeting someone else at dawn," Coventry

replied.

"And you knew this before we left Sussex?" William could not believe it! Why wouldn't Coventry confide in him?

"I knew it was a possibility. I did not know if the challenge would be issued or accepted."

"Who challenged Chellenham?"

Coventry's gaze met his, as if asking him to figure it out for himself. Going over the bets placed, his gut churned...and he knew without a doubt. "Coddington!"

"Lady Aurelia's uncle?" Michael O'Malley asked. "What does he have to do with ye marrying Lady Calliope by Special License?"

"The first part of the bet denied Lady Calliope had been in need of rescue," Coventry explained.

William's gut stopped roiling and iced over. The chill had him fighting the tremors of anger surging through him. He believed Calliope, but more, trusted she'd told him the truth. Chellenham would pay. "Coddington's not a young man."

"Neither is Chellenham," Coventry added.

"What is yer plan, yer lordship?" O'Malley asked as Rory and Dillon Flaherty filed into the entryway.

The viscount studied O'Malley and his cousins, ranged shoulder to shoulder, and silently thanked the duke for hiring the loyal men. Men who would guard your back—and guard your extended family if asked.

"When and where will they meet?"

"Tomorrow at dawn," Coventry disclosed. "Chalk Farm."

"Who is Coddington's second?" William needed to know. He would stand at the ready if Aurelia's uncle—Calliope's benefactor, needed his support.

Coventry looked pained. "Edward."

"You're not serious." The viscount could not believe what he was hearing. How had things escalated to such an extreme from one man's utterance...most probably while foxed at the time?

Coventry met his gaze. "He and Lady Aurelia should be arriving any time."

William could not believe the tangled web he'd been caught in. Extended family, wife-in-name-only, wrapped in strands of envy choking him. He had to set this right. "Coventry, might I have a word?"

The duke's guard was listening intently but, at Coventry's nod, silently filed out to man their posts.

Jenkins moved forward. "Captain Coventry. Good to see you've returned." Jenkins helped them out of their greatcoats and accepted their gloves and the viscount's top hat.

William speculated why Coventry never wore a hat, mayhap it interfered with his line of sight.

"Thank you, Jenkins." The viscount waited until Jenkins glanced his way before saying, "I trust you heard that the earl and Lady Aurelia are expected tonight."

"I shall be on hand to greet them, rest assured."

He thanked the butler and followed Coventry to the duke's study. They entered and William closed the door behind him. "How can I prevent Coddington from dueling Chellenham?"

"You would deny his lordship the right to avenge Calliope's and Aurelia's honor?"

"Aurelia's? The wager and subsequent *on dit* does not concern her."

"Doesn't it?" Coventry's one-eyed gaze had William wondering what he'd missed. He'd been so consumed with protecting his wife's reputation, he never considered Lady Aurelia's. "Good God, she's Coddington's niece."

"And would once again be the subject of someone's ill-timed and vicious slander."

"I repeat. What can I do to prevent Coddington from meeting Chellenham on the field of honor?"

"Nothing."

"Maybe one of the O'Malleys could be convinced to detain the man for, oh…say the next six or eight hours."

Coventry chuckled. "They might at that, but what of your

own need to claim satisfaction?"

The viscount pulled his timepiece out of his waistcoat pocket and noted the time. "Think Chellenham will still be at White's?"

"Why don't we start at his residence? It's closer."

"You don't need to accompany me," William told the man.

"Ah, but I do. The duke would be displeased if I did not see this through."

TWENTY MINUTES LATER, they were admitted to Chellenham's town house. His butler had not wanted to admit them, but the viscount insisted, using his cousin's position as his entrée into the lord's town house.

The older man appeared, still garbed in his evening attire. He glared at Coventry but did not include the man in his greeting. "What is the meaning of this, Chattsworth?"

"An urgent matter, my lord."

"What's this? Urgent you say?"

The viscount glanced at Coventry who's green eye gleamed with anticipation. His slight nod was the signal they'd agreed upon. *Get it said, issue the challenge, and leave.* "You have insulted my wife and impugned her honor. I demand satisfaction!"

Chellenham's jaw dropped. He collected himself to demand, "You didn't challenge me the other afternoon at White's."

"You swore you did not place the wager. Now, I know that you were the one who placed the wager that started the slanderous gossip among the *ton.*"

"See here—"

"I shall have my second call on you with the details."

"No need," Coventry advised the viscount. "I am here now." To Chellenham, he said, "Chalk Farm at dawn."

Chellenham's face flushed a deep red. "Already engaged at that time."

William noted Coventry did not look away from the man. "Six o'clock then, you should have finished with your first appointment by then."

"How do you know about that? Damn your eyes, Coventry!"

"Eye, Chellenham...only have one, you know."

"You're a cold fish." Chellenham decried.

"I suppose you would know, being one yourself."

The man's mouth opened and closed twice before he thundered, "Leave at once."

William already had Coventry by the elbow, tugging him toward the door. "Tomorrow," he reminded the man. "Six o'clock!"

The viscount nodded to the hackney driver who'd waited as promised. He stepped into the carriage and waited for Coventry to climb in before asking, "Is that done?" He'd never heard of a gentleman fighting two duels of honor in a row. Two days in a row, yes, but not one right after another.

Coventry settled against the seat across from him and shrugged. "We shall be there and see what Chellenham does."

"Is Coddington a decent shot?"

Coventry slowly smiled. "An excellent shot."

"Then there will be no chance for satisfaction if he wounds Chellenham."

"There is a bright side to all of this. He could put paid to Chellenham's account."

William bristled. "Not the outcome I am hoping for. I want a chance to knock him off his feet."

"He would never accept a bare knuckle fight challenge," Coventry advised.

"One can dream, can't one?"

"What do you intend to do tomorrow?"

The viscount fell silent. His mind raced from one thought to another. "As far as which body part I plan to aim for, either his black heart or his great gullet."

Coventry's gaze met his. "Ever seen a man take a ball in the gut?"

"I have not."

"It's a slow and painful death watching a man bleed out from it."

"You've shot a man in the stomach before?"

"Nay, my time in His Majesty's Royal Navy involved cannon fire and deadly splintered spears from masts and quarterdecks."

Knowing even that small bit of Captain Coventry's past was a window into the man's time in the navy. "Yet you're here now, able to talk about it."

Coventry's green eye gleamed. "Enough about the past. Let's talk about the future—tomorrow."

William agreed, speculating, "What if we were to arrive before dawn?"

"Go on."

"Not sure what I'll do yet, but think I should be there if nothing else to support Coddington. After all, he took Calliope in after that dastard cousin and his wife beat her."

"She confided how she came to live with Aurelia and her uncle?" Coventry questioned.

The viscount nodded.

"Never say you believe the slanderous *on dit* about Coddington and your wife!"

The need to punch something nearly overwhelmed him. Drawing on his steely control, he met Coventry's gaze and growled, "I do not."

The duke's man-of-affairs nodded. "That, your lordship, is the first hurdle in our quest to clear your wife's good name."

"We?"

"Did you doubt His Grace and his brother? They would never leave Calliope or you twisting in the wind while Chellenham spouted lies and then placed a wager to profit from those lies."

"I hadn't thought past my need to avenge Calliope's honor."

The carriage came to a halt and Coventry surprised the viscount by getting out and sending the driver on his way. "Do you intend to stay the night?" He thought it a bit odd, but it was close to midnight.

Coventry grinned. "There's a happy thought, but no. I need

to speak with Earl Lippincott."

The viscount was poised to knock on the door when it swung open. "Thank God ye're here!"

He wondered why Michael O'Malley answered the door and was about to ask when the raised voices distracted him. "What's going on?"

"Difference of opinion, my lord," Jenkins replied as he stepped in front of O'Malley to take their coats.

"Sounds quite heated, Jenkins."

"I daresay it is, your lordship."

"That sounds like my wife," he ventured. "But it couldn't be. She promised to stay in Sussex."

"Believe that if it comforts, yer lordship," Michael O'Malley chimed in from where he still stood in the entryway.

"Is that my wife?" William's patience was growing thin.

When neither the butler nor O'Malley immediately answered, he strode toward the argument taking place behind closed doors. Not caring if it was rude, needing to discover if his wife had truly ignored his orders and followed him to London, he burst through the door.

"Ah, Chattsworth," Earl Lippincott effused. "Good of you to come. I appear to be outnumbered by the fairer sex."

Aurelia and Calliope stood shoulder to shoulder—a feminine wall of silken beauty. Captivated by the flush on his wife's cheeks, he walked over to stand in front of her. "My dear, have you trouble hearing?"

She tilted her head to one side, studying him. "No."

"Then why in God's name are you here?"

"Wrong question," the earl mumbled to Coventry who had entered the room behind the viscount.

"He hasn't had a chance to experience married life as yet," Coventry said in the viscount's defense. "Give him time. He'll learn."

"If you thought I wouldn't follow you, you are a very dense man."

"Warning shot fired across the bow," Coventry rasped to Edward.

The earl grinned.

"When I give an order, I expect it to be obeyed."

"Have you more than one wife?" Calliope asked.

He frowned at her. "That's a ridiculous question when I have but one...you."

She smiled and he lost his train of thought. Her pretty face was flushed a delicate rose. Her lips begged to be kissed. He nearly gave in to the need but managed to stop. He regained his composure, needing to get to the bottom of why his wife was standing before him.

A horrible thought occurred to him. "Tell me you did not travel without escort."

"Do you think I would travel all this way—arriving after dark, unescorted?"

"Her cannonball just took out his topsa'l," Coventry quipped.

Edward continued to smile at his wife's friend. "Lady Calliope has come into her own while living at Chattsworth Manor. She'll make a fine viscountess."

Coventry was about to agree, when the viscount pulled his wife against him. "You will not defy me again!"

Calliope pushed out of his arms. Placing her hands on her hips, she glared at the viscount. "I shall do whatever I believe necessary to see that you don't do something so foolish as to engage in a duel without my being there to support you."

"What are you thinking? Your reputation has already been called into question. That is why I made the bloody trip back to London in the first place!"

Her hands slid to her sides and she closed the distance between them. Ignoring the others in the room, she lifted her hand to gently cup the side of William's face. "I love you and cannot imagine my life without you in it."

He grabbed her hand and pulled her roughly against him. "You've yet to have me in your life for more than a few hours,

Calliope. You don't know me."

She smiled at him. "I believe we've already had this conversation, William. I would risk your anger. I would risk my reputation to be where the man I love stands. Whether it be in the duke's study, or in the dawn mist at Chalk Farm."

Edward urged his wife to follow him. Coventry followed and made certain to close the doors behind him.

"Calliope, I cannot bear the thought of what you will face if I do not avenge your honor."

"Public censure?" she asked. "I have lived with that most of my life. Polite society frowns upon poor relations and tends to take the side of the relatives who must support them."

"You do not deserve anyone's censure."

"I have survived that and more at my cousin's hands...until Aurelia's uncle took me in and treated me as if I were Aurelia's sister."

The viscount watched tears fill her soft gray eyes and spill over. Moved, needing to do something to ease her sorrow, he wiped them away and held her to his heart. "You know Lord Coddington challenged Chellenham."

He felt her nod against his chest but couldn't quite make out what she murmured. "What did you say?"

She leaned back and stared up at him. Her tear-stained face and red-rimmed eyes had him maintaining his stance. He would avenge her, whether she wanted him to or not.

"Aurelia and Edward told me when Mary Kate and I arrived."

Curiosity piqued, worried because he'd seen how she'd handled a horse just a few short weeks prior, he asked, "Tell me you did not ride here on horseback."

Instead of the lilting laughter he remembered, she snorted out a laugh. Surprised, he watched the play of emotions across her face. Sorrow changed to delight. "You remember correctly. Mary Kate has never ridden a horse. The third time she fell off, Seamus and James offered to take us in the carriage."

He sighed aloud. It had been one of the contingency plans

he'd discussed with the men left to guard his wife. "Are they still here?"

"Of course. I believe they're holding a meeting about tomorrow."

He hoped they didn't intend to interfere. "Tomorrow?"

"I think they plan to be on hand in case Aurelia's uncle has need of them."

He frowned. "I see they do not trust Chellenham either."

"Sean O'Malley worked for him before the duke hired him as part of his personal guard."

"And his brothers and cousins?"

Calliope replied, "Were spread out between Sussex and London and delighted at the chance to work together for the duke."

He traced the line of her jaw and stared at her mouth before lifting his gaze to meet hers. "I'm glad you did not attempt to ride alone."

"I had planned to come with Mary Kate."

He clenched his jaw to keep from saying something inflammatory.

"You're not still vexed with me? You've forgiven me?"

The hope in her gaze was his undoing. "I cannot stay mad at you, love." He lowered his head and pressed his lips to hers. Her soft sigh and sweet mouth were a balm to his worry.

She slipped her arms about his neck. "I cannot lose you, William."

He slid his hand down her spine to her waist, pulling her flush against him. "Have faith in me, Calliope."

Her heart kept time with his as he searched her face for the answer to the question he'd yet to ask. Lifting to her toes, she pressed her lips to his. "Make me yours, William."

"Calliope—I have to be on the field in a few hours."

"I won't beg you."

"Ah, sweet, but your eyes do." He dipped his head and plundered her lips, taking all that she offered.

She melted against him and he was lost. Lifting her into his arms, he stalked to the door. Shifting her in his arms, he locked it, and walked back over to the settee. As if she were fragile, he carefully placed her on it. "Be sure, Calliope. Once done, it cannot be undone."

She reached for his hand. "I am sure."

Never taking his gaze from hers, he removed his frockcoat and waistcoat. "I will treasure this moment and the gift of your love always." He pulled her close, inhaling the elusive scent that had haunted his dreams—sun-drenched roses.

He reached behind her to unbutton the back of her gown. Easing her back, intending to pull the dress over her head, he paused. The apprehension in her eyes was quickly replaced with a heady mix of passion-laced trust. Holding that trust to his heart, and with a gentleness he'd never sought to use before, he undressed her with care.

Calliope traced the width of his shoulders and the breadth of his broad chest with the tips of her fingers. He shuddered at her touch, burning for her. Afraid the leash he held on his desire would snap, he yanked back control. He needed to show her he valued the gift of her virtue. The vicious rumors the whole of society believed were untrue.

He wooed his innocent bride with whispered words of praise and feather-soft caresses.

Slowly at first, William showed his wife what was in his heart. She trembled in his arms—not from fear, but from desire. He urged her to trust he wouldn't willingly hurt her. "Look at me, my love,"

Her eyes were drenched with wonder, brimming with tears. "I promise to stop if you ask it of me."

She nodded.

"Do you understand that there will be pain our first time together?"

Again, she nodded, but he needed her to tell him. "Do you want me to stop?"

Tugging on his neck to bring him closer, she traced a line of hesitant kisses along his collarbone.

"Calliope," he groaned in pain. The wait was killing him.

"No."

He froze and tilted her face to look deep into her eyes. "No don't continue, or no, don't stop."

She smiled as she slid her hands from his shoulders to his waist and back again. "Don't stop."

Their passion flared until it was a living, breathing entity. Whispered words of praise were followed by soft sighs and tangled limbs. He wanted Calliope, but more—he loved her.

They moved together as one, and he finally spoke the words he'd wanted to say, words he knew she longed to hear. "I love you, Calliope."

As the night waned, he carried her to the bedchamber where she'd left her bag earlier. With what little time they had left, he pulled her close, listening to her soft sighs as she fell asleep in his arms.

Beyond tired, energized by making Calliope his wife—he let his thoughts drift forward. He knew what he had to do. In a few hours' time, Chellenham and Coddington were in for a surprise.

CHAPTER TWENTY-EIGHT

V ISCOUNT CHATTSWORTH DISMOUNTED and waited for Coventry to do the same. "Do you think Coddington and Chellenham are already here?"

The two men tethered their horses to low hanging branches and walked toward the mist-shrouded field where two men would duel against the same man!

In a quarter of an hour, Lord Phineas Coddington would stand on the field of honor to prove he had not dishonored Lady Calliope—now Viscountess Chattsworth.

A short time later, Viscount Chattsworth would take to the field to prove he had not dishonored Lady Calliope, nor had he anticipated their wedding vows.

"Chellenham will not be victorious," William vowed.

"Did you wish to speak to Coddington before he takes the field?"

The viscount shook his head.

"Ah, so you are here to support Coddington and his niece, your very distant cousin by marriage, Lady Aurelia Lippincott."

"I will do whatever I deem necessary." He was not about to tell Coventry the whole of his plans else the man would try to stop him. He could not risk harm coming to the older lord. Chattsworth owed Coddington far more than he could ever repay. He'd taken Calliope in at a crucial moment in her life.

The sound of carriages arriving had him snapping to attention. "They're here."

Chattsworth watched Chellenham and his second climb down from the first carriage. Keeping the distance, and the mist, between them, he waited for Coddington and Lippincott to disembark from the second carriage.

But no one emerged. Curious, he wondered if Coddington was waiting for the physician to arrive. "Have you ever acted as second in a duel before?"

Coventry was quick to reply. "Nay."

"I attended a duel once—acting as support for a friend."

"Unusual," the duke's man remarked.

"To tell the truth," the viscount admitted, "I was there to ensure no one interfered with their duel."

"Not so unusual. Do you think someone will try to interfere?"

"I do not believe so." He would try not to interfere—he bloody well planned to interfere!

The sound of carriage wheels alerted them to what they assumed was the physician's arrival.

Coddington and Earl Lippincott climbed out of the third carriage. "Who the devil—" William muttered, as he watched the earl stalk over to the carriage and pull open the door.

He and Coventry did not approach but watched the scene unfold from their vantage point.

"Is that Lady Aurelia?" William could not believe either the earl or her uncle would condone her attending such. His question was answered moments later.

"Did I not forbid you to attend, Wife?" the earl's anger reverberated through the mist toward them.

Coddington boomed, "You will leave at once, Aurelia!"

By Heaven, the countess stood her ground and did not retreat. "I do believe Lord Chellenham is waiting."

"Let him wait," the earl fumed. "The physician has yet to appear."

"Aurelia, at least wait inside the carriage," her uncle pleaded.

She turned to do his bidding and William's heart stopped. A small gloved hand pulled Aurelia back into the carriage.

"Good God," Coventry exclaimed, "you don't think your wife—"

"She was asleep when I left."

"Did you not tell her to remain home?"

"Last night. I didn't want to wake her before dawn to remind her to obey me."

Coventry snorted, then pretended to clear his throat. "I see."

The need to remain unseen was imperative. The need to see his wife safely from the field was just as imperative. William was torn between wanting to stalk over to the carriage and demand his wife and her friend go home and the need to remain hidden.

"Do you think Aurelia will remain in the carriage?"

"Along with Calliope?" Coventry questioned.

William's throat felt tight as fear for his wife and her friend filled him. The worry that Coddington would be defeated added to that fear. "Coventry would you go over and—"

"See that the women remain in the carriage. Of course." He slipped through the mist undetected.

Alone, William knew his plan would be put into motion. If Chellenham acted without honor, as he suspected he would, William would be ready. No one would be able to stop him.

A few moments later, the man the combatants waited for arrived. The physician was introduced to the seconds. Dueling pistols were chosen, primed, and loaded under the discriminating eyes of the seconds.

The mist thinned, allowing a glimpse of Chellenham and Coddington standing back to back, pistols in position. At the call to take twenty paces, the men strode away from one another. Chellenham took fifteen, turned around, and stood waiting.

William sprinted toward the field.

"Aim, fire!"

The lead ball struck William in the arm, forcing him back a step. He ignored the pain, as the report of Coddington's pistol was punctuated by a scream of anguish and Calliope calling William's name.

"You bloody fool!" Coventry exploded as he rushed to William's side to keep him from falling on his face.

Odd, his legs seemed to lose a bit of their starch. He hadn't been hit by Coddington's lead ball, had he? No, he knew he hadn't, but then who had?

"What were you thinking?" the man demanded as he tore off his cravat and tried to stanch the flow of William's blood.

"You saw what happened. I couldn't let Chellenham kill Coddington."

Coventry swore as he pressed against the viscount's wound. The feeling in his arm returned with a vengeance. William bit back the need to groan. Instead, he hissed through his teeth, "Hurts."

"It bloody well should," Coventry swore.

"His lordship is stronger than ye know," a familiar deep voice assured the duke's man.

Where did Michael O'Malley come from, and why was O'Malley here?

"Sure and he'll be fighting to regain his strength for Lady Calliope's sake."

Seamus Flaherty? Had he been followed by the duke's guard?

"William!"

His head felt light as if he were floating. "Thought I heard Calliope's voice."

"Aye, ye did, yer lordship."

He let the floating feeling envelope him. The last thing he heard was his sweet wife cursing a blue streak.

HE AWAKENED LYING on the damp ground. "Blasted cold today, Coventry."

The duke's man chuckled. "Glad to see your wound didn't keep you down for long."

"What happened?"

"Blood loss, your lordship," the physician intoned. "Chellenham's come around once already, but given his advanced years, his constitution is not as strong as yours. Not surprising he's lapsed back into unconsciousness."

"What about Coddington?" William wanted to know, then he remembered his wife's colorful language and looked around to see where she was.

"Did my wife leave?"

Coventry smiled. "The earl tossed his wife and yours in their carriage and demanded the coachman return them to the duke's town house immediately."

"How long ago?"

"Not five minutes," the earl groused walking over to join the group. "What in the bloody hell were you thinking, Chattsworth? You could have been killed!"

He shrugged and instantly regretted it. "Couldn't let Chellenham have the advantage by not taking the full twenty paces and shooting Coddington in the back! Calliope and Aurelia have lost so many of their loved ones. I would not let them lose another."

"What about you?" Coddington demanded, stalking over to stand at the viscount's feet.

"Me?" William wondered if the blood loss was affecting his ability to reason.

"Your wife loves you," the older man growled. "Would you sacrifice her love, too?"

He didn't know what to say. Nothing had gone according to plan. Chellenham was every bit as dishonest as Sean O'Malley had warned him. He never had the chance or time to shove Coddington out of the way. Chellenham had cheated.

"Chellenham never took the last five steps before turning around."

Coddington and Coventry agreed. "That scream you heard was a combination of the man's anger and pain," Coventry stated.

"Anger that his plan to shoot me in the back was foiled," Coddington said. "He knew when he posted the wager it was a lie."

The viscount was not quite ready to get up, so he asked, "Why do you think he did it?"

"The coin he hoped to earn. Both Lady Aurelia and Lady Calliope are much admired among the *ton* after their appearance at the end of last Season," Coddington replied. "Both are known to be women of high moral fiber and kind. Their acts of kindness have not gone unnoticed. When others are quick to fan the flames of adversity and gossip, my niece and Calliope are the ones to douse the flames, befriending the ridiculed and downtrodden."

Pride in his wife filled him. He knew her to be all that Coddington said and could not wait to hold her in his arms. Pushing himself up with his good arm, he wavered a bit. "I need to see Calliope."

The physician frowned. "I need to stitch you back together. There are two wounds—the entrance wound and the exit wound. I would prefer to have someplace a bit warmer to attend to you."

The image of the physician's fingers sinking a needle in his skin had the viscount's field of vision shrinking.

"Bloody hell," he rasped as the darkness pulled him under again.

⟫⟫⟫⟪⟪⟪

"AURELIA, I CANNOT just leave him!" Calliope ignored the tears streaming down her face and implored her friend, "Please have the coachman turn around."

Aurelia's shook her head. "You saw how angry Edward and Uncle Phineas were that we did not stay inside the carriage."

"How could they expect us to when William leaped onto the field trying to use himself as a target to save your uncle. I cannot believe Chellenham is so dishonorable."

Aurelia sighed. "I certainly can. One would think your husband would have asked how much experience Uncle Phineas had on the dueling field."

Calliope mopped her tears with the handkerchief her friend handed her. "Has he?"

"I shouldn't be discussing uncle's penchant for defending those whose reputations have been impugned."

"How many?" Calliope asked as another thought occurred. "Was he directly involved with those he was defending—or was it out of the goodness of his heart?"

Aurelia's eyes widened a moment before she leaned close to confide, "Uncle does not know that I've been keeping track of his duels."

Calliope's tears slowed as her interest was redirected for the moment. "Really?"

Aurelia sighed. "He's such a romantic."

"Has he had many...er..." How did one ask about one's romantic liaisons?

"Affairs of the heart?"

Calliope smiled at the term. "That sounds lovely—not sordid as proper ladies would have us believe."

"Uncle has always been highly respectful of the ladies he has escorted to various balls and gatherings in the past. But hasn't really shown any particular interest in squiring any one lady in the last few years."

"Mayhap he was more concerned with finding the proper husband for you," Calliope suggested.

"I suppose."

"How many," Calliope had to know.

Aurelia smiled. "I know of half a dozen."

"Do tell."

"No," Aurelia shook her head. "I will not betray a confidence."

"Very well, if you'd rather not tell me." She really, really wanted to know. Lord Coddington was still a handsome man, though he was approaching his middle years. She could see why the ladies of the *ton* would be entranced by his laughing green eyes and lovely temperament.

"He is still quite a catch," Aurelia admitted. "Mayhap now that Edward and I are wed, he'll accept more invitations and meet someone who will capture his attention for more than a fortnight."

Calliope covered her mouth to keep from snorting with laughter. "That long?"

Aurelia narrowed her gaze at her friend. "Do not make fun of Uncle."

"I wouldn't dream of it!" Calliope made an X over her heart. "Promise."

"What were you laughing at then," Aurelia demanded.

"The length of time some of his former lady friends held his attention. It's not very long at all, is it?"

Aurelia sighed. "No, but something always has him losing interest. I've often wondered if he was only looking for someone to pay him attention the way Aunt Minerva did. They were so in love, Calliope. Between my parents and Uncle Phineas and Aunt Minerva, I had wonderful examples of what true love is."

"I vaguely remember my parents but know they, too, shared a love that spilled over onto me—until father died and then mother."

"Don't think about that now," Aurelia urged, "You're going to have to concentrate on keeping your head."

"Of course. How could I forget William's been shot!"

"Not only that," Aurelia rasped. "I heard the physician warn against wound fever from the lead ball."

Calliope's hand flew to her breast. "What can I do? Edward and Uncle Phineas wouldn't let me stay with him."

"The physician may bring him back here to tend to his wounds. The threat of wound poisoning is still a possibility."

"I didn't recognize the physician, did you?"

"I overhead Edward and Uncle Phineas speaking last night. The physician has been working with Dr. McIntyre."

"Does he live close by?"

Aurelia shook her head.

"So there is a very good chance they will be returning to the duke's town house."

"Yes. The time for tears is over. Edward asked that I tell Mrs. O'Toole and Mrs. Wigglesworth what occurred, if they haven't already heard through the grapevine."

"You mean from one of the duke's personal guard."

"Exactly."

"Did you know they were there?"

Aurelia admitted she did not. "I should have realized they would be. After all, Edward was Uncle's second, and the duke would want to ensure nothing untoward happened to either of them during the duel."

"Or to you," Calliope reminded her.

"Or you, to that end," Aurelia was quick to reply. "You know Jared and Persephone consider you a close family friend—and not just because of your friendship with Phoebe and me. They have from the beginning."

"I wouldn't want to do anything to cause them to revile me."

"That would never happen," Aurelia stated emphatically. "They know you too well. I know you too well."

As the carriage rocked to a stop, the women grasped one another's hand. Aurelia spoke first. "We shall not speak of this morning to anyone!"

Calliope added, "Other than our husbands."

Their gazes met and held as the door to the carriage swung open where one of the footmen waited to help them alight.

No one spoke as they were quickly ushered inside. Jenkins was waiting for them, his lips in a firm disapproving line.

Calliope and Aurelia nodded to the butler but did not let him help them off with their cloaks.

"Hurry!" Aurelia urged as she pulled Calliope toward the door to the servants' side of the town house.

"Is there a problem, your ladyships?" Jenkins asked their backs.

Neither one paused to answer him.

A few minutes later, Michael O'Malley and Seamus Flaherty arrived. "The physician's on his way—his lordship's been shot!"

Jenkins did not so much as blink as he inquired, "Why would Lord Coddington not go to his own town house? He'd surely be more comfortable there."

Flaherty paused and shared a telling look with O'Malley. "'Tis the viscount who's been shot."

Jenkins froze for a moment, before his normal unflappable mien resurfaced. "I believe their ladyships are alerting Mrs. O'Toole as we speak. Shall we direct them to the duke's study when they arrive?"

The duke's guard hesitated. "'Twould be a right bloody mess—the lead ball went clean through his arm. Two wounds to close."

Jenkins grimaced at the pronouncement. "I shall send them directly to the kitchen. Mrs. O'Toole will no doubt be prepared for any eventuality."

Flaherty and O'Malley agreed. "We heard how she took charge until the physician arrived the night Hollingford held Lady Phoebe hostage at knifepoint after gouging the earl's arm."

Jenkins agreed. "Mrs. O'Toole is stouthearted." Meeting their gazes directly, Jenkins straightened to his full height and announced, "I stand at the ready to assist."

"Ye're a good man, Jenkins," O'Malley told him.

"Aye," Flaherty agreed. "We're proud to be working with a man such as ye."

Jenkins' eyes widened at the praise, but that was the only emotion he allowed. There was much to be done in quite a short amount of time. As the men were about to open the servants' door, he called out, "Will someone send a message to His Grace?"

"Aye," O'Malley replied.

With that, the men slipped in through the door and closed it behind them.

Fifteen minutes later, Jenkins opened the door to Edward and

Coventry supporting the very pale viscount, the physician right behind them.

He didn't bother with pleasantries normally extended to those entering the duke's town house. "The kitchen!"

The men stopped and changed direction.

Mrs. Wigglesworth appeared bearing a cup. Handing it to Jenkins, she relayed the brief news. "It's bad, his lordship has lost a lot of blood. I overheard Mr. O'Malley tell Mr. Flaherty he'd seen worse."

Jenkins didn't quite know what to say. He accepted the cup of tea and nodded his understanding.

"Drink up, Jenkins. You know the household depends upon us to carry on no matter the circumstances."

Their eyes met and held for long moments before he replied, "You are a jewel among women, Ophelia."

Mrs. Wigglesworth smiled and placed her hand on Jenkins' forearm. "You are the steadfast rock the staff and the duke's family have always depended upon, Peter."

The strait-laced, straight-faced, longtime butler winked as he emptied his cup. Handing it back to her, he ordered, "Back to your post, Mrs. Wigglesworth."

She was smiling as she dashed back to the kitchen with his empty cup.

CHAPTER TWENTY-NINE

C ALLIOPE WAS FORCIBLY removed from the kitchen for the third time in an hour. She struggled against Lord Codding-ton's hold, but he did not let go until he'd had her in the entryway...for the third time.

"You cannot and should not be in the kitchen."

Tears filled her eyes, threatening to overflow. "Please, let me go back. I need to be by William's side."

Aurelia's uncle raised his eyes heavenward and sighed—a deep gusty sound that reminded her of the bellows she'd often used to keep the fire going in her cousin's home. "The pain is excruciating, and the blood loss, worrisome. You have got to let the physician concentrate. William's life depends on the man's skill."

The first tear fell, and then another. Calliope did not blink, did not make a sound. "Why have you let Mary Kate stay?"

He harrumphed, before answering, "Your maid has a steady hand and stout heart." He held up a hand to keep her from interrupting. "Did you know her mother is a healer of some renown in Ireland?"

Calliope shook her head, then nodded. "I forgot. She did mention it..."

"She jumped right in and began to apply pressure to your husband's arm at a crucial moment when the doctor was threading the needle a second time."

She felt her stomach heave and fought to control the spasm. She could not and would not show weakness in front of the man who'd done so much to save her from her relatives.

"Blast!" he grumbled, hauling her into his arms and calling for a bucket.

Before she could tell him she'd conquered the urge to relieve the contents of her stomach, Jenkins came running with a large container.

She stared at the butler, and at the brass cylinder that normally housed any number of walking sticks and started to giggle.

He frowned at her while Lord Coddington told her to be still.

She could not seem to stop.

"His lordship is asking for ye," Seamus Flaherty called as he shoved open the door into the hallway. Flaherty paused to stare from Calliope to Lord Coddington and then at Jenkins holding the brass holder, as if prepared to catch something. In a flash, the man surmised the situation.

"Shall I tell his lordship ye're indisposed?"

"Nonsense," Calliope replied. "Please put me down, Uncle Phineas."

He set her on her feet while Jenkins returned the brass holder to its position in the entryway.

"This way, yer ladyship."

Calliope was ready to scoot around Flaherty when he cautioned her, "He's lost a lot of blood, yer ladyship. They'll have cleaned most of it up before ye enter the kitchen. Turner's fetching a clean shirt."

"I see."

"Even a brave woman such as yer ladyship, should not have seen all that ye have today. After he sees ye, will ye wait upstairs in yer bedchamber? Michael and I will be helping him up as soon as he's satisfied Lord Coddington didn't tie ye to the duke's desk chair like he threatened."

"I promise, Seamus, and I apologize for making a spectacle of myself. I should have been more reserved and not interrupted the physician."

"The doctor knows it was out of concern for his lordship."

She nodded and let him precede her into the room. The first thing she saw was the parchment pale face of her husband. His brilliant blue eyes were pale, his cheeks hollowed out. This was not the same man who'd so valiantly leaped into the fray to protect Aurelia's uncle from the lord who sought to cheat and take his shot before the signal to fire was given.

She rushed to his side and dropped to her knees beside him. "William!"

"There you are, love." He tried to smile, but that required more strength than he had at the moment. It had taken most of what had been left to demand they let him sit in a chair to greet his wife.

He locked gazes with her. "A beautiful woman should never cry. You should be happy always."

"I'll be happy when you've been tucked into bed upstairs where I can sit beside you and tend you."

He felt a warm glow inside at her words, but it faded as he realized, "I may not be able to make the trip unaided."

"Not to worry, yer lordship. O'Malley and I stand ready to assist ye."

"Thank you, Flaherty."

As the men moved into position to help him stand, Calliope stood back and dug deep to control the worry threatening to paralyze her. *Dear God,* she prayed, *don't let him catch wound fever—or worse,* she thought, *lead poisoning.*

Her maid reappeared a few moments later and did not look as worn out as Calliope felt. Then again, she'd insisted her maid stay behind this morning since Aurelia would be accompanying her to Chalk Farm.

"Let me help you," she offered.

Calliope wanted nothing more than to say yes, but knew Mary Kate deserved a bit of time to herself. "You were wonderful assisting the physician. Thank you, from the bottom of my heart."

"My mother would have been disappointed if I didn't use all I learned to help your husband."

"Please do be sure to rest. I can manage now that I know my husband has been patched up."

Her maid nodded. "There are a number of herbs my mother used back home to fend off fever. I'll ask Mrs. O'Toole if she's familiar with them and see about procuring them."

Overwhelmed with Mary Kate's willingness to help and share her immeasurable healing knowledge with her, she hugged the maid to her heart. "Thank you," she rasped.

When she eased back, Mary Kate promised, "Do not worry, we'll have the viscount on his feet in no time."

Five hours later, Calliope was fighting back tears as her husband thrashed about, drenched from the fever that grabbed hold of him and refused to let go.

"Lady Calliope," Mrs. Wigglesworth urged, "let me watch over his lordship while you stretch your legs and have a bite to eat."

She stared at the man in the bed, willing him to keep fighting to conquer the fever. "He has to get well," she whispered.

"He is a strong man," the housekeeper reminded her. "Fevers always seem worse at night and in the early hours of the morning. Do not lose faith."

"Without faith, I'd be lost," she admitted. "What if he rouses and calls for me and I'm not here?"

"I shall fling open the door and shout for you," Mrs. Wigglesworth proposed.

Her words lightened Calliope's heart. "Do you promise?"

The older woman held open her arms and Calliope collapsed against her. Crooning nonsensical words, the kindly housekeeper soothed the worst of the fear building within Calliope. She'd been stricken with terror watching William's pale face flush bright red. Though she knew it was the fever, the heat radiating from his skin shocked her. She didn't remember ever suffering from such a high fever—ever.

"What if Mrs. O'Toole cannot find the herbs Mary Kate's mother swears will bring down the fever from a pistol wound."

"She will," Mrs. Wigglesworth assured her.

"How does Mary Kate's mother even know about such things?"

"Mrs. O'Toole knew exactly which herbs Mary Kate recommended. Why don't you ask her when you go downstairs for a cup of tea and a bit of broth and bread. It'll sooth your aching stomach."

"How did you know my stomach was bothering me?"

She sighed. "I've been around long enough to have seen any number of ailments, some physical and some that started from fear for a loved one. Don't let yourself become incapacitated by not taking care of yourself, Lady Calliope. His lordship needs you."

Calliope blinked away her tears. She did not have time for them. She had a mission—take care of herself so she could take care of her husband. He would battle and beat back the fever that held him in its grasp. And he would get well. She could not bear life without him by her side.

"I shall be back shortly."

"Take your time and be sure to speak to Mrs. O'Toole about those herbs."

"Thank you, Mrs. Wigglesworth, for your care and your kindness."

"Don't hurry back," she warned as Calliope softly closed the door behind her.

Rushing down the back staircase, she stumbled on the last step and flung out her hands as she burst through the door.

"You must be near starved, your ladyship. Have a seat while I serve you up some of my soup. It'll put a bit of color back in your cheeks. Lord knows, his lordship will appreciate seeing you looking your best."

When Mrs. O'Toole finally let her get a word in edgewise, she thanked her and asked about the herbs. "Any word from the apothecary yet?"

Mrs. O'Toole paused, soup ladle over the pot. "Now why would you think one of the apothecaries would be carrying the herbs you need for his lordship?"

"Where else would you acquire them?" She certainly had no idea.

"Well now, I've a friend who grows herbs she brought with her from home years ago."

"Where is home?" Calliope asked.

"County Cork," Mrs. O'Toole replied. "My husband and I left years ago, before I was hired to work for duke."

"You don't have the same accent as the men in the duke's guard," Calliope pointed out.

"When we first arrived, we were told if we wanted to work for one of the titled gentlemen, we'd best lose our accents." Mrs. O'Toole sighed. "It was work, but it was for the best."

"About those herbs," Calliope began.

Mrs. O'Toole nodded, "My friend has been tending to her herbs and been giving away cuttings to those who have a way with growing things."

"And those that do not?" Calliope had no idea if Mrs. O'Toole was handy growing plants.

"Deidre dries the herbs to use in various remedies and keeps a supply on hand for those of us from home in need."

Mrs. O'Toole placed a bowl of soup and sliced bread on the table. Calliope sat when the cook pointed a wooden spoon at the empty chair and then at Calliope. Without a word, the woman made her wishes known. She'd best listen, or else the woman may not help William.

"That kind of thinking will get you nowhere."

Calliope paused with the spoon to her lips. "What kind of thinking?"

"'Tis written all over your face."

"What is?"

"Fear that I won't be helping you, if you don't do as I tell you and fill your gullet."

"Will you? Help me that is."

Mrs. O'Toole shook her head. "I would never turn away a soul in need. That man of yours...his lordship is in great need of my help—mine and Deidre's. We'll do all we can to get him back on his feet. Depend upon it."

Calliope had to ask. "And the herbs?"

"Are steeping in the small pot on the back of my stove."

Relief tangled with desperate hope. Sobs wracked her body as she buried her face in her hands.

"There now, you shouldn't bottle up so much worry and fear inside yourself. It isn't good for you."

Calliope managed to stifle the worst of her sobs, putting the back of her hand against her mouth.

The cook handed her a large towel and ordered her to blot her face and eat her soup. "And be quick about it."

Used to being ordered about for most of her life, she did as she was told and felt immeasurably better having done so.

When she finished her buttered bread and soup, a cup of tea appeared at her elbow with the admonishment to drink every last drop.

Her cup empty, her tender belly full, Calliope rose from the table and placed her dishes and utensils in the dry sink and prepared to wash them.

"You'll be wanting to freshen up before you go back to your husband," Mrs. O'Toole reminded her. "Why don't you use the pitcher and bowl I keep in the pantry and wash your face and re-pin your hair. You'll arrive looking more like your beautiful self, your ladyship."

"Thank you, Mrs. O'Toole." She hurried to the pantry to do as the cook bid.

A few minutes later, she returned, looking far better than she had a short while earlier. Mrs. O'Toole beamed. "Well now, don't you look the picture of health? Your husband will not worry about getting well if you don't wear your fear on your face."

Calliope thought about the advice and realized she'd heard it before, years ago. "My mother used to say as much."

"You'd do well to remember her good advice."

"And yours, Mrs. O'Toole. I cannot thank you enough. I do feel better and more like myself, ready to tend to William while he recovers." Eyes bright with conviction, heart ready to believe her prayers would be answered, she vowed, "He will recover!"

"God will see that he does. You but need to ask it of Him."

Calliope smiled at the cook. "I already have."

"Well then, best be on your way. I'll be sending up the herbal draught for his lordship shortly. See that he drinks every drop."

"I will." Her spirit light, her belief that William would fully recover, she dashed up the back staircase ready to do battle at his side.

CHAPTER THIRTY

T HE DUKE'S PERSONAL physician, Dr. McIntyre, had called every day, for the last few days, checking on William. His last visit, a few hours ago, assured her the worst was past.

She held back her tears as she fervently thanked the doctor, asking him to relay her thanks to Dr. McIntyre's associate who had tended to her husband immediately after he had been shot. Dr. McIntyre left with the assurance that he would relay her message to his associate along with his instructions: Viscount Chattsworth needs to rest and eat in order to build back his strength.

Enjoying the calm after the storm of the last few days, Calliope was reading at her husband's side, relieved he was sleeping the deep sleep of health—fever free when Jenkins appeared in the open doorway.

"Coventry is asking to see his lordship."

"I don't want to wake him, Jenkins, he's only just fallen asleep."

"Shall I tell Captain Coventry to come back tomorrow?"

"That won't be necessary, he may have something important to relay to William. Would you ask Mary Kate to come and sit with William? I'll be happy to speak with Captain Coventry in a few minutes."

"Very good, your ladyship."

Mary Kate was happy to relieve Calliope and pleased the viscount's fever had broken, and he was in a healing sleep. "Why don't you take the time to stretch your legs and grab a bite to eat? I'm sure Mrs. O'Toole has something sweet to tempt you."

Calliope smiled. It felt odd to do so after the last three days of constant worry for her husband. "I might just do that. Can I bring you anything?"

Her maid shook her head. "I'm fine, thank you."

This time, Calliope paused to check her appearance in the looking glass in their bedchamber before exiting the room. Tired, but no longer resembling the washed-out woman of the past few days, she waved to her maid and slipped from the room.

Taking the main staircase, she wondered what news the captain had to impart. "I wonder if it is news about William's father." Mayhap it was news Chellenham has been forced to flee to his country estate—no, she realized that would not be possible given his advanced years and what she'd heard Edward and the others saying about his wound. He would have to heal before that would be possible. News of his dishonorable conduct during a duel of honor continued to be the topic of discussion at home, White's, and the endless round of entertainments the quality so desperately sought on any given day.

Jenkins met her at the foot of the stairs. "I didn't want to disturb his lordship just now by staying too long."

She nodded. "Thank you for your consideration."

"How is his lordship this afternoon?"

"Sleeping," she told the butler. "Peacefully."

Jenkins cleared his throat and confided, "The staff has been praying for the both of you."

"The both of us?"

"Mrs. O'Toole reminded us that you needed prayers for strength to continue to care for his lordship."

"Thank you, Jenkins. Please thank everyone for me and assure them his lordship is on the mend."

"Of course, your ladyship."

"You don't need to announce me."

"Ah, but I would be quite remiss in my duties if I did not, and His Grace would be quite vexed with me if he found out I was derelict in performing my duties."

"Lead on, Jenkins," she said with a smile.

"Lady Calliope," Jenkins announced.

"Your ladyship," Coventry said, walking toward her. "I understand from Jenkins the viscount has turned the corner in his recovery."

"It is a relief to see him no longer in the grips of that horrible fever."

Coventry's brilliant green eye never wavered as he held her gaze for several long moments. "I am quite sure he owes his recovery to your excellent care."

She felt herself flush. "I do not know about that."

He smiled at her.

"I don't believe I've ever seen you do that, Captain Coventry."

He immediately relaxed his features into his normal serious expression. "Rare occasions warrant such. I do believe the news I bring may add to the speed of his recovery."

"Won't you sit down?" she asked, seating herself on one of the occasional chairs facing the fireplace.

"Thank you." He sat on the edge of his chair, watching her.

What was he waiting for? "Your news, Captain?"

"Forgive me," he murmured, "I simply must tell you. If I had not already heard the good news from Jenkins, I would be able to surmise as much just from looking at you."

She shook her head at him. "I am sure I have no idea what you mean."

He held her gaze as he told her, "The tension is gone from your brow, and the worry no longer in your eyes."

"Oh." She didn't know what else to say. That the captain was observant did not surprise her. William had mentioned his talent for such more than once.

285

He sat back in the chair. "The news I was waiting for arrived. Earl Chattsworth is alive and due to arrive later this week."

Calliope gasped. "Alive?"

Coventry nodded. "And well, all things considered."

"What kind of things?" she asked. "Where has he been? Had he been too ill to travel?"

"I don't want to divulge too much before I am able to speak to the viscount first. But suffice it to say, he made an unexpected journey of some length and is on his way home."

"Quite cryptic," Calliope grumbled. "Are you certain you cannot tell me more? When will we see him?"

"I am not at liberty to say. However, when his lordship wakes, please do share my news."

He rose and bowed before her.

"I will. Thank you, Captain."

"My pleasure, your ladyship."

She was still sitting there staring at the fireplace when Jenkins came looking for her. "His lordship is awake and is asking for you."

Calliope fairly flew out of the duke's study to the bedchamber where her husband waited for her. Her hand was on the knob, when it turned in her hand.

Mary Kate was smiling when she opened the door to greet her. "His lordship is most anxious to speak with you."

"Thank you, Mary Kate." The sight of her husband clear-eyed and rumpled, sitting up in bed, banished the memory of those long hours bathing his face and chest with cool water, trying to bring his fever down.

"You look remarkably well for someone raging with fever not five hours ago, William."

He raised his hand and beckoned her toward the bed. "Would you sit with me while I am lucid?"

She carefully sat at the foot of the bed. He shook his head at her. "Closer."

Calliope scooted up a few inches.

He smiled at her. "Closer."

She moved up a bit further, but not close enough to touch him. She didn't want to jostle his injured arm. "I think this is far enough for now, William. I wouldn't want to hurt you."

"Ah, Calliope, don't you realize that by not being close to me you wound me?"

"I'm afraid I do not understand."

His heavy sigh had her springing to her feet to lay the back of her hand against his forehead. "No fever," she pronounced.

As she was about to step back, he nabbed her hand and held her by his side. "Maybe you should check the way you would in the early morning hours."

"I didn't think you would remember that."

"I remember more than you realize, my love."

Calliope leaned closer and pressed her lips gently to his forehead. She was smiling as she repeated what she'd just said, "No fever."

His smile was just this side of wicked as he tugged on her hand, pulling her to within inches of his sculpted lips. "My mouth feels like it's on fire. You should check one more time."

With a half-hearted attempt at irritation, she brushed her lips across his only to have him let go of her hand and band his good arm around her as he seared her lips with a kiss that promised unbridled passion and more.

She staggered and nearly fell when he broke the kiss.

He caught her to him. "Having you so close to me and not being able to make love with you drove me to the brink of insanity."

"You were beyond the brink of sanity while in the grips of that fever, Husband," she reminded him.

"Calliope, you wound me."

She shook her head at him. "Never on purpose." Her eyes met his and she whispered, "I thought you were going to leave me, Husband."

"Never willingly, my love."

"Until Mrs. O'Toole prepared that herbal draught for you, nothing I did broke your fever."

"Sit beside me, Calliope," he rasped. "I need to hold you."

"You'll tell me if I lean too heavily against you, won't you?"

"My darling, Chellenham shot my other arm."

"I will not sit until you promise."

He raised his eyes to the ceiling and was quiet for so long, she was afraid he was going to ask her to leave. "I promise, now please sit next to me."

She gingerly sat on the edge of the bed until he scooped a hand beneath her and settled her on his lap. "Much better. Now, what is the latest on the dishonorable Chellenham?"

Calliope proceeded to fill her husband in on the latest *on dits* concerning the lord who'd dared to flout the unwritten code of honor and turn before he'd taken the full number of paces. Let alone fire before the command had been given.

"Hah! If he were well enough to travel, he'd have headed for the country by now. And we'd be well rid of him! By the by, has Coddington gotten over his pique at me for interfering?"

As Calliope answered his questions, she slowly relaxed against him. She slid off his lap and lower on the bed until she was leaning against his side in the cradle of his arm.

She yawned, then gasped. "Oh, my goodness, I almost forgot the most important news!"

"What would that be dearest?"

"Captain Coventry stopped by to see you. He needs to speak with you but did impart a bit of good news that I know you'll want to hear."

"Have your cousin and his wife paid back the money they stole from you?"

"Er...not as yet."

"Well, then it can't be anything I'm anxious to hear. Why don't you close your eyes and get some sleep? You've had precious little these last few days taking care of me."

"I'd do it again in a heartbeat. Too much sleep is just as harmful as too little, you know."

He chuckled as her eyes slid closed of their own volition.

"Calliope, love?"

"Hmmm...yes?"

"What news did Coventry share with you?"

Curled into the warmth of his side, she murmured, "Your father is alive and due to arrive home by the end of the week."

Her husband's reaction pushed her to the edge. She hung on for a heartbeat before slipping off the bed.

"Calliope, are you hurt? I didn't mean to shove you off the bed, but the news...the wondrous news! Are you certain? There's no mistake?"

She rubbed the sore spot on her elbow and hip bone that took the brunt of the impact. "I am sure."

He leaned over the edge of the bed. "What time is it?"

"I have no idea. After six o'clock, I would imagine."

"Splendid! Summon Turner if you would. I intend to bathe but will need help getting in and out of the tub."

"Couldn't you wait until morning? You may have more strength tomorrow."

He smiled at her. "Please ask Jenkins to send Seamus Flaherty. I need to speak with him."

"Botheration!"

"That reminds me, my dear, where did you hear such a colorful expression."

"Botheration?" she shrugged. "If you must know, Persephone uses it quite a bit."

"Not that expression, the more colorful one," William said with a grin. "The one having to do with the devil and his blue—"

Calliope shot to her feet and clapped a hand over his mouth. "Please do not repeat what I said. It's mortifying enough that it slipped out in a moment of extreme duress."

"You were under duress?" he asked.

"You'd just been shot!" she declared.

"Ah, so under extreme circumstances you use such expletives

that you heard where?"

"If you must know, Uncle Phineas."

"That makes more sense. Now, please speak to Jenkins about sending Turner and Flaherty to me."

"And just what am I to do?" She'd thought to spend the evening with her husband—alone.

"You'll want to rest up. I am feeling quite energized by your news."

Her gaze met his, the brilliant blue of his eyes twinkled with a combination of devilment and desire. Hand to her heart, she nodded. "Just how much rest do you suggest?"

"As much as you can get. In those moments when I was not in the fever's grip, I hungered for you until I thought I'd go mad. I'm no longer feverish."

She brushed the tips of her fingers along the line of his jaw. "I confess all those nights bathing your face, and chest with cool cloths had me praying you'd recover quickly."

"It would seem your prayers have been answered, my love."

CHAPTER THIRTY-ONE

C ALLIOPE STIRRED, SLOWLY stretching muscles that had been used so deliciously the night before. Opening her eyes, she stared up into the face so dear, so beautiful, it brought tears to her eyes.

William frowned. "What's wrong, love? Did I hurt you?"

She blinked the tears away. "When you took to me to paradise the first or the second time?" she teased.

His smile returned. "Apparently, I've married a lusty wench."

She felt her face warm at his words. Wanting to show him that she would conquer her embarrassment, she quipped, "Who knew?"

He trailed the tip of his finger along the curve of her cheek before following the line of her jaw to her chin. "I am beyond grateful to have married a strong woman."

"I'm not nearly as strong as I'd like to be," she confessed.

William pressed his lips to her forehead. "Your strength is in your heart. You've courage and conviction to do the right thing, no matter if there are consequences you would suffer."

"I may be a poor relation, but I've not forgotten the lessons learned while my parents were alive."

"Were, my love. *Were* a poor relation."

She wondered at his words but wouldn't ask if he'd had a reversal of fortune now that his father was no longer missing. *Had someone wagered on Earl Chattsworth's return? Where else would he suddenly come into the coin she knew he so desperately needed?*

Calliope would not ask him. She would trust that he would tell her eventually. "My life changed for the better on Hogmanay."

William's face paled. "When I knocked into you and nearly sent you to your death?"

"You saved my life, pulling me to safety and changed my life for the better when you married me."

"I should never have turned my back on you, Calliope."

"You had reasons why you felt you had to."

"I regret not sharing those reasons with you, my love. Can you forgive me for failing you?"

"You did not fail me," she reassured him. "I confess I was not looking forward to explaining my reasons to Uncle Phineas. I just could not trespass on his generous offer, nor could I envision living in his home once Aurelia and Edward married."

"But he'd offered you his protection and a place to stay where you were not mistreated by your relations."

"Without Aurelia there, it would have been awkward as we are not related."

"I am certain the duke and duchess would have been happy to vouch for your character to all and sundry." He locked gazes with her and was silent for long moments before asking, "That is what concerned you wasn't it? The threat of malicious gossip?"

"Life isn't always sunshine and rainbows, William. I've been the brunt of more than one relative's harsh criticism and slander."

He wrapped his good arm around her and breathed in the scent that was uniquely Calliope...*sun-drenched roses*. "Life is a balance. How we balance the good and bad, harsh and easy will only make us stronger."

"What if someone else spreads lies about me? Aurelia and Edward survived those horrible things said about them last year, only to have Aurelia's name attached to the inexcusable gossip about her uncle and me. Guilty by association."

William tucked her close and rolled onto his back. A curtain of her silken honey hair surrounded them. Wide gray eyes stared down at him. "I vow to stand by your side though the storms life will assuredly blow in our direction. Together, we are stronger than apart, Calliope."

"But what if—"

"Stronger together." Tugging on the strand of hair that tickled his chin, he whispered, "Come closer."

She slowly smiled. "Together, William."

"Would you add insult to my grievous injury? Forcing me to lift my shoulder?"

Calliope fell against him and held on for dear life.

His groan of agony was silenced by her lips. "I'm sorry, William."

The pain was soon forgotten as the life-giving sustenance of his wife's sweet lips met his.

IT WAS WELL past the noon hour when Calliope emerged from their bedchamber. Her husband's list of duties, still to be performed for the duke, was clutched in her hand. She didn't even have to ask Jenkins or Mrs. Wigglesworth where the earl and Aurelia were. The couple were standing at the foot of the stairs waiting for her.

Worry filled her, twisting her belly into painful knots. "Is something wrong?"

Edward and Aurelia shared a glance before smiling at her. "Not at all, Calliope," Edward was quick to reassure her.

"How is William this morning?" Aurelia's expectant look had Calliope wondering if there was something amiss that they were afraid to tell her.

"Have my cousin and his wife managed to abscond with more funds from my allowance?" She shook her head. "Never mind, Uncle Phineas and the duke promised that my cousins would repay the monies they'd taken and not be able to siphon off anymore."

Aurelia rushed to her side as Calliope reached the bottom step. Hugging her close, Aurelia whispered, "You look radiant."

Calliope felt her cheeks warm as memories of last night filled her. "Er...thank you. I finally caught up on much needed rest."

Edward chuckled, then promptly cleared his throat at his wife's pointed look. "Amazing how restorative a bit of *rest* can be."

He could not mean...how could he have guessed? *No*, she thought to herself. *He could not have known how she and William passed the night. Could he?*

"Do cease your teasing, Husband," Aurelia ordered. "Ignore him, Calliope. Edward does so love to tease. Besides, I can highly recommend the prelude to rest my husband speaks of."

If a hole would only open up in the entryway, she could disappear and not have to face the happy couple smiling at her. They knew—*knew* she had spent the night making love with her husband.

Husband. There is nothing wrong or untoward with passing the evening doing just that with one's spouse. Time for her to become accustomed to innuendo from her dear friends who are so happy.

Thinking of the whispered words of love as their passions cooled and they drifted off to sleep, she thought once again that her life had forever changed for the better on Hogmanay. When the handsome, dark-haired viscount strode into the church and captured her heart.

"Edward, aren't you forgetting something?" Aurelia asked.

He stared at his wife for long moments before answering, "Ah, yes. Roxbury sent word that he has urgent business to discuss with you."

"Me?" Calliope recognized the name. Why would the duke's solicitor need to meet with her? "Did he mention meeting with my husband, as well?"

"He did not, but that would not preclude William from attending the meeting with you if he is up to it."

"Must I go to Mr. Roxbury's office? I'd rather not leave William until he is fully recovered."

"Given what has occurred in the last few days, I felt it my duty to respond on your behalf, asking Roxbury to come here," Edward informed her. "I do hope that will meet with your approval, Calliope."

She nodded. "What time is he expected?"

"Three o'clock this afternoon."

She turned as if to go back upstairs when Aurelia called out to her. "Let William sleep for now," she urged. "No doubt, he'll wake up soon."

"What makes you say that?" Calliope had no idea how Aurelia could make such a determination.

Edward laughed. "I daresay, he'll wake as soon as the chill hits him."

Worry speared through her. "The chill? Do you think the fever will return?"

Aurelia soothed her friend. "Edward, take yourself off! Can you not see you're upsetting Calliope?"

His gaze met Calliope's. "I beg your pardon, that was not my intention."

She nodded and Aurelia whispered, "He cannot seem to keep his comments to himself as of late. I apologize if his words upset you."

"Edward does have the best of intentions," Calliope agreed. "I'm trying to become accustomed to actually having my husband with me instead of living our lives separately."

"You'll be surprised how quickly you become used to waking beside him and falling asleep in his arms."

Calliope sighed. "He's just so beautiful, my heart seems to skip a beat whenever he looks at me."

Aurelia nodded. "It's those diamond-bright blue Lippincott eyes. Terribly attractive."

"The width of his shoulders."

It was Aurelia's turn to sigh aloud. "And the breadth of his chest."

They shared a secret smile. "Our husbands are devastatingly handsome, are they not?" Calliope asked.

"Without question," Aurelia agreed. "Now, about your meeting with Roxbury, would you wish for Edward and me to attend and lend our support?"

"Would you?"

"Of course. We can be there whether or not William is up to attending."

"Thank you. I am quite sure William will approve of your suggestion."

"What is next on your list for the day?" Aurelia asked, nodding toward the papers still clutched in Calliope's hands.

"Oh, bother! I was supposed to speak to Edward about William's list of duties from the duke."

"Why don't we see about getting you something to eat and ask Jenkins to find my husband."

"By that time, maybe William will have missed me."

"Calliope!"

The deep rumble of her husband's voice echoed through the vast entryway.

The women jolted then started to laugh. "I do believe your husband grew chilled without you," Aurelia teased.

"Where the devil is my wife?"

"Coming!" Calliope called, retracing her steps to her bedchamber. She was out of breath from rushing to his side. "What's wrong? Are you in pain? Is the fever back?"

He grabbed hold of her hand, pulled her in the room, and closed and locked the door behind her. "You weren't there when I opened my eyes."

His accusatory tone took her by surprise. "I didn't want to wake you," she soothed.

His gaze met hers. "I woke up cold...and alone."

"In the future, I promise to wake you if I leave before you rise."

Her words seemed to ease the tension in the bedchamber. "Why did you leave?"

"It's well past noon, William. I thought to ask Edward to help with some of the duke's duties left unfinished while you were so ill."

He surprised her by agreeing with her idea. "A sound notion."

"I'm glad you aren't upset with me."

"On the contrary, I am a bit put out."

"Oh? About what?" She could not think what she could have done to cause him to feel that way.

"I not only woke cold and alone, but you were not there to kiss me good morning."

She smiled. "It's afternoon."

"You should beg my pardon for failing to kiss me good morning, and for completely ignoring the fact you should be kissing me good afternoon."

She slipped her hand from his to wrap her arms around his neck. Tilting her head back, she whispered, "Forgive me, William."

"Kiss me, Calliope."

"Only if you promise to be present at my afternoon meeting with Mr. Roxbury."

"Can you put him off a day? I should feel ready to climb aboard a carriage tomorrow."

"Edward anticipated your request and asked Mr. Roxbury to meet with me here."

"What about?"

Calliope frowned. "I really have no idea. It's not as if I need his advice on handling financial affairs, having very little to my name."

He tipped her chin up and rasped. "All that I have is yours. Even though it may not be much at the moment."

"When my cousins finally repay what they stole, it's yours."

"You don't have to—"

"You've given me a home and before you risked your life interfering in that duel, you gave me something far more precious. Your love. Let me do this one small thing for you." She hesitated before adding, "I am not certain it will be very much, but it may help."

"Calliope, your generosity knows no bounds. If you insist, we shall put it to good use at home."

"Home," she sighed. "That has such a lovely sound."

"Are you anxious to return to Sussex?"

"I do prefer the country and your staff made me feel welcome."

"We shall leave as soon as we settle matters here in London."

"Where do you suppose your father has been this last year?"

William did not answer right away. Was he worried about the state his father would be in, or was it something more…something that had to do with his father's disappearance?

"I intend to find out the answer to that question and more when we see him."

"You'll take me with you?"

"I must speak with Coventry to find out where and when to expect the earl." Easing back from Calliope, he asked, "Would you help me dress?"

"I've never helped a gentleman dress before."

"I sincerely hope not, my dear. If I promise to keep my hands to myself, we might actually accomplish this feat before your meeting with Roxbury."

"Mayhap I should summon Turner to assist you."

William sighed heavily. "Are you back to being afraid of me?"

"I'm not afraid of you, just not accustomed to my new role," she admitted.

"Am I asking too much too soon?"

"Not at all. Let me help you out of that dressing gown."

It was harder than she envisioned dressing a man from the skin out. He held her gaze while she blushed. The man seemed to delight in the fact that he stood there without a stitch of clothing on! One more thing she would have to become accustomed to being married to William.

Tying his cravat proved a bit more than she could handle. "Best summon Turner then, my darling."

A short while later, she was ready for the meal she had missed. "I am quite famished. Do you think Mrs. O'Toole would be willing to prepare a light meal for us?"

"I am feeling a bit peckish, myself. Shall we?" William held out his arm to her. When she slipped hers through his, he replied, "I would imagine she'd be delighted. She and Mrs. Wigglesworth have been taking excellent care of me."

"I could not have managed your care without their help these last few days."

"My cousin is most fortunate in his staff."

"Mrs. Meadowsweet and Hargrave are devoted to you, William."

He patted her hand as they made their way down the staircase. "The feeling is mutual. I've known them all my life. They deserve to be pensioned off, living as comfortable a life as they have given to my family."

"Between us, we shall see that they do."

"Thank you, Calliope."

"For?"

"Everything."

Jenkins was waiting for them. "Your lordship. Lady Calliope. Mrs. O'Toole has prepared a light luncheon for you."

"Please thank her for us," Calliope said.

"I was also instructed to remind your lordship that Dr. McIntyre will be by later this evening to attend you."

"As you can see, Jenkins, I am much recovered."

Jenkins dared to frown at him. "I am to remind you not to overdo."

"Doctor's orders?" the viscount asked.

Jenkins cleared his throat to reply, "Mrs. Wigglesworth's."

William and Calliope were smiling as Jenkins swept open the

door to the dining room with his usual flourish. "Enjoy your meal."

"Thank you, Jenkins."

Calliope's stomach rumbled loudly.

"I daresay," William drawled. "You are hungry. I'd best feed you."

She shook her head at him. "Dr. McIntyre would be most displeased if you tore open your stitches by doing too much too soon. Have a seat and I shall serve the both of us."

"It's lowering to admit I cannot even dress myself without help."

"Not for long," she said. "Before you know it, you'll be back to doing what you always do...by the way," she mused. "What do you do all day?"

"You shall soon learn, my dear."

"Ah, the life of a gentleman."

"Just what is that supposed to mean?"

She set a plate of front of him. "Most gentleman seem to spend an inordinate amount of time purchasing horses, visiting their tailors, meeting with other gentlemen at White's...shall I go on?"

William shook his head. "You're not that far off the mark. You must understand, that is not the life I lead. Only while in London, handling the duke's affairs, do such things occur. At Chattsworth..." his voice trailed off.

As she poured their tea, she noted the expression on her husband's face. He appeared somehow to be lost. "Are you all right?"

"Hmmm? Yes. Quite. Just thinking."

"There is much still to be done at your home."

"Our home," he corrected. "Hargrave mentioned you had a list."

While they ate—and Calliope helped William manage with the use of just one hand, she shared her thoughts on what could be done.

Before they'd finished eating, Edward and Aurelia arrived, trailed by one of the footmen bearing a tea tray filled with sumptuous desserts.

"We've already had our meal while you two were otherwise engaged," Edward announced. "We sweet talked Mrs. O'Toole into preparing a tea tray for the four of us."

Calliope beamed. "Thank you, Edward. I confess I'm still a bit hungry."

His blue eyes sparkled with merriment. "Strenuous work dressing a gentleman, I hear."

Calliope's gasp had Aurelia frowning at her husband. "Do cease your teasing, Edward."

"How did you know I helped William dress?"

"The walls have ears—and eyes. Our staff is always on hand to assist, whether they are summoned or not."

"I see."

"You'll become accustomed to it," Aurelia advised.

"I used to be part of the staff," Calliope whispered.

"You're not any longer," William said softly. "I shall help you adjust, my love."

The group polished off the tea tray. While discussing the merits of spending time in Sussex, Jenkins knocked on the open doorway. "Captain Coventry to see your lordship."

Edward and William shared a look before Edward asked, "William or me?"

Jenkins responded, "Viscount Chattsworth. He's waiting for you in the duke's study."

"Thank you, Jenkins."

"Shall I accompany you, William?"

"If you would, my dear."

They followed after the duke's butler. Calliope held on to her husband, determined to support him no matter what news Coventry would share.

CHAPTER THIRTY-TWO

WILLIAM SQUEEZED CALLIOPE'S hand as Coventry relayed the news that Earl Chattsworth had, indeed, been pressed.

"How is that possible? No press gang would dare to press an earl!"

"My contact in the Admiralty insists their *recruiters* did not know the unconscious man they'd hauled aboard the *HMS Albatross*, along with the other men who were convinced to serve in His Majesty's Navy, was an earl."

"But his clothing...his signet ring with our family crest on it! Surely they'd recognize him as a man of consequence."

Coventry's gaze met and held the viscount's. "He was dressed in ill-fitting clothes...a bit on the ragged side."

"What about his ring?" William demanded.

"He was not wearing a ring."

The magnitude of Coventry's words hit him with the force of a blow. "Someone wanted him to disappear."

"Aye," the duke's man agreed. "It is a wonder he survived the rigors of life as a sailor. One without rank."

"Wouldn't someone recognize that my father was not a commoner from the way he walked and talked? Wouldn't the ship's captain want to see him returned to his family as quickly as possible?"

Coventry seemed to be weighing his answer before he replied, "Mayhap your father did not wish to be discovered as a titled gentleman."

The viscount shook his head. "There wouldn't be any reason for him to—"

"What about the debts he owed?" Coventry asked, "or the worry that whoever wanted him to disappear would be waiting to finish the job when word reached shore ahead of the earl that he was found alive."

William chewed over those questions, all the while wondering who had been behind his father's being mistaken for a drunken commoner and pressed into service. Unable to fathom it, he blurted out, "Father cannot swim," William rasped.

"Not many sailors can."

"Why in God's name would anyone willingly board a ship if they could not swim?"

Coventry sighed. "Surely not every passenger who boards a sailing vessel has the ability to float or swim."

"William."

Calliope's calm voice calling his name snagged his attention. "What?" he barked, immediately apologizing, "Forgive me for snapping at you."

She frowned at him. "Would it not be a better use of your time and intelligence to try and piece together the rest of the picture? Who would have reason to send your father so far from home—pressed into service to the king?"

"I would imagine the length of time most vessels are at sea is one reason," Coventry remarked. "The perils they face, not only due to the weather, but in battle for king and country—or against pirates, would be additional reasons."

William was not surprised his wife had come to the similar conclusions as he had. The worry of the reason behind his father's disappearance swept through him. He raked a hand through his hair and promptly winced.

"Best keep a clear head and not use that arm until it has fully healed, Chattsworth."

"Sound advice," he admitted.

Coventry smiled. "Hurts like the very devil."

Calliope turned her attention from her husband to the man across from them. Noting once again his black eye patch and black sling, she wondered if he'd been shot. Before she could ask, her husband did.

"Ever been shot, Coventry?"

The slight inclination of the captain's head was his reply.

"How long did it take to heal?"

"Longer than you will."

"Why would that be?" the viscount challenged.

Coventry shrugged. "I'd been hit by more than one lead ball. A blunderbuss is quite effective fired in close quarters."

"Dear God in Heaven!" Calliope could not contain her shock. "Is that what caused your injuries?"

"My dear, I do not think it prudent to ask such a personal question of the good captain."

"Please forgive my impertinence," she whispered. "After caring for William—who'd only been hit by one lead ball, I cannot imagine how excruciating the pain must have been."

Coventry agreed, then told her, "To answer your question, cannon fire destroyed a top mast, sending splintered projectiles that took my eye and rendered my arm nearly useless."

"Now I understand why my cousin and his father championed the cause of those who fought so bravely to defend king and country," William stated. "Thank you for your service, Coventry. I would hope that the Admiralty awarded you for your sacrifice."

Coventry shrugged. The viscount wondered if they had. Had he been so broken when he had returned that they'd shuttled him aside like so many others? He would revisit that discussion another time.

"Shall I ring for tea before I leave you to discuss what's being done to uncover who is behind your father's circumstances?"

William was grateful for her question as Coventry appeared

distinctly uncomfortable continuing with the other line of discussion. "Tea, Coventry?"

"No, thank you."

William motioned for his wife to remain seated. "If you have something more pressing, by all means. If not, please stay."

Turning his attention back to the duke's man-of-affairs, he mentioned, "Having already spoken with Lord Andrews, I do not believe his recommendation of the shipping company Father invested in was meant as anything but what it appears—advice, having invested in the company himself."

"I'd come to a similar conclusion, your lordship."

Grateful to note Coventry was quick to collect himself, William nodded. "As to Lord Darnley, I am not quite certain about the man. Our discussion was not as in depth, leaving me with more questions than answers."

Calliope made an inelegant sound. Suspiciously sounding like a snort of laughter.

William stared at his wife. "Calliope?"

She coughed. "Please forgive me. Do go on, William."

He frowned at her. He'd ask her later what had amused her in the middle of such a serious discussion.

Coventry, however, was smiling. "I take it you've had occasion to attend one of Lord Darnley's musicales featuring the...er...talents of his daughters."

Calliope agreed. "Quite astonishing performances."

William grumbled. "Could we please wax poetic about his daughters another time. We have more pressing topics to discuss before Roxbury arrives."

"Roxbury is expected?"

"He's coming to see me shortly," Calliope informed him.

"I hope he has good news to impart, your ladyship."

"Thank you, Captain."

"The duke arranged for another meeting before I was called away to Sussex," William said, reaching for Calliope's hand once more. "I met with Chellenham."

Coventry's one-eyed gaze connected with his. "And your thoughts after meeting with the man?"

"Were confirmed the other morning at Chalk Farm."

"You are not wrong in your judgment. The duke and I are in full agreement."

"Are you going to question Lord Chellenham?" Calliope queried.

"The Admiralty has requested my presence when Earl Chattsworth arrives."

"Do you think Chellenham will be well enough to attend the meeting?"

Coventry shrugged in answer.

"I would like to be in attendance at that meeting."

Coventry paused as if considering. "I shall ask my connection."

"Thank you."

Coventry rose as a knock sounded on the library door.

"Enter," William called out. "Yes, Jenkins?"

"Mr. Roxbury to see her ladyship."

Coventry's gaze met William's.

Calliope smiled. "Thank you, Jenkins. Please tell him I shall be there directly."

William stood and held out a hand to his wife. "Please let Edward and Aurelia know he is here. We have asked them to attend the meeting with us. My wife and I shall be there directly."

Jenkins nodded and left to do the viscount's bidding.

She put her hand in William's and slowly stood. "Thank you for sharing your news with us this afternoon, Captain Coventry."

He bowed. "My pleasure, Lady Calliope." He held out his hand to the viscount. "I shall be in touch."

Watching him leave, William turned to his wife. "Let us not keep Roxbury waiting."

MR. ROXBURY WAS standing when Jenkins opened the door to the sitting room. "Viscount Chattsworth and Lady Calliope," Jenkins announced.

"Delighted you were able to attend, your lordship."

William nodded. "Fortunate to be here. We have asked the earl and Lady Aurelia to join us." He guided Calliope to the settee facing the fireplace. When she'd made herself comfortable, he joined her while Roxbury sat across from them.

"You do not mind that the earl and his wife will hear personal news?"

Calliope shook her head. "I'd welcome their support."

"Very well, then I have no objection to their attendance."

A few moments later, Jenkins returned to announce, "Earl Lippincott and Lady Aurelia."

Once everyone was seated, Roxbury addressed Calliope. "I bring wondrous news, your ladyship."

"I cannot imagine what that would be."

"I am given to understand you are aware there was an allowance left to you," Roxbury stated.

"Yes," Calliope answered. "Although there is a bit of confusion as to when I will be able to make use of those funds. They have yet to be returned, and I do not know the particulars of the allowance."

Roxbury slowly smiled. "Today."

"Today?" William asked.

Calliope did not want to get her hopes up. Mayhap she misunderstood the solicitor. "I'm afraid I don't quite understand."

"Lady Calliope, I have been tasked with handling your inheritance and your dowry."

Hand to her heart as if to slow it down, she glanced at her husband first, then the solicitor. "I am not supposed to receive my inheritance for three more years when I am five and twenty, and I do not have a dowry."

He nodded, silently contradicting her. "It would appear that you do. As to your inheritance," he said with a quick glance at the earl, "apparently there was a miscommunication. You were to begin receiving monthly stipends when you married."

"How much would that be?" Calliope asked.

Roxbury cleared his throat. "Ten thousand pounds a year."

She gripped William's hand tightly. "And the dowry?"

"Twenty thousand pounds," Roxbury said with a nod. "As I was not prepared to handle money outside of my office, I am hoping you will accept my apologies for only bringing a small portion of that amount with me today." He reached into his waistcoat pocket and retrieved a small leather pouch and handed it to Calliope.

Her hands trembled as she accepted the coins, not bothering to ask how much was in the bag. She'd never held a bag full of coins before and was more than a bit intimidated. "May I ask who provided the dowry? I am quite certain I did not have one."

Edward looked quite pleased with himself but did not offer an opinion. Neither did Aurelia.

Roxbury shook his head, advising, "The person wishes to remain anonymous for the time being. But asks that you accept the gift and put it to good use."

She glanced at their friends, who merely shook their heads at them, confirming without words what she suspected, Lord Coddington and the Duke of Wyndmere had something to do with her good fortune. She looked at her husband before asking, "There is no mistake? You have not mistaken me for another Lady Calliope?"

William chuckled. "I daresay, I've not met another lady with the same name, love."

Roxbury beamed at the couple as Mrs. Wigglesworth knocked on the open door, followed by one of the footmen. "Tea?"

"Thank you," William replied as Calliope was staring off into space.

"Is there anything else?"

Calliope turned toward the housekeeper and thanked her.

"This looks lovely. Thank you and please thank Mrs. O'Toole for us."

The housekeeper smiled and motioned for the footman to follow behind her. "Ring if you need anything."

"We will," the viscount promised.

Calliope was glad to have something to do with her hands. Though they still trembled a bit, she managed to pour without spilling, while Aurelia served the cream tarts and currant cake.

William passed the teacups and dessert plates to their guests before accepting the one she passed to him. "Thank you, my dear," he said. "May I suggest you drink up while you digest Mr. Roxbury's news?"

The older man took a sip and sighed. "Delightful. Can't remember the last time when I had occasion for tea in such pleasant surroundings."

"Don't you have time in your day for afternoon tea?" Calliope wondered.

"A cup while I work," he replied.

"Then I am glad you are able to join us today."

Roxbury finished chewing and smiled. "Delicious. My compliments to your cook, Chattsworth."

"The duke's cook," he reminded the man.

"Of course. I wonder," he speculated aloud. "Would she part with her recipe for the cream tarts?"

"I shall ask her for you." Aurelia set her cup down and started to get up, but Edward shook his head. "Why don't we finish our tea first?"

"Capital," Roxbury beamed.

When they'd eaten their fill, Aurelia walked over and gave a slight tug to the bell pull by the fireplace.

Jenkins arrived a few moments later with a footman in tow, anticipating the need to remove the tea tray.

"Jenkins would you please ask Mrs. O'Toole if she'd share her cream tart recipe with Mr. Roxbury?"

"Of course, your ladyship."

Once the remnants of their tea had been cleared, they settled back to discuss the particulars of Calliope's inheritance and her dowry.

Roxbury reached for the leather folder he'd brought with him. He opened it, rifling through the documents he'd brought with him. Finding the one he wanted, he pulled it out and showed it to Calliope and the viscount. "Here is signed statement of the account that has been opened in your wife's name," Roxbury explained, "and yours, your lordship. You can see the amounts are listed separately with your inheritance at the top and your dowry beneath it."

"I never dreamed it would be so much. Mother never hinted it would be."

Roxbury glanced at Edward and Aurelia a second time before speaking. "A minor miscommunication. I am certain you shall put the money to good use."

Calliope knew then, despite the fact that her cousin and his wife had not repaid her, and that her inheritance from her great-grandmother would never have amounted to so much, she had the duke to thank for her dowry and Lord Coddington for her inheritance.

"And you are certain my benefactor does not wish to be thanked?"

"Not at present."

She turned to William and asked, "What shall we do with such a great sum?"

"Why not visit the modiste and purchase a new wardrobe?"

Calliope frowned. "What on earth for?"

The men shared a glance. Edward shrugged while William stared at her. "Doesn't every woman desire a new wardrobe whenever possible?"

She glared at him. "How would one such as me know that? I am a poor relation, you know."

He fairly growled his response. "Have you forgotten so quickly? Your circumstances have been elevated by marriage to me."

She clasped her hands tightly in her lap and stared down at them. "I apologize, William. There are times when I cannot seem to wrap my head around my good fortune. I can only plead exhaustion."

He immediately apologized. "I beg your pardon. Of course, you are tired, having spent the last few days caring for me."

Roxbury cleared his throat to call attention to himself. "I would be happy to make a few recommendations as to investments when you are ready. If you could come by my office next week, I'd be happy to go over the particulars in more detail."

"Thank you, Roxbury."

"My pleasure, your lordship." He rose and thanked the couple for their time and was about to leave when he paused in the doorway. "A word of caution, your lordship."

"What is it?"

"Be on your guard," he warned.

William nodded.

"Once news gets out about Lady Calliope's good fortune, unscrupulous individuals will no doubt appear out of the woodwork with suggestions as to how to spend the money."

With that prediction ringing in the air, the solicitor departed.

"I believe I'll have a word with Roxbury before he leaves," Edward said. "Come, Aurelia."

With a glance over her shoulder at her friend, she quickly followed.

William pulled Calliope to her feet and held her close. "It would appear you are now an heiress, my love."

Heiress. Just what her husband had planned on marrying. But as they were already married, the dowry would belong to him. Would her inheritance belong to him as well? She should have asked Mr. Roxbury.

Instead of elation, Calliope felt as if her world just crumbled. William had come to care for her when she was penniless...would he treat her differently now that he was once again a man of wealth?

"You're awfully quiet, Calliope."

"Digesting the news. It is a bit to take in all at once."

"I would imagine so. Come, I need to speak with Edward and Aurelia."

Calliope let herself be led from the room. What did he need to speak to them about? Did it have to do with her dowry? Mayhap her inheritance? Had they already known of her good fortune? Was it the duke who gifted her with a dowry? That would explain why the couple offered to attend her meeting with Roxbury.

Would her change in fortune find her back at Chattsworth Manor, living alone while her husband settled in London in a new town house?

Time would tell.

CHAPTER THIRTY-THREE

W ILLIAM FROWNED, NOTING the way Calliope clung to Aurelia. Was something amiss? She'd just become an heiress! How could she be worried when her fortunes had changed for the better?

Their fortunes. He wondered if she was concerned that, as her husband, he had the control of the lion's share of her windfall. It would certainly be within his rights to spend her dowry as he saw fit. If she had been in possession of a dowry before they'd wed, it would most definitely be his to control. That they'd received it nearly a month after they wed should make no difference.

Should it? Mayhap he should ask Roxbury the particulars. He really never paid much attention to such trivial matters as the coin to keep Chattsworth Manor afloat. *Mayhap he should have.*

He shook his head and watched his wife closely. Were those tears? "Calliope, are you unwell? You should rest. It has been exhausting for you, these last few days, my love."

She shook her head at him and wiped away her tears. "I'm fine, William, truly."

"Calliope and I are going to have a coz, just the two of us. I'm sure you and Edward can find something to do to keep yourselves occupied."

William looked from Aurelia to Calliope and then back again. Something was wrong. Why wouldn't his wife confide in him?

Mayhap because it is about you, his conscience suggested.

Impossible. He hadn't done anything...except interfere in a duel of honor and get himself shot. Calliope had lost three days' worth of sleep caring for him. Why didn't she let one of the servants sit with him while she rested? He would put the question to her later...after she and Lady Aurelia finished talking about whatever they planned to discuss.

Aurelia whisked Calliope from the room and through the servants' door to the kitchen.

Mrs. O'Toole smiled at them, but after one look at Calliope's face, set down her paring knife. "Is it his lordship? Has the fever returned?"

"No," Aurelia reassured her. "He is fine. Calliope needs to have a good cry."

"That's all right then. Cry it all out, your ladyship. You'll be the better for it."

"Sage advice," Aurelia whispered as she tugged on her friend's hand to escape prying eyes and big ears.

Once they were on the staircase to the second floor, Calliope whispered, "Is it safe yet?"

Aurelia shushed her.

When they reached the top, she hurried down the hallway. The last door led to the servants' staircase to the third floor. She opened it and quickly closed it behind Calliope. "Almost there, hang on!"

Calliope nodded while her chest grew tighter and her throat felt constricted. When Aurelia thrust open the last door at the end of the long hallway, she closed it behind them and said, "Go ahead. You can cry now."

Calliope sank to the floor, covered her face in her hands and sobbed her heart out.

Aurelia wished she could help but knew help would come after the purge of tears. When Calliope had nearly run dry, Aurelia poured water from the pitcher into a bowl and dampened the soft linen cloth beside it. "Come," she urged. "Sit down."

Calliope dropped into one of the chairs beneath the window and sniffled. "What am I going to do?"

Aurelia handed the cloth to her. "To start, wipe your face. You'll feel better."

"What if William sees this as his chance to return to the life he was accustomed to, before his father—"

"Gambled away their fortune on shipping cargoes and the turn of a card?" Aurelia finished for her. "Why would you think so? It's obvious he truly cares for you."

"But only just recently, and then the duel, and now…now— I'm not certain. What if he's sorry he didn't wait to consummate our marriage?"

"Do you have attics to let?" Aurelia demanded, her toe tapping a furious staccato beat waiting for her friend's reply. "Edward and I have never seen a man so besotted as your William."

"Money changes everything," Calliope whispered. "Look what it did to my family. My father died. His brother moved into our home, claiming his right as father's heir, while at the same time kicking us out of the only home I'd ever known."

Aurelia sighed, but before she could speak, Calliope continued, "The prospect of money is what lured every one of my distant relations to take me in. Although they knew I was the poor relation, there was the possibility of an inheritance from my mother's side of the family."

"Is that why your dastardly cousin and his wife took you in?" Aurelia demanded.

Calliope nodded. Her head hurt and her heart felt sorely abused. Would he do his part to beget his heir and a spare and then pack her off to the country while he remained in London surrounded by the Season's *Incomparables*?

"Can you not speak to him about this? You may be creating problems where none exist, my dearest friend. Do not torture yourself," she urged. "Ask him."

"I could not bear it if I am right. To finally have my heart's desire only to have it ripped from my grasp…" Calliope let the words trail off. Mayhap she should leave before he set her aside.

Once the thought took hold, she could not shake it free.

"I do not like the look on your face, Calliope. Tell me what you are thinking."

She shook her head. "How do I know you won't tell Edward? Edward will surely feel it his duty to tell William."

"What are you planning?"

"I don't want to talk about it yet. Would you mind if I stayed up here, alone, for a while? I'm so tired that everything hurts."

Aurelia shook her head at her friend. "I shall return for you in an hour. Try not to brood."

"Ladies don't brood."

Aurelia smiled. "Uncle Phineas has told us on more than one occasion that they pout."

"Leave me to my pout," Calliope whispered. "I'll feel better for it."

"Very well. An hour," she reminded her friend.

Calliope waited until her friend's footsteps faded and the silence surrounded her. She rose from her seat and opened the door a crack. Peering through it, she noted the hallway was empty. No sound. No movement.

Talking the back staircase, she waited at the bottom before opening the door to see if anyone was about. Luck was with her as she scurried to the bedchamber she shared with William. Packing the small bag she'd brought with her, she opened the door and nearly collided with her maid.

Mary Kate's eyes widened. "What's happened? Where are you going?"

Calliope blinked back the tears. She refused to let one more tear fall. "I have to leave."

Mary Kate reached out a hand to Calliope. "You cannot go alone. Give me two minutes to grab my bag. I'm coming with you."

She started to refuse, when she realized the wisdom of her

maid's offer. "Why would you want to go with me?"

"Even though you are my mistress," Mary Kate remarked, "I thought we were friends. Friends don't let friends run away."

Calliope frowned. "I'm not running away—exactly."

"No?"

"I'm returning to Chattsworth Manor."

"Now? Without telling your husband?"

"If you're coming with me, you'd better hurry."

A quarter of an hour later, Seamus Flaherty noticed the two women running toward the stable.

WILLIAM AND EDWARD were discussing the list of repairs necessary for Chattsworth Manor's tenant farmers, staff, and the house itself when James Garahan burst into the room.

"She's leaving."

William's blood ran cold. "Calliope? When? Where?"

"Flaherty's got a bead on them and following."

"By God, my wife better not be aiding and abetting your wife," Edward thundered.

Aurelia rushed into the study. "What are you shouting about, Husband? Aiding whom?"

"Calliope," Garahan repeated. "I've got to catch up with Flaherty."

"Wait! I'll go with you," William called after the duke's man.

"Ye'll slow me down. Don't worry, Flaherty and I will protect her ladyship."

"How will I know where to find you?" he bellowed, chasing after Garahan.

"Where would she go?"

Aurelia's eyes filled with tears. "Home."

"Where is home?" William asked as Garahan tore down the hallway.

Aurelia laid a hand on his arm. "Don't you know?"

He shook his head. "I thought she didn't have a home—" He felt as if he'd been headbutted in the gut. "Chattsworth Manor," he rasped. "She said she felt as if she were home there."

Aurelia grumbled at him, "Take the carriage and follow her!"

William stared at her.

"Well don't just stand there! Get going! She doesn't believe you want to stay married to her. You have to tell her...you have to show her. She loves you so much, William."

"Did she say why?"

"Does it matter?"

"It might help me convince her how much I love her."

"You do?"

"I'd be a fool not to."

"She thinks you'll use the dowry to repair and rebuild your family's home and coffers while you remain in London in your new home."

"What new home?"

"The one you will purchase with the funds from her dowry."

"Has she lost her mind?"

"If she has," Aurelia whispered, "it's because she so in love with you."

The viscount ran toward the stairs, Aurelia hot on his heels, yelling, "You'd best get ready to grovel!"

William had more to worry about than groveling. The keeper of his heart had left him! He had to get her back.

He would get her back!

CHAPTER THIRTY-FOUR

E DWARD WAS FROWNING at his wife when William arrived in the stable, bag in hand, heart on his sleeve. "Is there a problem?"

"Aurelia."

William groaned. "I have my own wife to worry about. Mayhap you should stay here until you sort yours out."

"I'm coming with you," Aurelia announced.

"Be reasonable," Edward urged.

"I am. I haven't kicked you in the shin yet to move you out of my way."

Edward's jaw dropped, and he seemed incapable of speech. While the earl stared at his wife, William slipped behind them and boarded the carriage. He was about to tell the coachman to leave, when Edward opened the door. "Get in then, Wife."

"Don't mind if I do." The sweet tone of her words belied the look on her face.

Edward was in for trouble. William remembered that he was already in the suds and sinking fast. "How much of a head start do you think they have on us?"

"Whom?" Aurelia asked. "The duke's men or your wife?"

William was about to respond when he noticed Edward trying to get his attention. The silent signal behind his wife's back—a finger drawn across his throat, had William shrugging instead.

Edward grumbled, "If we are to reach Chattsworth Manor in one piece, I suggest you stop antagonizing William and be nice."

"Botheration! I am being nice."

"I daresay, William," the earl said with a sigh. "If your wife ever starts using Persephone's favorite expression, do be careful and watch your step."

"Expression?"

"Botheration," Edward advised.

"Ah, duly noted."

When they stopped for the second change of horse, Edward suggested they stay for the night. "It's getting late. No need to risk a run-in with a highwayman or broken wheel in the dark."

The need to push on until he held his wife in his arms nearly had him begging the earl to continue. One look at Aurelia and William knew he would have to agree. While the innkeeper showed Aurelia to the room she and Edward would be staying in tonight, William asked, "Do you think they've stopped for the night or pushed on through?"

Edward took in the haggard look on his friend's face. "I know what's on your mind—"

William balked. "How could you?"

"Were I in your shoes, I'd see about hiring a horse to ride all night until I reached Chattsworth Manor."

William nodded. "I could easily make it."

"Or fall off your horse as exhaustion claims you," Edward grumbled. "You're half-dead and have yet to recover from Chellenham's treachery."

"I know that I—"

"If you are bound and determined to continue on, at least share a meal with us before you go. Oh, and I'll have your word that you'll stop at the next posting inn."

William was about to disagree when a twinge of pain from his injury jolted through him. "You have it."

Edward nodded. "Excellent. Let me go see if I can hurry my

wife along while you see about hiring a horse."

An hour later, refreshed and feeling ready to ride further than the next inn, he noted the look in the earl's eye and sighed. He'd given his word. His word was his bond, he'd not break it. "The next inn and no further."

Though the earl wanted the footman to accompany William, the viscount refused, insisting he'd be fine. The ride south was familiar and the quiet soothing. He had much to think about. Foremost in his mind was the gut-wrenching realization that his wife had left him.

"Why? What did I say, what did I do?"

His thoughts haunting him, his heart empty, he was surprised to see the inn ahead of him. "We'll stop here for the night," he told his mount.

The horse whickered in reply. "Bet a handful of oats would be welcome. It's bloody cold tonight."

The viscount saw to his horse, settling him in for the night with the help of one of the stable lads. Walking past the huge barn where a few carriages were parked for the night, he froze. "The duke's carriage!"

Rushing over to be certain his tired eyes were not deceiving him, he was grabbed from behind. "What in the bloody hell?"

"Yer lordship?"

He breathed a sigh of relief. "Flaherty."

The duke's guard released him. "We didn't think ye'd catch up to us tonight."

"I left Edward and Aurelia at the last posting inn and hired a horse to continue on without them."

"The earl agreed to yer plan? What about yer injury?"

William sighed. "I had to give my word not to travel further than this inn."

Flaherty nodded. "Are ye after seeing her ladyship tonight?"

William bristled at the question, but knew the man was only protecting Calliope. "I had thought to ask the innkeeper to deliver a message."

Flaherty looked as if he wanted to say something, but hesitated.

"What is it?" William had a feeling he needed to know.

"Her ladyship will not be expecting ye."

"Why not? I'm her husband!"

The other man grinned. "That ye are, yer lordship, but she doesn't think ye care enough to follow after her. Why did ye?"

"She's my wife."

"Sure and that's true," Flaherty agreed, "but don't ye have another reason for riding past exhaustion to be with yer wife?"

William's voice broke as he said, "She's my heart, Flaherty. I have to make her understand that. She doubts my love. I don't know why."

Flaherty nodded. "That's what ye need to tell her, what's in yer heart. Trust that she'll listen if ye say it plain."

"I've already told her I love her."

"Aye, but have ye told her she's yer heart?"

William could not believe he was standing there discussing his problems with the Irishman. "I have not."

Flaherty grinned. "Well there ye have it."

At the end of his patience, he barked, "Have what?"

"Yer answer. Tell her what ye just told me. Garahan and I can delay our departure tomorrow and wait for his lordship and Lady Aurelia to arrive for a change of horse."

"Why would you?"

Flaherty shook his head. "I can see ye're new at this planning and plotting."

William decided not to take umbrage at the man's words. Biting his tongue, he vowed to listen to Flaherty's reasoning.

He nodded and Flaherty continued, "Ask the innkeeper if they have another room for Mary Kate to stay in."

"Why?"

"She's staying with her ladyship."

"Very well."

"Then ask him to send a note to Lady Calliope. Tell her ye're here and need to speak with her."

"And if she refuses?"

"Ye'll ask the innkeeper for the key to yer wife's room."

"Would you have me burst in on her?"

"I'm thinking ye won't have to."

"You're either a brilliant man or addlepated," William grumbled.

"Sure and me sainted ma has said the same more than once."

"By the by, where is Garahan?"

"Having a chat with the lovely Mary Kate."

"I thought she was sharing a room with my wife?"

"That she is, just not at the moment."

William thanked the man and put his plans into action. The innkeeper was happy to accommodate the viscount, relaying the message to Lady Calliope. He handed William the spare key to his wife's room, while he confirmed there was another room for his wife's maid.

More weary than he wanted to admit, he waited while the innkeeper relayed the message to Calliope. Would she refuse to see him? Would he spend the night sleeping at one of the tables in the main room of the inn?

Patience. Calliope was no doubt just as tired as he.

The innkeeper nodded to him as he reached the bottom step. "Your wife is waiting for you."

He nearly asked the man to repeat himself but came to his senses and thanked the man for his assistance. The older man smiled and went back to the patrons in the main tap room.

Standing before room number three, he hesitated for a moment to collect himself. He knocked and the door swung open. "William?"

"Calliope." When she only continued to stare at him, he asked, "May I come in?"

She stepped back and opened the door wider. "Of course."

He waited for her to close the door, watching her every move. All the while wondering what he'd said to push her away.

"I did not expect to see you so soon."

"Didn't you?"

She shook her head. "I thought you'd be busy with the duke's appointments, meeting with Coventry and Mr. Roxbury."

That last name was said with a hint of derision. Was there a connection between Roxbury and his wife's running away from him?

"I have the duke's affairs to attend to, and I am expecting Coventry to relay more information about my father."

Her hands were in fists at her sides when she asked, "And the solicitor?"

Ah. He might have discovered the root of the problem. "I do not have any intention of meeting with him any time soon. I have far more important things to do."

Interest piqued, she asked, "What is more important than the money you've gained?"

The question was a slap in his face, but he let the cutting reply die on his tongue. He needed to understand his wife. She needed to understand him. "The money means nothing to me."

"I do not believe that for a moment."

He closed the distance between them. She stepped back and would have fallen on the bed had he not caught her to him. "What have I done to engender your distrust of me, Calliope?"

A tear escaped.

"Do your vows mean so little to you?"

Her gasp was exactly the response he'd hoped for. She was angry. Far better than sad.

"A wife who trusted her husband would not sneak off without telling him where she was headed. Do you not know the dangers that await a woman traveling alone at night?"

"Mary Kate accompanied me."

He raised an eyebrow, silently questioning her.

"Apparently Seamus Flaherty saw us leave."

"And?"

"He and James Garahan followed us."

"At least you and Mary Kate were safe with them guarding you."

Her eyes lifted to meet his gaze. "You sound as if you care."

He eased back to stare at her. "Bloody hell, Woman—I love you!"

Tears gathered but she blinked them away.

Appalled at her lack of trust, he nearly turned from her...when Flaherty's words echoed in his head. *"Tell her what's in yer heart."*

"I planned to return to Chattsworth Manor after I'd fulfilled my promise to the duke, completing the tasks he had for me."

She was listening.

"With my father arriving at week's end, it would only add another day or so to my stay."

Calliope didn't speak, so he continued, "If it's the dowry that troubles you, you can give it away for all I care! Coin is no comfort compared to holding the woman you love in your arms. Waking in the morning to streams of sunshine and her face smiling up at you."

Her sharply indrawn breath and the tender look shining in her quiet gray eyes gave him hope. "Your face is the last thing I want to see at night. Yours is the body I need to feel curling against mine as we sleep."

"Me?" Calliope rasped.

"Aye," William replied. "The woman I love."

Her eyes filled but she blinked the tears away. "And you truly love me?"

He sighed. If she still needed more words, he'd give them to her. "I do. Calliope, you are the keeper of my heart. When you ran from me, you left me gutted."

She wrapped her arms around his waist and clung to him, mumbling and crying at the same time.

"Don't cry anymore, love."

"I'm sorry. Fear took hold of me when Mr. Roxbury told us about the dowry. I don't know who gave it to us, but can't you understand that money has always been at the very root of the problems in my life? From my uncle to my cousin."

"Money doesn't have to cause problems, Calliope. Whatever charity you would like to donate it to, we shall."

She leaned back to study his face. "You mean that, don't you?"

"I always say what I mean, Wife. I hope our living together at Chattsworth Manor will convince you of that."

"I look forward to returning home."

Their gazes met and held. "I look forward to earning your trust, my love."

"Did you mean…"

He frowned at his wife. "I always say—"

"What you mean," she finished for him. "I would like to make a donation to the widows and orphans of those who have served in His Majesty's Royal Armed Forces."

When he waited for her to say more, she added, "And another donation to those who were injured and find themselves without means to provide for their families."

He was so proud of this woman who had toiled most of her life. She'd been given the gift of a generous dowry and thought of helping others who would have no other means to provide for their families. He had a strong back, his father was about to return from the dead, and his wife had received her inheritance and a generous dowry. They would be able to pay Chattsworth Manor's faithful servants—pensioning off all who were ready to go, make repairs to their tenant farmers' homes. And because of his wife's generous heart, those who'd served in the armed forces and were injured, and widows of those who'd died in service of the Crown would no longer be on the brink of starvation.

He knew all he had to do was ask the duke's advice, and the three of them would be able to formulate a plan to see that his tenants had seeds to plant and the materials to repair their homes until he and Calliope had a chance to meet with Roxbury and see that funds were allocated to that end. If Hargrave, Mrs. Meadowsweet, and MacReedy were not willing to retire, he would act as servant to his father before he let their elderly staff perform tasks beyond their strength and ability. A lot could be accomplished with one's two hands and a solid work ethic. His wife had shown him that.

He pressed his lips to hers, gently at first, coaxing her to open her heart to his. Her body relaxed against him, and he groaned as he fought to savor her lips, not plunder as he was so tempted to do.

Tasting and teasing, he kissed a path from behind her ear to the base of her throat. When she softly sighed, he tucked her against his heart. "Say you believe me and won't try to leave me again."

Her gaze met his. "I believe you, William, and I promise I'll never leave you."

The journey was catching up with him. He had to sit down before he keeled over. "Calliope, do you mind if I sit?"

She giggled. "Where are my manners? My darling husband, would you care to join me on the bed?"

"On it not in it?" he teased.

"You said you wanted to sit."

"I would be most grateful to."

She led him over to the bed and eased him onto it. "Would you like me to help you remove your coat?"

"You did say on, did you not?"

She laughed, a lilting sound that wrapped around his heart. "Yes, my darling. I did. Now, if you'll let me help you out of your frockcoat and waistcoat, you'll be much more comfortable."

"Are you trying to get me into bed?'

"I've already got you there."

He smiled. "So you have, my love. Planning to have your way with me?"

She traced the line of his jaw with the tips of her fingers, and then with featherlight kisses. "I am tempted, but not if you are too tired."

William was smiling as they undressed one another. He sighed as he pulled her close, cradling her to his heart. The deep ache that had slashed through him when she left lessened as their hearts beat in tandem.

"Love me, William."

"I already do," Calliope."

Her snort of laughter had him chuckling. "Forgive me, did you mean to ask me to make love with you?"

"Yes, Husband. Please?"

He was smiling as their lips met. When he could bear to end the kiss, he whispered, "Make a life with me, Calliope. Be my wife...be my life. Bear my children and I swear I shall love them as I have come to love you."

Her eyes echoed the love in his heart. "I do believe I'd like a dozen children."

His mouth opened but no sound emerged.

Her laughter had him frowning at first, but then joining hers. "Make love with me, Calliope."

"I thought you'd never ask."

Later, as the lovers lay entwined, the beat of their hearts gradually slowed as they fell into an exhausted sleep. When Calliope stirred, William pulled her back against him, wrapping his arms around her.

"Don't let go," she whispered as she roused.

"If I do, we'll never have those dozen children you asked me for."

"William?"

"Hmmm?"

"Do you think—is it possible that we...?"

"Worried that we haven't been successful granting your request, Wife?" he teased.

"Yes," she whispered.

"There's only one way to ensure that we have," he told her.

"Oh, and what is that?"

He rolled her beneath him and smiled wickedly. "We'll have

to keep trying."

"I love you, William."

His heart stuttered in his chest as her declaration filled him. "As I love you, Calliope."

As the first rays of sunlight lit the room, William opened his eyes to see Calliope watching him. "Your face is the first thing I hope to see every morning for the rest of our lives."

William tucked her beneath him and marveled that she loved him and wanted to have a family with him. But more, she was unafraid to work with him to rebuild the legacy they would leave for their children. He would ensure the Chattsworth line continued.

He pressed a kiss to the end of her nose. "About those dozen children."

A KNOCK ON their door woke them from a deep slumber. "What is it?" William called out.

"Do hurry up and get dressed," Aurelia urged from the other side of the door. "Edward and I would like to arrive before this evening."

Calliope hid her face in the crook of William's neck, stifling her laughter. "Do you think she knows what we've been doing?"

"A happily married woman like Lady Aurelia?" William queried. "I should think so."

Calliope slipped out of bed and turned to see her husband watching her. "Is something wrong?"

He got up and pulled her against him. "Aside from having to leave this bed and my wife, to go out into the cold? Not a thing."

"We'd best hurry if we are to arrive by late afternoon," Calliope urged.

CHAPTER THIRTY-FIVE

THE VISCOUNT ACQUIESCED to Edward's suggestion that he and Calliope remain in Sussex, while Edward and Aurelia returned to London. Edward would handle the last few requests his brother had tasked William to complete, and then he and Aurelia would return to Sussex and settle in once more at Lippincott Manor.

William and Calliope were breakfasting when Hargrave entered the dining room to announce, "Earl Chattsworth."

William shot to his feet. "My father is here?"

Hargrave smiled and stepped aside.

"Father?"

William rushed over to embrace the man he'd thought had died. "It's so wonderful to see you. What happened? I searched for you for so long."

The earl eased out of his son's hold and smiled. "All in good time. Coventry will be joining us for breakfast. We're half-starved, you know. Rode straight through the night after I was released from my...er...duty to His Majesty."

"Chattsworth!" Coventry called out as he entered the dining room. "I see the earl has already made himself comfortable."

"I intend to enjoy life to the fullest, now that I'm no longer aboard the *HMS Albatross*."

"Will you tell us what happened?"

"In good time, Son. Where are your manners?"

Calliope laughed as she walked over to stand beside her husband. "I don't mind, my lord. William has been so anxious to see you. We were planning to leave for London directly after breakfast."

"Coventry suggested you needed another week or two to rusticate in the country while your wound heals." His father frowned at him. "It would appear you have much to tell me, as well."

Calliope cleared her throat. "As my husband is too preoccupied, allow me to introduce myself."

The earl smiled. "I've heard tales of the Lady Calliope who made a donation to the widows, orphans and injured seamen, marines, and those who served in the regiment."

She smiled. "It was my pleasure."

"It is an honor to meet you." The earl reached for her hand and bowed over it. "Welcome to the family."

"Thank you, my lord. By the by, it was William's suggestion that I donate a portion of *our* dowry to the charity of my choice."

"Having served aboard the *HMS Albatross*, I can assure you the money will be well spent and the families beyond grateful."

Mrs. Romney arrived bearing a tray of food. "What have you got there, Mrs. Romney? Kippers?" The earl beamed. "You remembered how I love kippers!"

Calliope burst into delighted laughter. "I do believe your father and I will get along famously, my love."

The earl was busy filling his plate. As he sat down, food in front of him, his teacup filled to the brim, he paused to bow his head.

Surprised, as his father had never done so before he'd gone missing, he waited for the earl to look up. When he did, he smiled at William. "I learned to pray while I was aboard the *HMS Albatross*. After he'd plowed through the meal in front of him, he paused to sip from his cup before easing back in his chair.

"You've waited patiently, and now that I've eaten, I'm ready to confess."

The viscount was confused. "Confess?"

"We'd sailed for a few days before word got out that one of the men who'd been pressed was titled."

"Why didn't you speak up when you boarded the ship?"

"I was unconscious, and it took a day to get my bearings and another two to get my sea legs."

Calliope reached for William's hand. He laced his fingers with hers. "And when you were discovered, what happened then?"

"Nothing."

William waited for the rest of what his father would say.

"I had a good idea who knocked me out that night, and I wasn't sure if it would be safe to find my way home after we made the first port."

William was anxious to know if his supposition was correct. He blurted out, "Was it Chellenham?"

His father met his gaze and held it. "Aye."

"Did you give him the *Chattsworth Emeralds?*"

The earl stared down at his hands. "I lost them along with a pile of coins in a wager I never should have made."

"Gambling," the viscount stated.

"Now that you know the truth of it, what do you intend to do?" the earl asked.

William's gaze met Calliope's. When she nodded and then slowly smiled, so did the viscount. Turning back to his father, he said, "Celebrate your return. We shall open the house to our tenants, neighbors, and friends."

The earl shook his head. "Didn't you hear what I said? I gambled it all away on the turn of a card."

William's smile widened. "We didn't give away all of Calliope's dowry. Did I mention she happens to be an heiress?"

While his father stared at him, the viscount continued. "Chellenham lost a duel of honor to Lord Coddington—"

"And shot you instead when you jumped in front of Uncle Phineas," Calliope added.

"Coddington's your uncle?" the earl asked.

"Unofficially adopted," Calliope quickly explained.

"So that is how you came by the pistol ball wound," the earl muttered. "Where is Chellenham now?"

"Why do you want to know?" the viscount and Coventry asked at the same time.

The earl looked from one man to the other before shrugging.

"When you've had time to settle in," Coventry began, "after we meet with the Admiralty, mayhap you and the viscount can continue your discussion."

The earl clenched his hands into fists. "He has my signet ring."

William was aghast. "You wagered great-grandfather's ring?"

"Nay. It was missing when I woke aboard the *Albatross*."

"He took it?" The viscount could not believe it.

"If I were a betting man," he said, meeting his son's gaze, "which I no longer am, I would say yes."

"Mayhap we can buy them back," Calliope suggested.

"I'd had the emeralds in my fist over the pot of coins for a heartbeat and was pulling it away, when Chellenham grabbed hold of my wrist until I dropped them on top of the pile."

"So you didn't mean to gamble them away."

The earl held his son's gaze as he answered, "Nay."

"Your lordship is quite lucky that I have excellent connections," Coventry began, "and have tracked down who purchased the emeralds."

"Purchased them?" the earl sounded confused. "From Chellenham?"

"Aye. He sold them to a disreputable pawn broker," Coventry clarified.

The earl's voice cracked with emotion as he said, "I do not have the coin to purchase them back."

Calliope pressed a kiss to her husband's cheek before announcing, "We do!"

The viscount knew it was time to share the heavy burden he

carried with his father. He'd already shared it with his wife. "While I did keep looking for you, I sought to find an easy way to refill the family coffers."

Calliope squeezed his hand, encouraging him to continue.

"Marcus and I sent missives to the Duke of Wyndmere."

"You and Marcus always were in one another's pockets and usually ended up in the suds."

William let go of the breath he'd been holding. "We thought to collect on our distant but familial connection with Jared."

The earl's sigh cut through the silence in the room. "I should have given you a better example. But after your mother died, I lost my way." He raised his gaze to meet William's. "Mayhap between us we can step back on the right path, put all of our efforts into bringing Chattsworth Manor, her staff, and tenant farmers' homes and fields back to their former glory."

"I'd be honored to." William turned to his wife, seeking her gaze as she was truly his partner in all things. "But first I must apologize to the duke for not being honest with him in the first place."

Calliope's eyes misted with unshed tears, and he knew she understood the bone-deep need in him to speak to the duke and ask his forgiveness.

"The Duke of Wyndmere," Hargrave announced.

William was on his feet and striding toward the duke before his father had a chance to stand. "Your Grace."

"Chattsworth," he greeted William with a nod before turning to the earl. "I see the rumors are true." The duke smiled. "Welcome home."

The earl shifted from one foot to the other and cleared his throat to speak. "Thank you for looking out for my son while I was...away."

"Family first, Chattsworth," he rumbled. "Lady Calliope." He strode over to her and bowed over her hand. "You're looking exceptionally well."

The sparkle in the duke's eyes were reflected in her eyes.

"Thank you, Your Grace."

The viscount stiffened his resolve. "Your Grace, I must speak with you."

The duke raised a brow in silent question. "Of course, in private?"

Calliope was suddenly by his side. He hadn't noticed that she'd risen from her seat. She looped her arm through his and the rest of what he needed to say filled him. "Not necessary," he replied.

He knew he was making a muck of things, and forgetting protocol, but he had to get it said quickly before he lost his nerve. "I was not upfront when I sent that missive seeking an audience with you."

The duke held his gaze, but the intensity in his blue eyes, so like William's, had him digging deep for the courage to continue. "I was looking for the quickest way to refill our family coffers— our staff and tenant farmers' situations were quite desperate."

The duke hadn't spun on his heel and quit the room, so William continued, "I should have been honest from the beginning and beg your pardon."

It was so quiet you could hear a pin drop. The duke slowly smiled. "I was well aware of your situation, Cousin, and expected to hear from you and a few of my other relatives."

William had been right, the duke had far-reaching connections. "You were?"

"You've more than met my expectations and revealed the man you are meant to be by your actions and the way you handled yourself while in London at my behest."

"Was it a test?" William had to know the answer.

"You may see it as one. I prefer to see it as your chance to prove yourself capable of taking on whatever life has in store for you. I wouldn't have entrusted Lady Calliope to you if I hadn't thought you capable of providing for her."

"Have you eaten, Your Grace?" Calliope asked.

He shook his head. "I was in a rush to get here," he replied with another glance in William's direction. "To make certain that my cousin was on the mend. Persephone was a bit overset to learn of his injuries protecting Coddington."

Mrs. Meadowsweet entered the dining room followed by MacReedy hefting a large tray.

"Won't you be seated, Your Grace?" Calliope asked.

He frowned at her. "I thought I'd made myself clear, Calliope."

At the blush staining his wife's cheeks, William looked from one to the other, wondering what the duke had previously made clear to his wife.

Before he could ask, Calliope spoke. "Won't you be seated, Jared?"

"Thank you, Calliope." The duke walked over to where she'd been sitting and with a hand on the back of her chair, waited for her to be seated. When she had, he smiled down at her and sat at the empty place beside her.

William sat back down and smiled at MacReedy and his housekeeper. "Thank you for anticipating our needs, Mrs. Meadowsweet."

"Couldn't very well let His Grace go hungry," she replied, setting a plate filled with eggs, sausages, kippers, and scones in front of him.

The duke eyed the plate like a starving man.

Calliope poured his tea and passed the clotted cream and raspberry preserves. "How is the duchess faring—and how are your darling twins and Phoebe?"

"Twins?" the earl asked before adding, "congratulations, Your Grace."

The duke finished chewing and took a sip from his teacup before responding, "Thank you, Chattsworth." He turned to Calliope and grinned. "She's glowing, and the twins and my sister are quite well."

"I'm so glad to hear it," Calliope responded.

"I understand that you're interested in making a donation to the widows and orphans of those who've served the Crown," the duke stated.

Her gaze met William's before answering, "I am."

"So the dowry and inheritance it is rumored that you've received is already being put to good use?"

She smiled as she met the duke's interested gaze. "I cannot thank you or Lord Coddington enough for your generosity, Jared."

"Well worth every pound to see you happily married and able to make a difference in so many lives as you've made such a difference in our lives." His gaze met hers as he added, "Thank you, Calliope."

Tears filled her eyes, but William noted with pride that she blinked them away as her beautiful smile lifted the spirits of everyone in the room. "Thank you for insisting I marry William."

The duke chuckled. "I can hardly take credit for that, seeing as how you two were destined to marry."

"Destined?" the earl spoke up.

"Of a certainty," the duke replied.

The earl's smile reached his eyes as he looked from his son to his daughter-in-law. "Tell me, Son, how did you and Lady Calliope meet?"

Calliope set down her teacup and leaned toward William's father. "It was just past dawn on Hogmanay. Lady Aurelia and I had just finished decorating the church for her wedding when the doors to the church burst open," she said as she glanced at her husband and smiled, "and the man I will love for the rest of my life strode in."

About the Author

Historical & Contemporary Romance "Warm...Charming...Fun..."

C.H. was born in Aiken, South Carolina, but her parents moved back to northern New Jersey where she grew up.

She believes in fate, destiny, and love at first sight. C.H. fell in love at first sight when she was seventeen. She was married for 41 wonderful years until her husband lost his battle with cancer. Soul mates, their hearts will be joined forever. They have three grown children—one son-in-law, two grandsons, two rescue dogs, and two rescue grand-cats.

Her characters rarely follow the synopsis she outlines for them...but C.H. has learned to listen to her characters! Her heroes always have a few of her husband's best qualities: his honesty, his integrity, his compassion for those in need, and his killer broad shoulders. C.H. writes about the things she loves most: Family, her Irish and English Ancestry, Baking and Gardening.

Take a trip back in time to Regency England for her new series: The Lords of Vice, coming in 2021 from Dragonblade Publishing! Venture back to the Old West with her bestselling Irish Western Series. Fast-forward to the present, stopping at the Circle G Ranch in Pleasure, Texas, before finally landing in Apple Grove, Ohio–Small Town USA–for a slice of Peggy McCormack's Buttermilk Pie!

This award-winning multi-published author's books are available in paperback, hardcover, trade paperback, magazine, e-book, large print, and audio book.

C.H. Admirand loves to hear from readers!

Made in the USA
Middletown, DE
15 October 2021